Make Not Provision…

A novel by Allan A. Leonard

PublishAmerica
Baltimore

First printing

ISBN: 1-4241-4232-6
PUBLISHED BY PUBLISHAMERICA, LLLP
www.publishamerica.com
Baltimore

Printed in the United States of America

Dedicated to my wife, Brigita, without whose advice and persistence this would not have been written; and to the memories of Allan Ashley and Barbara Ann.

TO THE READER

Love is the top of a mountain, available only through a long, hard climb which promises to put in your way huge boulders to be moved or skirted and great chasms to either leap wildly across or painstakingly complete after building a bridge. It has slippery ice and scattering scree, distances unimaginable, sudden peaks and thin air. And once you're there, you can fall off it or slide down it, or finally make a nest as an eagle and remain there, soaring at will or living the high life forever in your nest.

This is the story of such a love affair. One-sided, to be sure, as the other involved had the misfortune of dying after it commenced. The sad tale of a man so in love he was shattered for the rest of his life. A lost man, who never really wanted to be found. A man, who for a time, became a spy. A man who was called a dangerous pilgrim.

This story is sometimes bitter. Death and sadness are on many pages. But in reading a love story, the reader may sometimes be taken away from the ugly and be graced with some tender talk to balance the destruction, and allow emotions to fly rather than flee.

Enter now into a man's life in the year of the Pilgrime Lord, 1650.

Eleven weeks in the life of Ashley Lyons of Plimouth—the Massa-adchu-ess-et—the Puritan colony of New England.

INFORMATION

Seen ever as the conscience within the English King's new Anglican Church, in March a.D. 1533, King Henry the Eighth ended England's official sanctioning of the worldwide and most Catholic Church of Rome, rebuking at that time its supremacy in all matters religious in which England and her territories were affected. In November, one year later, the August King Henry was proclaimed—through the Act of Supremacy—titular and ever "Head of England's Church."

Replacing the Catholic Church was the Anglican Church. In England—in the 1500s—for one to "be with the Church," one had to be an Anglican.

The Anglican Church was denoted "Anglican" after the cultural tie of all Britons with the Germanic peoples already in England, and for those who had entered, compromised with, and joined other North-Germanic Saxons more than a thousand years previously. Initially known in the era about a.D. 500 to a.D. 1066, as "Saxony," England's mix of Angles and Saxons which fixed the country and inspired the culture dissolved slowly their heritage into the term "Angle" (Angel) as the Kings of those thousand years seemed to associate their heritage with the warrior-Germans, especially after the French/Norman invasion/takeover of England in a.D. 1066. After 1066, the Angles and Saxons called themselves "English," and they took their religious beliefs seriously.

In the middle 1400s Gutenberg invented the printing press, and by the 1500s had made the Bible the book for all peoples; so with the combination of readily accessible Bibles and the printed word, the outcries presented by the likes of Luther and other churchmen, and the growing hatred in England of worshipping images and using priests as "middlemen to God," the people in England saw King Henry's Church as a place of open religion. There, in the Anglican Church, mandates and reprisals from Rome caused no fear. The time of the non-Catholic, the "protest-ant" (the Protestant) was here. That was the 1500s.

NOW, it was anno Domini 1650, with a DIFFERENT religious order—the Puritans—running the Protestant Church and England herself. A civil war had overtaken England and carried away her former rule, substituting the Puritan Church (a more reformed and strict body) for the Anglican Church. And now in England…THERE WAS NO KING!

PROLOGUE

Duxbury, the Massa-adchu-ess-et (the Land of the Blue Hills), one league from the Puritan (Pilgrime) colony, where the Pilgrimes landed in the year of their Christian Lord (anno Domini) 1620.

SUMMER: a.D. 1650

She was there for him, waiting. She was always there, no matter when he arrived or what day it was. In actual fact, the days now meant nothing to him at all, as each day began the same and ended the same: him, alone. But he woke for her and imagined her and saddled his horse only to go visit her. He was immersed in a routine of longing, craving, needing, desiring. She completed his day and his life: he put everything aside for her and cared about no one nor anything else. Just her.

She would never now be to him the way she was; he knew that in his soul but erased it from his heart; but that wasn't important. They had lived together twenty-four months and eleven days. Just because they were apart at night didn't mean he couldn't be with her every day. Every day. Every day.

He dreamed of her at night, visualized her with him, spoke to her, did things for her that he had done with her. His life was not totally complete, but he was satisfied. She did that for him, gave him a purpose, filled a blankness, forced him to get through each night without her…but every day he went to see her, be with her.

She was there for him, waiting, her arms outstretched and her lips warm and moist. She wore the same dress every time…the white, lacy one he liked so much which covered her completely but let him be aware of her whole body; and what a body! Petite and graceful, exciting, calling out to be touched, caught up in his strong arms and lifted high off the ground so he could hold her and kiss her and comfort her as she comforted him. She always comforted him, especially these days—when there was no comfort.

She was small. He towered over her and she had to tilt her head to see him speak. She loved to hear him talk; they always enjoyed their talks together and their little secrets and those small fun-things lovers and those married do together. At first she was frightened when he picked her up, cradling her in his long arms as is done with a child, and bringing her close to him. He loved to hold her, inhale her, kiss her everywhere and have her seem a part of him...and she returned all she got from him and gave even more than before.

He never even bothered to tie his horse when he saw her...he'd just ride up and look, see her waiting or know she'd be there, almost propel himself off the big horse, leaving the reins dragging on the ground and rush to her, expectant to hold her, feast his now-thin body with her look, her touch, her being.

Then they would be as one, holding, clinging, not even breathing they were so tightly together, wrapped, mingled, compressed: two people in one. Here was Heaven. Right here. They had always been happy together but these days were different...it was more than just happiness, it was the purest love and the finest joy.

After an intimate time with her he often felt playful-enough to ask: "What did you say your name was?"

Then he'd have to hold his arm as a pillow, to protect himself as slaps would careen across his ears, head, neck...them they'd fling themselves together again, holding, touching, kissing, playing...so happy...God! So happy!

Anna. Anna. His Anna. Petite Anna with her smile which lit her face—like having a halo of light around her head. Anna, whose tiny hands could touch him anywhere and he'd get great jolts of lightning inside him and need to take several gulps of air because he'd forgotten to breathe whilst he thought of only her. Anna, whose skin was as beaten cotton and warm as a summer zephyr on a cheek. He more than loved her; he existed only while she was around him, and nothing but hungry for her when they were apart.

A lot of times he didn't even have to talk to her...sometimes didn't even have to look at her. They'd lay there in the dark, holding each other...she knew what he was thinking, even when he'd deny it to himself. Never knew how she could do that...he could say something and she'd come back with: "You're saying that but you're not saying..." or, "I know...I understand...I know what hurts you and what makes you happy..." She was so far ahead of him...way down the road ahead of him...like they were the same person but she had been there before him and now only wanted to ease him through it because she already knew what it was like to be him and what it was like for him, but she hadn't been anywhere or done much at all herself and wanted it that way.

How in the world did he ever get her? She was a prize.

He put his lips on hers...feeling her body tremble...God, it was so good to hold her!

"Captain Lyons?

"Captain Lyons, sir?"

"What?"

She was gone.

"A message, Captain Lyons, from Captain Standish. Begging your pardon, Captain, but Captain Standish told me to personally hand you this message...and said you'd be here, in the cemetery, where you are every day."

Lyons blinked, reached automatically for the paper in the courier's hand.

"The militia is saddened at your wife's death, Captain Lyons. She was a fine woman and...well..."

"Yes, I know. Thank you. I'll read this later."

"Captain Lyons, I was ordered to tell you to read this right now, as Captain Standish must see you immediately."

"Standish see me immediately? The militia just met Saturday and...I guess he wasn't there then. He says I must read this immediately?"

"Yes, sir; and I'm to accompany you to him—if you please, sir."

"I hadn't..." He tore open the wax-sealed paper and glanced at it. "All it says is that I am ordered to come immediately to his office under accompaniment of the bearer of this note."

"Yes, sir. I was there whilst he wrote that. He said for me to come here to the cemetery where your wife was buried and fetch—get—you and stay with you whilst you went to him."

"Then, let us go." Ashley Lyons turned and looked a moment at the small stone under which his Anna lay.

"I'll be back, Anna."

CHAPTER 1

The tall ship glided rather than sailed into her place at the long, wooden wharf, responding—it seemed—gladly to the hawsers which now anchored her and pulled her to the wooden structure which reached as a stubby finger into Plimouth Bay.

She was the three-decked *Sovereign of the Seas*, a completely English-designed and built three-masted, hundred-gun warrior which challenged every Spanish galleon and finally gave the French ships worry. *Sovereign* carried the newly placed style of sails and showed square top-sails and royals above the top-gallants. She was meant for speed and was the forerunner of England's Frigate-Navy, being the newest style and the latest design and most-recently launched sea-fighter. Her first cruises were to deliver mail, but the English admirals thought they wanted to see if she would deliver the speed and turning-ability the designers said she would, so now she carried mail; soon she'd carry England's ensign around the world.

The ship safely secured, *Sovereign's* master had the gang run out and the eternal business of adding supplies began, but not before five gentlemen and their rather large clothing-chest came across to the wooden wharf.

"So this is Plimouth. Not so big as they led us to believe." Luke, with his thin lips, had been the first to speak.

"I've seen tinier..."

"At least it's clean. London..."

"Enough about London; it's here we are." A definite. That's the way Johnathan was, but the other four didn't take offense.

"Where from here, Johnathan?"

"I've a list of contributors...several are here in Plimouth. Luke, you begin the maps, cautiously, tho'...none need know what you do. Mark, you hire a horse and get up and down the close coastline to see gun-emplacements, whatever. Report on those. Geoffry, a rental coach, please; something to take the weight of all of us and our chest. Perhaps four horses...see what they have. It'll have to take us to Boston and beyond, and allow us to nap whilst we go about our business. Matthew, you're here with me; I find comfort in foreign lands when I stand in your shadow."

Big Matthew smiled. He was a giant of a man, well over two meters tall and about twenty-three stone in weight.

"Here; coin for everyone. We shall probably be in...what's that name over there? Bayhouse Inn? That looks to be a tidy rooming-establishment for the evening. Everyone should be here for the evening meal, what? Does that all sound safe and comfortable? Lively, gentlemen...there is no honor for laggards."

These five were old friends and traveling companions. They had each known the others for a decade—a score for two of them. Each was well-trained, casual but guarded, ready with a quick knife or musket. They were close, personal friends within a friendship which had been forged ten years...forged by Johnathan, driven by his desires and observations and likes and money. "Fingers in a glove," he said of them. "Each for the other; all for the King!" Here on business of the King...the present King of Scotland who strove to become also the King of England, and rightly so, as his father and Johnathan's had been King of England until very recently...when his fortune and luck ran out and he was rudely treated and publicly executed through ugly means.

So Johnathan was here on the business of his half-brother, the King, who waited impatiently, wanting to soon become what his father had been: King of England, Scotland and Ireland.

Matthew, Mark and Luke—not their given names—were all chosen by Geoffry. Luke first, as Luke enjoyed "being close" with a man and Geoffry appreciated that; then Johnathan claimed him. Mark and Mathew had soldiered together in England for a decade, then gotten out when their King was sought, caught and a lesson taught. They had liked the old Army and admired their King; now they worked to install a new King, the old one's son. Yes...all smiles and no worries; just complete the things they were hired to do and wealth was theirs.

Perhaps, as they had been told, they might have to sail to Spain, France, the Dutch Provinces...but that was no worry to men such as these. And more then "no worry," it probably would be pleasurable.

As to the names they had chosen...Johnathan decided he should hurt the Puritans of England so he named his band after the Puritan's main Bible characters. It was only convenient that he was already a "John."

Geoffry refused to change his name; said it was what his mum wanted it to be. *Interesting*, Johnathan thought...*that a dedicated killer and multi-imprisoned man would want to keep so obvious a name because of his mother*.

It would seem such a man might be too woman-like, too unwilling to fight or seriously defend the Cause. Not so, about Geoffry. As he loved his mother, he loved life and pleasure, but he also loved killing people: that was his true love.

So there they were: Matthew, Mark, Luke, John and Geoffry: the Good News Workers for Charles the Second, King by the grace of God and through the acceptance of the people of Scotland.

CHAPTER 2

Captain Ashley Lyons, Plimouth colony militia, a tall man and now thin with long legs and a great reach. Hooded hazel eyes. Chestnut-brown hair turning salt and pepper. A man of thirty-two years with full lips which mostly stayed apart as he breathed through his mouth; and with widely spaced shoulders as tho' made for draping frontier shirts across them.

A man from England who had grown up within the Plimouth colony and whose past was troubled and tangled and forced itself into his present, making him ever aware of what he had done, where he had gone, those whom he had feared, she whom he loved.

Not his past as an adult so much, but as a child—twelve years of age then and not prepared in the least to take on the job he did as a crusader for a god.

Only twenty-four months and twenty-nine days before, he had wed.

Anna. Short for Hannah. Anna, his wife.

He asked her one time why she chose him over other men. She gave him that precious smile, intimate and inviting…"Because you told me when you looked at me your mouth got dry and I never heard anyone else say that. Was that true?"

Embarrassed. "Was true; is true."

That was how much they loved each other.

In a million-pound raffle he had won, and Anna was the prize.

Anna was not an outright beauty, but a beginner in beauty. She was petite and graceful as a tiny, lithe child can be but she was almost his age. Her attraction was her size, and people marveled that she was of a certain age but looked as a child. She was cute, inviting, had a timeless face and tiny features, but was not a raving beauty as some of the northern European women were in Boston—with their flaxen hair and pronounced cheekbones and willowy figures and smiles which excited every man but those whose wives stood nearby, watching.

He wished he could see her now, but she never came to him until he was in the cemetery—unless it were a dream or a thought, and then she was only there a short while. That's why he spent so much time in the cemetery...she was always there for him, waiting.

At those times she'd hug on him, hang on him; they'd kiss and hold each other and sit under the old maple tree on that wooden bench someone had built—not him, of course: he could hardly hold a hammer, much less "build" something of use.

Hours. They'd hold each other for hours. Then she'd just disappear...and he'd leave. No goodbyes, just...gone.

But while she was there, they were totally together.

God's reward or punishment: he couldn't tell which.

At their wedding, Ashley's new father-in-law pulled him aside.

"I have thought about this and my only advice to you as a new husband, is to listen to your wife with interest, but never offer advice.

The best information he'd gotten about marriage, and he used it daily.

During that time they were married, if they were rich in love they were poor in wealth. Ashley's militia-pay covered their rent and both sets of parents invited them for meals, then forced "extra" food upon them as they left. Meats from the woods and vegetables from Anna's garden gave extras; they ate well or they didn't: the Puritan way. God would provide after prayer and physical effort.

When the first child—a son—was born, Mister Pennyweight (Ashley's stepfather) seemed to empty his Plimouth retail-store of goods for the baby and mother. Anna's parents handled the funeral expenses five months later—the baby had died during its sleep, devastating parents and family who put their hope and love into this child.

Before they were married, Anna asked one time if his position in the militia were a dangerous one, would he have to go somewhere and fight and either kill people or himself be killed. She was wary, frightened that this future husband would die also—as her first husband had—and then where would she be: after losing two husbands the community might think she were a witch; so she had reason enough to ask the question.

"No," he had told her, lying through his teeth. "No danger in this job. I might fall off my horse or cut myself as I shave my beard, but there is more danger at home—with wasp-stings and stray-dog bites and blankets of mosquitos—than there is in the militia."

She seemed relieved—not that he'd be injured at home, but that the militia was not the way it used to be, fighting hand-to-hand, hatchet-to-hatchet with Woods-People or having an arrow in your side as you passed a large tree or being pulled off your horse to be scalped or otherwise ambushed whilst going through a stream. He neglected to tell her he already had such adventures and in all probability would have even more, as the Europeans who arrived daily ever were aggravating the local tribes and getting killed or frightened, causing the militia to assemble in haste and dash after retribution—the European's idea of honor (which was to kill the other person in every instance).

When a soldier or militiaman fights with a sword, he inflicts horrifying injuries, and in truth expects the same inflicted upon him. The militia usually only wanted to arrive, show they had responded to an incident, were prepared to fight, then take apologies and write a report about their level of courage, their style of envelopment, their dangers which could have been. Then leave.

That's what they "wanted" to do. Ashley realized what often happened was that the militia assembled too late, had never enough men, and scarcely attended to the original plan. They'd arrive and get shot-at, arrowed, pulled off their horses and tomahawked, end up causing even a bloodier mess than if they hadn't answered the call. When they arrived too quickly they surprised a foe whose bloodlust was already heightened and they'd just continue the fighting—to the sorrow and loss of the militia. This was a different way of fighting than the European Armies waged: no standing upright to shoot or forming a line or expecting the Indians to do the same. They couldn't fight the Woods-People this way.

Left alone to run away, the hostiles could be taken piecemeal, one or two at a time, in different places without their entire village of braves being bloodthirsty at once. Most of the time the village chiefs abhorred the deeds done and would either tell Captain Standish who did the bad deeds or punish them within the tribe, sometimes banishing them. Ashley had been involved in wholesale slaughter but would never tell Anna, nor would he admit the job of the volunteer soldier on the edge of an ancient civilization which did not especially want Europeans there was precarious at best and deadly at worst.

She never knew how bad—dangerous—it really was on the frontier. Thank God.

When Ashley had first joined the militia he was sent to a faraway frontier fort to observe what and how they were doing and to see if anything they did was different from what Captain Standish taught. If someone on the frontier knew differently from Miles, Miles wanted to know, to learn. Standish was an avid learner and absorbed everything military, business, religious or political. His mind was open to everything but what he felt was illegal, immoral or alcoholic. Ashley had become Miles' eyes and ears on this information-gathering assignment.

The Indians inland were not so friendly as the Algonkin along the coast. These Woods-People were tougher, braver, prouder...would rather kill a man than have to deal with him.

One of the local militiamen somehow stole an Indian girl, bringing her back to the fort late at night for the rest of the men as amusement. He had already done some personal damage to her and now was about to sell her or her use. Ashley told him, "Give her back! At least let her run away!"

"No, by God!" was the answer. "She's here to be used and used she shall be!"

Ashley went immediately to the commander of the fort, woke him and told him. The man screamed at Ashley for being awakened. Ashley said no more, packed rapidly, saddled his horse and took whatever food he could grab, then rode pell-mell out of the fort, and as far as the then-exhausted horse could take him before he let it rest—them pushed it further, toward safety.

At morning, the log fort was surrounded and burned. The Woods-People shot flaming arrows into everything they could, hiding all the while from the scattered musket shots. The admired and polished cannon never was discharged, as there was no particular target for it. The more arrows were put into the log walls, then buildings, the more fire broke out to frighten and drive the soldiers from the walls, then there were less to soldiers at the walls to prevent the Woods-People from scaling them and entering the fort. The great log gates had burning brush placed against them; that stopped those inside the fort from trying to get away.

No one. Not one was left alive in the fort. It never paid to steal a woman from any of the Woods-People, but these especially. Each of their villages was a big family, and they all thought alike. They became as hornets when a nest is endangered.

Ashley's report to Miles was complete and detailed. Mile's interpretation of that report when he told the men of the Plimouth militia was a lot briefer: "For God's sake and your own, remember your religion and the Ten Commandments!"

So...here he was, on his way again to see Captain Miles Standish. To work for Standish was one thing; to be summoned to his home accompanied by a "guard" was something altogether different; no good could come of this. He

HAD to see Standish; there was nothing he could do but go there: a request from Miles Standish was an order he must obey.

Miles Standish...former soldier in the war for the Netherlands and devout Puritan was still—at age sixty-six—considered a stalwart man, a man who continued to be the military leader of the Plimouth settlement. He had withdrawn the previous year (1649) from his position as assistant governor and treasurer of the colony, and thirteen years earlier had moved with his second wife to Duxbury, to this home. It was a handsome house when built and backed up to the marsh and river, beyond which lay the great ocean which had become the only means of establishing contact with England. Miles had his office here, but preferred to work in Plimouth—where the action was—as the governing force of Plimouth lived and worked there: a place of energy and fury at a time of personal courage.

Miles Standish was not a tall person. He'd had a raised chair with a step made especially for him in his office-home so he didn't appear to "jump backwards" in order to sit, and had a platform behind his desk to stand on, that he could be "eye to eye" with visitors. The now long-gone-but-not-forgotten Thomas Morton had written of Standish that he was "a shrimpe of a man." (Not too much later after that printing, Morton was arrested by Standish and placed on a penal island, then rescued and taken back to England.) Others in the colony (within themselves) referred to Standish as "Captain Redbeard," or "Captain Temper," or...as the militia playfully put it: "The Short Shooter."

Standish—for all his years—was the same personality he'd always been and was just as sharp in his mind. Thanks to him, London banks and investors poured money, material and people into this New England. Miles truly was the beating heart of the colony. As well, Standish was a learned man who spoke several languages, including seven dialects of the Algonkin Woods-People, and it seemed he never stopped learning.

The path from the cemetery gave access to most of the trails in Duxbury. It was a too-well worn and frequented path a score of years in age. Captain Ashley Lyons and Standish's messenger left it, wound along the trails, cutting across grassed areas to go as directly as possible to where Standish waited.

There was no specific road from the cemetery to the home of Miles Standish, but instead a cluster of traveled paths as in Boston: cow trails overridden by horses and oxen, shod and unshod, oxen pulling carts and people walking—kicking up sand as they followed the animal trails. That was the way Standish wanted it; he didn't need unnecessary people coming to his home. His first wife had died shortly after he and the Puritan group had chosen to make

Plimouth their sanctuary (during that first, horrid winter) and when he chose to re-marry he had his house placed far enough away from all those old memories there but closer to the community cemetery. He jokingly said he lived so far from Plimouth to keep the "talk between women" held to a minimum, as his present wife—so far from Plimouth—would have little chance to hear from gossipers those old tales about him or be able to invent new ones. Others—including Ashley Lyons—thought that Miles was simply "moving closer to his wife" when he chose to build his house there.

Miles was standing, door open, seeming anxious. A short man with faded red hair and a sour look. This was the "protector of the colony" and—by God—you'd better remember that! No matter his physical size (or lack thereof) Miles Standish was proud, strong and passionate in his beliefs: a man who lived up to and loved his image. Everyone knew, adored or feared Miles Standish: that was the one thing everyone in the colony could say about him.

Ashley dropped the reins of his horse across a hitching-rail and went right to his commanding officer. The horse had been "ground-trained"...not by Ashley—who had neither the time nor patience for that sort of thing—but by the original owner of the blonde-haired gelding named "Joe." Joe might graze, but he wouldn't stray.

Standish's wife usually answered the doorknocker and greeted guests but this day was nowhere in sight. Not a good beginning for a summoned militia leader. Standish greeted Lyons with a hesitant handshake, one he ended as quickly as he could. That wasn't a good sign either, as Miles was ever the host, making guests feel very comfortable and at ease, then he backed quickly inside, waving Ashley to follow him into the small room by the front door he used as his combination office, command-post and trophy room. Ashley entered, noticing the armament hanging from the walls or leaning against them. On one wall were the antlers of an elk, taller than any deer and wider. Ashley wondered if this was the one Miles had shot when the colony was first beginning. All the original adults had talked (when he was a child) about that "last and biggest elk in the Massa-adchu-ess-et."

"Are those the antlers of your elk? I heard about that..."

Standish disregarded that, gave him a stern stare instead.

Ashley looked harder at Miles' desk. In the true Puritan fashion of using what was handy and not spending money for something more, it was not a "desk" at all, but a large drop-leaf table with one of the leaves removed so Miles could get his legs under it comfortably. Ashley smiled to himself. A similar drop-leaf—albeit smaller and made of cherry-wood—took up the area before the window. A Bible lay on that table and another—much bigger Bible with a wooden fastening—was on a shelf over the fireplace. The whole room shouted that its owner was a soldier and Biblicist as well as the chosen protector of the Plimouth colony.

The leader of our people, Ashley thought. *A little, redheaded man who frightens everyone.*

"You have missed militia meetings!" Standish barked.

"Yes, I have. Two. I made it last Saturday."

"Indeed, Lyons...indeed. You were there, a captain of militia I had appointed, DIRTY! Dirty, ragtag, same filthy clothes you have on now! Have you no shame, Lyons? No social grace? Your position as captain is one to which all soldiers must aspire. Then you show up dirty, clothes with holes in them, unshaven! What is wrong with you, man? I gave you the highest position in this colony, my own position, and you present like that? It is the duty of an English militia leader to be clean themselves and dressed the part...it helps educate the men and also gives them incentive to be clean themselves and strive to be more than privates!"

Standish paused to focus sternly on his militia captain. "You remember I gave you this assignment because you helped the colony so much, could speak the Indian dialects, and your parents were so well-respected."

Well-respected, thought Ashley, *means they're rich.*

"See here, Captain; it isn't as if you must wear a uniform of the English Army; all we expect is a shaven face and clean clothing." He paused, moving about a bit at the table, shuffling papers as if he were looking for something but giving the impression he was withholding something or leading up to something.

"I'm sorry about what happened at the meeting, Captain Standish...My wife's death..."

"Oh, I heard about that. Couldn't make it to the funeral; you have my condolences."

Standish went slowly up to where Ashley was standing (there was no chair other than Miles' in the room), holding up a hand to stop Ashley from moving, then put a hand on Ashley's shoulder. "We all—everyone in this colony—grieve for her passing, but it was God's mercy which took her from here to Him. Gratify her memory in that, lad."

"And the child? God wanted the baby as well?"

The hand pulled back fast!

"God's will is not to be judged or questioned! He saw fit to take the two of them together and will care for them together. This is a hard and short life, Lyons; all we have is prayer and God's mercy."

Standish went back to his desk. "You know what you have done to my reputation, Lyons? By being slovenly and dirty at a militia meeting? By having an un-groomed horse? By wearing clothing with holes? Man, what is the matter with you? You represent ME whilst you stand there as captain! I put this militia together thirty years ago! Do you drink wine or spirits, Lyons? Are you also a drunkard in addition to being slovenly and incompetent?"

There was no remark but a call to duel for that blast, but Ashley only responded meekly: "No...I do not take spirits. I touch no alcoholic drinks."

There was only a slight pause as Standish seemed to ready himself for the next pronouncement. "I have no recourse but to remove you from your position as captain." He turned and reached for the paper he had pushed around on his desk earlier. "Here, Lyons, this tells it all. You are summarily and immediately relieved of your command and will take part in the militia only as called-upon until I say otherwise. Turn in your hat and badge of office, your identification papers, your commission, musket, knife and...was that our horse?"

"No," Ashley replied, tight-lipped. "The horse is mine."

"We did not loan you that horse?"

"I purchased Joe from his breeder up in New Hampshire and have those papers, still sealed in wax. My horse."

"From one of those Anglicans up there? Are you Puritan or Anglican, Lyons? Do you trade often with those reformers? Did you get him from some Anglican up in Exeter?"

"Not from Exeter, Captain, but Hampton. Good Puritans."

"Those Antinomians are just the same..."

"God, Captain Standish, I got him from a Puritan!"

"I hope so. Then, turn in all other things mentioned. I was sure you had no horse."

"I have two, Captain Standish, two of my own. I never required a horse from the militia."

"That settled, go now to Plimouth, to the Great Hall, and return those items there...before you are further humiliated by someone coming to your house to ask for them."

Well, that was Standish. You loved him or you hated him...but...that was only his job—protector of the colony—and as such he had difficult decisions to make. So he had made this one.

Standish sat. The meeting was over.

Ashley turned to leave, then paused. "So...our business is done, Captain Standish? I am relieved of my command and released of my oaths to the colony?"

"All oaths specific and pertinent as a leader of militia, yes. To live here, you need respond to the laws. Ashley, go see Elder Otis and make your peace with God. What you said about the child...you'll need that."

Now there was the Standish he knew and respected.

"Thank you, Captain Standish."

Embarrassment over; anger building. "It's just as well, Captain Standish; I have neither the nerve nor imagination to lead further. I am better off without all of this, and you better off without me. If you'd like I'll write a letter of resignation."

"No!" Standish replied, his face terse. "You are discharged immediately! I'll not give you a chance to say you left voluntarily! You disgraced the militia and SHOULD be discharged in shame, and herewith are!" Standish could get angry also; he could live up to his reputation as Captain Temper.

"Well, thank you for your candor, Captain."

"You're a bad liar, Lyons, and a drunkard, it would seem. A beard, unwashed, clothes dirty and torn...you're a disgrace! Leave here and do not return!"

Ashley went out to his horse. "They even wanted me to give you away, Joe. Well, as Paul said, 'to Rome,' we go now to Plimouth, then home, Joe."

The New Hampshire gelding snickered. Joe was handsome, intelligent, and loved attention; but he had a peculiarity which his former owner could not abide, and why he sold him.

Ashley swung onto the small saddle and headed for the Great Hall in Plimouth.

CHAPTER 3

He urged Joe on. Everything Miles had said he must return was with him, mostly in his saddlebag as he hadn't bothered to take out anything he received from the militia and had to use it almost every Saturday when the militia met anyway…so he always carried it around.

He'd never fired the matchlock except at militia practice—he had his own musket at home—theirs hung in a closed scabbard from his saddle, signaling all who saw it that its owner was in the standing militia.

Joe would be glad it was gone as it forever bumped against him all the time. Wasn't much of a weapon anyway—a matchlock; Ashley would have preferred a rifled arm such as the French had begun to make: one of those flintlocks he had only heard about…and couldn't understand how they might work.

The whole thing about his captaincy was only a gesture on the part of Miles Standish anyway; Ashley hadn't wanted the commission as captain. It happened some six years back. A gang of a dozen or so Woods-People braves (it was always the young ones who got everybody in trouble) had been cheated by an English trader and killed him, in the process arrowing the cow and pig of a nearby farmer and tipping-over the farmer's water-barrel (a capital offense, as drinking water was a real necessity). The farmer ran to the security of Plimouth, telling tall tales of "Indians on the warpath" and "people grievously slain along with farm animals."

Miles Standish called for an emergency raid upon the Indians, and Ashley—a member of the militia simply because he was present in town at the time—joined the squad of mostly older men. They easily found the Indians, who had taken refuge in previously built fortifications upon the top of a rounded hill, but were reluctant to charge up that hill to kill them, as the "murderers" held the distinct advantage.

The appointed leader of the militia demonstrated against the Indians by ordering the firing of almost all their ammunition and powder at them (the braves merely ducking down as the shot went wildly over their heads or plunged into trees)...then it was decided that a messenger be sent to Captain Standish to request more ammunition, powder, etc., men and a plan of attack. Ashley, actually recognizing one of the young men up the hill, called to him in the Algonkin language of the coastal Woods-People, then walked without weapons up the hill to parley with them. By this time, the Indians were almost ready to run away, but the matchlock shots had aggravated them and the repeated yells by the militiamen made them angrier yet, almost angry enough to fight these men hand-to-hand. The militia had thus far been lucky the "cowering coastals" hadn't already charged and eliminated Miles' brave army.

Ashley, having been adopted by the Anakapi and able to speak the language of the "coastals," tried to reason with them. "Melt into the woods, brothers, and go away from the English who would kill you and all your families or make them slaves in the faraway islands. I can keep the men from the colony away a few hours so you may gather your belongings and flee beyond the river. The elk are there but no tribe lives there now, as they died from the white man's disease. I will lead the soldiers away from your village long enough for you to go in safety."

"You will do that for us? Why?"

"You hear me speak? You believe I am Uhu, son of the Mugquomp from the Lavrador, and learned to speak your language there?"

"Yes."

"Then leave."

They did. Simple as that. The Woods-People accepted their world as it was, not how it might be if they changed it. They didn't want or need change, just a decent understanding of what would usually happen. They saw good in everything: weather-change or local happening. Acceptance—however simple—gave them routine, and an acceptable routine could be modified for future events (like the coming of winter or summer). To live was all. Everything else was easy. They knew they could change nothing; they had no power nor usually didn't want any.

Ashley returned to the militia to tell them the Indians said they only wanted to pray for a while (behavior instantly recognized and condoned by the Puritan militiamen) and then they'd give up. The militia—mostly old men and frightened at the thoughts of battle—readily agreed.

Hours later, led by Ashley and rearmed with fresh powder and shot, they advanced steadfastly up the hill to find the top deserted. Ashley then led them on a false trail until dark, when they decided it would be advantageous to return to Plimouth rather than stay overnight in a dangerous forest. When Standish was told of the escapade he instantly was angry that the militia hadn't charged up the hill and hand-to-hand killed the Indians, but Ashley told Miles (alone) the truth—that he knew the Indians and they hadn't harmed anyone before and that trader they killed was not a Puritan but a scoundrel chased out of the colony and probably deserved that death for all the damage he previously had done in several townships—the finger of God finally touching him. And—at that time—Standish was being pressed by the colony committee to "clean out the heathens" anyway, as the colony committee wanted their land.

So the story developed that Miles had sent the militia after the Indians, and following a fierce fight (in which none of the militia was injured except Old Billy, who had fallen after stubbing his toe on a rock) the entire tribe had run away for good. Standish pointed out the gain of the land for the newly arriving settlers, the excellent job the militia had done, the "zero" rate of deaths and but one injury (he didn't send in the bill for the extra powder and shot until the following month's meeting), and the increased safety for the colony with the Woods-People gone. Miles was lauded by the committee, each of the militiamen received a written commendation and had his rank increased (with the resultant increase in pay), and Ashley was appointed captain of militia. Miles had told him, "I can't pay you, but I'll give you a commission—a captaincy; I'm allowed to do that—that will give you a monthly stipend. I'll send the recording of all this today. Thank you, Captain Lyons; I, the colony, and your King are indebted to you."

Now, Ashley was no longer in the militia and there was no King. He used to wonder if his father were proud of him as a captain of militia... if they might meet in Heaven some time and talk about that and all the things they hadn't talked about and those they had—although Ashley was only six when his dad died. Not much talking going on at age six, so they'd have a lot to discuss when he met him. But now—without his commission as captain—whyever would his father or anyone be proud of him... probably wouldn't talk to him at all. But that would be too different from the Heaven he was told about... where only love existed and good times. Religion was too difficult to figure out. Let the elders do it.

Ashley Lyons was not a man who hid in strong drink or used tobacco: the leaf which was smoked, because the Woods-People called their pipes "tobacco," not the weed. He held everything inside...all the hurt, all the pain, all the embarrassment and rage. His wife of twenty-four months and eleven days had encouraged him to talk to her, but even as much as she loved him, his stories about Brendan Splaine and "the others" were things which made her clasp her Bible to her chest...things which made her frightened and caused her to cry. Her husband's early life had been more than "difficult": it had been as scary as if he had gone awhile and stayed in Hell. And for a Puritan, that was unseemable.

So, even with her—with Anna—he could never tell the complete story. "When I have a child, I shall tell the child everything," Ashley had thought many times in those married months. "The child will have no fear of my stories." But now—as before—the child was dead and so was Anna. Their first child—a son—had died suddenly, unexpectedly, at the age of five months; died in his crib at night. This time Anna had died while attempting to give their daughter birth; she and the baby died together.

Anna, short for Hannah.

Like the Hannah of the Bible, the Lord had shut up her womb.

Anna was a woman of sorrowful spirit, but Ashley knew why. She had told him why.

Their wedding had been large—for the community involved—and well-attended. Whatever his stepfather, Mister Pennyweight, had available in the store had been used for decoration and atmosphere. It was held outside at Anna's parents' home and the prayer-group had brought foods of all kinds while the ladies of the church had baked cakes and pies. Those on the frontiers of Plimouth had brought in meat from animals of many varieties: fare from the forest and ponds for their favorite militia-captain and his new bride.

The whole colony knew Lyons and Anna, and showed it. The ceremony was a time of happiness and thanksgiving: the two previously lost souls had joined in wedlock and would now return completely to the church. Everyone was happy.

The wedding day—June fifth, Ashley's birthday so he would never forget the date of their wedding anniversary—was a glorious, sunlit and cloud-scattered day without high humidity or any wind. Clearly, these two were meant to wed this day.

Now, there was no one left to talk to, tell the stories to. Even Rufus Case—Ashley's friendly storekeeper—didn't believe everything Ashley had told him about those bygone—lost—years. And there'd never be another Anna.

He needed Anna to stay on compass, keep his life on course, show him and tell him what she could, what he needed. He wanted so much to have her back, to whisper in a warm, rosy ear, to feel the natural swells and curves and depressions of her body, just to know she was there and agreeable in a difficult world. All he wanted was what Anna freely gave him: her love for him was shown him daily. No wonder she could never be angry with him, even when he forgot to do the chores or walked rudely through her newly planted garden or stayed too late at militia meetings and her hot food turned cold and her cold food turned hot when he didn't show up on time.

When she died he penned a trifling little poem:

> "My wife lies here, whom I hold dear.
> A wife and child taken together, forever.
> Both to God before their time,
> To taste the dregs of Death's cold wine.
> She wanted only to live and laugh,
> And in epitaph
> I find I love her more
> Than ever before."

He took this raveled poetry to the stonemason, asking what it would cost to have it chiseled on her stone. The price was more than a year's pay and then some...so he re-wrote it on parchment and covered that with wax, then when she had been buried dug into the freshly turned earth where Anna and the child lay and interned it there, hoping somehow she might be able to read it. He said prayers aloud, wept without shame, then sat on the old, wooden bench under the spreading maple tree. That was the first time she had met him there. After that, he needed no poetry.

In Plimouth he completed his business at the Great Hall, then, as directly as he could, had ridden home without concern. Let Joe walk as fast or slow as he wanted. Didn't matter when—or if—he got home now: no one was waiting for him...worse than before he was married, as he didn't know any better then, just had wandered from here to there and never concerned himself with much, certainly not arriving anywhere on time except for militia meetings.

Joe gave the kind of ride which would let a man sleep as he moved...almost a cradling, so long as the rider stayed upright and didn't lean to the side, then—in sleep—fall. But the accomplished rider slept head-down, body leaned forward, reins slacked. The knights of Olde tied themselves onto their horses, as when all that weight shifted, mere muscle couldn't halt the avalanche of armor when it tipped outside the limits of the saddle.

Anna's horse—Bess—didn't allow a rider to sleep. She was all movement, short enough to force a rider to feel the rippling effect of her canter and a bouncing which Joe didn't present. Probably just as well, for if anyone tumbled from Bess, she'd just keep running. Joe would have stopped and either looked back while he grazed or gone over to nuzzle his fallen rider.

Single again; alone again. Awake several times each night thinking Anna was still there...then missing her all over again. Wishing she were there, praying for her immortal soul. Lonely.

Tired. Sad. Aching for her.

Had the child lived...had the first one lived...just so alone.

Anna had said that a child completed her; she then had reasons to live and enjoy. She lost the first child without warning or reason but never talked about it after the funeral...only mentioned it in her nightly prayers. Then she insisted she could love another baby. Wanted that for them both, so she could become "a real family." Ashley felt the same: he could re-live his childhood with a son or daughter, telling the tales he had lived and heard, teaching the ways of the woods and the coastal Algonkin Woods-People. He could do things for and with a child...those things he wanted his dad to have done with him, things he was cheated from doing when his dad died and Ashley had just turned six, things he never even knew until he had already grown up and realized he could—he should—have known them as a child, things he'd make up as his child grew. To give those things to his child...image-healing for the adult, based on his missed things. Now, all that was gone.

People told him to marry right away to get out of the mood he was in and presented to them, to give another good woman a chance at a husband and family, to give something to God—for as everyone knew, the reason FOR man to marry was to create and re-create, to continue life in the glory of God, to maintain in and with God's love. Ashley couldn't do that: there was too much hurt.

He missed Anna. Whatever incentive he previously had, there was none now. Everything they had wanted to do together, the places they wanted to go together, the children they hoped to raise...all these things and more were just...gone. Just gone. There was no incentive anymore, no initiative, no reason to do anything. The future of their past was the present and there now seemed no future but for others, as this present—to Ashley—would ever be his past. It had to be, for he never wanted anything else to change, only wanted to remain inside his memories of Anna and what they did together, what they planned together, what together they wanted. Without her there was no future. She anchored him to his past better than a hawser on a ship holds it against a pier. So, if she were there, Ashley wanted to be with her there. Now...later...always with her. Always. Her death had torn into his soul and collapsed his life.

Finally, Joe had gotten to the cabin. It had been a hot summer thus far this year...hot and muggy. The horses seemed to need water every hour; they had cut back on their eating; they became tired easily. Too much heat...so much water in the air it felt like living as a fish.

The cabin was really "a cabin"...log-sided and chinked with mud, but someone—some other renter—had covered the north side—the weather side—with clapboards, and another had added more to the east wall. It was a cabin with but a single room, divided with blankets hanging from ropes. There was the traditional stone and brick fireplace and chimney. Usually the size of the chimney denoted the amount of fireplaces in the house; Mister Pennyweight's store/home in Boston had seven fireplaces, a brick oven and a heating kettle for water, but he had insisted the chimney be no larger than others in the area as he wanted compliance and acceptance from neighbors rather than showing a great chimney and thereby boasting of wealth. The chimney of this cabin was tiny.

The mud mat at the front door was about worn through and had probably seen several winters. Ashley usually kicked his shoes and boots against it, hoping most of the mud and straw and manure he'd picked up from the small barn would fall off so he wouldn't have to remove his footwear. Strange how that stuff clung to shoes. Anna always wanted him to build her a mud room...a small, enclosed front porch where shoes and boots and rainwear could be removed and slippers or dry clothing substituted, and wet items left so they wouldn't get inside the cabin.

"Can you build me one?" she had asked.

"Can't build onto someone else's house," he had answered.

"Ask if you can do that."

Yeah...ask. He never bothered to. Another disappointment for Anna and to Anna. He wished now he had just gone ahead and built the damn mud room...had pleased her at least once. He always seemed to disappoint her...wasn't ready to go places on time, wasn't social when he got there, wasn't even too happy to return here once he got away from the cabin. Only was happy with her and she wasn't doing anything except concentrating on him—and he on her.

Just themselves…just together. Forget the world and the mud rooms and the rain-soaked and drippy coats…just the two of them together: that was his dream and his world.

Cake without jam: just her!

This cabin had a small back porch, open to the weather, just a few boards placed at the rear door. Ashley had replaced the rotten floorboards and stair-step as Anna liked to take lunch there, admiring the growing vines she had planted and which crawled up one of the posts. Now—often as possible—Ashley would sit in her chair on that porch—a ritual of a sort, honoring her and imitating her while he thought about her. He tried to eat her favorite foods on this porch: boiled potatoes, beets, bread, drink her favorite liquids, talk to the vine: tell it how well it was growing, how big it was getting, how proud he was of it—all things Anna would do.

He was hungry, but drank water to put off that hunger for a while more. Even the water was stale. When he was standing—just looking without seeing, lost in thought—there was a pounding on the cabin's front door which jogged Ashley back into reality. As he opened the door his landlord was standing there, his horse and carriage just behind him.

A bent-over man of aging years whose bushy eyebrows were more "salt and pepper" than Ashley's hair and whose long, oval face and sunken cheeks made him appear far more stern than he actually was. He wasn't one of the original Pilgrimes to this land but had arrived three years after their landing and with coin from Leeds had gotten several small properties, in one of which he resided and let-out the others for monthly payments or food or work. This cabin had cost only one pound, six, passage back to England for its original owner and already it had returned that cost through the rent.

"I'm gladdened to find you home, Captain Lyons; I've been by four times when you were not."

"Oh, the rent."

"Yes, the rent. Seven weeks you owe me."

Ashley tossed his money-purse onto the table. "Take it from that; I have no great concern about money; Anna always paid you."

"Yes, of course…and now she's gone and we have all prayed for her soul and the baby's."

"Thank you; I appreciate that and I'm sure she does as well." A simple statement, made in gratitude; his landlord thought otherwise: that Ashley was being sarcastic.

He counted out the coin he wanted and wrote a receipt in the new manner of a businessman, then pushed the paper toward Ashley.

"I've taken a rent payment exactly to today. Please read this and sign that."

Almost absentmindedly, Ashley signed the receipt and the landlord retrieved it.

"Where is your cat?"

"My cat? Anna's cat? I don't know...wherever it is cats go, I'd imagine."

"No, you wouldn't know, Captain Lyons, because you didn't bother to feed it and it went to a neighbor who would."

"Good for the cat. She was a nuisance."

"And who feeds your horses?"

"I do."

"When they're fed."

"What do you mean by that?"

"You're never here. The horses have no hay. Your neighbor has to feed them and groom them."

"Who told you things like that?"

"I know you're never here...you're at the cemetery every day, all day, until night falls. You are late in your rental agreement and you don't feed your animals."

"I DO feed my animals and what the bloody business is it of yours?"

"Careful with that talk, Captain Lyons...or should I say, 'former Captain Lyons'?"

"Oh...that's the way of it, is it? You have a long ear, to hear about my personal business so fast!"

"Everyone knows. The colony knows. The dismissal has been published at the Great Hall. NOW how do you propose to pay for rent and animal feed?"

"None of your bloody business! You have the coin, now leave!"

"I wonder where you'll be in a month's time."

"So you can collect your rental payment?"

"You're a man without a job, a wife..."

"Keep your bloody mouth shut about my wife! You can just go to bloody Hell, but leave here!"

The landlord actually blanched! From a smile, his face went into terror! Ashley could see what color there had been in that old face had left...the house-owner looked as though he would faint and fall through the floor.

"You cursed me! In the Devil's name you cursed me!"

"Pull yourself together, man!"

"A witch! You are a witch! You told me to go to…a witch!" He turned and "traveled" as fast as he could in his stunned condition, through the open door, then looked at Ashley as he backed away. "I'm telling the elders! They will deal with you, witch! Please don't burn my house; I can smell the brimstone already!"

"That's cat-pee under the step!"

The landlord scrambled to his waiting carriage and yelled to the horse as he snapped the reins, and the horse responded immediately, carrying him away from the witch.

With great sadness, Ashley realized what he had just done to himself—not meaning to, but done, nonetheless. He had frightened the landlord and lost his rental—Anna's rental—that he would live with, but the worst thing a person could be called was a witch. James, King of England, had so feared witches that when his mother commissioned a printing of the Bible to be assembled for him, she insisted a word other than "witch" be converted to "witch" and made that word and those charged with it the most hated (and usually the most tortured and killed) persons alive. Actually, for more than three hundred years previously, people had been charged as witches, tortured, tried and killed grievously in almost every case. True, most had been found in France, but it seemed that every Catholic country produced witches, and killed them in most hideous ways. Plimouth was not France and Puritanism was not Catholicism, and those Catholics who sought witches were not here…but the mindset of King James and his witch-hating Bible was the mindset and Bible of the original people of Plimouth, the Massa-adchu-ess-et, and being so close to the land as they were, their fears of witches who would sour cow's milk and turn hay brittle and indulge in anti-God affairs like May-Pole dances were extremely real. At the least, a witch would be shunned and have to leave the community; at worst, the accused witch was grievously slain, after confessing whatever sins his or her torturers wanted to hear.

Now, all that fear about witches was here in Plimouth, believed by the saints. The saints of Plimouth—that's what the Puritans called themselves: saints. Now maybe these saints would want blood from witches, blood from him! How saint-ful was that? Call a person a witch, torture and get a confession, kill the person because he confessed, then say justice in the name of God was served and everything was right with God? They were so God-fearing that they'd kill people in God's name! What justice would await THEM in death?

So…there would never be a better time to leave here.

Leave. Leave Anna's home. Leave the first house he had of his own—as Ashley stayed with his family in Boston most of the years previously to Anna and this rental place. It was good he had rented: it would be burned now by the townspeople. It was too far from his relatives and Anna's family anyway.

He had gotten on very well with Anna's parents. They had insisted, though, before the wedding he and Anna have a home of their own to go to... Anna was the youngest of her siblings and because she had a married sister and two married brothers, there were always "guests" at her parents' home. Her parents were right in saying the newlyweds had to have a place of their own without anyone bothering them on a regular basis. It truly was hard enough for Ashley and Anna to get used to keeping the rental-house going and feeding the animals without having to be courteous twenty-four hours a day to in-laws in a parents' home.

Ashley thought back: that first time they kissed was in Anna's parents' house, with them outside while he and Anna had gone in to get the evening meal to take outside and be eaten there.

He'd said, "I don't know what love is, but I think I love you." She hugged his neck and raised herself way up—she was tiny and he was tall—and touched her lips briefly to his. "I wondered if I'd get a tingle when I kissed you," she'd whispered.

"And you didn't?"

"No."

"Oh."

"I got it when I reached for you and it lasted after I kissed you."

After they married she said to him, "Does it bother you that...I'm an...experienced woman?"

"You mean because you were married before?"

"Yes."

"No...it doesn't bother me. Your life before me was years ago and your own. Now your life together with mine is ours...and we'll make our own experiences."

She cried.

Sat there and cried.

Then she dried her eyes on her dress, lifting it high enough to expose her pale, thin legs; they both hugged and kissed and she whispered, "I love you more than anything or anybody and will ever be yours. Let's do an experience now."

And, of course, being together gave them the time they wanted to really see and talk with one another. Anna loved being at home, having a garden with vegetables and herbs, having a cat, enjoyed watching her husband do the myriad of chores for a frontier cabin—this wasn't a "town-built" house, but a real-life cabin people in Plimouth talked disparagingly about which was on the very edge of the Plimouth settlement. There was a brook with clear water not far away which held seasonal fish; the woods had deer; turkeys strutted around within sight of the cabin's rear window. Not the comfort Ashley was used to or wanted to give his wife...but the place was quiet, solid and theirs.

Anna knew about flowers...all kinds of flowers. She'd see wild-flowers and have to transplant them into her garden, would gasp when Ashley took her into the woods to see the little, white "Indian Pipes" and suffer when they were touched and folded. Those she never transplanted—they wouldn't have lived anyway and she knew it...they were wild things and needed the wild; she understood that. Sometimes she thought to herself that she was just like them. But the tiger-lilies and the daisies and the flowers of the field and the birds and the squirrels put there were hers to admire and smell and care for...just the same way she loved to care for her husband...and her first child.

Now he had to leave. According to the landlord, Anna's cat was gone and having a better diet at a neighbor's place; there truly wasn't enough money to buy horse-feed AND pay the rent, now that his militia stipend had ended. Without Anna the walls here were cold and close; the bed was hard; the fireplace took too much wood to keep the place warm in the winter and it was too hot inside to have a fire for hot water in the summer. Some difference from his mother's home in Plimouth and later, Boston...but then, with Mister Pennyweight doting on her the way he did, his mother seemed to have more than enough comforts wherever she lived.

But Anna occupied his thoughts right now.

After Anna died, Ashley had cried when he had to move her things...Bible, knick-knacks, stones she had found in digging her gardens and saved, and round stones from that rocky beach in Plimouth. He almost had to close his eyes so he could move her clothing from the bedroom—that he wouldn't look at them while they left those places Anna had put them. He tried to tell himself he wasn't moving "her," just the clothes...But he didn't believe himself. Everything was Anna: everything held her touch—that tiny, warm touch. He kept a lock of her hair with some of his son's in a small bag tied around his neck but had given the rest of the cuttings she had made just before the birthing process began to her mother, along with her framed likeness her father had painted. So he packed more of her things now—personal things—wondering all the while how he could ever take those to her parents' house: how could he do that? Dropping them off as if he didn't want them, had no use for them, wanted to give away his wife, forget her the same way he seemed to be forgetting all her items. This was the worst job he ever had to do! He thought losing her was bad, but looking at, touching her things, then dumping them at her parents' home? Just ungrateful. He was ashamed of himself that he didn't have the courage to keep all these items, saying, "These are my wife's and I shall damn-well hold them in love for her!" Yeah...that's what it seemed to mean...that he didn't want any part of Anna so he was giving it all away—and, by God, that was not ever—NEVER—the case! He simply couldn't keep them all, had no room, didn't even have the cabin now. Tears filled his eyes and he openly wept.

He wasn't even counting the times each day he cried...there were too many crying-episodes to keep track of. God, he was lost without that woman!

In the drawer of under-linen he found little, sewn bags of wildflowers, which he assumed would have given perfumed scent to her garments. The things a woman does...the things Anna did. He could hear the songs she liked to sing, the verses she would most quote, those funny little sayings she would use, especially when he was in need of comfort or understanding. She had songs for everything: life, love, happiness, sadness. Snippets of song, mostly, enough to make a point without going on for several minutes. Sometimes simply rhymes, sung or spoken.

This morning, Ashley had decided to wear some clean clothes, the ones last washed by Anna that he had—until now—refused to wear. The refusal had been to keep something that she did as "fresh," but maybe she'd rather have him wear those clothes. After all, she had hand-washed them while about to give birth specifically for him to wear while she was unable to do the washing, and maybe his refusal to wear them would be an insult to her memory. He only had three shirts and two pair of pants. Had the militia realized their captain was so poor they'd have taken up a collection for him as they did for the needy: those dirt-poor farmers and old men and indentured servants. But in the end, after all the going back and forth about the fresh clothes, he couldn't bring himself to change into those washed clothes.

The shirtsleeve cuffs he wore were a bit worn but usable. The shirt had been white when it had been made in Lancastershire but now was almost a yellow; faded, thin, worn in many places and showed it...the fabric a great wrinkle with slight holes and tears and ragged edges which its maker never imagined for it. His mother had requested it; Mister Pennyweight had ordered it; the shirt was nothing he would have wanted or worn without Anna's insistence, but here it was upon him, his "best" shirt at present and none other available nor wanted. He preferred to wear no shirt at all, but his mother and Anna joined in their cadence against him looking like "a heathen savage," and the men of the militia—themselves champions of the shirted colonist (some of them even admitting to wearing underlined or shortened nightshirts in place of expensive "ordered" shirts) forced a form of "male colonist identification" upon him. Now he not only wore the shirt but slept in it, ate in it, worked in it and seldom removed it. The rain and beckoning rivers washed it—and him. His shoes were good, and all they required was a splash of water across them to carry away some mud and manure. His pants were fine; perhaps smelly from the horse and sweat. Ashley's saddle had been made for him and Joe, and it had a lower cantle with no knee-roll. It had "shined" the seat of his pants and wore it thin, putting tiny holes in the fabric. Soon, he'd need these repaired—as he wouldn't get different ones: whatever would be the reason for new pants be?

The clothing reminded him of Anna…everything seemed to remind him of Anna. Handling everything in preparation for leaving was as traumatic as it could get…except when he thought about Anna, and he thought of her every night; she was included in his morning prayers, along with prayers for the dead and thanks-be to God. He prayed for her, remembered how she looked, how she moved, how she smiled…her touch, her laugh, her determination in whatever she did…the way he felt with her: safe, happy, ready to do anything she asked (except build a mud room).

She always seemed frightened. When they were married she said to him: "Please never show me a temper so terrible I recoil from you for the rest of our marriage. I lived with such a thing and could never again." Anna's previous husband had literally purchased her from her father. He had rented the horses and plow to Anna's father when her father gained the land he settled his family upon in South Duxbury, then sent over indentured servants to help Anna's father chop and remove trees and brush and assist in the plowing and planting. Her father couldn't pay until the crops came in, as the crop's sale would pay for everything and more so. The spring rains held off, coming down too far away from the newly planted fields, then the summer sun scorched the dry earth, killing off the already weakened plants. No fall crop meant no way to repay. More credit was needed for the next year—and readily given—but somewhere along in the two-year process a request for Anna was made and accepted. Anna was the older child living with her parents and at age seventeen, she already should have been married. Her father and mother had hoped for "more than a farmer" for their daughter, but...to lose the planting and the farm with no way to return to England? Well, that would have been a disaster no husband wanted. Yes, the colony would have—for a while—fed and clothed them, but they might have then been shunned—as Puritans helped the needy but not those who did no work at all, and this was all Anna's father could do except paint portraits—a skill not at all appreciated by the colonists who felt that was not "real work" nor "God's dividend." So the only way out of the crop-failure-mess was to indenture his family or give Anna in marriage to a man thirty years her senior, with a great beard and a smell which turned people's noses and stomachs.

Well...what must be done was done, and she was married to him. Almost immediately she realized he fermented dandelion wine—about 140-proof—and drank that on a nightly basis. He didn't beat her, but he abused her...and so much so that one particular night he was almost blind and slobbering from the drink and Anna opened the door, led him outside, and locked the door after she went back in. He ultimately fell to the ground and in the morning was found by the farmhands, his fingers still grasping the door handle. The surgeon from the settlement felt his swollen liver and saw the effects of alcohol-poisoning on his face and skin. "Dead by his own hand," he told the elders, "with help from an illegal substance and the coldness of winter."

The women of the colony, however, wouldn't forgive Anna that she locked the door on him and took no pity for his cries all through the night. She was shunned and moved to Boston. There she met Ashley's mother in Pennyweight's store, and the rest was history. She found out what a husband really was, and he, how a woman could change his life for the better. But she was ever haunted by the stigma from her previous marriage. She and Ashley found that cabin to rent in the furthest part of Duxbury, inland—not toward the marshes or the sea—and settled there, mainly because her family still had its (now prosperous) home in Greater Duxbury.

Ashley sighed. Old history, all of it now.

He turned, seeing himself reflected in a poorly backed mirror on the wall...the one Anna always used to see if her hair seemed all right before she went out. She even looked there when she went out to the garden. Ashley smiled warmly, then stopped smiling as he didn't recognize himself: the reflected image did not look like Ashley Lyons. His eyes were lidded and his cheeks sunken; his hair was long, snarled, and had even more started to turn from chestnut to white—it gave him what his mother called a "salt and pepper look." And that beard. Not him. He saw a tiredness he hadn't known since Bren and the trip north. "God. Is that truly me?"

He saddled Joe again and put all the things he wanted to take with him and whatever tack and horse-feed he could find—which wasn't much—into a Rufus Case-designed pack on Anna's mare's back. Nothing held him here now. Anna and the babies were gone forever. Damnation, but it was difficult without Anna! He had only known her four years, but that twenty-four months and eleven days he had spent married to her made him feel more alive and wanted that at any other time. They'd lost the first child—a boy born less than ten months after they were married.

He was a happy, beautiful infant (of course—aren't they all?), but at the age of five months they had found him dead in his wooden (borrowed) cradle. Anna wept for weeks, and Ashley had to take her to live with his mother for that length of time…Which meant he had to return home to Pennyweight's combination store and home in Boston, by the Great Wharf. His old room was always left vacant for him—but it was a "third-story loft room" neither of his two half-sisters wanted as it was far too small and distant, and much too difficult to climb up those steep stairs. No guests of Pennyweight were bedded there. Fine for Ashley: all his belongings stayed put. Even Anna didn't move them when she was there. The corner where he had hidden Gair's unopened chest remained empty; the window which overlooked the Great Wharf and the ships of Boston Harbour still had oiled-paper on it.

Rufus Case, the storeowner and would-be inventor in North Plimouth, had an open stable in addition to his having a post-relay for the mail between Plimouth, Granite City and Boston. Maybe Bess could be left there for a while.

Ashley looked around for the last time. Cooking utensils and furniture would have to stay; he couldn't take them with him. He'd ask Anna's brothers to clean out the cabin and take whatever they wanted. He just had stuffed clothing into a sack and would carry whatever else there was in his hands…then took the horses, Anna's Bible, and left.

CHAPTER 4

HE was living in a tent!

GOOD GOD!

HE was living in a TENT!

Oh, he had before been "in" a tent, stayed a while IN one, but never "LIVED" in one!

For a short time in England—at age twelve, while his father fought and won the battle of Edgehill in the Civil War—he had stayed in his father's tent in a field. It then seemed quite fun at the time, but now…there was no fun, no excitement, no father. And his tent was not so large and certainly far less comfortable than his father's had been.

Several weeks ago he was sent here, and here he stayed, trying his best to make a go of it whilst he waited for the Scots Council to improve his life. They had sent him here. He had applied for asylum, had switched his religious support from Anglican to Scottish Presbyterianism (although in his heart he remained faithful to his father's Anglican ties, his mother—whom he loved dearly, as any twenty-year-old should—wanted him to convert to Catholicism and did manage to press his younger brother into that conversion, mainly because they had fled to France) and then they sent him here to wait for their decision as to whether he should fight or run.

Here, dressed in old clothing which had ripped for lack of repair, was Charles the Second, newly made by the Scots, King, and recognized officially by them as King of Scotland, France, Great Britain and Ireland. His father's son, a tall, handsome man of twenty years with an oval but sour face and large nose, who liked to wear a long and curly black wig as a formal accessory. He had heavy, black eyebrows and sunken cheeks (from the lack of food), but he was surely his father's son, looking almost the same as Charles the First of Great Britain and Ireland, the sickly and tactless son of England's James the First—the just, the loved, the religious James who feared witches.

Here Charles was, living in a borrowed tent, waiting for the Scots Council to cease their constant arguments among themselves and agree to give him the men, money, food and permission to let him fight an offensive battle against the English Army. The Prize? Why, freedom of religion for the Island's people and his return to London as its one and only King! What other reason could a King have than to fight a just battle for the true religion and religious freedom? It was all for the people, not for him—only for the people—and he sincerely believed this.

His close friend and personal instructor had just entered the tent to bring him news: "The representative from the Swiss is here. He wants money."

"Damn his soul! They know I have none! I live as a pauper, on handouts from relatives and my subjects; there is no money!"

"Still...I think you should grant him an audience."

"God help me...I need the Swiss so badly and they argue so pettily about money. They're the best mercenaries ever; they swear to whomever pays them and never break an oath."

"Then, my King, you should speak with the Swiss emissary. All is not lost...we shall have the money soon."

Charles ran a hand across his face, wiping at his eyes. He was tired to exhaustion. "I don't feel like a King. Two years ago I engaged in a naval demonstration on the Thames in hopes it might better make the people more aware of the plight of their King, so they would turn him free. It cost all the monies I had left to do that, and nothing came of it but bile." He signed. "Just months ago I signed for that damn Cromwell a blank piece of paper in which I agreed to any terms Cromwell would consider—even my life, which you know he wants—if he would just release my father from the prison. He scoffed at me and killed my father—beheaded him publicly!"

"Your father went bravely to his death, a martyr who would not renounce his religion to that 'reformed Puritan religion' they now preach!"

"On an improvised scaffold in front of the banquet hall, yes. That rotten Cromwell! My father refused to enter a plea because Oliver Cromwell the farmer had no right to arrest a King! So they executed him for not giving a plea, not because he was found or even supposed guilty! It's all that Cromwell's fault!"

"Cromwell will pay!"

"Yes...after I pay. Pay my Army, pay my bills, pay my debts...the Scots elected me King, but gave me no money nor credit. Thomas, I have sacrificed my honor, my conscience and purse, have abandoned my former friends in

England, have argued with my brother, have separated from my mother, and now live in poverty—a proclaimed King and son of a King—living in a used tent! The Scots make me a King, now argue amongst themselves and put me off to one side, directly in front of the English Army, only leagues away. Even my brother, James, commander of the French Army, rejects me."

"You gave him English and Irish troops."

"Which he lost because I couldn't feed them and he wouldn't!"

"You could return to the Netherlands; they treated you fairly well."

"So long as Spain paid them! They stopped that. This is it, Thomas: I live or die here in Scotland. Here we fight and win or I am taken into custody to be executed as my father. There are no further choices: we have done them all, spent all the money, used up all the relatives and friends, taken all the favors, exhausted all the options but this one tent in a field and these few and hungry Scottish soldiers."

Charles hung his head, blinking his eyes. "God help us."

"What shall I tell the Swiss?"

"He's not dressed for court, is he? They always come so well-dressed...I'm ashamed to greet these people in old clothing. I AM King, after all."

"But you are the King under duress, a monarch who fights valiantly for his people and Great Britain. No matter how you dress, my sovereign, you are always the King."

"Get me something to throw over this torn shirt...I never have a tailor when I need one. Why haven't you gotten the tailor out here?"

"My King...he is on his way. I've sent soldiers to get him, but we are at war, and people—especially tailors—are afraid to come to a battlefield."

"It's not a battlefield yet; General Fairfax has honored my father's memory by quitting as commander of the English Army in Cromwell's absence and the English Army has no leader. They stay in their camp and don't threaten us, except by their presence."

"Cromwell will come to command; he has to."

"He fights in Ireland. And he himself is no warrior: he was a farmer! All he ever did militarily was head a troop of horse and then became a Member of Parliament; and I still laugh when I remember my father fired him from that job!"

"Shall I tell the Swiss you'll see him later?"

"Cromwell, that rotten scoundrel! He hanged my father, hanged a King!"

"The Army has wept for months, my King…we must surge forward, now, whilst the English Army has no leader!"

"These Scots won't move unless they are paid! Shall I use your salary to do that?"

"My Lord, if the Scottish Army would fight for a ducat a month I'd gladly give it."

"Now you're being smart and smug! I hate it when you're like that!"

"My gracious Lord…if I have offended you, my heart cries our for forgiveness. All I want in life—in this world—is to serve you well and faithfully."

"That is why I keep you around; you comfort me more than ten women."

"I heard it was twelve mistresses you had. What shall I tell the Swiss?"

"How much does he want?"

"A hundred thousand francs…"

"A hundred thousand? He asks a pauper to find a hundred thousand?"

"Francs, my Lord, not pounds sterling…only about eighty-thousand pounds, and that should be here soon from the colonies; I can tell him that."

Charles the King sighed again. "When will that be here?"

"Less than a month, my Lord; less than a month."

"Wouldn't you think that with all my father gave to Scotland they'd respond to a call to arms without the need of advance pay? I told them I'd grant restorations and I had pledges from New England arriving soon."

"It's not the pay; the men are here in Dunbar. It's all the pettiness between Clans and Kirks—their churches. You must appoint some Scotsman to be the head of your army; then they'll all join you and give support; it's a Scottish thing."

"It all sounds so easy when you say that…"

"What shall I tell the Swiss?"

"Tell him to enter."

"What about your torn shirt?"

"Let him see me as I am: fighting for my country. Be so good, though, as to get my wig for me."

CHAPTER 5

Rufus Case was a long-time resident of Plimouth, an accepted Puritan, and a sharp businessman who had learned the hard way—by doing—but arrived in Plimouth with only one reason: to establish a business for trade with England. This he did—and did very well. His General Store & Fur-Trading Post was in North Plimouth, actually more northwest of the settlement but called "north" only for differentiation. Even Plimouth had moved: the settlement was now further away from the coastline of the land called "the Massa-adchu-ess-et": the Land of the Blue Hills (which in all reality was west of Boston, but land developers being what they were applied the name to all of the Crown's land, here in New England, and they began to call it "Massachusetts").

Rufus had recently expanded his store. His original one was but a single room and out of that he ran a tiny post-office (with a stable for post-change riders), a grocery store and a general merchandise store which also purchased local goods and furs. The fur trade "made" the store and Rufus continued its prosperity with maple syrup and sugar from the local Algonkins as a springtime addition to his wares. England loved his products and returned a healthy profit for him.

He ran the business alone for years, a man who loved what he did and did what he loved, a man older than Ashley by about a decade who seemed driven by life; recently he had hired a stableman/store-clerk, as the business was far too much for one person and sometimes too much for two. He had arrived in the colony and gained permission to open a store, then—to the distinct pleasure of the local storekeepers—located it about two leagues from Plimouth, on the Boston Post Road but still along the frontier. There he became a mail-stop and relay-station. Here, settlers, frontiersman, trappers, traders and Woods-People were each welcomed. City people—the ones who frequented Pennyweight's store in Plimouth (Penny's)—didn't bother to travel so far as "Case's Places" (as they called it).

Rufus—for all his dabbling in different things—was not seen as a "character," but instead as a very knowing and active individual. He tinkered with "inventions" and tried diligently to test and sell them. Whatever he saw that was newly imported he'd try to make better or cheaper for his customers. Rufus Case let no grass grow beneath his feet and tried not to let any furs run past his door, as it was the booming fur-trade which brought him here and anchored his business activities.

Ashley walked Joe into the stable, bringing along Bess. All the businesses here were under one roof, in a semi-circle. Michael, the stable-hand cum store-clerk, asked, "Is that a sorrel horse?"

Ashley thought that was a joke: "No, and not a green one, either."

"I don't think sorrel is a green color." Perplexed.

Michael was usually seen and not heard, which was a wonder, as Rufus ever said Michael could and would do anything, and if he didn't know how to do it he'd ask and learn. Michael stayed friendly, but didn't ask about a sorrel horse again, and Ashley took off the saddles and gear and tossed them into the tack room, then walked the short distance to the store.

"You've cared for your horses?"

"Yes, thanks to your stable-hand. How did you know…"

"That you were here? I built this place so I can see everything from this window."

"Well, hello, Rufus, it's always nice to get a greeting from you when I arrive."

"You need a shave and a bath."

"Thank you again."

"Shave off that beard. Michael will do it."

"The stable-boy? Let the stable-boy shave me?"

"He needs the practice; he aspires to bigger things. Point being, I'm not a barber and my water is for drinking. Why are you here if not to receive a shave and a bath?"

"You're nothing if not direct, Rufus; I'm here because I don't want to go to my mother's and I can't go to my mother-in-law's."

"Why don't you find a woman to whose house you *can* go?"

"Touché! That one hurt!"

"Sorry…I live alone and forgot…"

"I've been ousted from the cabin."

"Ousted? By whom?"

"The landlord. He came by and collected the rent—to date—then told me to leave there."

"How pleasant of him. Did you put a boot up his arse?"

"Actually I did worse."

"Ah! I thought there'd be a story here! Hahahahahahahaha. Tell me!"

"When I got home the landlord was there..."

"But you said you paid him."

"Yes...but then he was smart with me and I lost my temper and told him to go to Hell..."

"Oh, no! Oh, good God! That was a witch's curse!"

"Don't I know; that's what he said."

"Oh, Ashley...start riding and don't stop until you reach China, then hide there."

"That's exactly the kind of support I need."

"God!" Rufus sighed deeply. "I'd rather fight an Indian war than have this community think I were a witch. All right...this is what you must do: go to Elder Otis and tell him everything...Ashley, look at me: Everything! Tell him it slipped out because you were tired, sleepy, tell him you'll do good works for the poor and the colony...*any*thing...just get him on your side. He almost controls the pulse of religion here..."

"He was at our wedding."

"Otis? Otis was at your wedding with Anna?"

"Yes; he knows her family."

"Merciful God! Thank you, Father. Ashley, go there NOW!"

"A bit late in the day..."

"Not for Otis! He reads his Bible every evening and takes visitors and leads a prayer-meeting...and he's really an understanding man. He helped me get through the prayer-meeting thing when I first got here...Ashley, go NOW!"

"Rufus, I don't think—"

"That's your trouble, Lyons: you don't think! Now listen to me and I'll do the thinking for you. The only way to stay alive in this community—and don't imagine I don't know—is to conform to their rules. They tell you to pray daily and you'd better. They tell you to attend prayer-meetings four times a week and you must! They hold their religion dear and practice it every minute. Almost every house in this settlement is literally a church. Only the differences held by the zealots separate prayer-meetings, and everyone, including their indentured servants, must be included in their prayer-meetings. The ones with large rooms in their houses are expected to use them to the spiritual aid and good of the community and the continuance of the faith. Ashley, these people are very strict. If someone says you're a witch, you can be killed by them!"

"You don't attend their meetings."

"I'm not accused of being a witch! Besides, I have a large room here and conduct prayer-meetings, whether or not anyone else shows up, because I know I have to be able to tell these people the truth: Michael and I attend. Now you listen to me, Lyons: you go to see Elder Otis NOW!"

"There's more."

"Whatever more could there be? Did you also curse his horse?"

"Miles took away my militia leadership and told me to go pray more."

Rufus groaned. "He literally said that to you? Took away your leadership and told you to go pray?"

"Among other things. He did say he was sorry about Anna."

"Oh, Lord...we're all sorry about that."

"I know, Rufus...you couldn't have been nicer when it happened."

"That bastard, Standish!"

"No...Miles is all right...He's pressured by the elders on one side and that new English colonel on the other. My own fault: I skipped drill twice and the militia looks up to its leaders almost as the English Army looks to its sergeant-majors. Being slovenly and a poor example is a thing unacceptable."

"Standish told you, you were slovenly and a poor example?"

"Well, I was, and I did."

"Standish takes his position in this colony too much to heart. He's dabbled in everything from trying to jump off the longboat from Mayflower onto the land first—to protect the boatload, he says—to being assistant governor; and he'd like to be governor! He still insists he's the protector of the colony, trying to emulate Cromwell as protector of England, I imagine."

"Well, he's had that job since he arrived here...thirty years! Whew! I know I couldn't last thirty years with that bunch."

They both laughed. The Plimouth Pilgrimes WERE a tough bunch.

It was late, but Elder Otis—a man of many years and much education—was wide awake, lights burning. He brought Ashley into the room he used for speaking with members of the flock.

"I hope you don't think I'm wanton with these lights...I like to read and I require perhaps excess light. If it bothers you that I use too much..."

"No!" Ashley was fast to answer. Otis was literally in charge of religion here and yet was frightened that someone might think he used too much light or oil. Poor man: trapped in his own religion, frightened he did too much or too little but never enough for the settlement.

"Some would say differently. But you are not here to discuss lights. Have you a religious concern, Captain?"

"Yes...a large problem...but first I must tell you I no longer am a captain...as of today."

"I heard that and it gives me great concern. Go on."

"You heard that already?"

"It's posted at the Great Hall, and three people have already come by to tell me...gossip about their reasonings and all that. How did all that happen?"

"I don't know what Captain Standish's motives were, but I skipped two militia meetings in a row and I was...well, as Miles put it, 'ragtag and dirty' at last Saturday's meeting."

Otis grimaced. What he had heard was true. "And your other problem?"

"I was...tired, I guess, and angry about losing my position as captain after all these years and, I...cursed my landlord."

"I heard about that also."

Ashley groaned to himself. Was there nothing which happened in this colony Otis didn't know or hear?

"Robert came directly to me after his upsetting experience with you and we prayed and I gave him encouragement. Then I suppose he went to everyone else he could tell the story to."

"Oh, oh, oh, oh." This was bad; the worst.

"First of all, I asked Robert to tell me all his story, as I shall ask you. And he did that, saying you were a witch and did curse him. I agreed with that and said that if it were true, then his house should be burned to the ground and that ground salted over such that nothing would ever grow or live there again."

"Oh, my God!" Ashley exclaimed. "You BELIEVE him that I'm a witch?"

Otis laughed and his belly shook. "No, no, no...I don't believe you're a witch but I had to convince him I was serious. When he realized he would lose his house and its income and never be able to use the land, he began to change his story."

"To...?"

"I suggested you had been so tired with all your efforts before and after your grievous loss that the Devil found an opening in your mind and put in that curse you uttered to Robert. Then I said that since you probably were not a witch and the council would decide that, then Satan didn't live in the house and we could simply pray there and all the evil would be gone; then he could feel free to rent out that cabin again. He liked that part."

"And he took that well?"

"Remarkably well. He now will agree that you probably are not a witch but was temporarily used to say what you did to him, and—of course—you will enter into a period of prayer with me so your mind can no longer be used by the Devil."

"What a relief!"

"Well, yes and no. Yes, that you probably will not be called to testify to the Grand-Council of Elders, but no, that you WILL be shunned and requested to leave Plimouth. Also, you must do quite a lot of reading and speaking with me, and take several tests—trials—to determine the level of your—apparently temporary—possession. Ashley, recite the Lord's Prayer for me, right now; and say the name, 'Jesus.'"

Ashley did that.

"Our religion says we are made in God's image, so we can assume what we say and do is permitted by God…but the 'rules' are interpreted in many ways. If you renounce the Devil and his works and invoke God, that will help you. You have made no spells nor sacrifice we know of, and no animals around you have died. These are all good things and in your favor, and I shall write them all down. Also, this seems to be the first and only time a curse has passed your lips, so there would be no demonic possession, as, if a demon were present he would not have allowed you to say the Lord's Prayer."

Otis HAD been frightened, Ashley thought, as he made him say the prayer before he talked further and had to be assured things were well.

"This is a very serious thing, Ashley, so you must take it seriously."

"I do."

"All over Europe, people accused of being witches are dying under torture. Thus far it has not happened here, and if God permits me, it shall not. We'll spend the rest of the night in prayer and talk, and in the morning we'll go to the elder's meeting and explain this to them. And you're going to have to praise God and Jesus and say the Lord's Prayer in front often. Then I'll tell them you are going to leave the settlement to become a hermit who prays constantly: they'll like that image. Then…leave here and don't be seen by any of the people for at least a year, all right?"

"All right…but what do I tell Anna's parents and how do I visit Anna's grave?"

"I shall tell Anna's parents myself, on the morrow, the whole story. I am sorry, but for at least a year you cannot—must not—return here, and even then you must write to me well beforehand to let me tell you if you are acceptable for a return—and that might only be a brief visit in the daylight. These people are so immersed in their Bibles that they fear everything, so you must not become a thing they fear...else..."

"I know."

"Now, we seriously pray, and with God's help you and I will get through the morning meeting."

The following morning, Ashley again rode to Rufus' store, the all-night session with Elder Otis (who fell asleep twice during that time) had been exhausting and the morning meeting with the elders of Plimouth was frightening at first; but all the elders voiced agreement that the curse was a one-time thing and Ashley was not a practicing witch. They gladly agreed that a year as a hermit, praying constantly, might be the better thing for him, and openly showed relief when Elder Otis told them the year of atonement would not be done in the Plimouth woods.

So he was free of Plimouth and would have to call Anna to him, as he couldn't go to her. She probably knew anyway; he had to take that position.

Missis Otis had told Ashley a courier carried the message that Rufus Case wanted Ashley to return to the store when he left Elder Otis, so he dutifully did just that, leaving Joe ground-tied outside the store while he went in. Rufus was standing there, apparently waiting for him.

"Will you have some tea?"

"No...I just want to water Joe and gather my things."

"You know I'm no busybody, but I would like to hear what happened."

"No, Rufus, I never knew that: I always thought you WERE a busybody!"

There was silence for a few seconds, then they both laughed: food for the soul. Ashley because it was a good joke and Rufus as he'd been caught in a pretense.

"It's good to see you laugh, Ashley."

Ashley sighed. "You caught me unaware. I haven't laughed since..."

"I know: we all loved Anna."

Rufus, seeing Ashley's eyes tear, turned away to his tea. "Sit, and I'll pour you some tea from China." He stepped to a side-server.

"Is that why I'm here, Rufus? For tea? You sent a messenger to Elder Otis which seemed important."

Rufus was a lot more serious than the day before. "I have a job for you."

"Rufus...cleaning stables and unpacking boxes is not for me."

Case laughed so hard he almost tipped over his tea. "I would have said the same thing, given your position. No, Ashley, not a job here: a job away from here which probably only you can do, if you will."

"What? Riding escort? Guarding your coin or trade-goods to the Woods-People?"

"Ashley, I've been approached by someone very high in this colony, to do a job…to find someone to do a job which may be extremely important."

"Who?"

"Can't tell you his name."

"Find who?"

"A man off an English packet, recently arrived in Plimouth."

"If he's recently arrived and you know the ship, anyone can find him."

"Find him—follow him when he leaves Plimouth."

"Sounds like you want me to be a spy; I find difficult the idea to snoop on people."

"These Frenchmen aren't 'people': they're jackals pretending to be dogs, men who would take our lives and our country so they can steal from this land."

"A little like the English have done here."

"Be here in the moment, not your taught history! Men fight for their homes when their failure to fight brings homelessness. I am unable to do this job; you are. England needs this colony and doesn't need France to take it. She has almost bested us for centuries, and think what would happen to the Indians you love so much when those black-robed Catholics got hold of them."

"Yes, they'd convert them to Catholicism rather than Puritanism."

"Have you no loyalty to England?"

"Rufus…I just don't know what to do these days…with Anna gone and me being sent away for a year…I just don't know. I need some advice but I don't know who to ask or what to follow."

"It's no weakness to ask and follow advice. The advice—of course—has to be good and should guide you well."

"Elder Otis tells me if he needed to go away for a year or so he'd go either back to England or to New Amsterdam. But with England at war over Ireland and Scotland, I don't think England's a good choice for me. Maybe New Amsterdam…Bren liked the Dutch and they'd have plenty of work for me."

"Join their church and they'll give you a choice of women as well!"

"Don't say things like that! Bren explained all that to me. It's their form of response to the wilderness and a new colony, just like the Indian. Just because one portion of their Church displays young women to be married…then the men can 'test' the women to see if they can bring forth children, which is necessary for the building of the colony…it doesn't mean their faith in God is faulty, only their social graces. The Woods-People don't get married either."

Rufus closed his eyes a moment. "Oh, God. Bren was no teacher for you! All right, where will you go? What will you do?"

"Boston, to see my mother...After that..."

"After that you have no place to go and nothing to do. Do this job and help your country. It is not to *be* a spy, but to *follow* one."

"Really?"

"Very really. A man I know who works on the Plimouth Dock was approached by three men who wanted to know if that was 'the wharf of Plimouth,' was that 'the only one.' When he said 'yes,' they all laughed, apparently because we only have one wharf and not too large a one at that. Anyway, they gave him a thruppence for his 'prompt answer' and walked away...but the big man said, 'Do you suppose Boston is the same?' and they all laughed. So they plan to visit Boston as well.

"It's not unusual for people to come to Plimouth or ask questions..."

"But to arrive in Plimouth and want to be sure *this* is Plimouth's wharf and not say anything about unloading or loading cargo? Oh, and one more thing: one of them seemed to be drawing a map, wandering about on the shoreline and pausing to draw the fort and the bay and things. I was told a suspected spy from France is here in Plimouth and that person wants me to find a trails-man who can follow—not approach or talk to—just follow him. Tell me 'yes' and I'll tell you more."

"Yes. What else do I have to do?"

"Good! He's here off the packet from England and seems to be very interested in the fortifications and tide-schedules in Plimouth; he carries a journal and writes in this; you should also."

"Get a highwayman to steal it and be done with it."

"He'd just get further protections, re-write the journal, then go to ground. No...he must be followed and his errands documented. When I learned I needed a frontiersman who could trail but also read and write, well...you're the only choice. Besides, you need to get away from this settlement for a while."

"I don't know whether that was meant to be good or bad. Is this really important? You're not just doing this to get me something to do?"

"Extremely important, Ashley. Truth be known, we think the spy is a bastard of Louie."

"Louie? France's Louie? The King?"

"Himself! This man looks like Louie and acts like royalty. He has two purses and a man-servant or two."

"Or two? There's three of them?"

"At least three…maybe two more, so there's probably five of them…that's one of the things you must find out: whether they stay together or go to different places. Right now, only three are always together.

"I have to watch *five* people?"

"Five are easier to watch than one."

"Rufus the understanding."

"The man in Plimouth has been able to watch there, and they stayed overnight, but they've rented a coach and four and may now have left for Boston—where they'll either leave the coach or go somewhere else in it. Can you leave soon? I have a pack and money for you all ready."

"Now?" Ashley sighed.

"Ashley, once you start this, there's no return until the end. You must find out who these men are, where they go—write the addresses down—and what they do. Send me a written report daily or as often as you can; I'll pass everything along to…that person."

"Rufus…I don't know if I'm able to do all those things…what use to France would any information from this colony be?"

"If they know the amount of wood we send to England they could realize the number of ships being built yearly. Is that an answer? If they know the size and shape and depth and tide-schedule in the harbour, could they not plan to sail a fleet into it, unload troops and take the town? Our 'fort' is a joke! Then, they could deploy soldiers. We have no cannon guarding Plimouth as Port Royal has in the Indies, or in Panama. To obtain a census tells them the possible food here, and manpower to gather it…So they would know the size of any armed force they would meet. Blacksmith-totals tells them arms and repair; granaries tell them food storage—all useful for an invading army. Local politics lets them know our loyalty to the Crown—well, England, as we have no 'Crown' right now…Or if we even would fight an invading force. In addition to all that, there was a law passed in sixteen-eight to protect those who fled from persecution of other countries. If a person can get into England, he's under the King's—in our case because we have no King, the Parliament's protection."

"So we can't bother spies?"

"Didn't say that. I said anyone who came here was under the country's protection, but—and this is a big 'but': if those persons welcomed to England do treason, they're considered traitors and executed. That's why we must document the travels of these Frenchmen and their conspirators, to prove them traitors. Enough answers?"

"Too many. How do I—*where* do I begin?"

"Bayside Inn in Plimouth says the three Frenchmen and several others off the ship stayed there overnight. A coach for six but with only four horses was rented, so they're not in a big hurry; the coach will be used to travel to Boston, there to leave it at Howard's Stablery. Boston is where you begin, at old man Howard's. You're up to all this? Chasing men around?"

"You know I have nothing else to do. But right now I'm pretty tired; I haven't slept since yesterday and with all the...excitement I've gone through...I'll fall asleep on Joe on the road."

"I'll tell my contact in Plimouth you'll do it, and since you've nowhere to go, there's a cot in the tack-room, off the stable. Use that for some sleep and you can leave whenever you're rested. I don't think you'll need a blanket: the horses generate a lot of heat."

Ashley leveled a stare at Rufus. "If I have to sleep in a stable, I'm calling you 'Joseph'!"

"Hahahahahahaha...that's funny!"

"What about breaking the fast?"

"None for me, thanks; I've already eaten."

"Thank you, kind host; I guess I will have a lie-down."

Rufus Case didn't go to Plimouth: he sent a courier and received an answer within hours, about the time Ashley Lyons was waking from his daytime nap. When Ashley went back to the store, Rufus was there at the table, drinking tea.

"Will you have some tea?"

"To go along with the non-existent breakfast?"

There was a silence for a few seconds and they both laughed.

"Under that napkin is your breakfast, and a lunch-snack for your ride."

Ashley sat, uncovered the meal and ate quickly.

"This tea is from China."

"What about the job?"

"Good pay, for a start."

"Good pay is always a good start."

"I sent off a courier earlier and received an answer in some detail. There's a purse of coin for you: silver and gold. You'll need it to pay lodging and people who will answer questions for you. I have boots and a vest I'll give you which can hold some of that coin. Empty the purse and I'll re-fill it."

"Very nice start: an always-full purse. Rufus, aren't we at peace with France? Why would the French King want to send spies here? And isn't France's King related to our former King?"

"Every European monarch is related somehow to every other there…it still doesn't stop them from starting wars and killing people."

"You really think these are French spies?"

"Yes I do! Two of them are dark as Frenchies; the others talk like Englanders, maybe from the east coast."

"How do you find out these things?"

"Let's just say someone who loves Plimouth is a vigilant person but he is not able to be a spy; wants me to use you as one."

"You know, Anna never wanted me to visit you."

"Why was that? We've been friends for years."

"Oh, she said you weren't a married man and unmarried men had the tendency to cause married ones to sin. 'Set a poor example,' was the way she put it. She'd say, 'That Rufus Case sets a poor example for a married man. Why isn't he married? What happens there in that store that he doesn't want a woman in his life? You stay away from him: he's trouble!'" Well, that was Anna: she loved everyone but was wary of them, and when it came to her husband, she was protective. Ashley wondered what she was thinking right then as he spoke with Rufus, with Anna either seeing him there or otherwise knowing about it. "But what *about* you, Rufus? Is there no woman in your life? No children?"

"No…not for a long while…since London. She had ideas about us and how our lives were to go…and I just wanted to go to work and 'do' something other than attend parties and visit people. I wanted less; she wanted more. She wanted me to do what she did and I wanted money and a business of my own. I shut her out…put a wall between us…and I've lived alone pretty much since then."

"She left you?"

"I had left her—in my mind and heart—years before she left me. She died…after all that she died. In my own way I still love her…the memory of her. It was an incomplete marriage from the start: I married her to become a partner in her brother's business, then when I earned enough I left his business and started my own…I had met enough people who would sponsor me by then. I could have changed my mind…about her, about work…but I didn't. Then she died…and…I came here. So here I am, working alone and having no time nor need for women, except as customers. I live so far from Plimouth for several reasons: first, I don't care for all their rules and I don't need to attend prayer-meetings four times a week plus Sunday services day and night, and have to speak nicely to all the people there. More important, I'm a fur-trader: there are no furs in Plimouth, nor do people there want any. I'm here to trade with the Woods-People: they know where I am and they bring furs here."

"You don't go to the camps to get them?"

"Ashley, please. Can you see me—who is afraid of the dark—in an Indian village? And how would I talk to them? I don't understand most of what they say in English! But you: you would go to the villages but I can't hire you to do that as you won't! You speak their language; you know how to set a camp at night, fend off wild animals, don't get lost...you could take horses and trade-goods: not me!"

"That's the way Bren lived."

"Bren was an exceptional man in an exceptional place at an exceptional time. Furs were plentiful in Mont Real and there were rivers for his canoe, which let him move rapidly with trade-goods and furs. Don't talk 'Bren': talk 'Rufus' here." He smiled.

Ashley smiled as well...the memory of Brendan Splaine in the Lavrador made him happy and sad all at once.

"Ashley, the placement of this store is perfect for me. The townspeople leave me alone, I get mail and messages twice a day from the riders out of Boston and Plimouth—and I feed them so they *will* stop. And the Indians bring their furs to me. Most of the time the men arrive, but two of the lesser chiefs now bring their wives and children. Do you understand how important that is?"

"No...not really."

Now Rufus had a wide smile, almost a grin. "When I first began to build this store I had several men from Plimouth over here to do it—don't think for a moment I built this myself. I had English investors and hired Plimouth residents to do it; also hired a guide to the Indian camps and we went with trade-supplies to them all. I did that for about two years...And I slowly got the friendship of the tribes and just as slowly convinced them to take money for their furs so they could buy the supplies I had here at the store or could order, but didn't have with me at that time. Of course I wanted them to buy here, but I was too small then and didn't have all the goods I do now, the things they wanted at once. But with the English coin they could go anywhere—any of the other trading-posts like your stepfather had in Plimouth, and the ones further south, toward Providence. Not many of them could understand the concept of using money for goods, but a few who knew the old Pilgrime Fathers did. Ashley, do you understand the idea behind that? Having the Woods-People use English money instead of wampum or furs?"

"Not really, unless you have... Unless you want to have Indians around who will work for money."

"Exactly! I had money to spare, not goods. After the store was built the Indians came here and built the original stable, hay-barn and fencing. I paid them as I'd pay Englishmen; they bought what they wanted and not what I had to take on horseback to their villages. Now they were 'customers'!

"Here's the other thing...and I'm so happy about this I could kiss those chiefs... when they started bringing their wives, the wives told other wives, and now the wives want to come here. Then they brought their children... children want six times what wives want in stores! See where this is leading?"

"Yes: more money."

"No! Integration! Think the greater picture: these Woods-People have spent their lives in poverty and fear. Now they come here in peace and safety to an English store, see and choose what they want to buy, live better, and their *children* are in at the beginning of all that. They're using English coin, talking our language, beginning to think like Englishmen...the Indians will prosper: they'll learn to trade and speak English and work in English ways and bargain with English coin. Ashley, no more Dutch muskets for trading; no more French talk or whatever the French bring for trade...the Woods-People will learn English ways and their children's children will be part of this settlement."

"I don't think so."

"I know they will! Every country and race the English have met around the world have eventually integrated themselves into English speech and manner. This colony is no different. The French want to keep the Indians wild so they can use them. The Spanish want them wild so they can steal from them. But the English *buy* their lands, treat them as 'people,' not 'savages'! However else could Plimouth still be here?"

"The English women of the colony will not stand for Indians living among them."

"I don't know about that. Those strong and silent braves do things with earnest which even English women appreciate."

Ashley didn't understand that statement and Rufus smiled inwardly at that thought.

"Since Cromwell put the noose to Charles last year, the trades-people and business-owners have come out ahead, paying more taxes but able to do more work and increase their businesses. It has helped me here... with selling and buying from England."

"When I think of Charles I think of Bren..."

"Your Irish friend in the wilderness up north."

"Yes...James was bad enough, I understand, but Charles sought money everywhere."

"He suspended the laws for favorites—who stole money to share with him and keep the rest themselves...a poor example of a King."

"Bren never lived long enough to hear Charles' neck was stretched. Bren was so afraid of Charles...he'd have loved to hear he was hanged publicly last year."

"Charles hated the Irish. He despised the Catholics. When they talked in England about bringing back Catholicism to the island the King had a tantrum! When that actually happened in Ireland a few years before...well...James was in a rage. That's what drove our Pilgrime friends to Holland: the thought of a great religious war in England and execution for their beliefs. When they opposed James they had to leave. Charles got back at them for ducking out on his father by levying additional taxes on goods shipped to and from our Puritan founders...There was a Royal Charter Tax and excessive customs taxes. He bled the merchants. A King without a conscience is soon a King without a country...Or in Charles' case, the country is now without a King! Good riddance, I say!"

"To think we'd see the day when a King is publicly executed."

"Fear not to kill the King; 'tis good he die."

"What? Sweet God in Heaven, Rufus, that is treason to say things like that!"

"Ha! An old Marlowe play, one of the times I returned to London. Just remembered it as it was so silly then, but that's what happened in our history and what happened to Charles the First."

"You went to see a forbidden play?"

"It wasn't forbidden at the time. Ashley, would you do another thing for me?"

"The job you mentioned?"

"No...I just remembered: my travel-papers to get me to London are with a man in King's Town. Could you go there and get them for me? I have buyers coming today and Michael is up to his ears in work."

"I can imagine just that—in that stable. Rufus, I'm not supposed to go there for a year—not even supposed to be *here*!"

"It's not too far a distance; you can be in and out without being seen."

"I won't have to see a play, will I?"

"That was years ago...here, I'll write the directions for you: it's a hard place to find unless you know how to get there. It's a big house but off the main roads; actually fairly close to the Indian village out there."

CHAPTER 6

Ashley couldn't remember when he had been in this area—King's Town—before. The land prickled with dunes and small hills, inconsistent in its level and sporting also dribbling creeks and strands of tall pine trees set upon sand and sheltering wide, wild meadows of tall grasses and flowering weeds. This was almost a community, with its four houses…a tiny neighborhood separated half a league from other habitats, making one wonder at the sight of these huddled houses and asking why these particular people and none others would be out here, so far from the town.

Milk cows could graze on the open leas; no lions had been spotted since the second springtime of the original colonists; nor had a wildcat been seen within that time either. Other parts of the colony, perhaps; not here, even with all the water around.

Far down the road was the culmination of this creek and others here; the land slanted and bled into a slow-moving stream which might be called a river, but it was a stream surely and the way it had cut into the low ground made it necessary for the colonists to build three wooden bridges across those tiny islands the stream forged. Their efforts upon the two sandy islets (the Bible used the spelling "iland"; the French wrote "ile"; the Romans called it "insula" in their writings, but each meant "a little island") the stream made forced the colony to acknowledge the unofficial name for the place as "The Three Bridges." Yes, there was a swimming hole, and yes, there were beaver and muskrat and a few otter had been trapped there along with a skunk no one dared approach to remove from the trap. But that was almost four years ago.

This was a good land, rocky but fertile, with plenty of rain in the growing season and enough warm days to make a man feel glad when autumn arrived. The wild grasses tamed fast under the scythe, and the berries lured pickers and the hunter's game. The olde men said England was the better place to be and grow and hunt, but Ashley knew otherwise: the Puritans now in power in

England fostered new types of taxes; business was the style, but try to start one with all the cost and documents; and so far as hunting deer to feed your family? If you could find one it was on someone else's land and forbidden to the point of death to shoot one, much less eat it! They'd hang the entire family for that! And if you didn't pay your taxes, you could/would be imprisoned.

He shook his head slowly, thought about Bren; Bren and his refusal to pay his tax. Had Bren only stayed here when he'd brought Ashley back from the Lavrador, he'd probably still be alive today; certainly he'd have had a longer, much less painful life for the length of time he did live. To rot away in a stone cell was no way for a man to live and die.

It didn't seem that Ashley had been able to stop for a while, rest peaceably at all, really gather his thoughts, get a decent night's sleep since all this with Anna and Miles and Otis. This just went on and on, a maze of action and effort coming from different directions such that he couldn't understand or escape.

From a widower to a witch to a spy to a man breaking the latest rule about not being in the colony...a fortnight of sorrow in a world turned on its side and not letting him right himself. What was next? Lord, what COULD be next?

Apparently washed clothing was hanging from a Plimouth-made rope at one of the houses and Ashley knew it would take all day for that to dry, the air was so heavy with moisture. Washed articles in London—where he was born and raised—were just put onto the ground to dry. Many a day he had—after being commanded by Anna—washed his own clothing and hung it across the rail on the back porch of the cabin, only to find at night it was still damp. He never dared tell Anna about these times, only put on the damp clothes—which made her happy that he was clean—and it wasn't long after they'd either dry by themselves or just get wetter with sweat. He normally got his pants so grimy that it took his big hands to wring them free of wash-water; her gathering and him getting water, then her washing and him wringing, and together hung the clothes and sheets. He felt needed then, more so than ever at his mother's home.

Rufus had told Ashley that the man he was to visit was "a fat man." "The fat man" he had called him, and not polite about it. There were some old men with big bellies in the colony, but Ashley had never seen one who was truly fat; it just didn't seem anyone could be, given the hardships and religious restraints on food. Anyway, this man lived in this grouping of four houses—then Ashley realized they must be reformed or breakaway Protestants—on King's Road, in the middle of a field of tall grass calling out to fill the bellies of horses and oxen alike. There was a creek behind the fat man's house—small one, but the whole area was crisscrossed with waters of all sorts and water was a practical necessity here (although the freshwater and saltwater mosquitoes it bred were some of the larger ones in the entire area). The road was well-kept: broad and not so rutted as most, having tall bushes along one side, with a ditch. It allowed a good view of the house on one side.

A local farmer in torn shirtsleeves who seemed in his twenties and his two barefoot sons walked beside an ox which pulled a hay-cart so filled that they had to tie ropes across the hay to keep it from falling off. A thin man with sunburned skin and longish, sweat-soaked hair. A man with sons like stepping-stones, probably a year apart and who knew how many others were at home. Most likely these were the oldest and he was teaching them the ways of the farmer and the use of oxen. Lucky man, to have two sons and so much to do that he needn't chase around, doing a job nobody else wanted.

The farmer nodded as Ashley rode past, and the boys looked—they hadn't seen many people on this road before. Ashley nodded back and waved at the boys. Felt good to do that.

The house of the fat man seemed to be a mansion—or the mental picture of a mansion Ashley held in his mind. Didn't look like the houses he remembered from London and certainly not those of Plimouth, but this—with its variously placed and steeply pitched roofs to slide off the snow—was no Plimouth house. It was two storied high in front and had what seemed to be a third in back…so many heights and angles on the roofs it was hard to tell at a distance. Regardless, the place was very big for a colony home. Looked like where a beefeater might live.

And the closer he got, the easier it was to see the windows: like tall, fat people standing upright against the house and wearing white shrouds—several of them on one side of the home, especially. A fat man's home; a fat man's windows. Ashley tried to think of what a fat man would look like; no one of the Plimouth men was fat.

The windows—on close inspection—were strange, reaching from the floor, wide as doors, several of them, especially along the bottom story…windows uncommon—never seen, even in Plimouth—which would have to let in the cold winter and bled out fireplace heat. Windows which must have cost a lot and their expense would be in heat-loss and repair (if local, little boys found them so they could toss rocks at them). Yes…far too many windows in this big house. Too easy with all these windows for an Indian raid.

Ashley rode to the front entrance of the house and tossed Joe's reins across the hitching rail. Joe wouldn't move unless he had to—but he could (to get away, say, from a dog or other pest); he was used to being "ground-tied" with the reins tossed anywhere in front of him. Ashley went up the step to the wide front door—which carried (of course, as did most doors of Protestants) the traditional "cross" built into it. Christian crosses were depicted all around the colony.

The job he was doing for Rufus hadn't been planned...well, it may have by Rufus, but it surely wasn't by Ashley. "A simple plan," Rufus had said, "nothing complicated; observe and report. Never approach, speak to or answer them. Stay away, only watch and record and send that information to me daily. No trouble to get into; no trouble to get out of. If they see you, leave. If you get frightened, leave. If you get fired-upon, run away and stay away. If you can't find them, come back and tell me. Try to never let them know you watch them: that is most important. Be a tree-frog who hides upon a branch, sees everything but no one sees him. Then they don't see you either. Stalk them as you would stalk deer: be invisible."

This was no kind of a job, going places for someone when he could just as easily go there himself—and probably do what was necessary a lot easier and better. Ashley should have stayed at the store whilst Rufus came here. Ashley could sell, having had experience—well, "limited experience" as he broke many of the things at Pennyweight's store and wasn't asked often to help out there—and could make change of coin or paper—a feat which daunted most young men of the colony. Rufus trusted him enough to get this job done, though, so this was what he'd do. And on his own in Boston, Rufus could trust him as well. That's all a man had these days: trust. He had to trust people that they'd do as they said, and they had to trust him to do the same. Proverbs said not to trust man, only God, but there were no Puritan elders here to explain why he shouldn't trust Rufus, just his history with the storekeeper. Oh, well...one fast visit for Rufus, then to Boston for Rufus and to see his family...and...probably tell them about Miles and the loss of his Commission. Anna would have cried real tears to hear what Miles had said and done. An old, grumpy, carrot-haired soldier who had his fingers into every pie in the colony. There were no "pies" in Boston for him, tho'. Miles Standish: you either loved or hated the man; there was no middle-ground with him.

Ashley used the large, metal knocker on the front door of the big house which had been built into one of the two neighboring hills—or tall dunes. On ground-level, the front door—set off with a chiseled piece of granite on the ground before it—was the main entrance. At the rear of the home—because it was built into the hill—going out the back door would allow a person to step onto level ground (the top of the hill/dune). Funny arrangement but one which was almost common in this area of un-level land. Probably a Putitan arrangement, as the builder didn't have to move much earth to get the house in place, used an otherwise-barren piece of property, and Ashley had heard these houses had rooms tunneled into the hill for more space—rooms which could be used to store vegetables, create bedrooms or form a secret tunnel, a way to get out of the house in case of fire or Indian raid.

He heard a voice calling, telling him to come in, so he pressed the wide thumb-latch and entered. There was a stairway immediately to his left, reaching toward the top of the house, and a large room on his right. Shutting the door behind him, Ashley turned toward the right, seeing the waving arm of a man in a room beyond this great room. Miles Standish could have fit his whole house inside this room, it seemed so large.

"Over here," a voice called, and Ashley walked toward the waving man.

This was a large man in a big, gold-colored chair. The man was obese. Old and obese. A man more than halfway through his seventh decade who counted upon reaching at least his ninth. Ashley truly had never seen a man quite so fat: he looked like two people! This man was a serious eater. And it wasn't as if he "wore" his clothes: he seemed to have them "draped" upon himself; the clothes hung "over" him rather than "on" him...but here and there Ashley could make out a button or two, so the clothing must have been hand-made for this huge man.

"Please join me in my salon." The man—already seated and not moving—motioned to a plus-covered chair near the one in which he rested. "Are you Lyons?"

"Yes...Rufus Case sent me."

"Do sit, Squire Lyons; our mutual friend says you'd like to understand some things as well as return to him some papers I have here for him."

Ashley looked around briefly: a person usually can tell about the homeowner and the way he lived just by seeing the front room of a house. Anna ever had hers clean, always expecting unexpected people who never arrived; she always said the front room of a home was a reflection upon the lady of the house. Ashley freely admitted he was a slob in his own home, throwing things and dropping clothing everywhere and anywhere. This room—this entire house—was spotless and has nothing out of place...but the tables were cluttered, minor mountains of piled paper to be cataloged and arranged. This salon was packed with bookcases, bookshelves, knickknacks and their shelving, piles of papers, pens and bottles of inks...a true "man's room"—this salon—but without a musket hung or standing, or a painting of any kind.

A huge fireplace filled the inside wall and angled such that some of the bricks—no stones here, but expensive, formed bricks—presented a work-area for food-preparation. A Dutch oven was built into the fireplace, and a huge, black kettle hung suspended over an unlit lay of fireplace logs. No signs of a woman or children here: a man's retreat with the golden leather of a bound Bible showing on the long mantle above the fireplace.

The fat man sat in his great, gold-colored lounge chair next to an extended table below an ordinary-size window to the side of the house. The table held a mess—a mass of papers with seals attached to them in differing colors, and tubes into which the documents—paperwork which seemed to have haunted his life with names, dates, places, things done and to be done—would be rolled for safekeeping in travel.

"Do you like my home?"

"It's very nice...very big."

"Yes, I wanted it large. Notice there are no draperies hanging here; no place for anyone to hide and overhear our talk, as happens in the palaces of Kings."

"I thought it might look the way a beefeater's house in London might look."

"Beefeater? Oh, you mean a yeoman of the guard! They have a common home...quite a large domicile close to the...well, formerly close to where the King lived. Theirs is much nicer than this, as there are a number of them and they pledge their lives to their sovereign. He makes their comfort and they protect his life...or did. I wonder how that all happened with them there...I can't imagine there are any of them left, especially with that Cromwell-person there...whyever would there be?

"Regardless, you have a sharp eye, Squire Lyons: I noticed your glance at my preparation-table."

"I apologize for looking..."

"No, no! Apologies are not necessary here. Here, everything is legal, legitimate, all business. I am completely honest and pay my taxes. Nothing you see here is secret or confidential. Perhaps askew, but not confidential. Do you know Latin? Tabularius?"

"Some Latin, but not that."

"Notarius?"

"Notary? A clerk who keeps and seals records for people?"

"Excellent! I am such a clerk. I keep and seal records for people...I loan money and receive tithes." He smiled, showing white teeth. Ashley wondered if he used the same white chalk his mother forced upon him to keep his teeth clean. "Here, around me, is some of the paperwork which has filled, defined…and sometimes haunted my life. Old papers, new papers, signed papers, unsigned papers. In the days when Rome owned and operated England as a business, the Primicerius Notarius kept the records, ever thinking the land of England would stay Roman. It didn't, but the job of seal-implanter persists.

"May I offer you some refreshment? I have a rather smooth Sherry…"

"No, thank you."

"Ah…the quintessential Puritan: no alcohol shall pass your lips…perfectly all right, sir…then let us meet one another. Please partake of some lunch, Squire Lyons; I have a cool lemonade and a crabmeat salad which some say is the most delicious they've ever eaten." He pointed to a nearby server with covered food and drink, then got up to get some, so Ashley followed the bulky man and took food also. They each sat and ate for a bit, then Ashley broke the silence: "The most delicious I've ever tasted!"

"Aha! Then we are in agreement! I do not concoct this food, but have it prepared for me and brought here. As you can tell, I enjoy eating and do so as often as I am able, for one never knows from day to day if the food they are eating shall be their last…but I request the food be good, and it's temperature specific to its application: cold food cold and hot food hot."

There was a set of empty teacups on the server as well. The teacups seemed thin as parchment paper, almost too thin to hold hot tea and certainly seeming they would break to bits were one to jostle them or touch one against the other. How did anyone make these? WHY would they want to make these so thin and fragile-appearing? Ashley felt cups should be thick—so as not to burn the hand or mouth—heavy enough that they would not tip over when put onto a plate, and have sturdy sides so an inexperienced person—such as he—could wash them, as he had done with two of Anna's cups and broken them. She never said a word about that—when he broke those cups—just presented a strange, strained, sad face with a slight turn or shake of her head. A "resigned look" his mother would have said that was: the kind of look someone has when they say, "Don't walk close to that cow; she'll kick you," and then some damn fool does and is kicked. That look. It's an "I knew that was going to happen all along and all my talk and worry isn't going to change that so why do I even bother talking to you." That look. The look you don't want to see because you remember it all your life afterward.

"Rufus tells me you are a well-traveled man but recently unemployed."

"Rufus gets around for a man with a store to tend."

Another smile from the notary. "Yes…Rufus is a mover and a shaker…if you were to do a job for me I could arrange some credit and things for you."

There was a pause. "No comment, Squire Lyons? Then I shall continue.

"My contacts are wide-spread and political. This is the way of the world community...we no longer live safely within a particular country's borders, but are challenged by foreigners who wish to steal everything we have—even our lives.

"Countries war with one another; treaties are made and broken; cousins declare war upon cousins; money in great amounts is provided for reparations and tribute. You see, we the world are all in this together, but the fastest and smartest are there first, gathering the fruits of the tree, such as they are. Do you get my meaning?"

Ashley nodded. He HOPED he had gotten the meaning.

"Two years ago, France and Germany signed the Peace of Westphalia. France had won peace with Germany and each could return to a better home-life. But for those who 'manage' those nations, those people returned to making more plans. Do you follow?"

"The peace is a lie: they only wish to re-arm and fight again."

"Ah...a man of the world. When a country is at war, all its people and monies and incentive are used to end that war. Now—after years—Germany and France are at peace, their talents and aspirations ready to be used else where. Two Januarys ago our former King Charles was executed under the auspices of Lord Protector Cromwell, Chief General of the Armies, with permission from the religious community of London. Cromwell has gone on to play his war-games in Scotland and Ireland, but soon—very soon—there will be a general peace in Greater Britain. You are still understanding what I say?"

Ashley nodded again and settled back into the comfortable chair. This man talked as much as he ate.

"Phillip of Spain has had a rough ride recently...I like that: sort of alliteration: rough ride recently. Rather redundant, wouldn't you say?"

"Indeed I would," Ashley responded, almost lost.

"This one is my favorite: a great, galloping gob of gelatinous goose-grease!" He laughed and Ashley smiled.

The man is funny, Ashley thought. *Odd but funny. There's nobody in the colony who speaks like that.*

The notary, still smiling, returned to his original thought: "Phillip has treated with the Dutch Provinces, ending a decades-long religious war, and is having some trouble with Portugal, especially since Portugal has joined with France and that Treaty...can't remember...begins with an 'M'...anyway, that was done two years back. All over the world, countries are freeing themselves of commitments and are plunging into business...worldwide trade, Squire Lyons, trade around the entire world!

"Did you enjoy your tea with Rufus?"

"It was a flavor different from what I was used to, but it was quite good."

"I had that brought from China. Imagine! *The* China Senor Columbus sought is now sending us in New England its tea! Did you try the coffee?"

"No, just the tea."

"Ah...The coffee is delicious! I flavor mine with cocoa-bean from the islands. Extremely tasty. So you can tell, Squire Lyons, that the world is now in a flux, a polyphony of rush to trade, a fast, futile, fury of finance. Ha! There's another alliteration for you!"

Ashley nodded again. "More seriously and to the point, less than two years ago the Presbyterians were ousted from Parliament and presently, England has no official religion to follow. Men turn to business, trade, money, investments, insurance...things we before could not do or have whilst war was waged. I believe the Frenchmen you are to follow are agents from either France or Spain, seeing the defenses of this land in preparation for conquest. For all I know—and I know a lot—they are from Catalonia, the Pyrenees, or are Jews. I can make cases for each. Yes, I see, Squire Lyons, you wonder why all this talk.

"Spain seems somewhat sinuously suspicious...mayhap the leader of these Frenchmen is from Spain: I am told he looks as though he could be. Peace will be Spain's next move.

"Meanwhile, I understand William the Second, of Orange, has become terribly ill and his takeover of the Dutch Provinces will come to naught. You can tell, can you not, Squire Lyons, the belt of business tightens around the waist of the world. Find this Frenchman or Spaniard or whomever he is and offer him the proposal I have in this letter."

He pulled a heavily waxed letter from the clutter on his crowded table. "This is my proposal to him. He—of course—is a spy and cannot answer me, but his master shall."

"So...you want me to go up to this man or group of men and give them your letter...then...walk away? Get an answer? What?"

"Was that a declaration or an admonishment; I believe I missed the point somewhere along the line."

"I'm told this man is a spy, and spies are hanged. If I walk up to this man and his companions—I've heard there are several of them—I believe I will be killed on the spot! Whyever would a spy in a foreign land take a letter from me and not be frightened I'd tell the sheriff? He'd be more afraid of me than I would of him. Rufus says these men are dangerous and I'm only to observe and write reports."

"Perhaps then, this man would not be the one to receive this letter...sad...I thought mayhap this was the time. But I can see how you would be reluctant to deliver it."

"Is this why I'm here? To deliver a letter?"

"Oh, no, dear man...I have all the travel-papers for Rufus completed and he wants you to take them to him. He's traveling soon to London and wants travel-papers and Letters of credit."

"I'll take them to Rufus and go along to Boston in the morning...I'd just as lief be behind these men as on the road with them. Before I leave I wanted to say your windows are...different...from those I normally see...all the way to the floor, as they are."

"Oh, dear man; those are not windows but French doors."

"Doors?"

"Yes, doors. They open all the way out. You know why they're called 'French doors'? These windows?"

"No."

"One of the French Kings put a tax on windows and the nobility were the only ones with them, so they changed their windows to these 'doors' to end the taxation! The idea caught on and voilà! French doors! Here in Duxbury, the colony committee is presently thinking about a tax on doors! Hahahahahahahahaha...doors! So all the poor will be without them and all the rich will shingle over them and not pay the tax, and we'll all be knocking on shingles and climbing in and out of windows!"

"Perhaps I should leave now. It's been very...informative, listening to you; but I should be going along. I have the horses..."

The notary leaned over and laid a great paw of a hand on Ashley's shoulder. "I'll gather what Rufus needs. If you want—or might change your mind—the letter is right there for you to take. Please consider it." He pulled back the hand and moved his great bulk to the desk—a real one, not the kind Miles had tried to fashion—where he chose several papers, put them in a pouch, and, turning, gave that to Ashley.

"I can't take your letter, as I might not be able to deliver it. Maybe the next trip, after I see what Boston has to offer."

"Oh...Then, splendid. You are as agreeable as Rufus said you were...A charming man, that Case. Please return at any time and we shall have coffee and more magnificent mentionings, chitchat, consolation, cockle, communication. You are a delightful young man to listen so intently to me, and we shall be quite friendly now." He shook Ashley's hand—his right one. Ashley was left-handed but used to that greeting between men. Then the notary sat again and gave a wave of goodbye as Ashley turned and left.

On the journey back to take Rufus his traveling papers, Ashley wondered about this "job" he was intending to do. Where would someone learn about a thing such as this? Who would teach it? How does a militiaman spy on a spy…and what WOULD happen if those five spies found out? He was glad he hadn't taken that letter from the notarius…but that was real question: what happens if the Frenchmen find out they're being followed and observed?

The Frenchman was a "real" spy who had the resources of an entire country plus several helpers with him and no one even knew why he was here or what he wanted and everybody was pussyfooting around him; maybe the notary's letter WOULD be the better way…but not delivered by Ashley! It seemed easy enough to follow these men, but everything to be learned would be secondhand, as these men would have already done things by the time they were seen and followed, and if they left, how could they be watched? Too many variables for just one colonist.

Joe, the blond gelding, moved along as if he wanted to get wherever it was they were going, instead of doing his usual slow walk. Joe. What a name for a horse! Ashley had found and purchased him on a trip into New Hampshire during all that religious squabble two summers before and it had been instant companionship for him and the horse. Prior to that, Ashley had used an older horse who—after Joe arrived on the scene—was turned out to pasture with mares in New Hampshire: one of the reasons for Joe's fast sale. Joe had been trained with affection and seemed to respond as a dog does to hearing his name called. Both horse and rider were as happy right now as each would be that summer…on this trip.

Rufus Case always seemed to be in his store. Well, there was no one else who worked there but the stable-hand, and he was always busy, what with the relay-horses, the coach-horses Rufus kept and running errands for Rufus.

Ashley handed the notary's packet to Rufus. "Who was that I just visited?"

"You mean the fat man? How'd you like him? Isn't he different? He's gentry from London, personally knew the King and knows everything legal."

"Well, he's as different as anyone I've met in Plimouth…I've met some really 'different' beings…but why did you send me there? You could have had a messenger go as well as me."

"I wanted you two to meet. He's a friend of mine...rich, eccentric...came here right after I did and invested some money in this place. Helped me to get the tack-room built...allowed me to purchase some weapons and things to store in there...in case we needed a place to dive if another Indian war broke out. He has the same thing: a tunnel out of his place in the event of an attack or fire. That's why he's so friendly to the local Indians; wants to keep on their good side.

"I thought you had London investors."

"I do...but they're very conservative and don't back my inventions or alterations...this man is rich enough to be able to give me money to create and test my inventions. That way I have no need to take money from the store and forge my books to try to hide the losses."

"You have losses?"

"Well, there was a ball-proof vest I made which soldiers could wear and the ball from an enemy's musket wouldn't penetrate to kill them...but the people who make muskets and powder and ball made better ones before I could sell the idea to the Army. My old vests wouldn't stop the newer rifled balls but I'm working on that. And a couple other things. This man loves the colony and will finance almost anything new, different or necessary to be used here."

"Standish must love *him*!"

"Miles threw a fit when he heard Foster—the notary—wanted 'different' things...said we came here to get away from all those European inventions and needed only the tools of the field and the Bible."

"What a—to use a phrase from the notary—'pretentious Puritan prick'!"

Case didn't know whether to laugh or act surprised. He just stared, nodding.

"So...you're ready to go along to Boston? It's confirmed those Frenchmen have rented a coach to go to Boston and drop it off near where your parents have their store."

"Convenient."

"You should go now so you won't miss them...before they leave there."

"The only thing I'll miss is going to see Anna and making the militia meetings."

"Old men and children, pretending they're soldiers every Saturday."

"It has its purpose...and Miles had soldiers come in to teach us different things...I was learning a French-style of fighting: using the legs and feet, kicks to the opponent's knees or groin which can be used if someone threatens with a knife or ready fists."

"Around here they threaten with a matchlock or musket; and so far as French fighting goes, I doubt French soldiers fight with their feet: they use cannon, muskets and bayonets; those are real soldiers, tough."

"Still…I shall miss the militia meetings."

"Do this, get it done and you can join the Boston militia. No Standish there, and they'll have you in an instant and teach you more about French fighting. Ashley…be careful in your endeavors…these Frenchmen are probably well-trained and dangerous. Only follow them and report what you can; don't press them; don't talk with them. Be cautious, please."

"All right. I'll go along to Boston to try to pick up the trail; first stop there will be stables, old man Howard's, and I'll try to find where they left the coach and where they went from there. The notary said Spain may be involved; why do these countries want to wage war?"

"Countries don't make war; men do. The men who run—not especially rule—them. Men get greedy, angry, ambitious, frustrated…the Kings are all related, but to find out which country will fight another, look to those directing the countries: the House of Holland, Louie of France, Phillip of Spain…who among them is the more greedy or rash."

"Who do you think?"

"Right now?"

"Yes."

"Holland, of Holtland. The Dutch are rich but want more."

"Not France?"

"It's what Kings do, or their advisors. France has twenty times more people in it than has England…how else can these people be used but to engage them in wars and pit them against a cousin who rules as a King in another land, but France is spent, and her latest wars have hurt. Only the Kings of Europe really know. What are Kings, when rule is gone?"

"Sounds like another of those banned plays."

"Shakespeare or Marlowe…who can remember? Each writes of the death of Kings and what the latest King will do. I suffered—as a businessman—under King Charles. Oliver Cromwell, who breeds business instead of children, allows me to prosper. I pity England if Cromwell dies in one of his wars."

"Rufus the soothsayer. England will survive Cromwell and all her Kings, so long as France stays in France."

"We've had a history of her not doing that."

CHAPTER 7

Boston was growing rapidly—adding height and girth as a hungry teenager. Almost a thousand people a week arrived in the daily ships. Pastures were being replaced by buildings and cow-paths with dirt roads. Houses and cabins sprung up daily and business establishments flourished. The Indians who used to live in and around Boston and who visited peacefully the original English settlers no longer were present—moved further and further away by the Europeans and their diseases; and the end of all the deer and turkeys removed all the ready food for the Woods-People.

It was still difficult to find good water in any supply in Charlestown and that had to be brought in from Shawmet. Regardless, in 1632, Boston had been made the capital city of the new Massachusetts Bay Colony, a governor was elected, taxes imposed, congregational churches flourished...Boston had become just like a small city in England.

Pennyweight's store in Boston had been established in 1631. He had recognized the possibilities of a store exactly at the waterfront, and got there early enough to have a building constructed for his store. Another thing he did early was father two daughters with Ashley's mother.

Originally an indentured servant to Pennyweight when she and her twelve-year-old son had arrived from Dockside, London, to Plimouth, Ashley's mother—a widow at that time—had shown her future husband (at that point her employer) a head for business and a talent for homemaking. They wed before her time of indenture was completed, and together produced two daughters: Esther—named for her maternal grandmother but also the Old Testament Book, and Ruth—called that for the Book of Ruth in the King James Bible wherein Mister Pennyweight had found wisdom. (He never told his current wife, but his previous wife—who had died in England—had the Christian name "Ruth" as well).

Esther was dark-haired, dark-eyed and had a dusky skin which showed off a beauty seldom seen in the colony. In features she resembled her father—save she had skin the color of old, spilt milk. Her long eyelashes turned women's heads and boy's hearts. Tall for her age, she was—nonetheless—gainly and not showing the clumsy manner of the usual teenaged girl. Her smile was not freely given, but her eyes sparkled as she watched people, viewing perhaps some traits and things not readily understood as a youth. She was quiet, usually, serious until she laughed—then her laugh was full and melodic and thoroughly delightful. Those who saw her were taken by her: she had the hidden beauty sought by many women but found by few. On the continent she would have been sought-after by royalty; in Boston, she was a virgin wasted.

Ashley's other half-sister, Ruth, was almost the complete opposite: fair of face but plain; two years younger than her sister Esther, covered with skin which sunburned readily and freckled as the women of her mother's line before her. Ruth took pleasure in embarrassing her big brother and in teasing him. Young men saw her abundant freckles and turned away; her light hair was ever askew as she flitted around being a girl.

The ride from the store of Rufus Case was the same length as always, but Ashley wondered most of the time about the Frenchmen and why they'd be here. Storm-clouds to the west looked as if they carried rain, but their distance and direction didn't bother Ashley. Clouds from the east, however, brought those three-day storms he and Anna used to like…there in their own home, snug, safe, satisfied. When it would thunder and lightning, he and Anna would lie abed, together and happy. Anna had said, "If God thinks we need more rain than we normally get, I think He causes thunder and lightning to let us know it's all for us—His children and His animals. He calls upon thunder and lightning to let us know He is there, watching that we get enough rain for the crops, the fruit trees, the fish, all His creatures and creations. I love thunder and lightning: it's God; and I love being with you in God's sight and care."

He wiped tears from his eyes. Poor Anna: she loved life so much.

She never thought she would die, nor did anyone else. Ashley felt he had neglected her but more importantly, he had made her pregnant and brought upon her the wasteful death. Now he couldn't even go back to the cemetery to visit her. A whole year before he could go back, if then. His worries wove a tapestry of torture in his mind.

Destiny—a Puritan's call-word for God—seemed to drive him on, calling to him in that seductive way, interesting and exciting him to do this, do that. taste, sample, achieve, conquer, become. Nothing was spared: not thought nor emotion nor friendship nor concern. It was as entering a vortex and ceding to it all whatever would be. No plan; no awareness of what was to come; no care. To do this was the only thing.

It was late when he arrived at Pennyweight's combination store and home in Boston. Mister Pennyweight had long before retired to bed, as he always rose early. Ashley's mother, however, was still up, completing some cooking.

"I'm surprised to see you. Glad, but surprised. You look terrible."

"I haven't...been doing much since...Anna..."

"Ashley, you can't blame yourself for Anna's death. In all honesty, things like that happen too often. Childbirth takes a woman closer to death than anything else. I miss that girl and we pray for her every day."

"She shouldn't have been with child after we lost the first one..."

"Did she say that? That she didn't want another child? Because she never told me that, not *ever*! Did she say that to you?"

"No..."

"Then, it's happened and it's past. You can't undo it or change it nor should you suffer for it. Yes, it hurts; don't I know as I lost your father and both my parents. Yes, it's awful. Yes, you wish it had been you and not her; but it *was* her...and she's gone to God with the children and you stay here with prayers, memories and no answers. There are no answers...so stop asking questions."

"Yes." A meager response.

Ashley's mother could play the harpsichord and ever hoped her son would do as well. He had gladly accepted lessons from her, but his left-handed style confused them both. About all he could do were the scales and the starting portion of "God Bless the King" (which was no longer played as there was now no King). They each gave up after that. She had given her harpsichord to the elder's council when Pennyweight's family moved from Plimouth to Boston—above the store—so the harpsichord issue for Ashley was over for all time. She had "mentioned" (well, she talked about it for months) that when her grandchild was born she'd get another to teach that child the instrument. For some reason she couldn't or wouldn't teach her two daughters to play that instrument and Ashley ever thought it was that the girls couldn't use that talent to any cause as they attracted husbands.

Ashley's mother had taken his son's death badly also: she cried for days and prayed almost steadily for weeks afterward. Then when—a while later—Anna became again pregnant, then died, his mother came to the realization that her son would never beget grandchildren for her. Now, her hope for grandchildren lay with the two daughters she'd had through Mister Pennyweight.

Situated as it was, across from the Great Wharf of Boston, Pennyweight had a recognizable location for his store and had built one large enough for not only groceries and household items, but marine needs as well. Never a follower, Pennyweight was a leader in retail business and a devout Puritan.

Ashley's room in Boston—the loft room of the store—was the one he had always used: an attic room with one window overlooking the harbour and ships. Two sides of the room had slanted ceilings into which were built clothing drawers and a small writing desk. He had put two black bearskins on the floor as rugs, and another wall possessed a small fireplace which Pennyweight had installed, serving to keep the room warm enough in the winters. It was built into and against the main chimney of the house; a mason had owed Pennyweight too much to ever pay, so the store owner had traded his apparent loss for having the fireplace built—a good swap either way, but a far better one for Pennyweight as he effectively had placed a teenage stepson as far from his wedding bed as he could.

There was a traveling-chest at the foot of the bed, which was wide enough for the clothing of a married couple, and blankets of several colors lay folded upon cotton sheets. Bleached cotton sheets were new to the colony, through Protector Cromwell's influence, and were now manufactured in England. (Previously, all the cotton sheets Pennyweight could get were made in India and became costly, having to be shipped through the Dutch East India Company.)

Next to the door of the room was a stand for a washbowl and a water pitcher; a fluffy, dark towel hung beside those. Because it was still summertime, Ashley had removed (again) the oiled paper from the window—both layers of it. As usual, he marveled at the view, the sights, smells and sounds of a growing young city along the waterfront.

After breaking the fast the next morning—family greetings said—Ashley rode through Boston, looking for the "probably five" Frenchmen and wondering where they might have gone. Old man Howard had passed away, his stable replaced by another, so all the stables had to be checked. The morning was a loss: no one he could find knew of the five travelers. The sun had gotten especially hot so he returned in the late afternoon with Joe to Pennyweight's store, then put Joe at the nearby stable Mister Pennyweight used for his hackneys. It seemed a shoe was getting loose on the blonde gelding, and that gave Ashley grave concern.

Standing in the doorway of the store, lounging really, keeping away from his stepfather but out of the sun, Ashley watched in slight surprise as five well-dressed men—most probably the Frenchmen—came walking in his direction, on the street across from Pennyweight's store. He quickly slipped inside the store and peered out the large front window. The five, clumped together, went past and turned onto the Great Wharf. The man in the middle of the group certainly did "look French," as well as the one who hung toward the rear, seeming to protect—certainly to observe—the back of the clique.

Ashley saw a skinny little boy in a red sweater standing there in the store, looking at merchandise. "A gold sovereign for you if you'll do a small job for me."

"A gold sovereign? I'll do it!"

"Good. Now, see way over there on the entrance to the wharf? Those five men walking away?"

"Aye."

"I want you to follow them, see where they go, then come back and tell me."

"They can only go to the wharf, sir...nowhere else—or a boat."

"All right...follow them at a distance; don't let them see you following them, understand?"

"Yes."

"Then come back and tell me if they go on a boat or what they do. Be careful, will you?"

"Yes, sir."

"Don't let them see you."

"I won't."

The five "Frenchmen" had seemed to wander the wide wharf with its areas of crates and cargo, but they had approached everything carefully, doing here as they did in Plimouth: mapping, drawing sketches of stockade and cannon-emplacement (of which there were precious few), noting where the meeting halls and gathering-places were. They had been to all the wharves now...this one was the largest and last for them and they would complete their affairs here, except for hiring a coach and two or four and whatever else was entailed in that.

The five were laughing quietly at the pathetic little ships and fishing boats they saw, and the incompetent way boxes of ship's cargo took up more space than would have been necessary upon a wharf in London. The way this cargo was handled was slowly and random: nothing like what they had witnessed in London.

"Johnathan, have you seen that boy in the red sweater way behind us who seems to be watching us as we go along this fish-wharf?"

"Yes…I have been wondering about him. I can understand why he might look at us on the street…but to follow us out here with no adult about…Geoffry, why don't you be a good fellow and snatch him over behind that stack of boxes so we can ask him? Luke shall observe whatever else is happening."

"My pleasure, yer…"

"Over here, men…to the edge of the dock. Cluster about and look seaward whilst Geoffry does an errand."

"I ain't finished the sketches yet, Johnathan."

"Hold off on those awhile as we distract a boy who seems to be—and don't look *anywhere* but seaward—seems to be following us."

"A boy following us? Whatever for?"

"We shall ask him."

"'Ere we are, doin' business an' 'e's doin' monkey business. Hahahahahahaha."

"Stop, stop, Mathew…you make me laugh too much!"

"That's why we get along so well, Johnathan: I likes t' be funny an' you likes t' laugh."

"All right…here by the water…oh! You two point out there. Yes! Like that! Now…go down to that next ship and when you get there, wave your arms a couple times. A little bit of subterfuge to get the boy's attention. Action captures the eyes of a child."

After a short while, Johnathan turned a bit, looking toward where he had last seen the boy. He was still there, but behind him, closing slowly, was the furtive Geoffry—Johnathan's "main man" and bodyguard. Johnathan smiled openly at his plan, then frowned as he thought with all the outward innocence in this sleepy colonial town, someone would want to watch him. That could not be tolerated!

They looked at the boats—mostly fishing craft—another minute, then Johnathan ventured another slight glance toward the boy. Geoffry was a short distance behind him, and Johnathan smirked at the thoughts of what he felt was to follow.

Less than a minute later, Geoffry—who had looked carefully about him to be sure none watched him—captured the child and lifted/quieted him with a handkerchief-bearing hand across his mouth, then carried him behind the rudely placed boxes Johnathan had pointed out.

The four then went there, after being sure they also had not been watched by cargo-handlers or fishermen on their boats or ship's personnel.

The boy was frightened, but Geoffry had his scarf across the child's mouth and a heavy hand on his neck. He squiggled, but couldn't really move.

"Geoffry, what have we here? A wharf rat? Hahahahahahaha."

"This 'ere is the one what was followin' us. Shall I cut 'is throat an' throw 'im t' the sharks down there?"

"This good lad? No! Of course not! What a nice boy he is...Geoffry, I think the boy wants to answer some questions for us. Of course...if he doesn't, *then* you may feed him to the sharks. You *do* want to answer some questions and then go home, do you not, lad?"

The boy in the red sweater—his mouth still covered with the scarf—nodded briskly in agreement.

"This is what shall happen. Listen, now, boy...you look like a bright young man; listen attentively to me, answer the questions truthfully, and whatever you're being paid, I shall triple. Do you understand 'triple'?"

The boy nodded.

"No yells; no screams; no one will hear you anyway, out here with the waves crashing. Just speak to me and you'll be gone from here in a minute, with coins jingling in your pockets. All right?"

The scarf came off slowly and Geoffry's hand remained poised, but the boy never screamed.

"What a charming lad. You'll go far in this life, young man. Such a quiet fellow you are, and so respectful of your elders. You must have fine parents. Here we go: question-time. Did someone tell you to watch us?"

"Yes, sir."

"Good! Did they pay you?"

"No, sir, but I was promised a gold sovereign."

"Then, my good lad, I shall give you *three*! So you shall have four gold sovereigns to spend instead of only one! Yes! We're getting along splendidly; money and freedom for you. Who was the man who promised you the gold sovereign and told you to watch us?"

"I don't know, sir...he's a tall man with white shirtsleeves in Pennyweight's store."

"Ah...the proprietor?"

"What is that?"

"The store owner. Was it the store owner who sent you here?"

"No, sir; he's an old man; this man was a lot younger and a very tall man."

"A tall man. Taller than that fellow over there?"

"No, sir; not that tall. Taller than you, sir."

"Is he employed at the store? Does he work at the store?"

"I never seem him as a clerk, sir."

"Fair enough. You don't know who he is and he doesn't live around here?"

"Please. sir...I don't know who he is an' I never saw 'im before."

"Then you are a truthful child and Geoffry has your reward. We're going to walk away, now, and when we're over by the water, Geoffry shall give you everything he has in his hand. Come, gentlemen; a brief walk to complete our business here. Be on the lookout for a tall man with white shirtsleeves over in that mercantile establishment."

Supper with the whole family that night was uncommon, as Ashley's mother had invited a female friend, and sat her across the table from Ashley. The seating was perfect: two on each side and one at each end. But as Ashley was used to sitting at the end opposite his stepfather, he was more than a little surprised when his chair had been moved to the side, next to his little sister, Ruth (with whom he hardly got along) and directly across from his mother's guest, whose name was Elspeth and who looked to be younger than he, but not by much. When his mother left the table for something, the woman spoke directly to him for the first time.

"I am very pleased to meet you finally, Captain Lyons. Your mother talks all the time about you and..."

"Yes, my mother talks."

They smiled. Understood was that his mother talked about Anna's death and that of the baby, and that now her unmarried son was available if she could get him to Boston. Ashley knew what his mother talked about.

"You must enjoy your work...men like things like that."

Who WAS this woman? She had watched him as an owl watches a field-mouse all throughout the meal, leveling her eyes at him and not diverting them when he looked at her. He had returned those looks, smiling outwardly and to himself as he saw her play with her soup, dipping in a spoon, blowing lightly on it, touching it to her lips...staring all the while she did that and it made him uncomfortable to see those lips pucker like that.

His youngest sister, Ruth, took all this in for a few minutes, then couldn't take it anymore. Bumping her knee against her brother's to get his undivided attention, she asked quietly, "How is the soup?"

"Very good."

"You haven't tried it yet." That's the way sisters are.

It got worse as the meal went on. He looked at Elspeth and saw Anna: Anna with the laughing eyes seated next to his mother as she used to, the two of them talking together the way they always did but also keeping up with the table-conversation, the stray glances at her husband which conveyed so much between them, the need in those eyes he wanted to fulfill.

But it wasn't Anna.

Why did it feel so good and hurt so much at the same time?

Ashley had also seen the smirk on his mother's face as she watched the two of them...another damnable attempt at a marriage arrangement as she had done with Anna. Not now; not ever; not yet, anyway. Then he thought he could perhaps scare away this woman. When his mother again left the table to go to the kitchen, Ashley said, "Actually... it's a bit difficult to say...and my mother doesn't know it yet...but I gave back my militia commission three days ago...so I'm no longer either a captain or employed." That should stop her plans to wed a captain!

"Your militia commission?" Pennyweight almost yelled. "Is that true?"

"Afraid it is...I...just didn't...need it any longer...so, Miles...said I could leave."

Ruthie kicked him under the table. Yeah, SHE was happy.

"Missis Pennyweight!" his stepfather called toward the kitchen.

She came in with a pie, berries out of season.

"Ashley gave back his militia commission! Just the *best* news!"

"Good! You never needed that anyway, dear; it only kept you from us; now you can live here in Boston!"

"I've always said a man in the militia is like having no man around, as he's always off doing things with his group!" Now Elspeth was involved in the conversation. "I imagine your mother shall be happy you no longer are a target for foreign invaders or savage arrows."

"I certainly am!" his mother agreed.

These people had suddenly ganged-up on him.

"I may have to come here to live."

Elspeth with the big smile: "Wouldn't that be nice."

"Hurry and finish eating, now, everyone; we'll talk later about all this. We have to get to prayer-meeting; I didn't notice it was getting on so late." His mother was putting off the subject so she could get more used to it and have more to say later.

Ashley finished quickly; he always ate fast. Anna used to try to get him to slow down, first by talking to him as he ate—but that seemed to make him eat faster, to finish so he could talk. Then she served herself before she served him, but he still out-ate her. Finally she decided to nibble while cooking, serve him and talk with him, then eat alone later. Not much worked: he inhaled the food; then try to get him to engage in any conversation!

The pie was eaten right away, but for six people it wasn't much more than a serving apiece anyway; no one really had to rush their meal to finish on time. Moments later, Missis Pennyweight asked, "Are we all ready to go to the meeting?"

"I am," Elspeth answered with a big smile for Ashley.

Oh, Lord, he thought; *This woman doesn't give up.*

Pennyweight bent toward Ashley: "Walk with us; safety in numbers, son."

Prayer-meeting was dreary. Ashley, however, wasn't too aware of what was happening as he couldn't seem to keep his eyes from Elspeth. He seemed to forget all else and was not even aware why the meeting had been called on an off-night anyway.

The sudden disappearance of a boy was the reason they all—and in all other churches and meeting-rooms and parlors around this area of Boston—prayed specifically for the safe return of a missing boy-child. Ashley just didn't bother to listen closely enough to grasp it all, he was too interested in the one woman in whom he insisted he had no interest.

Afterwards, Ashley's mother got him off to one side. "Isn't Elspeth a nice girl?"

"Yes, very nice."

"Ashley…you know I loved Anna…"

"Yes, Mum; and I still do."

"But life is for the living…those gone with God live there now, like your father."

"And what would Anna think—or my father—about me seeing some Boston woman right after Anna's and the baby's death? Right after they took up residence in Heaven? Think Anna might grumble at that? That I didn't wait long enough? You mourned a full year in London after Daddy died…I've only been at it less than a month."

"That was different."

"How was that different?"

"What a surly child you turned out to be!"

Pennyweight came over to the two of them: "How did you like the message? Even tho' he did read it all…?"

"Very specific," Ashley responded, happy to get off the previous subject.

"Exactly! To the point of the meeting! Refreshing to hear something other than Romans..."

"Put on the armor of Lord Jesus Christ..."

"Every meeting in Plimouth, four nights a week..."

"Every week..."

They smiled together...probably the first time in twenty years, for Ashley and his mother had come to Plimouth in sixteen-thirty as indentured servants of Pennyweight. That year, Ashley had been kidnapped by Lavrador Indians and his mother had married Mister Pennyweight. The differences and concerns between the two never were settled nor addressed, as Pennyweight refused to believe the boy was taken, rather that he had shipped aboard to England and that way returned, some time later.

"Ashley, you walk Elspeth home."

"Her parents are here; won't she go home with her parents?"

"She came with us and she's our dinner-guest, so we have an obligation to at least walk the girl home...what would she think of us, abandoning her here? Go and do that."

"Someone do something," Pennyweight interjected; "I need to go home and sleep: morning comes quickly. Ashley, you can go with Elspeth and her parents; I have a big day tomorrow at the store."

His wife smiled that knowing smile mothers do. Hadn't HE performed well!

Ashley tagged along "after" Elspeth and her parents; not "with" her. Like a cow's tail, following everywhere she went. He felt as tho' he were a child again, tagging after Mum.

At Elspeth's home her parents went inside immediately—Ashley still not understanding why they seemed so disturbed—leaving Ashley and Elspeth alone. Somehow they moved together to the bench on the grass outside her home, slapping at mosquitoes as they sat there.

Her hair was long, longer than women usually wore it. She had a small braid from the top, down each side, forward of her ears. None of the women he knew chose to wear their hair like that: it was a strange look, pleasant but strange...almost inviting. He seemed to want to hold those braids, pull her head close to his and kiss her...and that very thought both pleased and shocked him. Good thing Elder Otis wasn't there...he'd be reading those thoughts like he read his Bible, getting ready to preach a lesson about them and their meanings for Puritan people.

"Elspeth is a lovely name. What's its origin?"

"Scottish. Difficult to say that, with us at war with Scotland."

"Well, it's a beautiful name…for…a beautiful woman."

"Thank you, kind sir." She waited a moment, then: "Your mother says you're thirty-two; I'm twenty-eight. I've been shunned for so many years it seemed as if no one would ever speak with me…your mother…she's different, different from most women I've met."

"Yes," he laughed. "She certainly is different from other mothers I've met, also!"

He stared at Elspeth: she was as a ship in a harbour, flying flags, waiting, expecting an answer from the shore.

She smiled, lighting up her face in the pale cast of the night sky with all its scattered, dark clouds. "I'd like to…I have to, tell you about me."

"No, you don't have to!"

"Oh, yes I do! Unless you know everything, you know nothing." She wiped her hand across her mouth and looked down a moment, seeming to be thinking.

"You know nothing about me," Ashley pressed. "Other than what my different mother has told you about me—and she over-tells and under-tells."

They each smiled.

"What I know about you is that you're a beautiful, sweet woman who helps strangers…and probably stray cats."

Her laugh was the sound of tinkling ice in a glass.

He paused to study her a few seconds. "There are parts of my life, times in my life, events of my life…what I'm trying to say is that…lots of things have happened—and still will. But I've always tried to do it right, and have had a lot of help in that. And…"

"You don't want me in your life."

He heard himself say it: "No! That's not what I'm trying to say! I *do* want you in my life, but I have something to…complete—if I can—here in Boston."

She nodded, uncertain. "I married a man who was twenty-two, a farmer from my prayer-group. I was fifteen. I guess I did it in defiance of my parents…that's the way girls that age are. I didn't know that at age eighteen my husband was taught by Boston whores…and he more raped me than loved me, and beat me more than my father had.

"I produced a child—a girl—and he gave her away to someone, saying, 'I'll have no girls around to eat my food and not help me with this farm and then run away with some boy. Give me a son, bitch!' What a husband. What a father he would have been.

"My next two carryings and births produced dead babies: boys. He beat me for weeks after each of those, then it just seemed I stopped living. I just existed. At first I had prayed…then I just didn't.

"Drunk again one night he beat me again, and I was knocked unconscious. When I woke—and this is the truth—my husband was dead in the bed, our kitchen knife in his upper chest." She paused—hardly breathing. Reliving it all...almost in tears and shock all over again.

"The girl across the street—my own age then and going through the same problem with her husband—heard me screaming and came over, saw what had happened, never said a word to me but broke my money-jar and took the few pence inside it, then left. I was too upset to even talk to her. She went to the sheriff and swore she had seen two men around my house and wondered why they would be there, but told the sheriff her husband wasn't home, and he had told her never to leave the house unless he was there, so she couldn't tell anyone about them or my screaming until he came home.

"The sheriff and his men saw the broken money-jar and saw that one of my kitchen knives had been used, and said it was the first time that a burglary had turned into a killing. They smelled the drink on my husband and said he couldn't have stopped them, but the two men probably became frightened when they saw a man, stabbed him, then took the money and ran away.

"About a week later—after the funeral the town had given my husband—I saw the neighbor again and thanked her for being such a good witness. 'In for a pence; in for a pound' was all she said to me. She never gave me back the pence from the money-jar. The same thing happened to her husband—killed by two strangers who had broken into the house to steal—but I had left there before that, so I was glad I didn't have to be a witness for her in that crime.

"So...that was what happened and that's why the congregation shunned me. Also, I believe in God, but do not think He is only on the side of the Puritans...not their own, special God who answers only their prayers because they pray in a certain way, at a certain time, in a silent voice. I believe God hears us all, and He loves us all, and if He knows everything, well, He knows what each of us does and He lets us do it here on Earth, but when we die and go to Heaven, then and there we get compensated or judged for the trials of earth and mortality. While I live with my parents I attend their prayer-services, but...I have killed."

"I killed also."

"But as a captain of militia, you were forced to."

"I have killed men—people—who shouldn't have been killed. Do you think because a man is an Indian or of another race he should be a slave or die?"

"If he has not found Jesus..."

"However in the world could a man in the wilderness find Jesus? These men—these Indians—they're out there every day, every day...They're feeding and clothing their families, taking part in their tribal routines, praying to their god...There are many gods, Elspeth; perhaps they pray to ours also. Could this not be true? Would not God protect the Indians even if they hadn't heard of Jesus? Because they haven't found Jesus in their hearts is no reason to kill them! They're men! They're people! Why do we enslave and torture in the name of religion? I believe in a God; one God. A God who knows everything and we are here as His children. He put us here and says, 'Go, live and multiply.' We do that and then we kill people...but God knows this. This is the burden HE must take, not us. We are His children and He knows we will be bad...mean...loathsome, killers at times. Eventually we will pay, but not here, not while we live. Another time; another place. But in that time and place God rules and knows all...and when He gets you there He'll be the Good Father and say, 'You were wrong to do that, but I know why you did that and I put all of you there, so the fault is mine. Next time I shall try to change a person before I let him be born...and then the world will have no murderers.

"Never think because you kill someone God does not love you. He *ever* loves you; you are His child. God knows; He loves; He forgives; He punishes the meanness, not the acts of desperation. I have thought about this exactly for a score of years, What you did was what you were driven to do, not what you wanted to do. God loves you; I know."

"That was the sweetest thing I've ever heard."

"I can't...express what more I'd like to say."

"Don't. Say nothing. Knowing now what you do about me, I don't blame you if you leave and never see me again. If you do, I promise I'll never talk to your mother about you, or tonight."

He looked at her there, just for a second...a woman torn by grief and deed—as had he been. His arms went around her in a natural movement and he held her there, breathless, knowing what would happen now. He drew her to him, her breasts touching him, lightning bolts of emotion all around, inside him. Anna never did this to him or for him; he felt himself ready to emit. He couldn't! He shouldn't! In almost a single gesture he was in earthly heaven, holding her as closely as he could, mosquitoes be damned! "I don't know what I'll tell my mother when I get back home tonight."

She smiled coyly. "Tell her the tavern on the wharf was open until midnight but as you were already inside, they let you stay with a few others while you drank and swapped stories."

"She'd never believe that."

"Can you think of something better?"

"No...and I don't want to."

They held each other for a few moments, realizing more and more the mosquitoes around and on them, then she led him into the house, to her bedroom on the ground floor and began rapidly taking off her clothing. She sat—nude—on the bed. "I don't know how I can be so blatant in front of you...but there's something..."

Seeing her there without clothing, the first thing he thought was, *Mum was right: she IS "thin as a rail."* Little girl's breasts on a woman's body which had borne three children.

He also undressed, standing near her. Pulsing blood warming him everywhere.

She touched a long scar on his hip.

"I got that when..."

She put a finger on his lips to quiet him. "It frightens me when I think you could have died then and wouldn't be with me here and now." She stroked the scar, kissed it lightly, then kissed him on the lips. Have you ever wanted to do something and knew it was the right thing to do at that time? That's the way I feel."

"It's hard to do the right thing...everything gets in your way."

"Want to stay for a while? Until the morning? You can, if you want."

"I'd like that."

They woke—almost together—probably two hours after their initial coupling. She turned on her side, toward him, and he kissed her but didn't get the response he expected. She pulled herself up on the pillow and he recognized that move: she wanted to talk, not writhe.

"You've been a married man and I've been a married woman. We both know what that means and the good things and the bad. I'll never again be driven to what I did...Now I know too many ways to leave a man or turn him from me. What I'm saying, I guess, is..."

"I know what you're saying." He put an arm around her and pulled her gently against himself: "And you don't have to say it. There's good and bad in everyone; I know someone who killed a man and didn't mean it...and I stabbed and killed a Lavrador Indian when I was twelve years old and still think about that...he killed my adopted father and...the knife just seemed to go there by itself. So I *do* know. I *do*! And there have been other things I can't tell you about now...some might seem as evil or demon-related, but I went places with people...just another long story too hard to talk about right now."

"So you feel the pain I do." She leaned over and kissed him on the lips—after the newest fashion in London—and Ashley—wantonly—kissed back.

"You know you don't have to marry me to get me in bed...I'll go any time you want. To marry a widow is not necessary for you, Ashley Lyons...you can have any woman, any girl, as a wife. I don't need a husband again, just a good man, and I think you're the same way: you don't need a wife right now, just a woman around to help you get through the nights and a reason to look forward to the days.

"Women live their lives as slaves...waiting from girlhood to be sold or given to some man—any age—who comes along and ingratiates himself to her parents. Women are used to breed children, pleasure men, keep a house, cook food and pretend to be gracious to the delight of the husband. Women have a hard life, even the better-off ones like your mother. They're taken from their safe, childhood homes to places and people that they don't know and don't want to know. They're given tasks and duties and chores and burdens and told if they 'do it right,' they might get a good word or a bauble...but the good word is forgotten and the baubles are ultimately pawned for drink or whores...and the woman never can return to her girlhood and safety.

"So, this is who I am...a woman who had defiled her sworn husband and her God in Heaven, and who leads a life in fear of death or discovery, for either seems too frightening to imagine. I shake with an ague and have nightmares and worries. This is who I am...I don't blame you at all for not marrying—not even liking me. I'm so sorry, Ashley."

"Elspeth?" Ashley replied. "I have a secret."

"After what I've said, whatever secret could you have?"

"I'm afraid I fell asleep while you were talking and didn't hear a word of what you said. All I remember is you saying something about loving me."

She smiled, tears cascading down her cheeks because there was no way in the world this man couldn't have heard every word she said.

She drew Ashley close, holding him in a way a frightened child holds a parent.

"You heard it all, my love...that was everything I said: "I love you."

When the summer thunderstorms arrived—at night—he and Anna would lie together in their bed, thankful that the plants were being watered and secure in their faith that they were safe from lightning. It was like that all over again with Elspeth: together, safe, happy. He was touched with a pride and a satisfaction and a heavy guilt when he caressed her, but the inner feelings he experienced from that contact shoved aside the shadow of guilt, cloaking it with sunshine and tingling excitement and warm emissions.

"I feel..." he ventured, "as tho' I have two lives...the one before and this one."

"Ummmm..." she murmured, running her hands across his body. "You had a child's life, a young man's life, a married life, and now you are living an unmarried one...getting ready for another life of some kind. We're always living a new life, always. It might not seem so, but it is. That's the only way I get through each night: thinking I have a new life each dawn...and fresh hope. And look at me now, with you here and me so happy."

She stopped talking but Ashley didn't speak.

"I hope I can make you happy tonight, and all the nights you remember me. I never want to change this."

He still didn't speak, but instead encircled her with his arms and pressed his lips against hers.

His pulse quickened.

This time the lovemaking was slower and more deliberate...Not the way the first time had been. They used different positions and enjoyed them, clinging to each other and touching. This felt so much better...Better than the first time, better almost than at any time he might feel. It was dark, but he knew she was smiling, happy, enjoying everything as was he.

Actually, Ashley was somewhat embarrassed, as he felt this was the best time he'd ever had with a woman in bed—enjoying himself with such abandon while thinking—knowing—he was disappointing Anna.

It happened between them again, then one more time. Then they fell soundly asleep in each other's arms.

This time when they woke there was sunshine coming in the small window and pieces of her parents' conversation coming through the thin door.

"Oh, Lord!"

"Get dressed quickly; I'll go out and come back to tell you when you can leave."

She was back in less than a minute. "Go now! My parents are upstairs, searching one more time for my brother."

At home, he was caught while going through the kitchen, headed for his bedroom stairway.

"You were either up early or out late." It was a statement. His mother didn't miss much, and Ashley had always thought it was because she had done the very same things he did, so she knew and probably beforehand; yes, certainly she knew: don't mothers all? Her hold on an obedient son had never occurred; he was ever a renegade, a will-o'-the-wisp who sought his own deeds and satisfactions, but she knew those as much as he did.

"Out late." No sense in lying; she probably had already looked in his room.

"Where are your stockings?"

"Stockings?"

"Yes, dear; you wore stockings to prayer-meeting last night."

"Oh."

"When are you going to shave that off your face?"

"Soon."

"Are you ready to break the fast? Mister Pennyweight had early business so he's late eating this morning."

"Yes...I'll have a breakfast."

"Ashley...change your clothes before you sit with Mister Pennyweight, dear; there's an odd smell to them."

"Yes, Mum."

Ashley changed his clothes—he had plenty in Boston and didn't have to think about the ones Anna had washed and folded so carefully and put away so lovingly. Those he placed in a separate drawer. He sniffed at the ones he removed, wondering as he did what it was that his mother smelled.

Put on socks; didn't shave. Still in a playful mood—thinking about Elspeth and the previous night with all the mosquitoes buzzing around and landing on them—he sat at his desk and penned a poem:

The Blue Hills in the west
Where sunset quickly dies
Give life to nightly creatures:
The owls, the bats, the flies.

Far now from woodland ways,
Where boughs confront the sun,
The towering hills proclaim their right
To shelter nightly fun.

So here they play the night away
Those mighty, flying things;
Inflicting into all they can
Their bites and chews and stings.

No report to Rufus this morning; yesterday's would have to suffice. He'd do "something" today...didn't yet know what. Then he could write it all tonight and send it off. Those Frenchmen really had put a mark on him...he needed to construct some way to go from here...some plan so he could find and watch them without being seen. And that little boy never came back to tell him where they had gone...but that's what little boys do: they never stay on a certain thing very long, always doing the "next" thing they think about.

Ashley sighed. He'd heard a talk about planning a raid upon a smuggler's hideaway while he was in the militia: the raid had happened almost three years before, but the militia leader of that group—he thought maybe the one in Granite City—gave the same talk to every militia-group in the New England area that all the men could learn from deeds and mistakes of their comrades. One of the words the militia-leader used was "thorough." It wasn't a plan unless it was "thorough," as, if you didn't know all about your enemy and his defenses and resources, and all about how to conquer despite all those, there was no reason to stage a raid, because it would fail. Thorough. He had to be thorough. He had to know as much as he could before he did much more, or he'd fail...and a spy who fails is a dead spy.

By the time he had gotten downstairs again, his mother was waiting.

"Mister Pennyweight has eaten and gone, long ago. What took you so long upstairs? And you still didn't shave!"

"Something I had to write to Rufus Case. I'm here to do a small job for him."

"You know he's Mister Pennyweight's competition."

"Mum...they don't sell or trade the same things. Rufus is no one's competition."

"Don't speak of him when Mister Pennyweight can hear you."

"I won't."

"You didn't mention that last night, that you were here to do something for that man."

"I think I did, but did not say much about it...and I was fairly busy last night, with the supper and meeting and all."

"While you were upstairs, Elspeth was here."

"She was *here*? And you didn't call me?"

"She wasn't here for you! Her brother didn't come home last night and she's out looking for him. He was with her yesterday and somehow left her and she never saw him afterward."

"Her brother? I didn't know she had a brother."

"Hush! He's in the store all the time; was here yesterday and you must have seen him: stands and stares at everything; the boy's a little slow. Thin child—like his sister—with the same, strange eyes. Always wears that old red sweater he likes so much, warm or cold. He pretends he's a Red-Coat in the Army."

"Oh, God."

"Yes, I thought you'd recognize the seriousness of it."

"Her brother."

"Everyone has eaten. What can I get for you?"

"No breakfast; I've got to see Elspeth."

"Well, I won't worry about you not eating…Anna always said you ate as you wanted and she couldn't keep a table for you. Go, go somewhere because that's what you always do…before you go, why would Elspeth think you're going to marry her?"

"Mum…I have no idea."

"What did you say to her last night after the prayer-meeting?"

"We just talked. I told her about Anna…Just talked."

"I think you did more than talk."

"You want the truth?"

"I always want the truth but seldom get it all the time."

"We talked; I went to bed with her, and we talked some more."

"Don't say dirty things like that to your mother!"

"She's been married and I've been married. If she thinks I'll marry her because…"

"Stop! Stop right there! You and Elspeth need to discuss intentions instead of old times. Anna didn't say much; so if you and Elspeth really talk, you're ahead of what you wouldn't do with Anna."

"Anna didn't have much to say. Anna needed to be loved and wanted, not talked to. She didn't talk because she held it all in; you don't know what she went through and I shan't tell you!"

"Well!"

"Elspeth holds no secrets…"

"Then if she has some, keep them!"

He shook his head in a resigned manner. "I'm going riding."

"You can't leave; Elspeth needs you here."

"This is too important."

"Too important? You're going RIDING! She's talking marriage and cannot find a lost brother and your riding is 'too important'? What is it you're doing for that Rufus Case? Mister Pennyweight never trusted that man and Anna…well…Anna…"

"I know what Anna thought of Rufus."

"Where are you going?"

"I'm doing something for Rufus."

"Why is he more important than what's happening here? I think you'd better stay right here!"

"I'll be back as soon as I can."

"I'm sure Elspeth will be pleased to hear that. What *are* your intentions toward that girl, anyway?"

"I have no intentions."

"She thinks you're going to marry her."

"Mum...I only met her yesterday. I'm going to see to my horse at the stable."

"Don't be gone long."

He went out to the private stable Pennyweight and nearby neighbors used, then chose a horse Mister Pennyweight owned—a chunky hackney—to give Joe a longer rest and to add to the "disguise" he wanted to maintain. This day he had changed his clothing to a different overall color. *I want to stay thorough,* he thought: *and that means asking about the horses and coaches the Frenchmen used as well as asking about them.*

There were only three stables in this area which were close enough to allow the Frenchmen to walk onto the Great Wharf—three public stables, as there were several privately owned and used ones which the business-community sponsored and used. Unless they had left their coach with a friend, he'd have to find the Frenchmen somewhere nearby; he couldn't discard any thought today. Yesterday he'd asked at old Howard's stable; but with a new owner, perhaps there'd be a different stable-boy there today.

CHAPTER 8

In the first stable, the manager knew Ashley's stepfather and held nothing back. "There were five men with a coach and four from Plimouth here just yesterday."

"Really? Them those are the men I seek. You don't know their names, do you?"

"The man who did the business with me wrote his name as 'John Smith.'"

"John Smith? He must be very old."

"Very funny for a store-owner's son. Laugh at this: his brothers were Matthew, Mark and Luke!"

"That's *not* funny!"

"Well, it's true. Five men: Matthew, Mark, Luke, John and Geoffry."

"That's taking the Gospels too far, mocking them like that!"

"He insisted those were their names. He had passage-papers with those names on them, and if England says that's their names, so do I!"

"Then they play games…and we shall see who shall win."

"Mister Smith did seem to be playing a game…"

"How so?"

"I said to him, 'You're all related?' and he says, 'Dear man…'; I have never had anyone call me 'Dear man' before. Then he says, "Let's go through this once and not again'; and he clapped his hands and said, 'Everybody! Travel papers!' and then they all showed me their papers and they were all the Smiths. Very embarrassing for me."

"The Smiths. Not French names?"

"I have never known a French 'Smith.'"

Ashley thought: *Their disguise is better than mine; not only are they arrived on an English ship, but they all carry English travel-papers.* He frowned, thinking of how smart these Frenchmen were.

"Did something to you, did he?"

"No...just that I seek his whereabouts. I must tell you that my coming here and all we have spoken about has to be held in secrecy."

"What does that mean?"

"You can't tell them I asked about them or you told me about them."

"That's not right...if someone asked about you, wouldn't you want to know?"

"These men may not be whom they seem...they could be involved in anti-Puritanical business."

"So is half this town! We're here *because* we're not Puritans!"

"Please? It's very important to me that they do not know I asked about them or that you told me. They might get angry...hurt you and I don't want anyone hurt."

"Well, I certainly am too old to be wanting to be hurt...I won't say anything to them, but it doesn't matter anyway, because I didn't have a coach large enough for all of them and I had to return the Plimouth coach, so I sent them over to Isadore Gold's Stable, across the street, there."

"But they brought the big coach here; they couldn't keep using it?"

"The coach was from Plimouth and they only have the one...and they need that for daily rentals around Plimouth so it could only be used for a one-way trip and I had to return it that night; I sent it back as soon as the Smiths left here. They wanted to keep it a week or so...Plimouth Stable charges on a daily rate—makes 'em more that way. Most of us charge weekly; much less cost that way. But I only have carriages which can accommodate two or three people, so they couldn't rent from me. Gold has everything: he's a good competitor."

Ashley thanked him and gave him a silver sovereign for his troubles, then rode over to Gold's Stable, a place where he had not been before. There he asked a little man with bad teeth and breath to match.

"Were you here two evenings ago?"

"Always here evenings if we're open; I sleep here. Only one full time; all the rest are partial-timers."

"I'm trying to locate some friends...Five men who rented a coach to go somewhere a day or two ago..."

"Five men. The Smith brothers?"

"Probably them."

"Only five men together I've ever rented to."

"Where did they go?"

"They rented to go to Salem, but where they went afterwards..."

"Salem?"

"North, along the coast. Roger Conant's colony in twenty-six. Governor Endicott established a fort there…oh…twenty years or so ago, to protect Plimouth and Boston from raids along the north coast. Big seaport there; lots of people."

"I'm glad I spoke with you; I didn't know that."

"I'm from there; born there. Ask me anything."

Ashley handed him a gold sovereign. "Thank you…I may see you again."

"Thank you, sir; come by anytime."

"Er…"

"Yes? Something else, sir?"

"Do you remember about Roger Williams?"

"One of our elders there. First Congregational Church."

"There?"

"Yes…he got himself into quite a pickle…arguing against the Church of England as he did! He went to Plimouth for a short time but came back…about the time the governor put the fort there…no…just before the fort! Let's see…I was born in twenty-eight and I was eight years old…so…sixteen thirty-six. Then he went back to England."

"Williams went back to England? I didn't know that."

"Surely. Long time ago."

"Many thanks."

"Happy to help a gentleman, sir."

Williams again. He was everywhere in this colony…places Ashley never knew existed and all over the ones he did. Perhaps his was the more famous case of a colony expelling one of its own. Williams seemed to go so far into religion that he developed his own way to practice it…certainly not the way the Plimouth elders did. He was so loud and obstinate that he was expelled from Plimouth…took a canoe with a couple of close friends and went up some big river…founded a community away from Plimouth where he could preach all he wanted, the way he wanted…providence. That was it: providence. God's providence in the wilderness.

Was it only historical or was there a tie-in between the Frenchmen and Williams…or where Williams went, here in New England. The Frenchmen came from England and went to Plimouth, Boston, Salem…would Providence be next in William's prior chain of places?

Anyway, it was no use to go to Salem…as the Frenchmen had gone there already and Ashley couldn't pick up a trail on them now.

By this time, the stableman was feeding again. Ashley walked over to where he was pouring mixed grains and drew a shilling from his pocket, then handed it to the man. "If you remember more about the Smith brothers, I'll come back in a day or two and you can tell me."

"Then you'll see them yourself."

"What?"

"They'll be here in two days...to get fresh horses to go south, to Merry Mount."

"The five?"

"The same."

"You didn't tell me they were going somewhere else."

"You didn't ask me where they were going, only if they had been here and where they went."

"But in two days they go to Merry Mount from here?"

"Already paid for the coach and four; be back late in the night tomorrow or the next day they said...he said, the one with the coin. The others didn't talk much. Paid in gold, he did, that Smith brother."

"And gold it shall be for you, too, good sir, if you don't tell them I asked about them." He reached into a pocket of the Rufus Case-designed vest and drew out a gold coin. "A gold sovereign now and another the next time we meet. Please say nothing to them about me."

"These are your friends and you don't want me to tell them about you?"

"This is a secret between you and me...I plan a surprise for them but must know where they are to find them for the surprise."

"Oh. Well, with another gold sovereign coming to me, I'll not say a word."

Ashley rode back to the stable Pennyweight used and left his horse there, then went to his parents' store/home. His mother (again) met him in the kitchen and his stepfather was already there.

"There's another prayer-meeting tonight; very bad news."

"What's that?"

"Elspeth's brother was found dead, early this morning. A wonder you haven't heard...everyone's been talking about it.

"Elspeth's...brother?"

"The reason we went to prayer-meeting last night. You didn't know why we attended on an off-night?"

"No..."

"Where is your head, man! Up your arse?" Now THAT was the Pennyweight Ashley remembered as a teenager.

"A particularly hideous death…his body found in the water, blood all over the back part of the northern pier. The tide must have carried the body between two pilings and it wedged there—at least the top part wedged there—the fish took all the rest."

"Mister Pennyweight! Please!"

"The boy has a right to know. A lobster fisherman found the boy under the Great Wharf, caught between pilings. He wouldn't touch him but went for the sheriff; and one of the sheriff's men got the remains."

"Good Lord, Mister Pennyweight, don't say that word."

"That's all it was: remains. The boy was almost all eaten by the sharks and crabs."

Ashley's mother burst into tears and covered her face by the apron she almost always wore while she worked in the kitchen. Then she sat and cried; whimpered, mostly—not a loud cry but the cry of a mother when she realizes a child is gone forever.

"Was he…wearing a red sweater?"

"He always wore that red sweater or jacket; that's what caught the eye of the fisherman. The boy wanted to be a soldier and got that red jacket because that's the new color of the Army jackets."

"Then it *was* her brother."

"Of course it was!" He pushed Ashley aside, away from his mother, and spoke quietly: "The child was murdered."

He put a hand up to Ashley's mouth. "Quiet! The boy had his throat cut before he was thrown into the water. Someone killed him and tried to get rid of the body, and they would have succeeded…the garbage thrown off the wharves brings all manner of sharks and fish who eat it…ah…a terrible tragedy for that family, for all Boston, as now we have a throat-cutter present here. So it's prayer-meeting tonight and you don't miss it! I know you like to go to your little places and do your strange adventures…but you be here for this, understand? Your mother speaks all the time about Elspeth, and—by the way—where were you so late last night after you walked Elspeth home?"

There was a lull in the conversation.

"Stayed with her, eh? Hahahahahahahaha. I'd have done the same thing in the same circumstances. So tonight she's a mourner, not a lay; and treat her with that respect. Your mother has lunch for you; give her some respect also: I'm busy. You be here tonight."

He left and Ashley's mother said, "Ashley, go to Elspeth. She'll need you now, more than ever. A terrible thing…awful…how could anyone do something like that to a child?"

Ashley hung back from conversation. He had CAUSED that! He had sent that child to watch the Frenchmen but couldn't—dare not—tell anyone about that. That could have—would have—been HIM on that pier...cut throat and all. Rufus told him to be careful and he wasn't; he'd better start to be.

"Mister Pennyweight says Elspeth has her parents and doesn't need a lovesick boy around her, but I think you should go see her."

"I'm no longer a 'boy'; I'm thirty-two." The conversation was over; Mister Pennyweight really was right: this was no time to bother Elspeth; and there probably never would be a good time.

He had killed the brother of the woman he had just bedded...and that would stay on his conscience and in God's memory for too great a time. He just hung his head.

He went to his room, wrote to Rufus about what he had heard at the stable, and waited in shame for the evening meal, to then attend the prayer-meeting.

Once there, the prayer-meeting was longer than usual, more boring than usual, and Ashley suffered as he kept remembering the dead boy was the boy in the red sweater he had sent after the Frenchmen, to the Great Wharf.

The topic of the prayer-meeting was "The Justice in Murder." They were all there to pray for the soul of the child, to relieve the sufferings of the parents, to speed the boy's entrance into God's Great Grace. But the congregationalists had another purpose also: every prayer-meeting had a topic—a sermon to add knowledge to the devotees while keeping them awake (these were hard-working people, awake and struggling since cock-crow). This topic—"The Justice in Murder"—was drawn from the Scriptures and meant to give the attendees some relief from this tragic end to the boy's life.

The speaker began: "The Law of Moses is very definite about murder; the crime itself is strictly defined in our readings. When God Himself decrees a death, it is not—never—a murder: it is Justice or Reward. In Numbers 35 we read: 'and if he smite him with an instrument of iron so that he die, he is a murderer.' And what is it then we are told? 'The murderer shall surely be put to death.'

"We have now some confliction. We expect God to slay the murderer, but then we read, 'the revenger of blood himself shall slay the murderer.' What does this tell us? First, we already know God will eventually punish the murderer and send him forever into the fires of damnation at the end time...so that part, in the end, is satisfied. Remember, through God, there is justice. But we see murderers being put to death by the Crown, the governor, the sheriff...are these deaths 'murders'? No. Those deaths are justified—not 'justice,' because only God has that—but justified because of several passages, especially, starting in Numbers 35: 'the revenger of blood himself shall slay the murderer.' This means that he who is murdered shall have revenge, for the Lord shall provide a revenger as well as justice. Who is the revenger? A chosen one. It is a representative of God or as God allows, a King or one chosen by a King. In other words, as we know it, the revenger is the law. We shall let the law take its course and find and punish this murderer.

"Remember: also in Psalms we read, 'The righteous hath hope in his death,' and, 'God will redeem my soul from the power of the grave; for He shall rescue me.' 'Lo, children are an heritage of the Lord...' Roland's soul is saved already and he exists now in the bosom of our Lord.

"I end this reading with Deuteronomy: 'Be strong and of a good courage. Fear not, nor be afraid of them, for the Lord thy God will not fail thee or forsake thee.'

"We are here this night to solemnly pray for the immortal soul of Roland Moone..."

It was all too much...Ashley had tried to keep his eyes from Elspeth and couldn't. When he looked at her, she was looking at him. Then each would turn away, trying to present some form of compliance to the prayer-meeting, but it was of no use. The reason for the meeting was lost to them.

After the meeting he was able to speak a moment with her: "I want to be with you."

"I want that also, but I can't. This...all this...my brother and I went out shopping two days ago and we ended up in your father's store. I wanted to talk to your mother so I told Roland he should learn independence and be able to be alone in this city. I left him...he went away alone, and because of me...he was..."

"It may not have been because of that."

"Had I stayed with him in that store...I sent him away to die and how in God's great love can I tell my parents that I killed their final child?"

Ashley sighed, knowing the truth of it, knowing he HAD to tell her it wasn't her fault that her brother was killed: he knew this, but he couldn't bring himself to say that. Yeah...really a good basis for a relationship with her.

He went over to his parents and they all started to walk home. He had forgotten about Anna...Elspeth had shut that door—made him aware that life WAS for the living and new urges and cravings fed that fire. Now he had closed another door...and he knew God had a special punishment waiting for him, and he knew he deserved it. So, now that love-match was over. How many men lose two women in two days?

In his room he tried to sort things through. So many things had happened...so many things to occupy his mind...but there was a pivotal point, a spike, a single thing which stood out. Only one person could occupy his mind now...only that one: that damnable murdering Frenchman!

The next day there was nothing to do but wait for the Frenchmen to return to Boston. He went out to the stable and got Joe ready to ride. Boston was big—compared to Plimouth—but not so big that five Frenchmen in a group could become lost within it, so he thought he'd just ride around to see if he might locate them.

He rode up and down the street by Gold's Stable, using different horses each time to get a glimpse of them as they returned from Salem without making people wonder why he rode back and forth. Pennyweight wouldn't care that Ashley used his hackneys as the horses seldom had exercise anyway.

Before noon he was back at home—having had no success at all; so much for being a spy. He thought about the prayer-meeting the night before. It would be hard to say God was urging him on in this chase, but...if He were doing that, then Ashley must be permitted to do it or God would have stopped him. He wondered what God would have to say to him about Elspeth...he had gotten carried-away with her, did just what he wanted, needed, longed to do to a woman, but what he shouldn't have done at all. His mother was right: he should either stop riding around the Massa-adchu-ess-et or tell her why he was doing that.

He went into the kitchen in his mother's home with determination to tell her...and Esther was there.

"Where's Mum?"

"Working in the store, where you should be."

"Can I ask you about Elspeth?"

"She says the two of you will marry."

"I just met the woman."

"Now she's 'the woman'?"

Clearly, Esther was not the one to speak with about Elspeth.

Esther had done a lot of planning, getting ready to attain the age when she could marry Alward and become "a woman." She had been treated by everyone almost as a bride and had gotten used to the idea...then Alward died and she was re-cast in the role of "big sister and helper to Mum" again. Probably when she thought Elspeth would marry her brother, she felt left out—alone once more.

"Is Ruthie here?"

"Don't know...She was in her room." Esther was so cooperative.

"She has a room of her own now? You two always shared a room."

"Look at me! Do you see someone who wants to share a room with a brat sister?"

"Can you get her for me?"

"No...Get her for yourself. I have things to do that *you* should be doing!"

"Esther...I'm no good with figures tho' I've tried to be...and have no interest in the business. I really don't know what to do with my life. I'm doing a job right now for Rufus Case from North Plimouth, trying to find some men from Plimouth for him...business that he has paid me to do. Right now I can't find them, and I just wanted to talk to you, talk to Mum, talk to someone." His eyes teared. "There's a lot happening..."

She gave him a single-arm squeeze, then moved back. "I know. I'll get her for you; then I should go into the store...it's that time of the day."

Ruth always seemed glad to speak with her big brother.

"You look like you need a friend."

"I need to talk...about Elspeth."

Her mouth formed an "O." "You like her a lot."

"That's not what I want to talk about...you've seen her, spoken with her...for how long?"

"Almost a month."

Anna had been gone about that time.

"How did she..."

"Get into the family?"

"Yeah! Get into the family: that's the question."

"She was in the store, talking to Mum, and suddenly she's here every night, talking, going to prayer-meeting with us, usually not here a long time, but just about every night after supper."

"You like her?"

"You don't want to hear that answer."

"Yes I do, I need to! Ruthie...I've just lost Anna and our child and I'm a wreck! This woman is here for me, with Mum's blessing, but...I can't explain it. She wants to do things..." He sighed. It was hard to talk with a little sister—even one who would be seventeen shortly.

"I don't know if I'm ready to think about getting married again, and if I did I'd have to live here in Boston and..."

"I don't like her; I'm sorry. She acts like she knows where she's going to step before she puts a foot down."

"Nothing to be sorry about...that's what I needed you to say."

"That I didn't like her?"

"No...your true feelings for her. So now I know."

"Don't stop seeing Elspeth because of *me*!"

"I think Elspeth was just what I needed at the time I needed it...someone to talk to...a woman instead of a man."

"So you won't marry her?"

"No; I never considered that. I just met her! Just that...she makes me feel more like a man than anyone has...and I get very protective and want to write poems when I'm around her."

"I think Mum would say that was love."

He sighed again. "Maybe it is and I don't know it or refuse to admit it, but it's very sudden and strange to me. I never wrote poems for Anna."

She suddenly pulled herself up and kissed him lightly on the cheek.

"That was unexpected."

"Good! Don't expect another!"

He rode once more, in the afternoon, then returned home and went to his loft-room to sleep, for he knew he'd have to be up early to start the ride to Merry Mount. He wanted to be somewhere along the road to watch the Frenchmen pass by so he could follow them the way a real spy would. Stared out the pane-less window for a while...Watching the ships in the harbour and thinking about the Great Wharf, not especially seeing anything, but just thinking. He'd spent a lot of his earlier years doing just this in this room.

Why was he involved in all this chasing around? Elspeth needed him right now and his mother was right: he should pay more attention to Elspeth. Who really cared whether these Frenchmen were trailed or spotted or anything else? He did want her more than anything else right now, so why even bother with foreign spies? Love flowers faster between strangers than friends.

At some point he fell asleep, but woke in the early morning to screams of: "Fire! Fire! Fire!"

Dressed in a nightshirt he ran down the steep stairs, the acrid smell of smoke in his mouth and eyes; all the family either following him or already there when he got to the lowest floor and the rear door.

The calls were coming from behind the store, and Ashley was just arriving in the kitchen as Mister Pennyweight—his pants over his nightshirt—plowed through the outside door and ran toward his shed, in the rear of his building.

By the time Ashley got to the kitchen door to look out, the flames were throwing shadows across the yard. The shed—not attached to the house for this very reason—was burning brightly with sparks snapping and popping, sending crackling noises into the otherwise still night air. A dozen or so men were there already. Fire was not an often thing, but in this tight town of wood, fire was an ever-threatening enemy. A fire-guard on the wharf had seen the first flames and yelled; neighboring men literally ran to the blaze, some with sand and others with water—all prepared and waiting by back doors. They practiced this drill as the militia practiced with their muskets, and were proud of their response-time, plus they threw themselves into the effort. No one wanted a fire in Boston.

It was—of course—an effort frustrated and denied. The shed burned to the ground, along with its flammable contents: the storage shed with the products Pennyweight had held so as not to over-fill the store was totally lost.

But…the fire had not spread. Confined only to the shed.

CHAPTER 9

The stable-hand at Gold's was there and wide awake well before sunrise; he lived at the stable and had good reason to be so prompt this morning.

Not long afterward, the five Frenchmen arrived to claim their already hitched coach and four.

"I beg your pardon, sir."

"Yes?"

"I feel a need to tell you that a man was inquiring after you yesterday."

"Oh? Which man?"

"I'm not familiar with him…well-dressed fellow with the shirtsleeves a store-clerk wears."

"A tall man?"

"Yes; much taller than me."

"The clark!"

"Hush, Geoffry…you saw which way he went when he left here?"

"Yes, sir…going south on the main street."

"Toward the Great Wharf?"

"Yes…just straight down there…I didn't watch him after he left here…had too much to do and thought just the idea of him inquiring after you would be enough."

"But you don't know him?"

"Haven't seen or rented to him."

"And you say he inquired after me? Specifically me? My name?"

"All of you; all five. He asked me where you went and paid me gold to tell him and also to tell him you've rented a coach to go to Merry Mount this very morning. I thought you'd like to know…and you might be pleased enough…er…he gave me a gold sovereign so I wouldn't tell you."

"Then, my good man, you must have a greater reward for your diligence and warning. Will you see him again?"

“No…although he said he’d see me some other time.”

“Then, he’s waiting along the road,” Luke grumbled.

“Here, here; not to be upset. Let’s pay this fellow and go along our way. Stableman, you say you are alone here this morning? I only inquire because I don’t want your employer seeing you receive several pieces of gold.”

“Several? Oh, no…no one here but me until well after the fast is broken.”

“Then, Geoffry, please take this dear fellow over there and pay him a handful of gold coin…he’s such a delightful fellow and so obliging.”

Geoffry left with the stable-manager, Johnathan beaming at the man’s information. “Luke and Mark, into the coach; Luke, give me a hand up, will you like a good chap? Mathew?”

“Yes, Johnathan.”

“Give Geoffry a hand piling lots of hay upon that dear fellow who warned us so politely and told the clerk our secrets…wouldn’t want to have him found too easily as we must return this coach on the morrow…oh, and get whatever coin you can from him: he won’t require it and perhaps we shall.”

CHAPTER 10

On the road beside the ocean, he could almost feel the earth rolling toward the sun—it seemed that close. Perhaps another hot day; almost the close of summer, a day when the sun felt as though it would make you melt. Wondering if the tide were warm or why it was not. Wondering why Roland had to die and if God would ultimately punish him for sending that child to do work assigned to him. Wondering why the Frenchman would have a child slain who only had—at the most—seen them at a distance. Wondering if that kind of death were waiting for him, for he also watched these men and reported their movements.

No ground fog this morning...the turning tide probably had kept it from forming. When ground fog commenced, a thick blanket of fog began at the ground and built, solid and dense until it rose to the height of a man's waist—then held there, seeming to wait until the longer, upper fog might join it.

Snuggled into a corner beyond the smelly, rocky beach of a tidal estuary from the sea, Merry Mount (a variation of its original name) was essentially a hotbed of religious fervor about which Ashley had heard but never confirmed. Elders in Plimouth had banished shunned people to there, but that had done that with Providence also.

Merry Mount was neither merry nor mountainous (low dunes with lots of water around most of it), but received its name in a rather bizarre challenge to the stern and organized Putitan/Pilgrime system of religion in effect at that time in the Massa-adchu-ees-et. The area of Merry Mount was an allowance of the Wollaston Company Land-grant; when the company moved to Virginia, a portion of the Wollaston's land to the east was re-named Merry Mount as a part of the tongue-in-cheek, conflicting approach presented by its beaver-fur baron, Thomas Morton.

Perhaps the Frenchmen, Ashley thought, had seditious fellows waiting to give further information. A landing of foreign troops along the beach, then a strike against any close town would be possible from Merry Mount. Foreign troops there would cleave the colonies, separating English soldiers in Boston from militia in Plimouth. Then the French troops could destroy the Massachusetts settlements rapidly and easily. A fire-ship brought in on the morning tide would detain the Navy in Boston long enough for soldiers and horses to be disembarked from other ships along Merry Mount beaches.

Oh, there was trouble coming. Ashley could just feel it as he let Joe set the pace toward a place he never before had visited and now which had become so important in his life. It wasn't long before they reached the crossroads he had heard about, where this straight road ended in a "T," and to the right lay Granite City and to the left was a marker for Merry Mount. Directly ahead was a clearing with grass and a small, abandoned cabin. He guessed he'd hide there, and Joe could graze behind the cabin. He felt bold, doing a bold move Bren would call a "coup de main"—a bold strike: a strike of the owl.

The grass was long and thick: Ashley vaguely wondered if this kind of grass was anywhere else in the world, then he thought he remembered seeing it in England. Wouldn't it be funny if the same grass were also in China? Probably so: grass must be the same everywhere...horses are the same around the world and they all eat grass, so why wouldn't all the grasses be the same?

Diagonally across the street was the water: toppling waves restlessly arising, streaks of white dashing as birds upon them. The vast bulk of the mighty Atlantic Ocean was so close, just beyond that beach. The sea which simultaneously touched England and the Massa-adchu-ess-et: deep as any mountain was high, filled with creatures as any forest on land, as enticing as a young bride and frightening as the worst fear. The only way to go to everywhere on earth, for it touched everywhere at once. The plight of the sailor; the sight for the traveler. The mighty Atlantic: no longer a plaything for its former owner. God, that was a long time ago: twenty years!

For the first half hour nothing happened. Oh, he heard dogs barking a long distance away and watched as seagulls flew overhead, seemingly seeking a way from the water which fed them. Crows cawed; squirrels scampered occasionally in the sparse trees beyond the clearing. The farmer who originally had this cabin must have planted the grass: it was a carpet perfect for grazing animals; maybe he had oxen. Ashley compared this grass to that of Duxbury, whose grass seemed thicker and courser. Perhaps the salt air made a difference, or just the soil.

This landscape was formed by the great glacier which pushed southward hundreds of leagues, carrying and dragging soil and rocks, grinding and splitting everything in its way. The depressions it left became ponds; the runoff, rivers.

An un-chinked place between the logs of the cabin allowed Ashley a view of the road to Boston, and presently he saw the Frenchman's coach approaching, then slowing and turning to his right. Five men and four horses, now headed east on the single road into the anti-Puritanical settlement. The Frenchmen had only paused a second before they turned east: they hadn't been there before but they must have received good directions, and the little "Merry Mount" sign helped. Only that one road in and out...not necessary to follow them unless...well, a spy would want to know the house to which they went. Maybe after they were gone awhile he could ride Joe to locate that house to which they must be going, so he could mail that information also to Rufus. Yes, that was the plan.

Shame on France, Ashley thought, *that it would send spies to such a small and weak community. Shame on those men for setting the fire—if that were true as he thought—which burned his stepfather's shed. Shame on someone who would do murder to a child, a child who caused no harm to anyone. Shame. And here I am, spying on spies, hiding and peering, writing notes of a man's movements when I know nothing else about him. Shame on me, also.*

The coach was now out of sight, so Ashley decided to saddle Joe and go slowly along the Merry Mount Road to find where it had gone. This was all so crazy...he was a frontiersman, not a spy, and lacked even those skills spies obviously held. So much to think about...so much to consider...so much to write down. He'd wait a few minutes more to let the coach get far enough down the road, them he'd follow—like a good spy.

The men in the coach had been much busier than Ashley. It was a decent-enough ride from Boston and the weight of the five plus their traveling-chest had about settled the coach on its worn springs, so they weren't jostled about too much. That gave them a condition in which they could think and plan.

"They's a rider ahead o' us—I've been seein' fresh hoof-prints on the road, maybe from new shoes. I'm thinkin' it might be that store-clerk."

Johnathan had other things on his mind. "Luke, this is a thoroughfare and the only beach road to Merry Mount, they say. Can you consider other people using this?"

Geoffry—sitting up front while Luke drove—agreed with his seat-companion: "Fresh prints, Johnathan; there's supposed to be a turn to the left up 'ere...yes, I see it now. We'll jus' see where these prints go."

"All right, Geoffry…you have a talent for what you do. You watch the tracks and the rest of us shall nod—not you, Lukey, you drive. Gentlemen, please do not watch the road or look about…if Geoffry is accurate and someone like the store-clerk may be ahead of us to observe, we should pretend not to know."

At the corner, they turned onto the Merry Mount Road, responding, it seemed, to the small, wooden sign posted on the ground.

"The shoe-prints went straight ahead," Geoffry whispered.

"Ahead of us?"

"No, yer Lordship…"

"Please…?"

"Aye. No, Johnathan. We turned because the road turned. The hoof-prints went on, into the grass, straight toward that old cabin. I think someone's in there, watchin' us…maybe the clark."

"I had conveniently forgotten about him. Apparently our little demonstration to his shed gave him no concern. No one look that way! Lukey, move along in the same manner. If we're being watched we don't want to hesitate at the crossroads. When we get down the road a bit, a couple of you slip off the coach and go to ground, to see if anyone follows us."

"An' if they do?"

"Why…I think we should inquire as to their reasons."

"Hahahahahahaha…yer a funny gent, Johnathan…'inquire as to their reasons.' Hahahahahahaha."

"The clark asked yesterday about us. 'E's followed us, watchin'."

"Yes…even after we gave him good reason not to watch…'a demonstration,' I believe I said it was. Apparently not a good-enough one."

"Maybe it wasn't 'is store, Johnathan. Maybe 'e jus' met the boy there an' watched from there, like 'e may be watchin' from that cabin."

"By God, Geoffry, that's why I have you around! Are you three listening to this man? You simply amaze me, Geoffry! Shall we turn this coach around and go see?"

"No need t' do that, Johnathan; I'll do it myself."

"No, no, dear man! I need you here with me. Let someone else do it."

"I'll go," Matthew responded.

"What do you say, Geoffry? Should we send the great man to look?"

"The way I sees it, Johnathan, at that rise in the road ahead we go over it an' two of us gets out an' slips back into them bushes. One waits there in case the clark comes through the woods an' one goes back down the road t' see if anyone's comin' or still in that cabin."

"Good thinking. Matthew, go all the way to the cabin and follow the hoof-prints out of there to see which direction they go, or see who's still there; then return and tell the waiter on the road. If all is clear and the clerk is gone, then you two wait there for us to send the coach back for you."

"An' if the clark is still there?"

"I imagine you should bring him to us. After all, that probably is why he's here...to see us and where we go."

"An' if 'e runs away?"

"I think you should stop him."

The coach went over the rise and Luke halted on the down-slope behind it. "Who wants to go?"

"I do," Mark volunteered. "This coach an' my arse don't get along. It goes up an' I goes down. Matthew?"

"All right," Matthew growled. "Is it pistol-time?"

"Yes, gentlemen...pistol time. Take them out from our chest, along with powder, ball and patch. Use them only if necessary."

"An' when is 'necessary,' Johnathan?"

"The circumstances will tell you, my great man. You will know."

Mark and Matthew got out, secured pistols and necessary bags and faded into the brush along the side of the road, loading their weapons. The coach went on, and Matthew started back to the cabin.

In the coach, Geoffry had swapped seats with Mark and now sat beside Johnathan. "Will there be food waitin' for us?"

"There should be. Still hungry, Geoffry? The blood from that little boy didn't fill you up?"

"Com' on, Johnathan...'e wasn't a speck! I need some good mutton in me t' quiet this stomach."

"There had better be some good food there; we're all hungry. Nothing like murder and raising money to make a man happy, but it's not very filling in the belly."

Johnathan's coach came to a stop outside a fieldstone, story-and-a-half home built off the ground: sturdy and safe-looking. Four steps led up to a veranda with more steps. Two of the family's men had been outside, awaiting Jonhathan's arrival and they notified those inside the house and guided Luke to the spot among many carriages and coaches and calashes where he must stop in order to let Johnathan walk on the gravel path. A man from inside the house came out and hugged Johnathan; Geoffry wondered if he would kiss him as well...these Royalists with their greetings and traditions.

Greetings given, they all started inside.

"I thought there were five of you."

"Two of my men are down the road, seeing if we are being watched."

"By the sheriff?"

"Some nosy store-clerk. Mathew and Mark will handle it."

"Then come in for the meal; we awaited your arrival to eat. Most of the people are here already and more will arrive later today. We all want to show King Charles our love and support."

"And you shall."

Ashley had waited and watched, then debated as to what to do. He had heard that the road to Merry Mount was a single one, straight as an Indian arrow, so if he followed too closely, those in the coach would see him. But to follow at all? That was a question to which he had no immediate answer. Even if he got to the old anti-Puritan settlement, he could readily be seen on that narrow road. But if he didn't go, he'd have no idea—as it had been with Salem—of where the Frenchmen went nor could he take anyone who knew this area well, to confirm the owner of the house or business where the coach had stopped. He pondered a few minutes, knowing all along what the answer would be.

Shaking his head as if to say, "Here we go" to himself, Ashley took the saddle and blanket out to the still-grazing Joe and saddled him, wondering again what lay ahead in Merry Mount, thinking also he needed help in doing things like this—but not any more boys.

Joe snorted and moved nervously.

"There, there, boy…another strap and we're done. Then we'll go along on our journey."

Joe snickered, his lips spitting saliva.

"What is your worry, Joe?"

"Maybe it's that a big man wi' a pistol is behin' you, store-clark."

Ashley swung around. True! A big man, a monster of a man who looked as tho' he might have strength to go along with his height stood there. Ashley was over two meters in height and this man was taller, and pointed a cocked pistol.

"If this is a robbery, I have no coin."

"Well, my Boston friend…this *is* a robbery, an' I don' care whether you 'ave coin or not, because I intends t' rob yer memory."

"What?"

"Yer the store-clark from Boston, am I right?"

"No…I'm from Duxbury."

"An' you sent the boy t' watch us along the wharves, right?"

"Don't know what you're talking about."

"Johnathan wants t' know why you chase us, clark?"

"I don't know what you mean…I was just resting my horse here."

"Didn't the demonstration make you want t' leave us alone?"

"What demonstration?"

"The fire, last night."

"There was a fire?"

"'Ere, 'ere, my man…I don' believe yer playin' the game wi' me. I think yer in somewha' o' a dilemma; tha's when you don' know whether t' stan' there an' be shot or run an' be shot, an' y' wan' t' run, but can't."

"You have a dilemma also."

"Which is…whether t' shoot you in the 'ead or the 'eart?"

Ashley smiled widely. "No…whether to shoot me and not have a shot at the man in the cabin behind you."

"Awwwwwwww…tryin' t' trick ol' Matthew…I was inside that cabin before I came out 'ere. I'm beginnin' t' like you, Colonist…you 'ave such a tender-lookin' arse."

"I'll just ride away now."

"Ride yerself over t' that cabin, Colonist, or I'll use this pistol!"

"And if I go there you'll use it anyway. Tell me who you are and what is happening: I don't know why you're doing this to me."

Matthew put the pistol to Ashley's head. "Go over t' the cabin." He didn't sound so funny this time.

Grudgingly, Ashley moved toward the cabin, hoping for a way out of this situation.

Tried to think what a militiaman would do, or a spy. The "play dumb, play stupid" technique didn't seem to be working.

In the cabin, Matthew gestured toward the floor. "Lie down 'ere an' talk from the groun' an' you'll not be thinkin' o' runnin' away."

So, all the man wanted was information. All right. Ashley lay on his stomach, on the packed-dirt floor.

"Now, Colonist, who are you? Why are y' 'ere?"

"I told you…"

The pistol was jammed into the back of Ashley's head. "Are your ears plugged?"

"I don't understand."

Matthew raised up, withdrawing the pistol from Ashley's head. "You know, Colonist, I'm abou' fed up wi' all this goin's-on. I 'ad a sick-t'-my-stomach ride 'ere, 'aven't been able t' drinks my beer, Johnathan treats me like a child wi' 'is fancy talk, Geoffry is the star o' the show, I 'ave to leave a bumpy coach an' walk a bloody distance t' get 'ere an' you're a bloody mummer…I've got the min' t' jus' shoot y' where y' lay! Do y' get wha' I'm sayin', Colonist?"

"I don't know what—"

"'Ere, 'ere! Stop that'! Let's jus' en' this little charade. Thank y' for saddlin' my 'orse…"

The explosion of the pistol was the last thing Ashley heard—if he heard it at all. The pistol—a French flintlock of the newest type—bucked as bad as Joe on a cold morning, and Ashley's shirt-collar and his hair at that point just…disappeared! Some of the surrounding hair caught fire.

Matthew tucked away the pistol and went over to Joe, who seemed nervous still, mounted without difficulty, and urged Joe to the road and toward Merry Mount. His weight was twice that of Ashley, but although Joe initially quivered at the added weight, he bore it.

"Well, get along, Joe," Matthew chuckled. "'Aven't 'ad an 'orse under me since the Army, an' this feels good. I feels much better, now, Joe…nothin' like shootin' inta a man's 'ead t' make a person feel good!"

It wasn't much longer—now that he was mounted—that Matthew reached the bushes where Mark waited, pistol in hand to halt the mounted rider.

"Com'on out; I've done the bugger in an' we rides t' Merry Mount a 'orse!"

Mark came out from the bushes, shaking his head. "You stole his horse?"

"'E's my 'orse now; dead men don' need 'orses."

"You actually *found* the clerk and that was the shot I heard? I thought he shot *you*, so I went deeper into the bushes to wait for him to pass by!"

"Hahahahahaha…'e wasn't much o' an adversary…folded 'is wings like a plucked chicken when I surprised 'im from behin'."

"And you shot him? Johnathan…"

"Coo…Johnathan wasn't there an' I was! The clark was in need o' shootin', so I done it! Now, my footman, do y' wan' t' ride t' ol' Merry Mount or walk behin' the gassy arse o' this fat 'orse?"

Mark mounted carefully. "Good thing this saddle is so small; the horse is long-bodied but I'd have a time with a proper saddle."

"Damnable little saddle chafes my arse…I wouldn't wan' t' ride too long on it."

Mark chuckled loudly. “Get a pillow for it when we reach the house.”

“By God, yer a fountain o’ knowledge! A pilla I shall get, t’ sit high an’ in bloody comfort on this beast.”

In not too long a time they had reached the house where Luke had left the coach upon the graveled path. Two armed Merry Mount guards plus Geoffry awaited them.

“Wha’ is this?”

“This is an ’orse, Geoffry…one rides it in the manner o’…”

“’Orse? ’Orse? ’Orse? An’ where did y’ get this ’orse? Is it the store-clark’s? Did y’ fin’ ’im?” Where is ’e?”

“Coo…too many damnable questions all at once, Mister Smith.”

Geoffry tucked the pistol he carried into his belt and drew his knife. “Mayhap I cut you inta several parts an’ each o’ them can answer the questions.”

“Now, Geoffry, I wasn’t bein’ smart; I’m jus’ proud o’ wha’ I done. I foun’ the clark an’ asked ’im some questions, but ’e got smart wi’ me an’ I ’ad t’ put a ball inta ’is ’ead.”

“You killed him?”

“Yes, I did. Shot ’im right proper in the back o’ the ’ead.”

Geoffry brandished his knife. He was known for his knife-work and short temper. “Look at me, y’ big bag o’ ’orseshit! You tell me the truth! To my knowledge you ’ave never killed a man, an’ now y’ say y’ did an’ are braggin’ about it?”

“I did kill ’im, Geoffry; I swears!”

“Tell me all; leave nothing out.”

“Yer beginnin’ t’ sound like Johnathan, Geoffry…wait! Don’ even think about yer knife! I come up behin’ the clark as ’e was chinchin’ ’is ’orse an’ I ’ad the drop on ’im wi’ my pistol…wi’ Johnathan’s pistol.”

“An’…?”

“I asked ’im who ’e was an’ if ’e was the clark, but ’e played funny.”

“Funny? How so?”

“’E wouldn’t answer an’ ’e played stupid.”

“Then by that display he tol’ you ’e WAS the clark! An’ then?”

“Well, I thought, ‘Wha’ would Johnathan do, an’…”

“You actually THOUGHT? You THOUGHT what would Johnathan do and did all that by yerself? All alone? Mark was not there?”

“Yes, Geoffry, all alone by myself. Was tha’ the right thing?”

"Matthew, I recant all the mean and miserable things I ever said t' you…you 'ave learned, my big man, t' understan' our leader an' follow 'is example. I am proud o' you, Matthew."

"Why, thank you, Geoffry."

"Did you think to search 'is pockets?"

"I did that, Geoffry, an' 'is purse o' silver an' gold is right 'ere in my pants."

"By God, Matthew, there's room f' you in our organization after all! I'll tell Johnathan 'is best man did the job!"

They all went inside to tell Johnathan, and he spoke to Matthew.

"I wasn't aware of your riding skills, Matthew."

"Y' gotta ride 'em t' steal 'em."

They all laughed.

"Stop, stop," Johnathan called. "You're making my sides ache! You're a good man, Matthew: my very good man. Now…shall we have a mutton dinner? And after that, Matthew may take his new horse and return to where he was, and…ummmm…clean up…what is there. William says he doesn't want the body of that clerk found there: the sheriff makes a point of riding out here every Sunday to see if any May-Poles are up or if any beverages other than water are being served. Ever since that Standish buffoon came here in thirty-six and arrested Morton and broke up the clan, the people out here live warily. You understand?"

"I do, Johnathan. No body, no trouble."

"Good man! I'd send Mark back with you but I really want him out watching the road and Luke is already back by the hay-barn in the rear. Can't be too cautious around here. Can you do all that alone?"

"Yes, I can, Johnathan, an' I takes it an 'onor that you'd sen' me t' do another job for you. I've said all along I only wanted t' please you."

"Well, you have done that swimmingly, my great man…swimmingly! Now! Let us all eat, for we have many visitors here and more coming tonight. And pick up a bit at that cabin so no one will find anything there—so in the daylight nothing shall look amiss. We may even stop by there on the return trip to be certain nothing is awry."

"I will do jus' that, Johnathan…er…I 'ave t' gets a pilla first."

"A pillow? How is that? You are tired, my great man?"

"Naw…for the saddle on that 'orse: it's tiny an' pinches my arse."

"All right…we'll have one for you after we dine. You be careful up there, sitting upon a pillow on that little saddle. If horsemen wanted pillows they'd have had then and they don't. You understand?"

"I'll be careful…jus' that now I'll be careful an' comfortable."

"You ever amaze me with you wit, Matthew. Oh!"

"Yes, Johnathan?"

"When you're out there, take your time about doing that job right. You have all night and may sleep in the coach on the next leg of our journey. Do it right—the way you already have."

"I'm the soul o' rightness, Johnathan."

The owner of the house came over to Johnathan. "Do you want to volunteer one of your men as a night-guard? We need all the beds we can get for those who will stay overnight and I think we need more men awake during the night; I only have the two."

"I'll give you Mark. I expect him to stay outside anyway, and he can sleep in the coach on the morrow, to Boston. But you have dogs; will you not leave the dogs outside at night?"

"The dogs stay in at night…too many things in the woods—like the feral hogs—to pull them away or make them bark; and if they start chasing raccoons, I'll lose them for days. No…it's better to use men out there with the dogs brought out if there's trouble…and if we had a break-in here, we'd need the dogs more inside than out."

"It was just the opposite at my father's home…"

"Yes, Baronet, but here we have a small community with several houses, and people who must sleep at night to work in the day. I hope that meets your approval."

"Quite. You know your business and these woods; so shall it be. I trust you implicitly with my father's eldest son."

"Thank you, your Lordship; tonight shall be a pleasurable one for you and the King."

"Then, to the meal. Your hospitality seems boundless, my old friend. And the plans we have for returning our King to England shall include you at the fore. The pledges of love and honor you collect here tonight shall go a long way in convincing our loyal followers in the island that there is a great movement of the people to return our land to His Majesty…and once that occurs, he shall remember his loyal friends and followers here in the colonies."

CHAPTER 11

Full night had fallen and the inside of the abandoned and run-down cabin at the Merry Mount sign was dark, regardless of moonlight and the holes from its non-existent doors and windows. Ashley, lying face-down on the dirt floor, groaned, then began to stir, his arms moving. At first he didn't remember anything at all, which frightened him terribly, but in a few seconds more he began to recall the huge Frenchman bringing him inside the cabin and...God! The back of his head was sore! Good God, had the man actually shot him?

He reached around timidly to the back of his head, expecting all the time to return a bloody, flesh-covered hand, and found the hair was almost gone, burned into little ringlets of crispness!

He felt and felt the injured area, but found no hole or indentation, and more importantly, no blood! What had happened?

The Frenchman must have struck him with the pistol...but the powder-smell decried that. Powder! He HAD shot him but missed, and it left powder-burns and a headache the size of a grazing cow! Ashley got slowly to his feet, wobbly and head throbbing. And his collar was burned—missing part of it. He felt his neck again, head, back and shoulders to see if a pistol ball had missed his head but struck or lodged elsewhere. No...only the powder burns and hair loss and a splitting headache.

Looking out the windowless window with the pale light of the moon bathing the cabin, he couldn't see Joe, so he assumed the Frenchman must have taken him. What a headache! And his ears hurt...sore outside and ringing inside, the tops burned as well by the powder. The man couldn't have missed...why would he miss? Certainly not to frighten him as the concussion had knocked him senseless for hours! "God. He didn't miss; he shot me!"

Ashley struck the wall with his fist, then hit himself. "I'm alive, and he shot me and left me for dead! I saw that happen once with an Indian...he shot a frontiersman point-blank but the man didn't die because the Indian had loaded the pistol but forgotten to tap in a ball! The Frenchman must have forgotten to load a ball and shot me that way! The powder burned my ears and hair and collar!"

Ashley fell to the dirt floor on his knees, praying thanks to God for his life and saying he'd re-dedicate himself to the Church and do good deeds in God's name. For a while he prayed, then stood and walked unsteadily out the doorway of the cabin. Joe was truly gone, probably taken by that Frenchman. Well...where now and what to do? It was a long walk back to Boston. Mmmmmmmmm...his head hurt!

He guessed going to Merry Mount was now out of the question...he couldn't be sure the Frenchmen were still there and it would be a long walk just to find no one, then come back here.

He heard the hoof-beats of a horse and ducked back inside the cabin, then saw Joe and the big Frenchman who had shot him come riding up to the cabin door. The man held a pistol but Ashley stepped out of the doorway anyway, angry.

"I see you ride my horse!"

"Oh! God's blood, y' frightened me! Who are y' an' why are y' 'ere?"

"I'm the ghost of the man you shot and killed, come to haunt you."

The pistol was pointed directly at Ashley but the man seemed to freeze in his movements. Joe was nervous, holding a heavy load and seeing his usual rider aground in front of him.

"You ain't no ghost." Not a decisive statement; just a spoken one.

"Didn't you shoot me in the head?"

"'Ho the bloody hell are you?"

With his eyes, Ashley measured the distance between himself and Joe. If he moved forward, Joe would block any view of him, plus, Ashley had an instant plan, based all on the reason Joe's owner in New Hampshire had sold him.

"Thank you for returning my horse."

"An a good 'un 'e is...but 'e ain't bein' returned." The pistol re-aimed at Ashley's face; the man was ready to shoot but still wary of ghosts.

"What have you done to the saddle?"

"Well, I added a down pilla t' please my arse so I'm comfortable as I ride, thank you. An' tha's yer last question."

Joe was a perfect riding-horse and trail companion, but Ashley knew he had a weakness: a loud noise or sudden move spooked him. Ashley had fallen twice from Joe: the first time when a little boy ran across the road in front of them;

the second when a rabbit—attempting to stay motionless in the sandy trail—suddenly realized speed was better than being trodden by a horse. The rabbit exploded in speed, startling Joe so much that he shivered to one side, causing his unsuspecting rider to slide off the saddle and onto the ground. THAT'S why his former owner had sold him.

Ashley suddenly screamed and with an accompanying long stride and arms waving, rushed at Joe! Joe startled instantly, snorted, backed up, swung his body around in an effort to get away, and got ready to run for his life! His sudden movements sideways and backward threw the weight of Matthew to one side, causing the pillow to slide off the shortened saddle, Matthew with it, landing on the ground, his pistol discharging as he struck it.

Ashley went directly to Matthew, checking to see his injuries, if any, keeping an eye on Joe. Matthew was dead: shot by his own pistol as his heavy body had hit the ground and his finger tightened on the pistol's trigger.

What was there to say or do? Ashley stood there a moment, re-playing that action in his mind. Yes, it really was true: he was alive and the Frenchman was dead. Joe had been returned and his prayers had WORKED!

He knelt and said a fast "thanks" to God, grateful, happy, astonished...delighted he was alive and the Frenchman was dead, because twice that very night it could have been very different.

He patted the pockets of the now-dead man: no papers, but his own purse was there and he retrieved it gratefully. Nothing else at all on the man's person. Well...he was with four other men, so they probably lived out of that big trunk they carried about and shared clothing, the leader holding the coin and travel-papers of them all. No matter: life was the important thing, and he'd received that gift twice more this night; but this dead man let him realize that the Frenchmen were in earnest and still in Merry Mount, and that decided Ashley's course of action.

Burned-hair or not, headache notwithstanding, his goal was to locate the house of the traitors to the colony. With a bit of pain, Ashley mounted the now-calmed Joe and headed him south, along the road to Merry Mount.

He was glad there was no fog this night...the whole area disappeared in the heavy fogs off the ocean...soup-thick and lasting into the daylight hours at times when even ships and boats couldn't move: the kind of fog smugglers adored. The locals would experience this and laugh, saying it was "London fog," but in reality, this was thicker: blanketing. Not the ground-fog of inland, but the kind in which you could extend your arm in front of you and not be able to see your hand. A heavy fog, quiet and frightening: that kind of fog: "real" fog.

Although it was the end of summer, there was a cool breeze that night, brought in off the water of the bay and sent far enough across the land to easily tickle horse and rider as they moved with determination back along the road Joe now knew by heart.

After some time, Ashley began to see the outlines of houses and the occasional barn or stable. He got out of the saddle and ground-tied Joe in a clearing off the road, then began to move slowly through the high bushes to see if he could locate the Frenchmen's coach at one of the houses.

Hard to find his way. No lights anywhere on the houses: too late at night. He didn't even know the time, but that was of no real matter, as it wasn't near sunup. No one should be awake at this time. Not much but pale moonlight, darkness and silence. He wondered if one of the Frenchmen was watching as he went parallel to the road, moving in and out of bushed places and light woods while he skirted some buildings. Now and then there was a graveled path—quarries right down that very street in Granite City, so there was plenty of crushed and broken stone to make mud-free paths and solid walking for horses at homes.

The houses here were apart—several of them...something like the setup at the notary's neighborhood: no one for half a league, then several houses in a clump, all occupants of them non-related, just happened to build or buy there. He walked probably two furlongs before he saw it: a two-story, raised house with a light on the ground floor and the Boston coach parked to the side of the house amid a tangle of other wheeled vehicles.

Lots of people here: dangerous place to be; had to have guards or dogs all around.

He circled back through the low bushes, which turned into sparse trees and a lawn. Here he'd be seen, but without the brush tangling around him, he wouldn't be heard. He crouched—doing militia-training—moving steadily, slowly, listening and watching all around, knife in hand, moving stealthily from spot to spot. This was the way the Algonkins of the Massa-adchu-es-et stalked the great bears, the timid deer, the fierce lion, and the huge moose and elk: slowly, steadily, stealthily, moving and stopping, waiting and listening.

In all actuality, Ashley had completed his mission: he had located the home of the traitors and Royalists, and the rendezvous of the Frenchmen, even had reduced their number by one. All he needed now was to return to Rufus or write to him, with his information. Maybe it was the shot to the head which made him bold or incautious, but Ashley "had" to find out more.

At the hay-barn he halted. Above him the overhanging barn roof, dark but outlined against the stars, its hayloft door wide open and the smell of recently cut, drying hay cascading from it as a net falls upon fish in a shallow pond. This was the home of a rich man who had a large house, a stable with horses, a barn with cows, and a hay-barn. Well…Ashley hoped he had enjoyed it all because after Miles Standish found out about the Frenchmen coming to do sedition and murder he'd return here to Merry Mount as he did years ago, arresting rogues and villains, putting a halt to non-Puritanical behaviors and correcting the manners of the colony by running out those people who used a maypole, lewd behaviors, strong drink and inflated profits in land sales! Yes, Miles Standish would show these Frenchmen a thing or two about English Law and English gaols.

Ashley went onto all fours, crawling across the barnyard, systematically looking around to be sure, getting direction, trying to observe for anyone else: a perfect militia-move. He made it to the hay-barn; the big doors there were wide open. Paused: someone could easily be inside, waiting. Went closer…as close as he dared without going inside…and heard—of all things—snoring!

A trick? A trap? Perhaps a tired guard.

He edged in as carefully and quietly as he could. The snoring was loud and regular—from the hayloft. Well…someone surely was there. He grabbed up the stone which was used to hold open the wide door of the barn during a breeze, and slipped over to the almost-indistinct set of very steep stairs to the loft above.

The hayloft was a "second floor," about three meters off the barn floor, forming a "U-shape" upon which was stored mown hay…an area high enough off the bottom floor that a horse couldn't strike his head if it were led into this barn to be shod or have injuries treated. This was a place cleaner than the stable. The loading door for the hayloft was open, giving a good view of the house and its back yard: a perfect observation spot for a nighttime guard.

The snoring persisted.

Rock in hand, Ashley went quietly up the steep set of stairs, not really knowing what he would do if confronted or if he found a sleeping Frenchman. The third step from the top creaked loudly, and as Ashley attained the hayloft floor, a voice from almost beside him suddenly startled and frightened him: "Almost morning? Where do I go to break the fast?"

Ashley paused, his heart throbbing almost loud enough to be heard.

"Where's the food? I didn't eat the supper. You're here to relieve me, aren't you?"

There was a pregnant pause; then, "Turn around." This time it wasn't a question but a command. Ashley turned slowly, backing away as inconspicuously as possible from the set of steps. Luke—who had been told to watch the rear of the house and wait for Matthew—had fallen asleep, but was now wide-awake and rested...and suspicious.

"Which one are you? What's yer name?"

Even with the small amount of moonlight coming in the open loft door, Ashley could make out the large knife in Luke's hand and the pistol in his belt. He wasn't the size of Matthew, but he looked meaner.

"Who the bloody hell are you...coo! You're..." He suddenly charged at Ashley, knife at the ready!

Ashley couldn't think, only react. His training in the militia was—compared to that of an English soldier—no training at all. What the leaders of the Army taught and expected was complete obedience; this, and only this, was expected. The soldier was taught to march and use defensive positions, to fire a musket or matchlock and use the French baïonnette, and to immediately, completely, unfailingly respond to any officer's command. Soldiers—after all—were expected to march into a position and stand there whilst cannon and musket fire literally cut them to pieces. Then, the survivors would—on command—be expected to fire their shoulder arms and either reload and be prepared to shoot again or be ready to charge upon order, with the baïonnette. Those who ran backward were shot by their officers; those who ran forward—if they lived—got to do it all over again, another time, another place. This was not the way of the militia—who savored life more than response to arms.

The militia was comprised of a volunteer force, mostly farmers and frontiersmen, as businessmen had to stay in the towns and literally run their businesses for the populace. So the militia had to train "differently": each man was an individual who was needed in the next fight, so he wasn't to be wasted in this one. The militiamen were brave and tough: they faced attacks by wild animals, wayward travelers, and many of the inland Woods-People. Running a trap-line was difficult and took talent and dedication far beyond that used by a businessman. What the militia was trained to do was be a showpiece for the colony—to parade for functions of the town and give a sense of security in a place where there was no sheriff. They already knew muskets, could use a bow, a knife, a hatchet. They tracked game and took furs and meat from the forest and ponds, and protected their own homes. All they needed—Ashley had thought as a captain of militia—was "in close" work. Too often a drunk had a knife drawn; how would a militiaman take it away? Only three ways Ashley knew to stop a man from gutting him as he charged with a knife: talk or throw something to divert attention, put something between you and the knife (a tree or shield of some sort), or get out of his way.

This time as Mark charged, Ashley literally jumped to one side. In the semi-darkness and just waking from sleep to see an enemy, Mark had forgotten about the stairwell. He saw Ashley move to the left, tried to compensate, put a leg out to turn—but the leg vanished into air: he stepped off the hayloft edge and fell to the floor below, uttering a great scream in the process, accompanied with a huge "thud" and a great gasp. Ashley knew the stairwell was there so he quickly went down to the fallen man, to subdue him. It wasn't necessary: Mark had dropped upon a hayfork and the tines had gone completely through his body. He wasn't dead, but dying.

Surely the scream had attracted attention! Ashley ran up the stairs again, and to the open hayloft door. He could see no one and heard nothing…but…if they came, it would be from the front, so…he turned and hung down from the open doorway, dropping the few extra feet onto the ground.

No one was there; no noise from the house. He crept back into the shadows and left as he came furtively, thanking God he had gotten away, then throwing away the unused rock he still grasped in his hand.

Back with Joe, Ashley pushed him along the road, letting him do the kind of cantering he liked, and the horse—no longer feeling Matthews (and Mark's) weight—went all out.

Got away! God! Got away and still alive! No angels coming for him; no trumpets sounding; no drums beating…just heavy breathing and a rush of thoughts, mostly about still being alive. He felt sore and heartsick before, but now—after this incident—had to stop thinking about a pounding heart, a sense of fright, a rush from completion…had to put away all those and concentrate upon getting away from here, far away, far enough away to let go of the fear and worry and the mixed emotions which wrapped him the way the notary wrapped his letters. Home. He had to get home. He'd done it all and was used up: exhausted. The flame of his soul was flickering because the wax was gone and only the wick left to burn.

Along the Merry Mount Road, thoughts cascaded through his mind. It was a warm night, turning a little cool, good to grow vegetables but not good for travel. Dampness. Maybe fog in the morning, maybe rain today: he didn't need that. In Duxbury—with Anna—the rains came in late in the day; here at seaside, there was no rumbling warning over the trees, just a sudden change in temperature and a quickening of the wind and the rain poured down.

It was either late in the night or early in the morning. False dawn in the eastern sky, probably about four of the clock, maybe later. His stepfather would be awake now, using a glass by lamplight to see his accounting books, his stock, his next planned project. That was the business way. Puritans were accountants of everything, and everything to them mattered. Everything was reduced to only two things in their lives: religion and business.

Ashley thought about the fire in the shed. That store had been there almost sixteen years and never once had there been a fire like that. "Bastards!" as Rufus Case would say. "Those French bastards!" Why, oh why, would they do that? The man who shot him said it was a "demonstration." They all could be dead right now, with half of Boston burned!

So much had happened...tired, almost to sleep...his head still sore, pounding, bones aching...his willingness to go after "more" at the Merry Mount house, then the Frenchmen's sudden deaths at the cabin and the hay-barn...and neither of those men spoke like the French: they seemed to speak unaccented English, the huge man sounding like the people in London he remembered as a child. It was all too much to unravel. In just a few hours he'd been surprised, shot, left for dead, had Joe and his purse stolen, almost shot a second time, then almost knifed to death...merciful Heaven! Was THIS the life of a spy? Whyever should he pursue it further?

Better to quit now and get out while the getting was good.

Joe had almost reached the deserted cabin where this all had begun. *A quick turn now and we're on the Boston Road*, Ashley thought.

Joe stopped running...stopped! Whinnied, backed sideways on the dirt and gravel road the way he did with Matthew; he didn't usually do that! Noises from the bushes, people talking, loud sounds: a trap!

Ashley almost leaped from the saddle, pulled Joe's reins and swung him around—as a barricade. Looked over Joe's back: nothing. The trap not yet sprung, the bait not yet in place.

What to do? The voices sounded closer, noisy voices, animalistic, grunts and bellows...hogs! Damnable hogs! Hogs the settlers let get away or lost, bred in the wild and now in a pack. Whew! Not a trap after all...good exercise for a militiaman; he'd have to tell them Saturday...then Ashley remembered he couldn't...and probably never would be able to pass along that knowledge to the Plimouth militia...not anymore.

He remounted, Joe still skittish and no wonder, after the past few hours of having different riders, him spooking Joe, now the hogs frightening the big gelding. Joe walked a couple more steps sideways...the hogs had something over there, something in the bushes...oh, Jesus!

Ashley suddenly felt heartsick. It could have—would have—been him. Instead, it was the big Frenchman who spoke gutter-English, shot him and took Joe. The hogs were eating him!

Ashley flipped Joe's reins and pumped his knees against Joe and the big, blond gelding responded, moving forward, obviously glad as his rider to be going away from there—them turning by himself onto the Boston Road and setting his own canter. No wonder. Who wouldn't be glad to leave there!

"God in Heaven, please judge the soul of that man as his body is being eaten, as that is what he planned for me. Amen."

CHAPTER 12

That night in Scotland, in the King's tent, supper was again dismal: watered soup.

A light rain; no decent food in the camp; no response from the nearby town, which had been requested to send a hundred sheep; no fish yet in from the Firth of Forth; three more disgusted Scot's chieftains complaining they'd take their men-at-arms and leave if conditions didn't quickly improve.

All day there had been interruptions. Constant bickering about the line of battle, wondering where the English would run when attacked, the Swiss demand fort money prior to service—whoever heard of such a ridiculous thing anyway: why pay for service "before" service? An impossible situation they forced upon him. The Swiss said they'd pledge to fight to their deaths, so they wanted money in advance to give them a proper burial, and something for their families left behind. Such a dreary thought before battle: fight to the death.

Then there was no meat, no fish, no food for the horses—the few they had; the Scots were sadly lacking in horseback fighters; Cromwell tried to put all his men on horseback and used even more horses to pull supplies and cannon.

And there was no agreement yet from the Scots Council. Things were not like this when his father were King; then, things got done! Difficult these days...his father murdered, his mother fled back to France, himself only twenty years of age and expected without training to command an army, win a kingdom, subdue rebels in Scotland and Ireland, destroy Cromwell the rotten scoundrel, pay his own army, perhaps have to pay an army in advance...almost too much to take, even for a newly crowned King.

England had been raped by Cromwell and his religion...those damned Puritans! The only way Oliver Cromwell could ever have attained what he did was because those Puritans and that outlawed Parliament had backed him. He had then become one of them, forgetting his past religious beliefs and decrying England's official church...all for the glory of command. He was as much a whore as those on Southwark's nighttime streets! He had been a FARMER! Threw out the true Anglican Church of Scotland, allowed the Puritans to take over and charge fines for Sunday travel or profanity in public…a FARMER! NEVER a soldier! A political appointee as an officer of a small troop of cavalry; now he was Lord Protector of England! *A rotten scoundrel! Beheaded my father, deported me! Sent my mother to France and made her a widow! Presently in Ireland, fighting those there loyal to me; killing my people! The KING'S people!*

The poor—the peasants. They did the menial jobs. Couldn't live with them but couldn't live without them: who would be the servants without them? They were all born dead anyway: never could change their lot in life and no one but King Charles the First ever cared if they lived or died. Charles had loved them, fought for them, fed them, acknowledged them…in their hearts HE would ever be their King.

He dismissed his staff and lay on the "bed" they had provided for him: furs over raised planks. He remembered too well the soft mattresses of feathers at his father's house and in the castle: THOSE were "beds"; these were…unsavory.

King Charles the Second dozed while he thought. This war was really only about whose religion was to be the religion of England. His father had been torn between religions, his mother and wife tending toward the Catholics and he attempting to appease the Scots with theirs, ever pacifying the Church of England, stepping gently around the reformed Puritans. In the end, he had no firm support: each religion refused him in his attempt to have them on his side. Then that damned farmer Cromwell was chosen as the champion of the Puritans and the Civil War begun. Everything about religion. Had Henry stayed with the Catholic pope, Charles the First could never have been challenged…or chased from his home and land and rule.

The dream came to him as he lay there, a dream wherein he had the Presbyterian Scots and the Church of England there, together with him. THEN he felt powerful enough to conquer Cromwell; then he knew he needed divine assistance in his endeavor.

A noise from the tent-flap startled him awake.

"My Lord King: Charles the Second of Scotland, Greater Britain, France and Ireland, I come with welcome news."

At least this man spoke English.

"And that is…?"

"The Council has agreed upon the appointment of David Leslie to the position of commander of the Army, under your gracious self of course, my King."

"Agreed? They have agreed?"

"Every one, Great King."

"Then those three chieftains aren't leaving with their men?"

"No one dares leave you now, King Charles: we are sworn to you, every man in Scotland."

"Then I shall not need the Swiss! God has shown the way! You have more to tell?"

"Only that General Leslie has made a Plan of Battle and feels he shall be victorious."

"Only that?" Charles laughed. "Why, dear man, that is precisely what your King needs to hear! Merciful God, thank You for Your intervention into this! England needs Her King and Cromwell needs to lose this war. Thank You for all You do for us, mighty and beloved God. Amen."

The Council appointee left, and Charles maintained his happiness.

From the kitchen a servant came in with a plate of mutton, placed it on the table and Charles—never into the role as King enough such that he could not speak with a servant—asked, "Mutton? From where?"

The servant went onto his knees. He loved his King, but a servant did what a servant had to do. "Dunbar has sent the sheep, plus all the vegetables they could harvest, as they feel no matter what course this war takes, some soldiers will eat them and it should be our Scots. And, my King..."

"More?"

"The fish for the troops is even now being distributed to them. The Council said the fish from the sea should be eaten by Scots, not Cromwell."

"By God, that's wonderful news! If only the pledges from the colony would arrive, we'd have everything we asked for in our prayers!" Charles crossed himself in the Catholic fashion, then knelt. "Merciful God, thank You."

Charles was technically an Anglican Protestant, but his mother was Catholic and it couldn't hurt to thank the Maker in each faith.

CHAPTER 13

Morning at Merry Mount. Table set to break the fast. The two night-guards replaced by different and more men, the night men sent out to the hay barn to tell Mark and Matthew to come in to eat.

Johnathan, Luke and Geoffry, the host of the house and his three sons just completing the morning Anglican prayers and Thanks to God.

"Where is your lookout? He's not here to break the fast."

"Looking out, I should imagine. Geoffry, fetch Mark here. Luke, where is my great man? Asleep?"

"The big man never came back, my Lord," the host volunteered. "My guards say he didn't return."

"Never came back? Odd. Geoffry, try this colonial food that I may eat; Luke, get Mark and then find Matthew; he's probably out with that big horse, riding back and forth upon a pillow. What a sight that must make!"

"How is London, my Lord? Several of us are from there and miss it."

"London is ever London…all the businessmen trying to act like Protector Cromwell, doing big business and throwing their weight around…in charge…even tho' Cromwell was by choice a farmer and of necessity a politician and never at all involved in retail sales. Just a busy place; no longer quiet and pleasant. I think when all this is over and Charles becomes installed as King, I shall open my own store and become a glove salesman."

They all laughed; Johnathan was the hit of every party and always had the latest news from London.

"You feel I jest, but in utter truth, my role as glove salesman seems predestined. Whereas my father had over eight hundred pairs of shoes, my grandfather James had more than a thousand pairs of gloves. I feel it runs in the family."

That broke up the table; Johnathan could ever be relied upon to have a funny story.

One of the day-guards entered the room and nodded at the host.

"Your coach is ready, your Lordship, and there's a basket with your lunch in it all ready to be put inside for you; and your trunk has been lifted in."

"Very good. I shall inform our friends in London that your services were exceptional, your party delightful, and the pledges of faith given in love of our King. Hmmmmmm...only my own guard seems to fail me."

Several minutes later, Luke returned. "Mark's dead, Johnathan: hayfork through and through, out in the hay-barn."

"What? Dead? No!"

They all rushed out to the hay-barn and two of the Merry Mount men went up into the loft. "Looks like he found a spot to sleep here," one of them called down.

"The loft door is open, so he probably was up here, opened the door for air and to watch the yard, forgot where the stairs were and fell."

"No! My Mark wouldn't have done that! My Mark would have stayed awake, on guard to protect me!"

"Perhaps he was awake, my Lord, but just missed the step in the dark."

"I'd much rather think that. I miss him already. My poor Mark...guarding me to the end...I shall ever remember him so."

"We'll take care of him, my Lord."

"You will give him a fine Christian burial? He deserves that, poor fellow. Perhaps I shouldn't have brought him here to this savage land just to die so far from his home."

"We'll give him a proper Christian burial, sir."

"He'd like that...at the end, and all."

Johnathan strode toward the house, calling to Geoffry: "Get our coach. No food; no rest: we must find my great man and get along to Boston. Already this place saddens me."

"Everything of ours is in the coach."

"Except for Mark and Matthew. Let us be off. Luke, drive; Geoffry, watch out for Matthew."

The coach had hardly left the gravel driveway when the homeowner spoke to one of his sons: "Pompous ass."

"What will we do with the dead one?"

"Put him in the hog-wallow beyond the creek. They'll take care of him there."

Luke drove the coach while Geoffry—pistol at the ready—watched the sides of the road. Matthew's failure to return was not a good sign, coming especially as it did upon Mark's sudden death. It wouldn't be that long—at a run by the horses after they were warmed—that they would reach the intersection where the road to Granite City turned toward Boston and the cabin was placed: where Matthew had been sent alone.

Along the way, Johnathan had given the impression of calmness, but underneath that demeanor he was seething: a spy they had to kill; a boy they had to kill; one good man dead under suspicious circumstances and another missing all night...whatever was happening to this mission? These men were hard enough to live with, in that they murdered without comment and remained crude in their talk, but now a quarter of his protection was gone and another quarter not accounted for.

Not much longer and they were there. Luke positioned the coach off the road and on the grass so the horses could graze while they waited and if Johnathan wanted to step out, there'd be a carpet of grass for his feet. Luke loved Johnathan.

"Geoffry, if you please?"

"On my way, Johnathan."

He took only a minute, then returned.

"What?"

"You don' wan' t' see this, Johnathan."

"Tell me."

"Matthew is dead...'is body—wha's left o' it—is over by the cabin door."

"Explain 'what is left of it.'"

"Looks like 'e was eaten by animals, maybe wolves. I turned 'im over t' see 'is face, but it wasn't there...but under 'is chin is a powder-burn. I foun' 'is pistol an' it's been discharged."

"Where is the clerk?"

"I looked in the cabin: no body, no blood. Matthew said 'e put a ball inta 'is 'ead...I don' see no bloodstains nowhere."

"Would he have shot him outside and the wolves carried him away?"

"Nawwww...'e tol' me 'e 'ad 'im lay down on the floor an' shot 'im there. No body; no blood."

"He wouldn't have lied."

"Nawww...'e wasn't a liar. A great oaf, but 'e didn't lie. Too frightened t' lie. 'E did somthin'...wha', I don't know; but 'e didn't lie."

"And now my great man lies there dead. How extraordinary. He was so large I never imagined anyone could do anything to him."

"No 'orse, either...but 'e coulda run away from the wolves..."

"Or another taken him. Probably the one who took the body of the clerk and killed my great man. He was proud, up on that big horse, sitting upon that silly-looking pillow...are you certain it is clothing for only one? The wolves didn't drag the clerk from the cabin?"

"Yes, Johnathan: certain. Only Matthew out there."

"Not the clerk."

"'E killed the clerk."

"He killed the clerk; he was sure of it, happy about it."

"Some frien' o' 'is must of either been wi' 'im or foun' 'im, then killed Matthew an' left 'im for the wolves."

"An accomplice. We deal now with another Puritan, one whom we do not now or can readily recognize."

Luke leaned down from the seat. "It seems thus. We should have expected that; these people always run in packs, like wild dogs. I should have gone with Matthew last night."

"You are right, Lukey...we must be better prepared in Providence. I shall write to Francis along the road to Boston and post it by fast courier once we're there. We must have more and better assistance in Providence, as the pledges there will be numerous and exorbitant."

"Wha' can we do abou' Matthew? We can't jus' let 'im stay there."

"I'll bury him, Johnathan, or we could take him back to the homestead and put him with Mark; he'd like that."

"Yes, I should think that also. Geoffry...are you up to...collecting...Mattthew?"

"Don' like it but I'll do it for 'im...'e was a right good mate an' 'e bunked wi' me in the Army."

"Use the clothes chest. It was a gift from my mother but it seems it now needs a different use, and our big comrade requires a tender repository after all he's been through. Pitch the clothing onto the floor; we'll have it all washed and ironed in Providence...and the next chest need not be so large. I just hope I remember to 'loser' it before mother sees it. They love us in Providence; mail comes from there monthly. Those in Salem were decent to my brother but I didn't want to stay there long...not the proper setting for us in that crude place."

"They gave a lot."

"And they'll realize soon enough they gave much more than they expected." All three grinned: they shared a dirty, little secret.

"Go along now: do the deed and let us return to the Merry house with our great man. Then to Boston, a swap of this coach for proper steeds, and a ride to King's Town to see our dear friend Walter Foster."

"What a surprise for him."

"Indeed...one long in coming. To think that all the years he worked for my father he was stealing from him as well."

"There are criminals everywhere these days, Johnathan. It's the Puritan-faction and their laws...they make men into criminals and force religious laws and taxes upon the population, the poor as well as the rich."

"But Walter was a greedy rogue...stealing from a man who needed his wealth to protect the poor; and then when he felt he needed to pay his Army and leave for France, that money had been pilfered. A filthy crime! One which none suspect I know about."

"He doesn't realize people brand him as a thief?"

"He and I communicate regularly; he has no idea at all I am aware he took the money and jewels. His bookkeeping hid much, but my father told me all."

"He has pretended to be your friend..."

"And I, his. If my father could have gotten from Scotland to France, he'd be alive today. The soldier's pay was stolen, father's jewel-box stolen...he trusted Walter with his life and Cromwell took that."

"You can't make it all return..."

"But I can bring some small satisfaction for the bad deeds to our family, and give him some long-overdue punishment for helping to kill a King. Walter shall understand my pain."

"Well, for a while, Johnathan...a short while."

"I still wonder what happened here, with Matthew."

"Had to be an accomplice. Someone came here, took the clerk's body, shot Matthew as he arrived, took the horse..."

"That being correct, now this task of ours becomes far more difficult as we may find the sheriff awaiting us in Boston, holding the clerk's body as evidence. Bad enough we struggle in a foreign zone with colonial rabble, but then we would have a band of zealot Puritans fall upon us, and we surely and soon would be hanged upon the gibbit."

"You think that's what it is? Them killing us off one by one?"

"What else must I think?"

"You think Mark...?"

"I do not understand the circumstances. Mark would not have gotten up into a hayloft to sleep while he waited for Matthew. Matthew handled himself so well...I feel we must have pistols prepared and be on the watch, especially going in to Boston."

"Matthew was not a killer; I never remember him doing in anyone. He says he shot the clerk in the head and I believe what he says...but I also wonder if he may have missed. A head-shot is not that easy, with the pull from these heavy triggers."

"What are you saying?"

"It's only my wonder."

"You think he shot but didn't strike the clerk, then left and the clerk remained here..."

"Then when Matthew returned, the clerk done him in, took the horse, rode to the house, maybe to the barn: the dogs were in during the night..."

"I remember that; it was strange to keep the dogs inside at night."

"He goes to the barn as that's the furthest building from the house, Mark sees him come in, misses his step—had forgotten about the stairwell—and falls..."

"Onto the hayfork that man said he left there! God! Ghastly to think such...but a distinct possibility."

"The clerk them rides away; the wild animals here smell blood and...about Matthew. The animals here are as savage as the Indians."

"Pray we don't meet any!"

"I ain't so smart as you, Johnathan, but if there were two colonists, one helpin' the other, they shouldn't have separated—letting the clerk be caught by Matthew. They'd have been covering each other and killed him."

"For now, your scenario is acceptable and probably the truth. Why would the clerk send a child when he had another man to help him? And where would that other be when Matthew first nabbed him? Without you, Lukey, I'd be lost. Geoffry protects me, but you think. So we probably still have that colonial killer watching us...maybe even now. It seems our shirt-sleeved store-clerk has become an adversary who is trained to do his job...and now we have lost two good men. The best thing I can think is if he operates alone, he has not involved the sheriff so far."

"Do we burn the clerk's store now?"

"God, no! We're in enough trouble and it's probably not his store; the little boy on the wharf said an old man owned it. That's why our little demonstration didn't work: he's not a store-clerk: he's some Army officer who is a spy, a trained killer against us, simple gentleman. We must be extra-cautious from now on. Always together, understood? Always together."

Geoffry had loaded the chest onto the coach and joined Johnathan. "Wha' about a spy?"

"Johnathan thinks the clerk is still alive and he is the one killing us—a trained spy."

"One of Cromwell's from England. Perhaps we shouldn't have taken that English ship here."

"We shall travel on a different carrier from Providence; I'll write Francis to book us passage. I'd go immediately to Providence from here but we must return this coach and four and get saddle-horses; a stolen coach is reported quickly and found too fast; we'd be easily hunted-down and cannot afford the fare if the sheriff follows us."

"An' Matthew?"

"Matthew must be returned to Merry Mount, to have him buried with Mark; we'll do that now. My great man would appreciate that and Mark will appreciate the company. So sad..." Johnathan sighed deeply. It was all too much. "The things we do for our King. The personal indignities we bear. Mother will get me a new traveling-chest; she's attending that cousin of Louis and may marry him. The sacrifices we make upon the altar of international intrigue, dying for the cause—that itself is heroic. We shall be remembered but not glorified, as we do the work of the King...too many want to join this crusade, but we spearhead it."

"Johnathan?"

"Yes?"

"We're going to do this. We're going to get Charles returned to England and proclaimed King. The people want it; only Cromwell and the Roundheads interfere."

"You truly care, don't you, Lukey. Yes...What you propose shall come true, with our diligence. Then, my Lukey, the world opens to us. A return to Spain, going to see my mother in France...The Dutch placated and friendly to their new King-cousin...Charles will reward us for all the tragedies here: that's the way he is, grateful for things his subjects do for him and his family. We're so close..."

Johnathan removed his cap and held it low. "God..."

Luke and Geoffry immediately joined him: "Save the King!"

CHAPTER 14

He pushed Joe. It wasn't that far and the big gelding was fed and rested, so he could canter a ways, then walk, then canter again. Riding this horse was like riding no other Ashley had been on…maybe the plain size of Joe or maybe his long back gave him his strength, but he surely could canter and make a rider easy in the saddle. Ashley knew he was far ahead of any riders Merry Mount could send after him; he just wanted to go home in safety…unless the Frenchmen had burned that also.

He tried to compose a letter in his mind which he would write and send to Rufus, telling him all the events and the description of the Merry Mount house. He also thought about Elspeth's brother…and his death. Never again would he involve a child in a man's work…although…that's what had happened to him, twenty years before. Wondered how Elspeth would take the news of who had sent her brother from the safety of Pennyweight's store and onto the wharf where he was slain…how in fact her parents would take it. That was the end of that torrid affair, no matter how much they wanted each other. He'd bear the weight of the world—as Atlas—to try to keep that from them if he attempted to court her, and that fire-brand woman would probably take a page from the Frenchman's book and cut his throat in his sleep if she ever found out he had sent her brother to his early and ugly death.

Another quandary: should he tell Mister Pennyweight and his mother about the source of the shed's fire? Although the shed and its contents had gone in that blaze, nothing else had been harmed. Bad enough for old Pennyweight; good for the neighbors and the city. His stepfather was at a loss as to why that had happened; Ashley realized he didn't dare tell him what he had learned, that HE was the reason for the fire. That was a one-time thing and the Frenchmen were gone now, what point was there in telling the fire was malicious but singular: a "demonstration" warning he didn't understand nor heed. Where were the heads of those Frenchmen that they would set a fire to send a message? Only the gentry understood things like that—subtleness. No one from Plimouth would think that fire was anything but spontaneous.

Well, he had seen the man who tried to kill him dead, and that one in the hayloft. Two strikes of the owl; wondered how the Frenchmen liked "that" demonstration!

If the shed hadn't been there, would the Frenchmen have fired the store? Probably. He'd have to write about this to Rufus…what a letter that would be. Rufus might come to Boston himself, once he read it. So…tomorrow he'd go back to the stable which rented the coach and ask about that…the stableman responded well to gold and Rufus had supplied plenty of that. After that…Rufus would know; he'd have a letter back from him by then. That was a really handy thing: having a mail-relay at your store. Rufus could figure all this out: he was an inventor, and they saw things differently from most people. Rufus had told him: "A look to an inventor is not like a look by most people. They see an object; I see a way to use that object differently—in other ways if I re-shape it or use it in a different manner or on different objects. I imagine. Ashley, as a spy, you must learn to imagine…imagine what will happen next, what *can* happen, what *should* happen…what if something goes wrong, what to do then. Think. Understand. Plan. Use subtle disguise. Always feel your enemy will counter your moves as in a chess game; think beyond what you do." Rufus was smart; no wonder he had his own business.

And what about Elspeth. She wasn't very reserved—came across as knowing what she wanted and beating a path to it; she surely did just that! He wondered if it was specifically him or was it just a means to an end—that end being married to someone, maybe even a man she didn't know but whose family she knew would help her get and hold him. Hard to believe that: she couldn't be so cold. She surely wasn't cold in bed…but…that would be her best move—almost every woman's best move with a man. God, that was good with her! He shuddered just thinking about that…then he knew how much he really missed her. He'd have to calm down those urges for her…and at the same time he was thinking this, he wanted more of her!

What would his mother tell him? Ha! "Marry her quick!" What about Ruthie…what more would little sister have to say about her?

He was pleasantly surprised when he came out of his thoughts and realized he was already in Boston, the streets filled with morning-people, the stable Pennyweight used not far away. Joe was walking differently…good thing they were already close to home. He owed the big horse his life and there was no complete payment for that. Maybe a shoe was loose.

He headed over to the stable...Joe came first.

The farrier told him Joe's favoring of that hoof was a real problem. Probably a stone-bruise from the gravel road, but he wanted to pull the shoe and inspect more. Ashley readily agreed, said he wouldn't use Joe for a couple days. He was pleased, really, as using one of Pennyweight's hackneys was another "change" in the disguise of his spy job. And they could stand some exercise; they were only used Sundays, for the carriage to the big Congregational church.

So...Joe would get some rest, grain instead of grass, all his shoes checked and a complete examination done, his sore foot treated...life now seemed less complicated.

Ashley walked over to his home. The kitchen—in back of the house/store—was this time empty. He went to the second floor of the "combination" building and found Esther, alone but moving about, assembling some papers to be sent with a shipment of trade-goods, inland, for a Boston fur-gathering company. Ashley, knowing he didn't want to do small-talk with Esther—she was much younger but actually a lot smarter as far as business, money-investing, new commerce and sales-inventory went; Ashley never cared about the store or its runnings. Esther had arrived at a time in the life of her father when he most needed a son to teach, and substituted his first daughter. He knew she'd marry sometime, but in the meanwhile she was there to listen and learn, understand and apply that knowledge. Even now she could run the whole business; she was getting to the point where she could even manage the trading and investing as well. All of which made her—to Ashley—a great bore and someone to stay away from.

"Oh! You startled me!"

"I've...been out all night."

"You're filthy!"

This younger sister acted like an older one. "I guess I am slightly dirty; was on the ground last night for a while."

"Ashley, there's water heated in the kitchen; bathe."

"Where's Ruthie?"

"Why?"

"I...have to talk with her."

"More about Elspeth?"

"Something like that."

"Where she always is, even when she's needed in the store, in her room."

"Thanks." He backed away, not wanting Esther to see his burnt hair.

At the door of Ruth's room, he paused. "Ruthie...I need your help."

"To do what?"

"Look at the back of my head and tell me what you see."

"Bugs?" A true "little sister."

"I...got burned."

"In the fire?"

"Er...yes!"

"Oh that's awful!"

"Could you wash my hair? Cut it? Make it look somewhat presentable?"

"Nothing will make *that* look presentable...but I'll try."

She washed the hair, causing some additional pain, snipped and combed, made him wince and squirm, finally brushed what was left and slicked-back the long hair in the front to try to hide the missing hair at the rear. Looking like that—especially from the front—it wasn't that bad-seeming, and he certainly didn't appear—with the beard gone—the way he formerly did: didn't look like any of the family with his hair like that. Then he knew this was the style he'd use as a further disguise. Yeah...further disguise. He wasn't through with those Frenchmen: they'd killed Elspeth's brother and ruined his chances with her...now they'd pay.

He thought that big Frenchman who had ridden Joe and shot him could have been the one who murdered Roland on the wharf...but the man wielded a pistol and showed no knife. Men who use knives live with them. They glory in them, show them off, play with them, always have them and always use them—like they're a part of them that does what the rest can't do. There was one of the militiamen like that with an Indian hatchet—a tamahanken—and he would "carry" a musket and he could shoot a musket, but when that first shot was fired, he dropped that musket and drew his hatchet, running into the fray as a wild savage, chopping and hewing much as Bar vom Dechlesburg must have in that story the wise woman told. Knife-fighters were like that. Assassins were like that. The blade was an extension of themselves and they relished that use. The big man with the pistol couldn't have been the one who cut Roland...and although that one in the hayloft had a knife, he was too clumsy to have been a real throat-cutter: those men are experts; that kind of person enjoys what he does, gets in real close and does his business then steps away and grins. Nope; not either of those. Another. Three others left, and probably not the leader.

He thought he had wanted Elspeth more than anything else in the world but he put this job ahead of her; ahead, even, of his family. The spies had extinguished any hope he'd have with Elspeth—because of Roland—but now Ashley thought to seek revenge in Roland's name. He'd be—as the prayer-meeting preacher had said: an avenger of blood. Oh, yeah. Vengeance for Roland AND himself—all at once. He'd get that one with the knife, maybe put his head on a post the way the heads of the traitors where put on posts in London. He'd make it his business...his only business.

Esther walked into his room like he owed her money. That's the way she was; he wouldn't have gone into her bedroom like that. (Ruthie's bedroom was different.)

"Post for you from North Plimouth."

Then she left. Convenient.

He opened the waxed and folded note, a mail from Rufus dated two days ago:

> *Ashley, I went yesterday to Plimouth to ask further about "our friends." This turned out to be rather an adventure for me as the packet had slipped her moorings and was being turned to set sail and leave. I hired a dingy and two to get me out to her and back. The captain—Per Liden—is a friend of mine, a Swede who has sailed rather extensively in the Baltic Sea. He told me the five got aboard outside London and "spoke English," but as Per is not so familiar with the accents or dialects of many languages, he could not place from whence they might be. Two were "darker" than the average Englishman. He will ask the person in London who arranged the passages as to whom they might be. At this juncture I must ask you to be particularly careful. It seems we have uncovered a plot which may be funded and forwarded from the highest places, and these five are most probably extremely dangerous. Take all precautions, I beg you! I am receiving your daily mail. Thank you.*
>
> *R. DESTROY THIS NOTE AND ALL OTHERS!*

He slept two hours and Ruth called him for lunch. Went into the kitchen not thinking about his hair; his mother standing there.

"What have you done with your hair? And your beard?"

"I asked Ruthie to cut them."

"Well, she certainly did! I've never seen your hair so short, and she really cut the back terribly, it looks all singed."

"It was too long—as you told me—and I must have moved when she was doing it."

"Well, it's an awful haircut…can't a barber fix that? There's a new one on the corner."

"I'll see today."

"And I'll tell Ruthie she's not to cut your hair again!"

Well, he had his latest disguise. Before, he'd had long hair and a beard; now he didn't. What was it Rufus had said about disguises? The easiest ones fool people the most. Wear a hat and remove it: they all looked for someone wearing a hat. Wear a red shirt, then change the color: they all looked for that red shirt.

Lunch went fast: warmed over seafood soup—Ashley's favorite, more a bisque with things cut into it, and fresh brown-bread warmed in the Dutch oven. Afterwards, Mister Pennyweight motioned to Ashley and they went out the back door, over near the burned shed.

"What business do you have today, Ashley?" Pennyweight was ever direct; Ashley couldn't get used to that, even after all these years His stepfather always seemed inquisitive and abrupt all the time.

"Just a talk with a fellow for Rufus, now done. I have heartfelt sorrow for your loss in the fire, and to think what might have happened."

"God lays burdens, but none we cannot shoulder. You're leaving soon?"

"Er…yes. Not right away, but sometime in the morning."

"We shall miss you, boy…your mother speaks of you often while you're away and is gladdest when you are here. I offer once more our deepest sorrows about Anna and the baby. We pray; they all pray for you and her at the meetings."

"Thank you; I need those prayers, especially now."

"You have them daily. Ashley, I want to tell you something."

"All right…" Expecting the worst, of course.

"First, I want to say I'm proud of you, that you're my son. I'm…" He couldn't finish: too many tears suddenly arrived. This wasn't Pennyweight: he seldom—over the past twenty years—acknowledged Ashley, much less spoke kindly with him; and never had Ashley seen the man cry.

"I know. Most of that was my fault. You married my mother and I resented you for that, that you would try to take my father's place."

"I'll never take his place…ever."

"I know that now—but then I didn't. I should have helped you more in the store or the fields…"

"God, not in the store; you always broke everything!"

They each smiled; Ashley had managed to break items easily.

"Son, I'm very sorry...I called you names..."

"I can't ever recall you doing that."

"To your mother and sisters...I called you a lazy boy, called you Lardarse, Anchorarse...and I'm deeply sorry I did that. I have prayed about that." He held up a hand. "Don't say anything; let me finish. When a man gets my age, family becomes more important than anything else."

"What age? You're still a young man."

"You're kind...but I'm almost the age of Miles Standish, older than most everybody around here, and these days I wonder if I can still make the walk to the prayer-meetings; I get exhausted by the effort and it's too close to use the carriage."

"Speaking of age, what is my mother's age?"

"You don't know?"

"She never told me."

"She never told me either! On her travel-papers she has the age of eighteen."

"Eighteen? When she came here? I was twelve!"

Pennyweight chuckled. "When I met her I fell in love with her and age was never discussed. You'll have to ask that yourself; maybe she'll tell you."

"And be chased out of the kitchen by her broom? No, thank you!"

They both laughed—for the first time in twenty years they were really talking.

"When I'm gone, you'll be the man of the house..."

"I don't want to hear things like that."

"Ashley...I know you tend to put off everything...you have your likes and dislikes—as we all—but I want you to run this business."

"Esther..."

"Esther can do it but she will marry and have children, and who's to say if her husband can or will want to tend a store. No...you. You have to do this; no one else is around.

"I don't think I can. How can I do that? I know nothing of the business or any other!"

"There's a chance for me to get an import license in New Amsterdam...of course, I can't go there, nor could I stay there. I had planned on Esther's husband doing that for me."

Esther's husband. Ashley had almost forgotten about that fiasco. Pennyweight kept talking, but Ashley's mind flashed back a few years. Esther's "to be" husband: Alward.

Esther had been admiring a boy older than she, who at the time was working in the store for Mister Pennyweight. This was a few years ago. Working for Pennyweight, but his mind was on the Army (probably as had been Roland's, well, probably "some" of the time Alward must have thought about Esther; who wouldn't?). The boy had will, but no education, although he struggled to get one by asking everyone he met about things. Pennyweight was—of course—interested in having an educated business manager for his stores (he started and now leased his Plimouth store, co-owned a store in Granite City, and had this one in Boston with aspirations) so he decided the best and easiest way to get a worker with education was to send him to a college. It didn't hurt that Alward said he wanted to marry Esther when she reached her age of attainment; that was a sort of "keep it in the family" situation which helped everyone. So a bargain was arranged: the "prospect" would be sent off to college, there to receive a proper and business-oriented education and all else college provided. After graduation—and Esther's attaining an age for marriage—Alward and Esther would wed, Alward would step into Pennyweight's businesses, and thereby become "the man of the house" and "partner" to Mister Pennyweight.

In 1636, the General Court of the colony decided to have a "college," and started this in Newetown (later re-named "Cambridge"). When the Puritan, John Harvard, died that fall and left his abundant endowment to the college, it was re-named for him. It was but a single house within a cow pasture when Esther's Alward attended it, but the instructors were European and Alward soaked up all the education he could get. He also applied to enter the King's Army—much to Pennyweight's chagrin—and as at the time the English Army was searching for business-trained young men, they readily accepted the style of accounting and business practice Harvard College taught. So upon completion at Harvard—to Pennyweight's expense—Alward accepted an appointment to the militia of Boston, and in a year he was an officer in the service of England, occupation. That fall, he succumbed to a disease and died. Ashley's thoughts returned to the moment: his stepfather was still speaking to him.

"So, there's a lot of money there, waiting for us…we only have to take the license and begin shipping goods—mostly furs—from there to here. What is most important is having someone follow the merchandise: it gets sent to the wrong port or is unloaded and shuffled away, lost, strayed or stolen unless someone is right there to watch it."

It was true: with so many ships and people in and around Boston, and so much cargo shunted across the wharves, theft had begun to plague the merchants. Whole shipments of valuable, re-sellable items would simply disappear; no accounting was available and no monitoring of shipments existed. Even on the roads, wagons of goods were hijacked. There was a committee to solve the problems, but Pennyweight wasn't secure in that group-thought: he wanted his personal representative right there—every step of the voyage—with the cargo.

Ashley realized that in doing this job, especially with the furs, he would be working against Rufus Case, Ltd.

"We're not talking 'pence' here...we're talking thousands of pounds sterling with each shipment. That's lots of money! Protector Cromwell has closed English ports to foreign ships, so the rest of the world waits to send products here, to New England, and so ships them to the Dutch in New Amsterdam, who then turn around and re-sell them to us and London, with English shipping. Very complicated but totally legal. Think about this, will you? You could get a start in the import business, learn how to pack and send freight, then later on return to Boston and run my stores. No real work, after you know what you're doing."

"I WILL think on that. Right now I do a job for Rufus Case..."

"My competition..."

They laughed briefly.

"Yes, but Rufus is more in the fur trade and you deal in household goods and clothing. When I finish this job for Rufus I'll go to New Amsterdam and see what I can do about all that...But I'll talk to you before that, all right?"

"Decidedly all right." He put his arm around Ashley's shoulder. "Decidedly all right. May I tell this to your mother?"

"Is that the eighteen-year-old we talked about?"

"Yes, that one: the young one."

Ashley sighed. "Yes, tell her. I have a lot of things I have to tell her also."

Pennyweight went along to the store and Ashley walked over to where Pennyweight's hackneys were stabled, saddled one and rode to Gold's. A boy was there instead of the stableman Ashley had paid for information.

"Where is the man who was here three days ago?"

"Don't know. He had the place open this morning but he's not here. I usually just help out a couple hours a day but I'm the only one here and can't leave."

"I would pay you for information..."

"I don't think I can give any; I'm only here in the mornings but I told a customer to tell Squire Gold, who lives in Granite City, that this place is wide open and smells awful. I can't stay here, but I must until Squire Gold arrives."

"I'm looking for three men; perhaps they go by the names of Smith. The Smith brothers."

"They had coaches out of here this past week...I thought they'd take one today, but I guess they didn't when they returned the last one."

"The one they took to Merry Mount is here? They've already been here?"

"All signed in by the stableman, and no further reservations for them...there are three horses missing, tho'..."

"Missing? Stolen?"

"No...not stolen; I think the stableman rode one and took a pair some place; that's probably where he is now. Probably was delayed; I'm going to wait until he or Squire Gold get here. I can't rent anything; I don't know how to write."

Three horses missing AND the manager of the stable missing...sounded like the Smith brothers' work to Ashley. The sheriff would probably find the manager in the ocean—if they found him at all—and the horses would be in another city, far away. He gave the boy a shilling and rode back toward the stable where the hackney was kept.

Back at the stable, thinking: where would those murdering villains go...there had to be a pattern. Plimouth, Boston, Salem...maybe further along the north coast, but after Salem they returned to Boston and went to Merry Mount. Then back to Boston, but that was to return the coach...they were decent enough to return a coach but they murdered the boy, set a fire, tried twice to kill him...how decent can they be? HAD to be them who took those missing horses...they've already gone north and east, and not much lies west...so maybe now they have turned South. Granite City...then nothing until...Providence. Maybe Providence.

This stable he was in: it held too many memories for him. As Boston was being built, a stable-owner from London chose this particular property for his stable, and as there was a small, tired, tidal stream off the water here, he'd be able to dump "whatever" into it and twice a day the tide would carry it away—as it did in London. He built his stable and it prospered, but he became alarmed when the officials of the newly developing town said they'd place a road across that tidal stream, filling it to the ocean and building there a wharf.

The land and the stable cost quite a bit at the time, the loss of which would sorely hurt the owner and the cost of having manure lugged away daily was prohibitive to profit, so the stable-owner proceeded to use cheap labor to have constructed a brick and stone tunnel—made in the Roman-fashion, like those in London—to protect the waters of the stream, then had all that re-filled such that hardly anything of the stream or tunnel could be seen. He then kept the tidal flow in place, and no one would see his refuse-system when the new road and wharf went in.

Well, it all worked out fine, still worked fine. Manure and straw were shoved down scuppers at the outward tide and most of it was carried far-enough out to sea, and the rest eaten by sea-creatures or reduced to mulch upon the bottom. When Mister Pennyweight came to Boston and bought land for his new store, he was close enough to use this stable as a place to keep his horses.

When Ashley was seventeen or eighteen, Mister Pennyweight—in a seemingly out of character move said to him, "I've bought you a horse."

"Me? You've bought me a horse?"

"Exactly that; all your own. Of course, you must take care of him. Can you do that?"

"Surely! May I see him now?"

"In a moment. You know I am a businessman, and as such, I deal in business. This is the business-offer I make to you: the horse is yours, free. The board, which includes feeding, I shall pay. You—however—must do the daily care and observation of both your horse and my horses. What do you say to that?"

"What care is that?"

"Oh, daily, check the feet and clean out any manure or debris in the hoof. If any of the horses favors a hoof, tell the stableman."

"I can do that."

"Once a week, curry and comb them. That will take some small effort, but they need and deserve that."

"I shall do it!"

"The stableman will be there every day—not at night, as he works days only—so if you see a problem, tell me or him. Will you do that?"

"Of course!"

"Now, let me tell you about your horse. He's a big, Spanish-bred gelding, a buckskin-color; they say he runs like the wind."

"Oh!"

"His former owner called him 'Cavy'—some sort of Spanish word I think. You can take him to the wild-cranberry bog and run him there…a full league of roads in an oval."

"May I see him now?"

"In a moment. I want to tell you all, then I must open the store. Remember, you must take care of your horse and see mine are clean and presentable for each Sunday, as your mother enjoys a ride that day. Is this all fair and agreeable to you? You'll care for all the horses daily?"

"I shall!" Famous last words.

"Then go to your new horse…oh, those Spanish horses? I think they're from Arabia, mainly. Cavy is big and beautiful and as fast as any here. Be proud of him."

"I shall."

To put it bluntly, he didn't. He hadn't cared after any of the horses. Following one ride, the "fast as the wind" horse came up with a limp (and that was why Ashley was so concerned about Joe—probably why he had bought him in the first place—Joe being big and a light-color horse, similar to Cavy). Even after the stableman had told Ashley what salves and soaks to use on the big Spaniard, he had little interest in caring for Cavy, the limping horse. His lack of interest spread immediately to Pennyweight's hackneys (themselves no little animals but bred big and strong to pull wagons and coaches), and when those carriage-steeds were found a second week in a row to be un-curried and having their hooves stuffed with manure, the limping horse was sold that day to whomever it is limping horses are sold. Ashley was afoot again, and in bad graces.

He put Pennyweight's horse into its stall and spoke briefly with the stable-boy. "Is Joe ready?"

"He's mostly lame…you shouldn't ride him for another few days. The hackney doesn't ride well?"

"I just exercise Mister Pennyweight's horses…do you have one I may rent to take to the Case Relay-station in North Plimouth?"

"That one over there, but he has to be returned here within the week."

"If I leave him with the relay-station, will they return him to you?"

"They'd bring him back the day he was ready to come here, with the mail-run; it'd save one of their horses. They all do us favors and we do the same for them. How would you get back here without a horse?"

"I may not be back."

"Oh. Well, three shilling in advance, since I know you."

"Cheap enough." Ashley paid and went over to Pennyweight's house for his clothing and gear. He'd have to poke around, looking for those three Frenchmen who spoke English; they were ahorse now, and certainly not in this area, with three stolen mounts. And then he'd have to end up at Rufus Case's place. Lots of things to do.

He went to his attic-room and shoved some clothes and raingear in a sack, looked around, then went back downstairs, to return to the stable.

"Good morning, Ashley." His mother greeted him as he came downstairs, headed for escape through the rear door.

"Good morning, Mum."

"How did you sleep?"

"Fairly well."

"Care for some breakfast? You were up and out early this morning."

"No...another time, perhaps."

"There's a note from that Rufus." She handed it to him and he read it fast.

> *Per Liden tells me all arrangements for passages are made by Excelsior Shipping Lines—a London-based travel company which arranges shipping and passages. Excelsior seems a legitimate (not Royalist) enterprise. You would do well to see in other coastal towns if the Frenchmen use this ship-line exclusively.*

No signature; no heading. Rufus must have been afraid this note might be "interrupted." Poor Rufus: too involved now and feeling it. Probably would have made this a coded message if they knew a code to use. Scared. Damn! Aren't we all.

"What do you have in the bag, dear?"

"Nothing...just some old clothes."

"Don't forget your boots, dear; they're in the mud room; I had them re-soled yesterday."

"I have my shoes, Mum."

"But you'll need them in the rain and for where you're going." Her face suddenly twisted; her mouth pursing as if she were about to cry. "I love you."

"I love you, too, Mum."

Finally—after twenty years of him slipping away—he had said a goodbye.

CHAPTER 15

The rented horse from the Boston stable was a mare who looked like Bess, but was a bay. She was ready for the ride, pushing her head at Ashley as he saddled her with that little, custom saddle he used…the one so uncomfortable for Matthew that he needed a pillow.

"Have to have a flat arse to ride this one," Ashley was told when it was given to him, "but it's great for the horse and fast for getting in and out because a portion of it is cut away." Ashley had said that was all right…something as that would make the horse faster and less tired and Ashley had a flat arse anyway—he'd been told. He really did like the saddle, once he was used to it: it did take some getting used to.

So…about the Frenchmen: South? How? One has to go down the Merry Mount Road and through Granite City to go south…unless they went west of Boston first!

He walked the mare to get her limber. tho' she cared to run right away; seemed she wanted to go faster and sooner…then, as she insisted she'd run, out on the highway from the city he let her out, urging her on to see what she had and how she would hold. Headed toward a road he hadn't used in years, wondering if he'd see the three Smiths—if they'd see him first and what they'd do as they no longer were penned inside a coach but could use cavalry tactics on him. Yeah…more militia-lessons…surround and attack your enemy: three against one.

In Watertown—at the big crossroads—there was a tavern which had been there near twenty years. He railed the bay and went inside.

"I'm looking for three men who might have come in here this very morning."

"No three men together have come in here all day."

"These men would have been dressed well."

"And you think my customers are not?"

"No...not at all. I just said that...these men would have been in dress-clothing, not work attire."

"Did you come in here to bother me, try to find someone, or are you going to eat and drink?"

Ashley sighed. He wouldn't find them this way. The Frenchmen were long gone from Boston. A hesitant: "Yes, I'll have some food and drink."

He sat at the table, thinking, recognizing how ignorant he was of spy tactics. All he could do would be to ride to Providence and look around...maybe they had gone there; maybe not. Just as easily they could have gone back to Plimouth, their job done here and them returning on a pre-planned passage through Excelsior.

For a short while he had felt himself within the bosom of Destiny as a real spy. Now, not as one.

Ashley was born June fifth, 1618, in London; itself a time of English destiny: the reign of James the Stuart at a time when England was in great debt and Her people were paying the price with their coinage over and over again, lining the pockets of the schemers who increased their wealth through raising prices that they might pay the King a goodly portion and thus endear themselves yet further to get more titles, tithes and the gratitude of their King—a gratitude not so far-reaching that it would include Sir Walter Raleigh, for James had executed this Discoverer of Land for England while he—the King—spoiled his son, Charles.

Ashley and his mother moved to the Plimouth colony in 1630, essentially missing the petty politics in London wherein Charles the First—the spoiled—had replaced his father as King, and Charles fought almost all forms of religion, increased the already-high amount of taxes while he imposed newer ones (especially on Trade), curbed religious preaching (they always said he was more Catholic than Protestant/Anglican), fought with Parliament and dismissed it, and thus brought down upon himself a civil war—which he lost—and for which he paid the ultimate price through being hanged.

The Civil War still raged, its flames licking all of England and scorching every religion in the land, forcing some to hide their beliefs and others to kill or be killed for them. A champion of the Puritans had risen, with the name of Oliver Cromwell, beating down the (former) King's Anglicans and slaughtering the Catholics, stealing land and valuables from Ireland, preparing even now to invade Scotland and remove their latest—and elected—King.

Destiny for England: hard times for her citizens, unless they were businessmen.

The potatoes were cooked hard, the mutton hardly cooked, the wine bitter and leaving a sour taste in his mouth. All right...not his mother's cooking, and surely not Anna's. Who could sell food like this for twenty years? Oh, to new customers all the time, as the old ones must have no taste or get their food cheaper. He ate it all, then paid.

"There was a man in dandy clothing in here early this morning. He got three breakfasts to take with him and inquired as to the whereabouts of the Providence Road."

He would have kissed him for that information but instead gave him a gold sovereign.

Providence. He knew it, but now he really knew it.

Ashley went out of the tavern fast, climbing onto the rented mare and pulling her around to go to see Rufus in North Plimouth. Rufus would have to know this, and he couldn't go all the way to Providence on a three-shilling mare as her time would run out and some lawmen would grab her and him together; lawmen hated horse thieves for some reason. Better to go to the store and get Bess, as he originally planned.

Providence. Of course! That was their scheme all along but he never figured it out until now. They were visiting all the Loyalist towns, places where Royalists resided, gathering information on coastal rivers and defenses which would be taken back to France, England's closest and toughest neighbor, enemy, religious antagonist. France had helped the colonists in the new world before, Bren had told him...they settled more to the north, but had explored the entire area of New England and inland and south years before the English. That was another steal: England's taking France's discoveries, especially in the Lavrador and around Mont Real. Bren had told him everyone stole from everyone else, countries were no exception. Poor Bren: dying alone and so far away from his beloved Ireland. All he ever wanted was his wife and daughter back. God. Too much old history.

Once there, Rufus was glad to see him but worried about him. "Ashley, is this is all getting too much for you? I don't want you harmed by all this...the Frenchmen, the long rides, Standish, the fire...Good God in Heaven, you've been scalped!"

"Ruthie cut my hair." He hadn't told Rufus he'd been shot.

"I knew it was different...she did more than cut it, she burned it!"

"Shot by a pistol at close range without a ball in it; burned by the powder."

"Good God! That ends it! No more of this for you! Good God! Shot?"

"I just need some sleep and have to get Joe's hoof and leg fixed..."

"He got shot, too?"

"No...just lame from the running, I think. I thought I'd take Bess."

"You shouldn't go anywhere! Sleep first, you look worn out. God. How do I explain something like that to your mother?"

"Don't!"

"How did you get shot?"

"All in the reports—there. Rufus, I can do this, but it's taking some effort. I think I know what's happening with the Frenchmen, where they're going...but sometimes they slip past me, like going to Salem."

"What was in Salem? Did you write about that? I didn't get it."

"Never got there. They were there a couple days and left, then I found out; but by then, they were back in Boston, headed toward Merry Mount...and all that's in that report happened. I don't know where they'll go after Providence..."

"That's where they are now? Providence?"

"Or on the road, at the least."

"Perhaps it's time to end the watchdog campaign and just pass all this along to..."

"Almost said his name, didn't you?"

"I think I have something to do...you sleep and I'll read your reports. Michael will take care of your horse."

"Too much, Rufus; I can't pay..."

"I'll put it on your account. When you inherit your stepfather's business I'll get my money then, with interest."

"Don't *ever* say things like that!"

Rufus came back two hours later, with some good food. "While you slept I scanned the reports you brought. You've had quite a week. You actually saw these men, then they killed the boy you sent to watch them? Beasts!"

"I've said a lot of prayers about what I did to that boy."

"You asked him to look at the men; *they* killed him! Not you!"

"Hard to understand the fault there...I sent him..."

"And *they* killed him! Suppose I sent you to a prayer-meeting and a highwayman killed you along the way. Would Elder Otis say I had killed you?"

"He'd say you contributed to my death; he'd say that."

Rufus sighed. "All right...you contributed to his death and you have prayed for him."

"I haven't told his sister or his parents."

"Oh; that's the guilt. Well, that's real. You should tell the parents the whole story, otherwise they'll ever think their child was a wanderer or just plain stupid. To tell them will dissolve a lot of grief for each of you. Promise me you'll do that."

"No promises right now; I have other things to tell you."

In the next hour, Ashley told Rufus the Merry Mount story and watched him react to that.

"And you still want to follow these men? Ashley, this is only a job; you're changing it into revenge. I'll get someone else to go to Providence."

"No one else can do this. I'm already a full day behind them, and I know what they look like. No one else can do this. My concern is not Providence, but how this all fits together. Why did French spies come to Plimouth when they knew we would see and follow them? I mean…five men? Five?"

"Only three, now. They'll be after you; they've seen you, too."

"Rufus…I think and think…wonder at the entire picture of this…thing. People just don't go to a place unless they have support or protection. I wonder about that. So much is happening…I have to tell you about a woman in Boston…"

"You *have* to?"

"All right: I want to. I spent a night with her; I'm very confused about what happened."

"Nothing happened. What could happen in a night? So you trifled with a woman…"

"Not a trifling, but a total abandonment of the love I swore to Anna and pledged in my heart when she died."

He confessed to Rufus as the Catholics seemed to use their priests, but Rufus was no priest and responded: "Life is for those alive. We all have feelings and needs."

"I never see nor hear about the feelings and needs of Rufus Case, the soothsayer. How do *you* deal with those?"

"I take business trips and go without sleep so I'll be too tired to think or act about that." Rufus the prince of tact. At least he didn't say he read from the Bible to pray-away his wants and needs, as others had told him.

"Ashley, forget about that woman. You need no woman to hold you on a leash and threaten you with a prayer-book."

"Definitely don't need that."

"That's why the sailors like the Indian girls so much…"

"Please don't talk about girls. I have to concentrate on all this."

"You're the one who mentioned the Boston woman..."

"This all seems like a big circle...But I don't know how big and I don't know where to start. Standish hires me and fires me...Standish broke up the colony at Merry Mount as it was too un-Puritanical for him..."

"Yes, that maypole thing, back in twenty-eight, with the indentured servants and the Indians and all that alcoholic drink; yes, I remember that. Standish put the founder of Merry Mount—what was it originally? Mare's Mount? Something like that...Sea Mount? Anyway, he put Thomas Morton out on one of those islands off Boston for a few weeks until he could be shipped back to England."

"But he returned!"

"So I heard, in a couple years, but not to Merry Mount...up north, somewhere."

"North of Boston? Salem?"

"I think...way north, not Norumbega, North Massachusetts."

"The Frenchmen went to Salem, then to Merry Mount."

"I read that, but this whole coast is just a big community...everybody going everywhere—not like England; not like, say, France going to the Indies or Spain going to the Grand Banks. Here...there aren't many places to go but visit people."

"Standish wanted my horse; I think he wanted me afoot."

"Your horse? Joe?"

"Yes, I have a bill of sale from New Hampshire for him, but I think Miles wanted me on foot and not riding after those five."

"Miles? I don't think so. You could always get another horse; I have three."

"So does my stepfather, but I heard Miles went to London for a year, recently. He could have met anyone over there."

"He was there in twenty-five and twenty-six; almost five years ago. He said he went there to get investors for the settlement and they did arrive here in twenty-seven, so he told the truth."

"Money, England, my horse...I'm no longer in the militia with any power...something, there's something here, deeper than the Duxbury Well but I can't put it together. Something is there but I can't get it to interlock and the colors aren't right...like a puzzle but too many pieces, like several puzzles together on a table, spread all over. Plimouth, Boston, Salem, Merry Mount, Providence, London...Standish calling me 'dirty'; I think Standish is the dirty one! I think he's pulling strings for these puppets to jump and jiggle between London and here."

"Miles was in the Provinces of Holland—the Netherlands, also. He met Braddock and Brewster and a few more there—before they established Plimouth."

"I didn't know that."

"That's how he got involved with the Plimouth colony: he was only a soldier and suddenly he was named militia captain for the colony. Captain Standish. A big jump from soldier Standish to Captain Standish; no wonder he keeps and loves the title."

"Another piece of the puzzle. Too many, Rufus; I just can't put them together."

"Well, anything to add before you sleep and go to Providence in the morning?"

"No…that's all."

"In Providence they'll see that radical group, just the same as they did in Marry Mount."

"What radical group?"

"Forget I said that; nothing you should know."

"Rufus, is there a plot happening?"

"Plot? Life's a plot. Yes, of course there's a plot but it's now beyond your head and mine; my job ends when I write to…"

"To?"

"Rufus lifted his teacup. "This tea is a splendid drink. I tried it with mint and some with cocoa, but alone it tastes best. There is coffee, also—a new shipment from the Far East came in last evening. That takes a flavoring."

"Well, it's not like annada tea, that's for sure, for sure."

"What?"

Just something Bren would have said. We drank tea at a woman's home for a while, when my eyes were blinded and the tea there was awful! I think a lot about Bren, lately; he would have done something about those Frenchmen who set Mister Pennyweight's shed afire."

"I never heard you were blinded."

"Something that was fixed."

"Like that snow-blindness thing?"

"Sure."

"Ashley…These men you chase are confident. They have unshakable faith in their cause and themselves. They will go to any end—the end as they see it. Never underestimate these people, for you will never know the force which drives them and never feel the power which pleases them. They will be unstoppable until they are stopped. They will not, they can not, admit defeat, failure: it's not in them. They'll kill themselves and you first. This is why you only "follow" them and chart their activities and the places they go: those places are very important as after they leave, the authorities will be able to act at those spots. You do nothing but follow them, all right? Never confront them; stay away from them; never let them know you watch them. Be especially careful...please."

Rufus was acting like he was sending his only son off to war. "If something goes wrong, terribly wrong, however will I know, you being so far away from here? Like you getting shot, as you were."

"In not knowing, not hearing from me, you will know. If I cannot post a letter daily to you, then that is not a disaster; but I shall try daily to send you some report, and if you hear nothing for a week or more...I think a week would probably be enough."

"And after that week?"

"Pray for me."

CHAPTER 16

"Walter? Are you home?" Johnathan called in the door.

"Here! Come in! I'm sitting in my salon," the notary answered.

"Do you always leave your door unlocked? Wouldn't the savages pounce upon you for doing that?" Johnathan and Geoffry went in, leaving Luke as a guard at the door.

"Good Afternoon, your Lordship; you're welcome in my modest home. After I received your letter I began to assemble the documents you requested."

"What a good soul. Geoffry? Haven't I always said Walter was a good soul?"

"You certainly 'ave, Johnathan."

"You are so in the country, Walter...without the good directions you sent, we should not have found you. Isn't that right, Geoffry?"

"Indeed it is." Being on his best behavior.

"Walter, you always were in the midst of people, dozens of them surrounded you. How is it you are here, no servants, no throngs? Simply alone in this great house?"

"Changed my ways, Johnathan."

"Oh...this life must be bitter for you, dear old friend. How are you caught up on the news from England?"

"I don't get much news from anywhere, here."

"Oh, that's a shame! Geoffry, Walter and I are dearest friends; he and my father worked together in London. Now he gets a chance to assist me. Walter, brother Charles has been elected King in Scotland, the old Stuart line, you know; and in England they have proclaimed him King in absentia. He *is* the true King, in every aspect. When he returns to the throne of England—and he shall—you can return there also without thought of prosecution for your role in forging the documents which led to the dissolution of Parliament and Buckingham's assassination."

Walter made no reply.

Johnathan laughed. "How was it you closed the Puritan House of Commons and then came to a Puritan village?"

"Easier to come here than stay in London with the mood there...and Cromwell's men."

"Why not to France, as mother did, where you would be welcomed? Or my home in Spain?"

"I prefer English as a native language."

"But the natives here do not speak English; they speak Indian. Tsk, tsk...here we are, standing. Who does that?"

"My sincere apologies, your Lordship. Please sit, gentlemen...all I require are signatures on these papers and I'll seal them as certified. These will get you any passage on any ship, so long as they don't take them to a bank, beforehand, as letters of credit are written in."

"What are the chances of travel-agents doing that?"

"They won't; they need the business too much to play snoop, and they're all insured. You mentioned there were five of you?"

"There were. Now we are three."

"Oh. Well, less work for me, then."

What was produced was eyed and accepted by Johnathan: three sets of documents which changed the names of Johnathan's band to others, plus letters of credit (good, except of course if they were presented to the bank upon which they were drawn, but done well enough for the acknowledgement of a ship's captain or any official who required proof of identity or citizenship or credit from a bank without first having to send them off TO that bank.) Also, they had travel-permits for the use aboard ships of English registration and her allies. With these, the newly named three could travel around the world without ready coin or explanation.

"Is this sufficient, Johnathan? All you requested?"

"You ever amaze one; your work is that of an artist. The seals are perfect; my own brother could not distinguish the difference. Yes...we now have everything we shall require, and then some. Excellent job—but, your work always has been excellent. That's why my father favored and loved you so much. Geoffry, fetch Lukey and have him come in here and sign so Walter can seal over his signature."

Luke came in, looking around in pleasure, signed, and returned outside to further watch and guard.

"Now, then…here comes the most important part." Johnathan gestured and Geoffry came over and laid an open pack of papers upon the strewn table in front of Walter.

"These are the pledges we require sealed. They list the amounts of money and credit and properties they 'would' give, were they to literally give them to His Majesty. Unsealed, they are pledges of love; sealed, they are worth every pence they mention. I want you to seal them all, that Charles may use these to re-build his torn army. I told them all that since the pledges were not notarized, they were no good—just pledges of love for their King, saying they had all this fortune and if he were here they would assist him because they were moneyed folk. With these notarized, Charles can give them to a moneylender and get the amount he requires to hire the Swiss army to invade England from the south while Charles and the Scots sweep down from the north. Isn't this a tender trap for these loyal subjects of Charles, over here? These Royalists who fled England and wouldn't stay with their King? Oh, not you, old friend…you played a closer role and we love you. But these colonists on the North Shore were the worst; now they shall get to lose everything because they have signed it away. Now, Providence shall be a different story: there we have those who use their own notary to give new-found money to Charles; they in that place came late and adore my brother whilst hating the Puritans."

"I shall have a chore, doing these."

"But you are the best, and we all are for Charles, so I know you will succeed in notarizing these, however long it takes."

"Of course, your Lordship…we all love Charles."

"Indeed, Walter…my, but it's good to see you once again; letters across the sea do nothing when it comes to face-to-face. I was hardly a man when you left London. I have missed you, old friend; only our letters have maintained us so closely."

"Thank you, Baronet; your friendship has been the only one which has mattered to me, since your father…"

"Yes…father. A cruel demise for one so loved and honored. He adored his people and they, him. We have a plan for Cromwell, and he shall have the same—plus more—as he gave my father."

"I should not notarize if the participants do not appear before me."

"Who appeared before you when my father's jewels were stolen?"

Foster just stared.

"Who appeared before you when my father's personal chest was rifled and lightened to the tune of a half-million pounds?"

No answer; just that shocked stare…surprise and fear.

"Who appeared in front of you when my father required funds to pay his Army and later to flee to France, then was completely unable as his funds were gone and them his Army and then his life? Captured, and Cromwell beheaded him publicly."

"Johnathan…" A weak response, almost a plea.

"Walter…old friend…it gladdens my heart that you will notarize these signatures. Doing this will erase your debt to Charles the First, and gain you popularity with Charles the Second."

"I…"

"No need to thank me, dear friend. Your signatures shall thank me enough, and then I shall be on my way, never to bother or require your services again."

"You swear?"

"I swear by Almighty God that I may burn in Hell if after this effort on your part and my departure from here I ever bother, write to you or send anyone to you for any reason at all. I so swear, by God!"

"I'm an old man…"

"And you shall be older, dear Walter. Begin to sign, that we all may not be too old when this is completed." Johnathan smiled that tight-lipped smile he used…like when you owed a man with a pistol a pound and you had just given him a pence. That kind of smile: not the kind which inspires nor bolsters confidence.

"How much older shall I be after I sign all these?"

"Walter…whatever age that is, I shall have aged the same. Do this, dear sir…that we all do not collapse of infirmities before you are finished. I have appointments in Providence which cannot keep and my men seek Providence women with large bosoms and little clothing. And I should think you would want the same. Do get on with this, so you may return to your women, wherever it is in this large house you have hidden them, for I know you of old and you always had a woman hidden away someplace, and Geoffry may sample Providence rump and I may enjoy my Lukey in peace."

Foster relaxed, blinked. Almost smiled.

"Yes…the inconvenience or assistance of a notarized statement, letter of credit…can win a friend or antagonize an enemy."

"Your signature, Walter, is more known around the civilized world than any other. You have a recognizable style of penmanship and a reputation for honesty which is accepted by bankers everywhere. Your seal is more known than any King's, and much faster accepted."

"It will take sometime to do all these..."

"We have no extra time left; you must do these now...please, Walter?"

"I...I shall try to hurry."

It took the remainder of the morning and a bit past noon for the notary to complete his work. Finished, he produced a pile of documents to be seen as notarized cheques de voyage, and which could readily be used as collateral by the Swiss. By God, Charles would have his Army after all!

"How thorough and prompt you are, dear Walter...just as always. I'm traveling still on the documents you made me years ago. I've been back to many of the old places...have you been to Spain?

"No."

"Marvelous place, Spain. Such a fine climate; nothing like that of London, or this...place. So. We're done? Everything notarized?"

"Yes, your Lordship, everything all signed and embarrassingly-legal-looking."

"I'm afraid we've caused you to get ink all upon your fingers, Walter...we're sorry for that."

"That's all right, your Lordship; I always get inks all over me when I do these things...nature of the work and all that."

"Geoffry, the travel-case for these papers, please? Have to protect our reason to return to the Misty Isles—that murky place."

"You don't care for this land, Baronet? I quite enjoy it here."

"Now that our business is done I can tell you I do not care at all for this savage land, nor its people."

"You didn't like Plimouth?"

"Walter...I tell you as a friend I cannot understand why you live here. It's so far from London and any culture or history...and the incomplete roads with their dirt...and the poorly prepared food. Oh! Just quite un-civilized! But I do find touches of civilization here in your home, Walter; you have a lovely home...the French doors are quite showpieces, the flower gardens, that marvelous staircase which winds on to the upper floor...all so unique in such a colonial residence. And the roominess of this all...fit for a King, wouldn't you say, Geoffry?"

"Indeed, Johnathan."

"Mother had gardens and olive trees in Spain...but there never was a wending staircase such as that, nor so many French doors. You would be right at home in France, Walter; you've never been there before?"

"No...I know you're used to better, being..."

"Ah, old friend...you know all about me: my likes and dislikes, my food preferences and my pleasures; but you always did know all about me; you did so much for me and my family...So many delightful memories I hold...But one thing escapes me, Walter..." Johnathan stepped close to the notary.

"Yes?"

"A question."

"What question is that, your Lordship?"

"Where are my father's jewels?"

"I don't know. They were pawned to raise that Army."

"Not the crown jewels, Walter; they went to Holland with the Queen."

"Why should I know more?"

"I know you do. You wouldn't have pawned them or sold them; I have inquired for two years about them and they are nowhere to be found...so you must still have them."

"Did you send someone here to locate me last year?"

"This is not like you, Walter...you ever gave of yourself for my family. We loved you. Walter, you never got rid of anything; you kept everything...I see old books here I saw in your study in London; that ceramic rose over there, and the tall jar: they were in your office. No...you don't part with anything but money, dear friend...which makes me wonder why you would part with King Charles' jewelry box. You couldn't; it's not in you to do that. You have it still and now I would take it." Johnathan's voice had turned threatening.

"I wrote a letter for...Was it you who sent the man here?"

"No...and now we need to get down to the truth. We've had our moment of meeting, and we've had our fun and games, you and I; now all that is over." He gave Walter a hard stare.

"Walter, I want my father's jewelry box, and it better have his jewels in it. Charles ever requires collateral, and I require funds to take to him."

No answer...then..."Please, Johnathan..."

"Yes...'Johnathan.' No longer a baronet or a lord, Walter, as you helped depose my father and stole his traveling money and took from me my birthright. You didn't realize I knew it was you who did that. He was trapped in Scotland...because of you, Walter, and your greed. To do what with it? Have this monstrosity of a house built in some remote colonial township where the savages will burn it? The whole of the English Army payroll is here in this house; you should be very ashamed of your filthy deeds. You took his funds, his jewels, his cache of money even the Queen knew nothing about...his very life, Walter...you took his very life. Cromwell the butcher caught him and killed him all because he didn't have the funds to get to France, where he would have been free and safe and still the King of England."

"I..."

"Thus far I have been a gentleman with you. I ask you as a gentleman, 'Where are my father's items?'"

"I spent the money...this house, as you said...some of the diamonds..."

"Was that an answer or a statement?" Johnathan shook his head. "I am rather disappointed with you, Walter. What does an old man have to look forward to but his hobby? Writing is your hobby, and reading. Walter, I'm about to interrupt your hobby. What would you do if your fingers were cut off. Walter?"

"Please, your Lordship..."

"I have found that an application of pain plus the realization of loss can be a rather effective tool."

"Too much pain and I'll die; I'm an old man."

"Yes, and a fat one, from eating my inheritance and Charles'! Oh, my dear Walter, whyever would I put upon you too much pain? Only enough to allow you to realize I am quite serious in my request. Geoffry? Have you observed the way our friend Walter signs his name, with his right hand?"

"Yes, I 'ave, Johnathan."

"And have you noted which finger he does not use in that effort?"

"'Is little one, Johnathan."

"Then...please give a demonstration to Walter of our intent to be serious."

It was more of a grin than a smile, more of a relishing than a piece of work, more of an eagerness than it should have been. Geoffry pinned Walter's right hand to the desk with a heavy grip, then substituted his knee upon it as he drew his thin-bladed knife. The notary tried to move his hand, tried to push Geoffry away, tried to scream...Ended up sitting there, crying. The fifth finger separated at the knuckle, blood spurting everywhere until Johnathan threw Foster's jacket over it.

Then Foster seemed to come back to life, enough so that he wrapped his finger with the jacket, but the crying didn't stop.

"Only a demonstration of our seriousness."

"P...please..."

Geoffry grabbed Walter's left hand and in almost one movement his knife had severed Walter's little finger on that hand as well!

The scream was loud and in anguish...Geoffry let go the hand and Walter quickly wrapped his lunch napkin around it. He sat there, eyes wide, staring at the pieces of himself which he had always seen attached to his hands.

"You swore you'd leave after the signatures."

"I swore, Walter, that after my departure from here you would never hear from me or mine again. That was my swear. Please be good enough now to live long enough that I may keep my oath. No more fingers, Walter...please. No more fingers."

Foster cried real tears...but managed to say, "The safe."

"Where?"

"The key on the chain around my neck opens the door behind you. Inside is a safe; in the safe is the jewel-box and all the money I have left."

"And the key to the safe?"

"Fitted into a compartment under the bottom of that Chinese jar."

"You old fox." Johnathan was happy with this information. "Please, Geoffry?"

Geoffry got the keys and started after the jewels.

"Why, Walter, did you ever desert my father? We all loved you."

"It was all happening...I saw it all coming...he dissolved Parliament, had Buckingham killed, made peace with Spain and France to stop bleeding his money reserves away, then beheaded Strattford..." Walter still had fresh tears in his eyes. "When he sent the Queen to Holland to pawn the crown jewels I was in charge of gathering all that for her...and...just..."

"Took a small advantage. Yes. Took not what the Queen knew about, but what my father had hidden from her with you. Eight years, Walter...you've been over here eight years: more than a third of my life. Now my father lies dead and my half-brother will succeed him, once the money for his army in Scotland reaches him. All his uncles and cousins in Europe will join against Cromwell then...England will be re-taken by us Stuarts and that farmer who would be a King shall be drawn and quartered after he is tortured; I promise that!"

Johnathan went to the door of the house and called in Luke.

"Ah. Here you are; everything outside is well?"

"No one anywhere, Johnathan."

"All right: get around to all the rooms in this manor and see if anyone else is here. You, too, Geoffry. If you find anyone; leave them where you find them, understood?"

"No."

"Kill them where you find them, of course; no witnesses. Move quickly, now, lads; we've much to accomplish."

"What about water for the horses?"

"Not now; later. We'll find some pond or something in this pestilent place...but go now and we should be on our way before others arrive to have papers sealed."

"You're leaving soon?" Walter called from his salon. "There's no one else in the house."

"Of course, Walter; whyever would we want to stay here? It's only that I wish no witnesses that I send my men throughout your domicile...otherwise, I would never be so brash as to go rampantly about a man's home."

Johnathan went back to where Walter sat holding his bloody and wrapped hands.

"This is all over, now, Johnathan? You have the signatures and the jewels and now will leave?"

"Really, Walter, your sojourn here has caused you to lose your manners when it comes to making your guests comfortable. But of course, old friend, whyever would we stay longer than necessary? I wait now only for my men."

In a few minutes more, Luke and Geoffry returned. "We've been into all the rooms. No one."

"There could be secret doors..."

"Most probably there are; my father had those. Are there, Walter? Secret doors? Are there people hidden, ready to spring upon us as we leave? Women hidden away, awaiting your call?"

"No...there's a door to the rear, in a bedroom. The house is built into a hill, so if you go out the second-story door, you're on a level with the ground. No other doors."

"Luke, be so good as to take the jewel-box and all that coin out to the horses and afix it somehow. Look around one more time out there, then come tell us how it stands."

Luke was back in a few minutes. "No one outside or around, from what I can see. No one on the road. Probably a good time to leave."

"Walter, it's been so good to have seen and spoken with you again." He turned to Geoffry, who was beside Walter. "Now."

The knife moved so fast it was hard to see. While blood still pulsed from Walter's neck, Johnathan and Geoffry left.

They rode out, Johnathan wildly happy about getting back his father's jewels and all the coin he had captured; Charles would embrace him in front of the court for all this. The family still loved him; only that tiny argument with Charles about...but why think on that now? With these funds, Charles HAD to recognize him, let him back publicly into the family. This cache was exactly what Charles required to complete his plan to return to England and become Her King. And then Johnathan's titles and fortune would return; he'd live well after that. What a thrilling few hours he had just spent! First, they intended to go directly to Providence to acquire more pledges, then go to Foster's home, but those plans changed—and seemingly for the better. Along the Providence Road—at a signpost which pointed to Plimouth—Johnathan had changed his mind, and, using the directions Walter had sent him the previous year, went instead to see the notary. Whatever pledges were gotten in Providence he'd have notarized locally, soon as a way to escape was attained and assured. His contact there would know a nefarious Notary he could use and remove. There would be nowhere the amount of pledges in Providence that Merry Mount or Salem had given anyway. It had worked out so well... Walter never realized he was a marked man when he tried to get back into the good graces of the family and he apparently didn't think he would ever be visited by anyone who knew about the jewels; even Johnathan's family didn't know: he was the only one his father had told...then, his father could tell no one else. What a secret! All his, and his alone.

Too, so far as leaving this remote and rural land, had they attempted to go from Plimouth, there might have been a complication. Leaving from the Narragansett would be safer. He almost felt thrilled as they rode along doing the King's movement: canter and walk. Charles would kiss him on the lips when their father's gold and jewels were returned: things were so good...actually, with all their adventures, this had turned out to be a fun place.

Providence might even be better—certainly the food should be better—then they would leave for London and Scotland...and a better life. He did wish he could have brought some of those hundreds of books Walter had stored in his shelves along with him...books were more than lessons: they were good friends and faithful companions to erase boredom for all one's life.

Walter's cherry-colored bookcases were so interesting, with all those bound pieces of precious knowledge...and Walter's table? What a mess! Whoever would know the color or design of that: it was so laden with paper that one couldn't see the color, design or function of it. In Spain, furniture was placed to show off the room, not cause a mess. And with that fleeting thought immediately missed Spain and had begun to return to his previous funk when Luke jostled him, saying, "Water ahead, Johnathan; we need to water these horses; they'll drop if we don't."

"Oh, yes... Water. Surely. You choose the place and we shall stop; look carefully about, for we need no one alive to tell that we have been here. A tale to Providence might ruin us all."

"Over at the side of that bridge there's a slope down to the river. We can take the horses down there and not be seen from the road. It'll only take a short while, then we'll be on our way and can push them easier, for longer."

They halted and dismounted, watering the horses and themselves and resting a bit in those few minutes. The horses were delighted to drink.

"Luke, did you see the mountains of paper Walter had on his desk and tables? How untidy was that?"

"Johnathan, I have a question."

"I should have taken that Bible, on the mantle. Did you see that? Golden leather on a bound Bible; mother would have loved to have that…but…she's Catholic now, anyway."

"Why did Geoffry have to kill him? He had given us the papers and jewels. Wasn't that another finger to point at us? His death? You always say you want to have quietness and calm, then the man is murdered."

"My poor Lukey…all upset. Walter had to die to settle an old debt you knew nothing of. Also, he knew us too well and I couldn't trust him. Who will miss him; he seemed to be living alone, despite his past practice of having women scattered about, and it may be a while by the time he is discovered." He put an arm around Luke's shoulders. "Worry not for the dead, but for the living, for us. Remember, we have a journey and a purpose, each to be completed. When we return to my father's home in London, we'll spend a little of this gold to enrich our lives. Think how it shall be there…in that huge bed of the King, with the fireplace alit…won't all that be pleasant?"

CHAPTER 17

Bess was another part of the spy-disguise.

She had been left with Rufus as there was no reason to take her to Boston, Pennyweight having three horses of his own, the private stable already was crowded, and she would have been an immediate expense—money he couldn't spare at this time, notwithstanding the advance pay he'd received from Rufus; and Joe would cost plenty. Worth it, but plenty.

Bess had come to Ashley as a three-year-old. A friend of Anna had raised the mare outside Plimouth, but the family was moving to Roxbury, so they couldn't take her and had given her to Anna as a marriage present. Anna loved her immediately and rode her—side-saddle with one of those footholds—as often as possible. Even fed Bess herself (for which Ashley was delighted).

The Romans had brought horses—good, sturdy steeds all—to England, where the abundance of grass and water allowed them all to increase rapidly in numbers over the centuries. And with horses of invading armies lost, strayed or stolen, England developed her own style of the horse. Then, the ones required in New England were transported there by ship and used to build a solid work-force and transportation for the colonists and their arriving numbers.

Bess was called a "light horse," a term designated for a horse who was used to give short rides or pull a carriage around the townships. She hadn't actually had any long rides, but as Rufus needed his carriage horses (in a pair) and Joe's hoof was still in question, she was Ashley's most prudent way to get to Providence. Bess was a mixed-breed with small shoulders, gave sort of a choppy ride, but she seemed strong and able to make the trip. Ashley wondered if she knew what was going on around her...being so long in a field, having different owners and riders and saddles...but she didn't seem to mind. Some horses would buck for no understood reason; Bess didn't buck, ever: she was reliable and really seemed to be happy; she surely wasn't disappointing as a companion or transportation. Being now a major portion of his "disguise," she was invaluable to Ashley, as he had ridden Joe all around Boston and the Frenchmen had not only seen him but used him (damn!). Different clothes and a different horse might throw off the casual glance of the Frenchmen, were they to see him now—a real threat—with them on horseback and upon the same long and lonely road.

He had heard that in England—on an improved trail—a dispatch-rider could go fifty-seven leagues in three days on a horse and the same distance in two days (all out) if he took a relay with him, changing-off regularly. Wore them out, but if they'd done it for the King, well...this wasn't England and there was no King providing horses; he wasn't about to wear out Bess. She didn't have the restful manner of Joe's canter and he imagined about those old riders of the King, in England: if they had Joe, they'd have made better time, but with Bess? They'd have had a churned stomach and a flat arse with her canter. She was better at a choppy walk.

Providence. It was a familiar story to all colonists...Roger Williams aggravating the Pilgrime Elders, pushing for more and more reforms, changes, allowances in the religious teachings and applications, finally becoming so anti-Puritanical that he had to be physically sent from the Massa-adchu-ess-et colony. The story was that he had gone with half a dozen friends, south, ending up in a Narragansett-Indian village and somehow wrangled or otherwise secured some land which he called, "God's Providence." That was in 1636.

Fourteen years later it was a city: Providence. Built on and around three hills—in the fashion of the Eternal City: Rome—and along the great Narragansett River such that it might become someday a world-known seaport in the tradition of London, Providence was less than twenty leagues from Boston. Not a large city, still, but there were several hundred people officially counted in its census and a few hundred more not counted but working there or passing through. More, actually, than Duxbury or Granite City, and more population arriving daily, due to the big river's access to the ocean and the interior—all at once (exactly as the Thames opened up England from the sea, so did the Narragansett invite settlers and pioneers and frontier-folk into the land).

Providence was founded upon "religious openness" and quickly the word spread that there was land and freedom of worship from an official religion here. That was the dream of Roger Williams: free and open worship for those who came in God's name to this new providence. Catholics and Jews were welcome...well, "allowed." The Puritan colony of Plimouth refused both—as they should, for they were a "Puritan" colony, not a colony which took whomever showed up. (Let them go to Boston!)

Ashley knew he couldn't push Bess the way he did Joe, especially as he didn't know how the roads were, whether there was danger along the roads from highwaymen or cougars, or when he'd be able to relax without fear on this trip. Encountering any danger, Bess might have to run flat-out, and he couldn't spend her beforehand so he let her do the King's movement: canter and walk as she desired, and she seemed to be up to that. He felt they shouldn't arrive there during the night, so he planned his trip to put him into Providence about mid-morning of the third day and would stop overnight at places which seemed safe. The ride wasn't that hard or long; he was glad to get away from a dismal area of sand and brush and wild trees which held few farmers. Along the ride he had encountered neither highwayman nor cougar, only frontiersmen who were friendly and some stray Woods-People from a tribe he hadn't heard about but who seemed to enjoy speaking with him regardless that his words to them seemed to be pronounced with a strange accent.

Though it was further south, there were not the butterflies of the Massa-adchu-ess-et here, the big, black-winged beauties of the woods and the orange-speckled ones of the fields. He saw different orange ones and the large yellow—and of course there were the little lightly-colored ones of the meadows, flitting about the edges of the road, but the smaller woods-butterflies were not present. Anna ever loved them and called them "Nymphs of the Woods," and the large, yellow ones were "Tailed flies." Anna loved everything.

The morning sky this day was menacing: a puffy purple all the way to the horizon. Plenty of rain there and soon to be here. This would be one of those two or three-day rains, heavy and pelting, the kind to cause flooding in Duxbury. He'd have to soon seek safe shelter.

Now, where would three men go...to the nearest tavern or the nearest stable...or perhaps the nearest blacksmith. There were several blacksmith sheds along this particular road, each seemingly busy more so with oxen than horses. Ashley passed by the individual smiths—smiling to himself at the name the Frenchmen had taken—and went along until he saw—at the entrance to the city—a large sign with an arrow which proclaimed:

Francis Lane, Blacksmith Oxen & Horses Shod & Remedied Rooms,
Food & Drink for Travelers.

It wasn't too far ahead that Ashley could see Francis Lane's establishment. Built originally as a fort with great, hewn trees upright for foundation-corners and smaller ones chopped and fitted into them for walls—and them those daubed and filled for insulation—Lane's Highway House was certainly large enough to comfort visitors and their steeds and carriages, with its wooden confines. The lowest roof was of slate; freshly swept plank comprised the second, and Ashley could see there were raised sleeping-areas above that. Probably had a great view of the river, well, the original fort would have required that, to watch the "locals"; and necessarily a good view to the forest-approaches. Several places acting as windows had been cut into the logs, and as no "forest friends" (the Narragansett) remained locally, no attempt to shutter those windows had been made. (There would be no raids by local Indians; they sold the land and kept their word to remain free and friendly in another place.)

Inside the old fort, woven cloths almost as tapestries hung on the walls, giving the structure nearly a "comfortable" look which seemed more friendly to Ashley than Miles Standish's office had been. This would be the place where the Frenchmen would likely stop!

He directed Bess to an open area in a large building, where three forges were in use at the same time. A boy rushed up to him.

"Welcome to Lane's Stables and More."

"Have my horse's shoes looked at; I need her in perfect condition."

"That we shall do, sir."

"Where would be Francis Lane?"

"Taking his meal by the tree, there," he said, pointing.

Ashley thanked the boy, slipped off his saddlebag and turned the reins over to the lad, also asking him to water Bess and feed her, then strolled over to where the owner of this extended establishment sat eating.

Lane was a middle-aged man with a dark complexion, shaven face which still looked as though a beard was growing, and bulging arm-muscles. He wore no shirt, but had a smith's apron on—a clean one. His eyebrows were dark and full, giving him a sinister, defining stare and he presented a look which went right through a person—the kind which screams that he already knew the answer before you asked the question and he was wondering well in advance why you would even ask. Oh, yeah: this man WAS the owner, founder, manager of all these buildings and enterprises AND a skilled smith: he looked and acted the part.

"Good day to you, traveler."

"A pleasant day to you as well, Squire Lane."

"Are you here on business?"

"No...seeking some men who might have stopped here recently. Three men on horses, dressed fairly well."

Lane showed a smile as sharp as the edge of a sword. "Your friends?"

"Acquaintances...recent acquaintances I heard were coming through here."

"Here to this shop or here to the Narragansett settlement?"

"Just to this area..."

"Is this inquiry an official request or just a friendly one?"

"On, friendly! Nothing official about it; just traveling through and looking for some men I met awhile back."

"If you're not a tax collector or a sheriff's man, I don't want to tell you anything about anyone who might or might not have stopped here. Not trying to offend you, good sir: just that so many people come by here...you understand?"

"Yes, I think I do; you protect your customers. I understand."

Francis put aside the remains of his lunch and stood: a heavy body and well-muscled. Ashley was far taller but Lane seemed far stronger. "Over there by those trees...that open space?" He pointed with a bare arm.

"Yes?"

"Merchants here want to put a hospital and food-storage area for the poor and immigrants there, for those who are arriving by ship. It's an expensive project to get funded. Would you suppose you'd like to donate to that? Say...well, I'd let you consider the amount, but most are giving a pound or more. It's quite a worthy cause."

Ashley reached into his purse..."Would two gold sovereigns assist in the building?"

"Indeed they would!" Lane responded immediately, taking them almost as fast as Ashley had gotten them in his hand, then tucking them into a buttoned pocket. "After you take your meal...you will take your meal here, won't you, good sir?"

"I...I hadn't realized it was that time of the day. Most certainly I'll eat here, Squire Lane."

"Then, after you meal you might want to go to the ship's agent on the waterfront...Excelsior Ship Lines. Perhaps the three went there to inquire about passage to London...after they located some friends here in town, on Lawn Street, by the bank."

"You've very informed about people's movements here."

"Sometimes yes; sometimes no. It's such a small community...but for money, yes, I do know where some people go."

"Well, thank you, Squire Lane, for allowing me to contribute to such a worthwhile town project and such a humanitarian cause through God's great love. I'll take my meal and be along on my way."

"Did I miss your name, sir?"

"Al...Al Gonkin."

"Ah...well, traveler Gonkin, go with God, in His merciful province. Providence welcomes you each time you visit here."

Bess was in good hands, so Ashley ate an abbreviated meal which he (this time) enjoyed—the cooking was far better than at the tavern in Watertown—then walked down the dirt road (another "disguise" as he used no horse) less than half a league to se the sign: "Excelsior Ship Lines: We Travel the world: India, World Ports & Europe."

The place was apparently closed, perhaps at the end of their work-day, and no others were around to answer inquiries about the bank on Lawn Street, so he returned to Lane's. A wasted day if he could do no more.

Bess was fine and had been fed, watered and rested, so he paid for her care and rode down the street where he had just walked, hoping to be able to easier explore Providence.

There wasn't much he could do...get an overview of the city, perhaps.

This time, there was an open door at the office of Excelsior, and Ashley rode over toward it to look inside. An easy place to find, Excelsior was the only small building at the beginning of the pier, and in addition to their sign on the road, had a smaller one at the beginning of the wharf. He left Bess tied at the hitch-rail (yes, she'd run at the first chance) and entered Excelsior through the open door.

An older man with a heavy moustache and pressed clothing (in contrast to the rumpled clothing Ashley wore) sat at a desk, papers neatly stacked in various-heightened piles in front of him. Ashley recalled the paper-mess on the notary's desk and imagined it should have looked more like this one. The ship's agent greeted his visitor and offered him a seat and a small fan, and Ashley sat on a low-seated, wooden chair similar to all those scattered around New England.

"Still look like rain out there?"

"Yes. I thought you were closed; I came by earlier."

"Very sorry to hear that, sir; an emergency, now over. How may I assist you?"

"Three friends of mine came through here in the past day or so; I'm wondering if they purchased passage on a ship from you."

"Lots of people come here, yourself included, sir; more arriving than going."

"These three would be going."

"Three? In the past day or so?"

"Yes, three. You don't have a favorite charity I could donate to, do you?" he asked, thinking he had learned a secret of Providence and was willing to play their game.

"No..." The man seemed puzzled at that. He pushed through papers much as had Standish. "Never was like this under King Charles...everything was on paper, then, and every ship was a crown ship and people needed permission to travel and paid taxes...here it is...three men from Boston, passage on *City of Leeds*, indirect to London."

"The name of the ship is *City of Leeds*?"

"Yes it is; I just said that. You can see her berthed over there...the heavy-masted one with the gold paint along her rail. She's an old French warship—carried a hundred guns, but there's only seventy-two aboard her now, to make room for passengers."

"Are we still at war? That's a lot of cannon."

"Not at war. There's still pirates and independent countries who allow freebooters their home ports. *City of Leeds* has a captain who refuses to lose his cargo—never has, to pirates; thus, the seventy-two guns and a full crew; that's the only way he'll sail. A passenger is completely safe aboard that ship. You want to book passage?"

Yeah, Ashley thought; *I'd be really safe with all those Frenchmen aboard.*

"You said 'in-direct'?"

"Oh, that means the ship is eventually going to London, but has some other places to go first, but will not come back here once she sails. Direct to London would be from here to there; no other stops."

"Do you know where the three men went from here? After getting their passages?"

"No...Just out. All I do is sell passages; don't ask where they go around the city like many. Are you here to purchase passage on *City of Leeds*?"

"Not this visit. Once I find my friends, perhaps I'll sail with them."

"Well, you'd better find them fast: *City of Leeds* sails with the morning tide, weather permitting. Excelsior Ship Lines guarantees your passage or your funds returned. We sail around the world, the Indies, China, all the Mediterranean ports...wherever you want to go, Excelsior is already there."

"The world shrinks."

"Yes it does: yearly."

"How long will it take her to get to London?"

"From here she runs to New Amsterdam, southeast. A stop there to unload and load cargo and pick up passengers...few hours there...another stop at Bedford after that to unload and load...overnight there at least. Then on to London, weather permitting. Excelsior wants safety, not speed. Probably less than a fortnight in all...you're sure you don't want a passage? See some sights and go to London? Completely safe ship with a remarkable record of runs back and forth across the ocean."

"Thank you...perhaps another time."

"Excelsior is here to serve and deliver. Think about Excelsior next time you travel: we go everywhere there's a port. Hope you find your friends."

Ashley almost ran back to Bess, to get away.

The Excelsior clerk hurried also, to quickly write a description of this man who had just inquired about his Lordship. This was the kind of man Squire Lane would like to hear about as well, and today the meal his Cookery served was the fish stew he enjoyed. Yes...a small chat with Squire Lane, a delicious free meal, and perhaps a coin or two when he told his Lordship on the morrow.

The groom who had taken Bess and told Ashley her hooves and shoes were in fine condition also had given him directions to Lawn Street, and Ashley rode there at Bess's fast walk. Several buildings made up the new street, the bank being on the corner, then several grocery and ship's goods' stores, and the street ended. No house...but...by the store with the sign:

Marine Supplies & More Sheets & Sails in one day

Ashley noted that the second floor of the building was not part of the store—as was Pennyweight's—because the windows were different and the second story had a "house look" to it. Had to be a letted apartment. He rode by slowly, not seeming to glance toward the store or the flat above it, and at the end of the street saw an open stable with several horses inside. Had to be where the Frenchmen ended; only "Lawn Street" in the city.

So, remembering the directions for writing in his journal to Rufus, Ashley then chose a different street and circled back so he could still view the store while hoping no one in the apartment above the store would see him. He noticed a tree encircled with a wooden bench—too similar to the one where he sat with Anna: a vantage-point for observation. *Now*, he thought, *I'm becoming a real spy, doing all the spy-things I imagined spies do. After all: the only thing I need do is mimic those things the Frenchmen have done to engage in spying: disguise, travel, carefulness, reports, destinations and return in safety...* Well, two of them wouldn't be returning.

He was glad he had changed his shirt: not only was the white one soiled and smelly, but in the shadow of the tree where he now sat, he seemed to blend into the daylight shadow the tree threw. One more use of disguise; he congratulated himself.

Bess had been tied, so Ashley decided to write his findings thus far, and the directions to the store he watched. Completing this, he just sat there awhile to see if any—or how many—people entered or left the side staircase of the store. The sky was gray, probably as the clerk had said, a rainstorm coming in. He'd wait until he saw people or it started to rain. The place from where he watched was a wooden seat around a large maple tree: just the type of place for someone to sit a while and perhaps enjoy the quiet or the view: the type place he sat with Anna. This gave Ashley no enjoyment. He was out in the open here, never quite sure if anyone were watching him whilst he observed the windows where he felt the Frenchmen had gone.

There was almost no one in the street...the occasional work-wagon, two older men, walking, no women at all. Then a horse and cart approached and the driver unloaded a large box of what looked to be groceries. The cart-driver struggled the box up the outside staircase and into the house—didn't bother to knock on the door, just went in as he could with the box. So they were still in there, and the food was for them. Little more to report, but they had been located and probably the Excelsior clerk was correct about them leaving on the morning tide, aboard *City of Leeds*. Ashley gave a sigh of relief, looked casually around him to see if anyone observed him, then got back onto Bess and went slowly from the tree, angling so he could see behind the store by going down an alleyway. He felt he should return to Lane's establishment to better understand his next move.

A wind had sprung up; seemed it would soon rain, and rain heavily.

He wondered if he could take all this upon himself...then realized no one else could or would do it: he was the edge of the English sword which had been handed to Rufus, perhaps the only person in all New England who knew what the spies seemed up to. Couldn't stop them, of course: who would listen to his story and who dared take responsibility for accosting three men to snatch away their collective maps and whatever. Would take a miracle to do that and he hadn't heard of any happening in New England and there surely were no saints around to lean on, so he figured he was pretty much alone in all this anyway. His duty was only to Rufus: only to "report" what he saw and record it truthfully and completely. Those damn Frenchmen! Then he thought, "Yes, I can take this upon myself; I can and shall do this; this is something Bren would have done." Pleased, he scanned one more time to try to locate anyone watching him, and, finding none, decided to leave the area for Lane's. Determined, tho'; convinced.

Couldn't change his mind anyway: too late and he owed these men too much for the way they killed and tried to kill him. Couldn't break off this job now. Back in Boston when he'd first seen the Frenchmen walking toward the Great Wharf he noticed they all looked alike. Oh, different clothes and different sizes and different shapes...but their faces—it was in their faces. Even from across the street he could make out their faces—not features nor coloring or teeth, just the impression they all showed. Each of them had a fixed stare, a look which most people don't have unless they're lost in thought or have just come through an harrowing experience. Some of the old soldiers he'd seen showed that cast to their faces, that look, that faraway stare even though a person stood beside them. Seemed like they were ever lost in thought but they still talked and responded...except usually their faces didn't change. Expressionless—like they'd already seen something so bad or ugly that nothing around them now could alter it. He hoped he wouldn't ever look like that—so determined. It gave him a queasy feeling just to think about it. What had these men seen that the wonders of Boston couldn't erase from their faces?

These men killed on instinct or for hire; they knew all the demons, and none seemed to frighten them. Maybe it was just that they already knew their immortal souls were lost and they had nothing more to lose: maybe that was it. They had at sometime gone so far they couldn't ever get back. Probably they were war-veterans: it took more than pure courage to stand in a line and receive artillery and musket fire, then to either charge with a naked baïonnette or receive such a charge from the enemy. That took training and resolve, dedication and calculated hate. After living through a war, its veterans would be cold and cruel to enemies, the death of anyone would mean nothing to them; they'd seen hundreds and thousands perish in each battle. Ashley knew he couldn't have gone to war and just stand there and take the punishment and watch the death all around. He'd have to be able to move about, hide, run...no, he never could be a foot-soldier: it was hard enough to be a mounted militiaman or be able to hide behind logs or sneak through the woods.

He had respect for these men...not that thy killed, but that the killing didn't bother them. Not that they were scum—for they were: all the deaths he knew about and all he didn't, proved that—but that they were determined. He liked that determination. Not that they were here, but that they had decided to come here, do their filthy business while maintaining some semblance of order. These men were doomed, damned. Absolute torture awaited them in Eternity, and they had to know that. From all the Plimouth elders preached, indescribable torment for ever awaited each. They had to be totally stupid or smarter than most: who knew which? There was a group in Europe—mercenary soldiers and Christians all—who did these things. Ashley remembered stories of them from his youth. The people of London said they were a secret society formed by knights who had rebuked their vows of chastity and poverty to become both businessmen and hired assassins. Perhaps these Frenchmen were such men. Hmmph. Who could fight THEM? Certainly not HIM!

He thought back: the big man—Matthew—was fearless to the point of being rash, self-seeking that he put comfort ahead of caution, reckless in not completely loading his pistol. He had spunk: walking up on someone obviously waiting in hiding, then taking over the situation totally. But he had been hasty and careless; now he was dead. The man in the loft was careless also. He must have gone there to hide, to sleep instead of staying outside and watching the rear of the Merry Mount house. Had he done his job and seen Ashley first, he would not have died so outrageously. First there had been five; now there were three, each an individual. One leader who directed, soldiers following. Not a non-commissioned officer but an officer. The fifth man doing all the talking, directing, ticket-buying, horse-renting, probably death-sentencing. Had to be an officer. They must have been through Hell with him, then got out of the Army and kept following him...becoming more highwayman than hero and more thief than workman. What could they want except plans for some other country. No other reason for these men to be here in New England. All the deaths they had caused. There wasn't much happiness to life for most, now there was deep sadness for some with the deaths these men had caused. "God, please stop these men from killing us."

He was headed toward Lane's business, going down the main street again. A Providence resident in a doorway waved and Ashley returned a small wave to him, at the same time looking towards the man's shop but seeing far beyond that—to the hill behind the shop. There was a man there, sitting—it looked—doing something partway up on the hill, one of the three hills of this town, looking over the houses and stores and the great river with its port. Drawing pictures of it all, probably: multiple-dwelling homes being constructed, a way-off Indian village…Indians: the Narragansett; the Pequots. More Woods-People taken in by the English and persuaded to cede their homeland away and still being killed and pushed off other land as the newcomers required more and more of the fertile area and wanted less and less "Indians"—never their name—around. He had seen this same thing build in the Massa-adchu-ess-et: get this, take that, want more still.

But as discomforting as it all was, the man on the hill was funny. Not laughable funny, as in the hearing of a funny story, but funny "strange": that kind of funny. Here the spy was, sitting up on a hill, writing down whatever it was he was writing about, and Ashley—observing him—was down here watching him, writing down about the spy watching him. Well, that man was probably drawing sketches of the land and river for the invading Army and Navy, but it seemed peculiar that each of them—on opposing sides—seemed to be doing the same thing.

Close in to where the Frenchman on the hill seemed to be looking was some sort of spring, or well…people gathered around it. Behind them not a big wharf—the way Boston built them—but more of a docking area at riverside. And there, another of those "Excelsior Ship Lines, now in Amsterdam, West Indies, Africa, China and all coastal ports" signs. Whew! Were there really such places? And why would anyone want to go there? Also funny (strange): not a mention of Boston or London.

He gave another glance at the man who was drawing: sent out there to draw a map of the city and show any fortifications, the dock area, the way the river twisted and ran, any buildings for an invading army which stored food or arms or resalable merchandise. They'd know where to bring their ships, to land soldiers, establish a toehold…directly between Dutch New Amsterdam and English Boston. These spies were good. He suddenly became worried: this man on the hill could easily have a sailor's glass or telescope. Only invented forty years ago in Holland, Galileo's Glass could watch the stars; why wouldn't it easily see him? Now he really became worried.

Those glasses were long, though…And probably heavy. He could easily be seen by the Frenchman if he were using one. Ashley's previous fears went away, replaced by new ones.

Where were the other two Frenchmen? He looked around cautiously, then thumped Bess with his knees and she started walking again.

He couldn't rely on any postal agent here; he'd have to take his daily reports for Rufus to a mail-relay station outside Providence, closer to Boston; maybe even take them all the way to Rufus by himself.

Well...tomorrow the Frenchmen would leave, but somehow Rufus should know in time—time to head off *City of Leeds* and have done whatever England wanted to do. This would soon be over. Rufus was right: "Those Royalist bastards!" Ashley hoped they'd get what they deserved: death.

The air was heavy, like it was about to rain but couldn't. Sweating. Not really hot, but he was sweating. Maybe the vest. He could smell himself, smell the sweat, hoped no one he met could or would smell that. Felt embarrassed about it, but every man sweats. His hair was wet from it; it ran down his arms and neck. Hoped it would rain to get rid of it.

The northeast sky was heavy with rain-clouds: there'd never be a better chance to eat and no fire could be made in the rain anyway, and although Bess might eat wet grain, Ashley didn't want her to eat wet food as her belly would swell and she'd be laid up a few days, recovering. He got to Lane's and decided they both should eat right away: wanted more of that good food he'd had earlier, the food that was better than Anna had made for him. He somehow felt saddened to think that—felt that he hurt her memory, hurt her cooking skills, which of course were less than his mother's to start with...but he had grown to like Anna's cooking. Now he was thinking some commercial cook in an anti-Puritanical town made better meals than his own Anna. Shouldn't even eat because of that...but it was true...so he put Bess into a stall to be fed and went into Lane's Cookery.

There was more food being eaten and cooked than Ashley had ever seen...all kinds, colors and preparations. He thought for a moment, then realized he must eat fast so he could leave ahead of the incoming rainstorm—maybe that way go right through it and out the other side. He opted for beef stew, but was told because it was Friday, the stew this day was fish. Providence had strange customs about food and the days they served it.

The fish stew was very good—as good as earlier, with all that butter floating around at the top—and it was better than what he'd had earlier. He didn't realize he was so hungry and had eaten two bowls. He never could stand to see the way Anna ate...she'd take small portions and pick at them, getting about half a teaspoon of food at a time, putting it with painstakingly slow motions into her mouth, chewing slowly and deliberately, taking so long a child could grow up while she ate a complete meal. She was ever after him to slow down his eating...she should have been raised by his mother, telling her to "Eat fast, before it gets away!"

Lots of seafood here at Lane's, like it was on the Atlantic but it was leagues from that, almost landlocked except for the river. The stew was good, fast and easy to eat, and although he knew he was wasting valuable time, he indulged himself; he knew he'd never be back here again! He had asked that Bess be fed and watered again—really too close to when she ate earlier, but…didn't know when she'd get to eat again on the wet trip back. He planned just to run for Plimouth, even in the rain. At least Bess was rested. That rest and grain would get her going and the rain and the smell of home would keep her moving. He'd noticed that the grass here was different from Duxbury; Bess would know that also. Duxbury had that sweet-smelling grass with those wildflowers in it she liked so much; she'd be glad to get home—home to the stable and turnout-pasture at Rufus' store, anyway.

Bess was a fun horse. The girl before Anna had spoiled Bess with treats and love, and Anna had kept up that menu. It was almost too long since Bess had been given such attention and she responded well to the little Ashley gave. He thought that when all this riding around was over he'd give her to some girl or woman who'd continue to spoil her, be light on her back, feed her molasses and apples, hang on her neck and talk right to her. Yeah…Bess deserved that—everything her breeder and Anna let her have.

He had taken a small table by a window and figured now would be a good time to write a few thoughts before he forgot them; couldn't write on the road in the rain and he wanted Rufus to get everything. He put down a skeleton-overview of what he had done, writing in the street names and the name of the business where he had seen what he felt were the horses of the three Frenchmen, and the ship's name and ports of call: New Amsterdam to unload and load cargo—few hours; Bedford for the same thing: overnight. Then to London, perhaps a fortnight in all, said the travel agent. Good information there; no specific place to arrive in London, but they all seemed to dock at Dockside and berthed west of there: everyone knew and understood that; that was the way of London since the Romans left. Though…too many factors controlled when and if the ship would arrive and dock.

So…next thing was to get Bess, go take the reports to Rufus, then maybe travel to London—if he could get there in time to spy on the spies. Now, wasn't THAT a novel thought: him going to London again, still doing his spy-job. Like that was ever going to happen! He surprised himself in thinking he could or would go to London. Must have been thinking as he ate, because the second serving of food was gone. Hmmmmm…always had eaten fast. When he was in London as a child, food was always scarce for a widow with a growing boy and no pension; his mother would give him things to eat but she hardly ever joined him in that eating. She'd say, "Eat fast, before it gets away!" He ever wondered what it was he was eating that might "get away"; his stomach turned as he thought that—but as a child he never questioned his mum. Probably just a method she used to get a child to eat and not play with his food. Perhaps. Maybe a reminder of what her mother used to say to her...her mother had been born in Ireland in the middle 1500s and perhaps the saying was relevant then and there. Anna hated that "eat fast" habit he had: she would serve him a meal, turn to get hers, and by the time she sat with her plate he was finished. Scolding helped slow him down a little...he tried to wait for her before he began to eat; she tried to give him "extra" to slow him down; she would put her plate on the table and sit, then say, "Oh, would you get your plate over there?" He still finished before she did. He always ate quickly. His eyes teared as he thought of Anna.

Ashley left the dining area and Squire Lane came up to him. "How was the meal, Traveler Gonkin?"

"Wished he hadn't used such an obvious name. "Very tasty. I never realized there was so much seafood and so many ways to prepare it."

"Fine. We take pleasure in your pleasure. If you like food, we have most everything; if you like lodging, it's here, plenty of rooms—well, usually plenty: we're almost full tonight. If you require your horse, ox or a carriage attended, my men will do it all."

"I must say you have an all-around place here, Squire Lane."

"You're staying the night?"

"I'm not sure."

"Look outside and you'll *be* sure, Traveler Gonkin; we have a heavy rainstorm coming in with lightning...neither you nor your horse will want to be out in that; horses get skittish in lightning storms and many a traveler has lost a horse due to them. But *here*, here we have a dry room for you, and for the price of a shilling you'll have the room, a full breakfast, and care for your horse. Is that a reasonable offer?"

"It certainly is."

"Come with me, Traveler; I'll show you the room myself." He led Ashley up a wide stairway to the second floor and down the hall to an end room, opening the louvered door with a flourish. "Here we are! A large, raised pallet, a window, two chairs and four chamber pots. There used to be four chairs but some of the guests..." The ending faded away.

Ashley looked in. True. A four-man pallet on a raised foundation which seemed clean, a window—but a window so small it could be used only for ventilation, as no one could squeeze through it and Ashley thought immediately that no "guest" could climb out such a window and run from a bill; and two straight-backed chairs of dubious strength. A four-man room, typical style in lodging houses.

"It seems quite serviceable."

"Go inside and look around; go right in! You'll take it? You'll stay the night with us? Remember, free breakfast—all you care to eat—and care for your horse as well, all included in the one price. Go right in, Traveler Gonkin; see how you like the room."

Lane and his money. If ever there were a pushy man for coin, it was Francis Lane. But…this was TOO good a deal, and breakfast free? But there did seem to be a really heavy nor-easter storm coming in; he'd already seem the lightning in the distance.

"Will the ships sail in the morning?"

"Oh, no! No ship at all will go out in what's coming tonight; a really terrible storm, those who have come in ahead of it say. The ships'll be here two or three days more, until the heaviest part of the storm and lightning ends. A miserable storm, I hear; a very terrible storm. You're lucky you're indoors as you couldn't travel at all in this, and neither could your horse."

Ashley pulled a shilling from his pocket and Lane snatched it. "I'll bid you good night, Traveler Gonkin."

"I…I'll go to see to my horse."

"Not at all necessary, there are several men already in the stable, bedding-down and tending the horses. We like horses here. My stable-hands have done everything already. He's a fine animal, your horse, but you've had a long ride from Boston and you must be quite tired. Go in and get some sleep; you deserve it. No one will bother you in this room; you'll be quite comfortable in here alone."

"I thought your inn was full, and with four pallets in here…"

"Well, we do have a lot of guests tonight, er, due to the terrible storm coming, but here is a fine private room for you, sir, already paid for and a free breakfast for you in the morning plus care for your fine horse."

"There's something I must get from my saddlebag."

"I'll do it for you! Go right in and see how comfortable the room is and I'll get whatever it is from your saddlebag for you, bring it right up. Go right in, Traveler Gonkin. Full service for the overnight traveler here, sir…just as Protector Cromwell says, a man must realize he has a talent, then use it to secure legal money, and thus he is a businessman. So that's what I do…I use all my talent. What can I bring you?"

"My thanks, Squire Lane, but I'd rather do it myself. It'll only take a short time, and then I'll be able to lie down in your comfortable bedstead."

"Excellent, Traveler Gonkin...have a dreamless sleep. See you in the morning for a free breakfast..."

"And care for my fine horse."

"Yes!"

Ashley wouldn't go into the room but went out to the stable and found Bess. No stablemen around at all: so much for the "free care of your horse." Oh, and Bess! Bess was a mare and Lane talked about her as a "he," so Lane didn't even know what Ashley rode. And that four-person room with only one in it...with the inn so full from "the terrible storm approaching"—which was now but a light rain, although it seemed heavy rain would start soon. But no lightning had he seen since he came outside. And that tiny window in the room? That room was no bedroom, but a cell! Once in, he'd never get out alive! Lane must be a Royalist, wanting the King returned to the throne of England and Cromwell out of the way. All that talk about Protector Cromwell...oh, and Lane had said "that long ride from Boston." How did he know Ashley was from Boston? A trap! The room was a cage and Ashley would be locked inside it with no hope of getting out alive and no escape and no "free care for your horse and a free breakfast!" And probably with his throat cut by morning!

He saddled Bess rapidly and then peered outside. No one there yet; perhaps Lane was giving him time enough to get whatever it was from his saddlebag. He led Bess to the open door, mounted and rose out, walking her carefully at first and making no noise, then giving her an urge to get along.

Finally, at a distance from Lane's, he put Bess into a canter and in spite of the rain which was now heavier, he relaxed.

The rain did get worse. And there was lightning—plenty of it and all around then it seemed—quiet lightning with crackles of thunder which made Bess and Ashley jump.

At a small farmhouse not too many leagues out of Providence, Ashley was forced to stop, hoping to find shelter in an open shed. Someone was trying to make a field from the woods, as trees had been felled, burned, and the stumps carried away to form a sort of clearing. With this rocky soil it might take a family of ten a lifetime to clear away the rocks he saw and imagined were there...that was the way of life for a settler-family: locate the land boundaries, place fieldstone on them to show the reaches, eventually construct a small wall from the rocks which would evolve to keep in stray animals like cows, sheep or goats—perhaps even small hogs—and then he thought briefly about the hogs in Marry Mount who were eating…whatever…that night. Hogs would root more, destroy more trees and eat what cows wouldn't while the liberally fertilized whatever soil was left after their rootings. This was the way of the settler/frontiersman. Sometimes grandsons removed the last of the original trees their grandfathers had cut years before but couldn't ever pull or cut out. He had seen that in Plimouth.

A pair of dogs ran up to Bess, startling her and making her jump about as they barked and growled. This was no place to stay, so Ashley tried to get Bess turned around to leave, but she faced the dogs and refused to respond to the reins, so terribly scared and determined to not have a rear hock bitten by one of the barking farm-protectors.

The farmer with a musket called from the house and the dogs stopped barking but stayed in place. "Who are you and what is your business?"

"Ashley Lyons of Plimouth and Boston, sir, and I only wanted to get my horse and myself out of the storm." His voice was carried on the whipping wind and the thunder reduced it, but they could see each other—the farmer and rider—in the lightning flashes. Looked like the farmer's wife had joined him at the doorway; she also held a musket. Were all these Providence people so determined and protective?

"Dismount and come forward."

Ashley got off Bess, leaving the only dry spot he had—his saddle—but he tightly held her reins. She wouldn't ground-tie as Joe, but would spring-away, especially with those slavering hounds present, if he let go of her. He made it slowly to the door, dragging her and the dogs following, still whining and shaking rainwater all around as they tried to stay fierce-some but obedient.

"Have you proof of how you are?"

Ashley thought a second. "I have a note from Captain Miles Standish of Plimouth in my saddlebag, with my name on it."

"Put your horse in that shed and bring the bag itself to this door. I'll read it before you may enter." He called to the dogs and they went into the house, shaking themselves and making the woman move back out of the doorway.

"Thank you for your hospitality…the storm…"

"Please hurry, sir."

"Of course." He stabled Bess. To their grand enjoyment the shed was dry, then he found the note from Miles and left it on top of his saddlebag items, closed the bag and carried it to the farmer—who remained with a pointed musket and them read it with an eye on his guest.

"Captain Ashley Lyons, Plimouth militia. Welcome, good sir, and come in. We were asleep so we have no food prepared…"

"No, no," Ashley protested. "Please. This is only a hope to get under cover for my horse and myself. The shed is fine; please allow only that; I require no further hospitality."

"Well, Captain Lyons, the house is so small and our children sleep in this room, so we wouldn't turn you away, but if you did stay in the shed..."

"That's where I shall stay, sir; the shed is dry and just perfect in this downpour."

"Oh, 'Woodstock' is my name. My family is located in the Rehobath Purchase and I have this farm here, away from them. The shed is small, but there's fresh hay for your horse and as a mattress." He returned Ashley's letter.

Once inside the shed, with Bess settled down and feeding, Ashley said prayers for his rescue from the rain—actually it WAS a "terrible storm" as Lane had predicted. The winds were getting heavy and this entire shed shook from them; and the rain came in sheets, blasting with little needles of wetness into everything. It truly was not a night to be traveling. He relaxed a bit and tried to bring Anna to him—but failed. All he could summon was her memory, and even that was no longer distinct. He was more alone now than ever.

The following morning when he woke—only a few hours later—the storm had intensified, with still-heavier winds and heavy, driving rain coming in waves, it seemed. There was a form of daylight, but no sun, and Ashley fell asleep once more. When he woke again, the rain was continuing but Woodstock's sons were out in the barn, milking and tending the stock. The farmer himself was using a grindstone to sharpen knives, hoes and shovels.

Ashley went through the rain to the barn.

"Good morning."

Woodstock laughed. "I suppose to get out of this rain and wind makes it a good morning...it's bad for me, but we'll get some odd jobs completed today. Seems like a three-day nor'easter coming in."

"You really think so? A three-day rainstorm?"

"Yes, I really think thus. Farmers have to keep a weather-eye to be able to plant and harvest, care for their stock and stay ahead of the blasted weather! I never thought it'd be so cold in this place; I was raised by the sea and it never froze the way it does here. And before you ask, yes, I wanted this land, and so I got it and am stuck with it." He laughed: a joke on himself.

"It freezes in Plimouth, but worse inland, so I understand what you're saying. You have a large farm."

"Ten hectares…but I have seven children: four boys. Able to do a lot of work with good help. And we have assistance in getting in the hay and crops from my family in Rehobath. We get by."

This truly was a three-day storm, and Ashley fretted all the while. Two full days and nights he waited in that shed, fed by the Woodstock family and worrying all the while about everything…mostly wondering if *City of Leeds* had sailed, thinking it couldn't. Still, he wondered.

CHAPTER 18

At Excelsior Ship Lines on the morning of the third day of the storm, the ticket-seller had come in early, as the rain was sporadic now, still off and on in waves, but getting less and the wind falling off from the gusts, even now from a different direction and more gusty than constant…not that strong now: still a hard blow at times, tossing around the clouds like sheets on a line, shaking them into wild patterns and shifting the grays and almost-whites, making blended colors in the sky, but noticeably weakening fast. Might be a sight God liked, it happened so often in the late summer here. Today, *City of Leeds* would leave late, the tide-schedule already posted, but the ticket-seller waited for passengers; he knew three who would board as early as possible.

As Johnathan's coach came up to the open gateway, the Excelsior Agent stepped out, waving at them.

"Did your friend find you?"

Johnathan looked puzzled, his mind on Scotland, not "friends." "Which friend was that?"

"The tall man…three days ago he came here looking for you. Before the storm."

"Wearing a vest?"

"Yes, a vest. So he did find you."

"The clark!"

"Shhhhh…Yes, he did locate us, but we did not speak. So good of you to remember such a long time…Geoffry, pay this man a silver sovereign, please, for being so good a gentleman. You can stay here until we get to the ship, if you know what I mean."

"Yes, Johnathan."

"You told him we would leave on this ship, good sir?"

"Yes, sir; Excelsior always tries to serve our passengers well."

"And he purchased a ticket from you?"

"No…said he'd be back, but hasn't, thus far. *City of Leeds* won't sail for a while yet, so he may still."

"How nice of you to give such service. When exactly will the ship sail?"

"Oh, three more hours or four…only the captain can say, but the tide isn't ready yet and the wind still is gusty from the wrong direction for the Narragansett; time enough to get aboard, stow your belongings and break the fast—which is happening shipboard right now, sir."

"Our plans have changed suddenly. Geoffry, you stay with me awhile. Driver, take us to the sheriff's office. You'll be here all morning, ship's agent?"

"That I shall…here alone all day, every day."

"In that case, we shall see you again shortly. Go ahead, driver."

The rented coach turned around. "How did 'e fin' us 'ere, Johnathan?"

"I knew we should have torched that store!"

"Gentlemen, gentleman…"

"Let's fin' 'im an' do 'im!"

"We shall do that in London, if he gets there."

"London, Johnathan? You think he'll follow us there as well?"

"Why not London, if he's a Cromwell spy? It seems he's followed us everywhere in New England, so why not back to London? That would only be a returning for him, getting more help there."

"Then we should do 'im 'ere, whilst 'e's alone!"

Johnathan patted Geoffry's arm. "If he were 'here,' we certainly would do just that. But we don't know where he is right now and we do have a schedule to keep. We'll get our law-friends to find him and do something permanent to him."

"An' if they miss 'im?"

"We shall be on guard and not think the colonials are all savages. We have six eyes to his two, and we must see him this time before he sees us. He has no contacts, if he inquires of stablemen, little boys and ticket-sellers…But, gentlemen, once we are in London, we have the advantage of home ground."

"I 'ave a bad feelin' about this clark…"

"Hush, Geoffry, my good man. Soon he'll be yours to do things with."

The morning of the third day of the storm, everyone at Woodstock's farm was bustling with activity, awake earlier than Ashley and busy. When he did wake, Ashley saw the barn full of Woodstocks and the animals being turned out, the place requiring lots of cleaning. He walked over to Woodstock. "The storm seems to be passing rapidly now, so I'll be on my way. You're all up early."

"We had butter and eggs and milk to deliver, so I sent my two older boys along with those to Providence already, as we've not been able to conduct any business these past two days."

"I didn't realize you sold farm products."

"Everything we can. The only way we can stay ahead buying grain at today's prices...I have a contract to supply milk, butter and eggs to several places in Providence...I can imagine they're jumping up and down with suspense and hunger, waiting there, especially at the Highway House..."

"You sell to food establishments?"

"We supply them with whatever milk, eggs, butter and vegetables we can; do it daily, always fresh to them and their customers. We missed them the past two days, what with the storm, so the two older boys have taken the wagon there this morning."

"To Providence by themselves?"

"Every morning we can; they're big enough and old enough to do that; besides, all they have to do is unload whatever supplies the taverns want and take a paper from them. They go to the same three places every day; the customers need our products and we need their coin and credit. Good swap."

"Then the storm was a bad one for your business."

"Bad for everyone: roofs blown off buildings, sheds tipped over. I had a neighbor here this morning who said he about lost his farm from all that wind. Bad storm; we seldom get those, but when they come, they're mean. I wouldn't let my boys go out on delivery the past two days and my wife wouldn't let me go; but so far as overall for my business, the old milk held and it'll be used today, probably already out in the restaurants. Everything else's the same—little wilting of vegetables, but...my only real concern was that Lane's would run plumb out of food before we could get him his re-stock; then they'd be mad and change suppliers...but Francis is usually understanding."

"We're speaking Francis Lane of the Highway House?"

"Yes."

"I must go. Your boys are probably already there, telling Lane where I am."

"So?"

"Very complicated to explain. I just want to leave."

"No."

"I'll go get my gear and horse..."

"No."

"No?"

"What happened, Captain Lyons? Things are fine until I mention Francis Lane's name, and then you turn pale and try to bolt away, telling me it's 'very complicated.' Un-complicate it for me!"

"All right…quickly. Are you Puritan or Royalist?"

Woodstock laughed. "Is that all there is now? Puritan or Royalist Anglican? No one may be Catholic or Jew?"

"I didn't mean specifically that…Francis Lane—I believe—is a Royalist."

"If you mean he wants a King in England and not the wars Protector Cromwell wages, then he is. I don't, especially, but I am no Puritan nor Anglican; we are Catholic here."

"I must speak fast and leave. I am here on the business of the Plimouth colony. Lane wanted to lock me in a room for some reason and I didn't stay there to ask why."

"Which is why you were riding in the storm."

"Just that."

"And why you fear my boys will tell Lane you are here."

"Exactly; I must leave."

"Go, Captain Lyons…I think I understand your concern." Woodstock looked down, shaking his head from side to side as Ashley grabbed whatever he had lying about. "I'm going after my boys. I'll try not to speak of you, but if I have to give you up for my sons, I shall."

"I fully understand."

Ashley saddled Bess and led her outside. Woodstock's wife came over to him with a bundle wrapped in a towel: "To break the fast, Captain."

He reached into his pocket, where just the night before he had placed a silver shilling for each of the children and two gold sovereigns for the Woodstocks. "I'll swap that breakfast for this handful."

"I cannot accept coin for Christian kindness."

"Take it for the children…I honestly do not need it. I'm headed home and don't know where I'll go from there, but I must leave now. Please say my goodbyes to your family for me; I have enjoyed staying here."

She took the coins and Ashley rode out, waving.

More worry; more concerns; more leagues to ride before safety.

A league down the road to Boston there was a long, steep grade rising the road and Bess slowed down, ending up walking by the time she had reached the peak. Ashley looked around, admiring the view—which was mostly pine and scrub oak with tangles of bushes and long grasses. As he scanned it all, he turned to look behind him and immediately saw a half-dozen riders or more, coming all out, pushing their horses in a sudden sprint.

No one would do that: run a horse in mid-point between the cities. HAD to be Providence Royalists riding toward him, trying to catch up, grab him! He was silhouetted on the top of this hill. Well…all downhill for Bess. He clucked at her, urging her to run, and she responded. Down the hill they went, far faster now than the Providence men—who soon had a long, steep rise to conquer after their fast run—and Ashley ran Bess as long as he dared, watching for good cover in the surrounding woods.

The "woods" was a tangle of brush and fallen trees, most of them over from the heavy storm just past, plus the usual growth and tree-fall. Hard to see into. But he was gladdened to see the natural cover, thinking, *Where would the average person go in here; I want to go into a dense place where they won't find me.*

To the side he saw a heavy stand of tall pines, many tilted to the side from that recent wind. *Yes! There!* He was as careful as he could be, slowing Bess and circling her from the road into the brush, hoping not to leave hoof-prints or break branches. He wove her around to the densely packed trees—most of them thickly branched but without much height—as that was where the average person would go: to a low cover. Ashley realized the hoof-prints would be tracked, so he went in a direction away from where he expected to hide himself. Way off to a side he chose a pair of tall pines which had fallen together at the tops, and although they weren't too branchy, had a full compliment of dense, upper branches way above.

He pulled off his saddlebag and turned Bess loose, slapping her rump to send her off toward some grass a distance away, pulled off his boots—quickly tying them together and putting them around his neck—used the saddlebag as a "hold" under a branch of one of the leaning trees, and worked his way up into the highest, thickly matted branches. Without his boots, his feet hurt, but there were no "slip-marks" from his boots made by his stockinged-feet. There he sat, hoping for the best and perched as Jimmy the crow, from the Lavrador. No musket, only his skinning knife for protection. These riders would miss him or find him, but he prayed they'd just keep riding on past.

The riders he had seen—who, indeed, had seen him atop that hill—were legalized sheriff's men. The acting-sheriff of Providence had been told that "Traveler Al Gonkin" was a wanted murderer from the Plimouth settlement. Well…being from that hated Plimouth was grounds enough for imprisonment so far as many of the Providence residents thought: Roger Williams was alive and well in the minds of Providence residents who told and re-told his trials and tribulations in religion at that dreaded Puritan place, and they listened well and re-told the stories. No Puritan OR murderer would survive Providence.

Life for any new settler was especially frightening as new arrivals heard distorted tales about savage Indians and wild frontiersmen, and they had no real confidence in local law. Better to band together with an informally appointed "sheriff" and capture an accused murderer than let him escape to murder more...and the reward the assistant governor proposed for the capture of murderers was tantalizing to many men. So these men were hard after the murderer "Al Gonkin"—a few of them realizing the tongue-in-cheek name and fuming at its use.

The band—eight of them—had left Providence at dawn, as the rains and wind had then stopped and they felt their "murderer" must be camped somewhere along the road: an easy arrest. They had stopped a short while before at Woodstock's farm after speaking to Woodstock himself along the road, and assured themselves the man who stayed at Woodstock's was indeed the man they sought, especially after getting a description from Woodstock's wife. Then they decided the Puritan could run toward Plimouth but they'd—by God—bring him back to justice in Providence or kill him trying. These were God-fearing men but not Puritan-fearing: those ones at Plimouth were of a different cloth. These men would just as soon shoot down a murderer as take him alive and think he might receive "decent treatment" or "only" a prison sentence. They—each—were prepared to use their new, rifled long-guns as soon as they got into range. If they all could shoot together—or almost together—and the murderer were hit by any one of the rifled balls, each could say he personally fired the shot which brought the murderer down. So there was fear, civic pride, personal gain plus resident-interest and legal justice which was at work within this posse.

The two riders most forward were sworn sheriff's men. The three riding in close were civic volunteers and righteous men who demanded "an eye for an eye" and a death for a death. Not the kind of group with which Ashley wanted to associate. They at first rode past the stand of pine where Ashley had hidden, then as they realized he no longer was in sight and there were no fresh hoof-prints showing on the damp dirt road, they stopped to figure out where the murderer could have gotten.

Jared Baker had the first idea: "I'd go into the trees. He's not ahead of us—unless on foot with his horse left in the woods—so he must be off to the side."

Lester Whitman agreed: "He's not riding any horse in that brush; he's afoot. You look south and I'll ride down and come back north. Check for prints going off the road and into those short trees."

The main sheriff's deputy concurred: "Old Tom, you stay ahorse here and scan all around. Watch to see if that fella is runnin' or has outflanked us on his horse. Bill, you do the same, back there, past the trees. Watch all over and around; see if you spot his horse. Be sure he hasn't doubled-back on us like that one two years ago, who showed his arse before we ran him down and re-paid him for our trouble. Fire a shot if you see 'im an' we'll all come a-runnin'. Samuel and James into the trees to the south. Lester, you stay here, ahorse, and supervise; you are our center, and we revolve around you. Watch everyone closely and look behind us as we pass places, that Gonkin doesn't slip out after we go by. All in the woods will meet in the center, somewhere. Be alert. This man has already killed and won't be taken alive. Shoot to kill, but—by God—be sure WHO in these woods you shoot at! My wife doesn't need a dead husband, you hear me?"

"Ain't what she tol' me!" They all laughed, knowing his wife probably WOULD like a dead husband so she could marry someone else who would stay around home.

Deputy Russell had been shot at and hit twice by other deputies and volunteers the previous year in the Narragansett Straits, when most of these men were hot on the heels of another alleged murderer—who had fired towards them and received for his trouble a barrage of shot and ball in return. Russell's shoulder still hurt and his knee ached all the time; his only relief was that he was hit by shot and not heavy-caliber balls. Each lawman took his assigned position. Not a man here was afraid. Worried, perhaps, but not afraid. This was a job they did often as a team, and they were quite good at it. They enjoyed their work, got paid too much (funny how the ones killed never carried coin) and had high praise from the community. "Russell's Raiders" they called themselves.

Charles—the assistant deputy—found the trail right away. "Here! Right here is where his horse went off the road."

Jared looked hard at the tracks. "He's on a small horse; can't outrun us and knows it. Riding a mare, looks like; that's why he went to ground; even our tired stallions would run her down. You glad now, Tom, I tol' you t' get a stallion?"

"Into the trees and be careful."

They spread out, rifles at the alert and pointing where they looked. Charles following the hoof-prints tho' he wasn't a tracker; didn't need to be with the rain-softened ground.

The eight did their usual encirclement: they had run scoundrels to ground for almost three years as a team and enjoyed the plan they used. Most fleeing men would eventually halt and take cover, as in fleeing they left open a trail and exposed themselves too much. So the way these men ran "their plan" was to observe, circle and observe, tighten the circle and observe. Every man a tracker: confident. Every man a good shot: ready.

It hardly took three hours, but they had all fanned out, then drawn close and covered each other, convinced that Al Gonkin had not either outrun them or anyway gotten away from them. Bess was found soon after the men entered the pines…her nickering caused them some excitement, but did not draw a one from his assigned post, as in the past they had lost criminals who had noises made and then when they all went to see the reasons for the sounds, the bad-men slipped away; this time they wouldn't waver from their sites.

Bess was approached by the lawmen who had her in their search-area, and only then as they completed their assigned circles. They saw she had no saddlebag and reasoned the rider had fled with it—probably taking gold in it and their thoughts burned at that idea. These were meticulous and patient men; they knew they had him and it was only a question of time before he shot, ran or gave up.

These men ever worked in pairs, one trying to watch for the other, and a pair went up a small stream and another down. One tracked; one protected the tracker. In an hour they had decided the fleeing man had not gone into or along the stream. Both deputies ascertained their prey was not under or mingled within the trees and probably not under bushes, yet they continued to feel he was still here; only a more thorough search was needed. He HAD to be here, still hidden, maybe looking at them Still here, nonetheless. On they went in their closing circles, doing their plan, watching, criss-crossing, marking any disturbance in or on the ground, ever vigilant: professional, relentless, enjoying their work, waiting for their man to flush as a grouse through the trees.

Still couldn't find him.

"Compass points, gentlemen," Russell called out. This was their final trick: each of four men went to a major compass point: north, south, east, west. Far enough to have some distance, close enough to be readily seen by their teammates, still covering each other.

"Where do we begin, Jared?"

"This man is a woodsman. No city man; he hides too well. He chooses his cover and stays there as an owl in the daytime. So where, Russell, do owls go in the daytime?"

"Up in trees; dense cover there for them."

"That's where we shall find him."

"Compass points, always observe the ground," Russell called to them. He didn't care if the murderer heard him; actually that might make him more frightened that his pursuers were not afraid to share their work with him; frightened, perhaps, enough to break and run—as many did.

"The three of us will stand apart, walk through the trees, looking up only. Old Tom on his horse in case the prey runs like a deer. Find him before he shoots you, gentlemen; I hate taking balls and dislike bringing back dead deputies. Hear me?"

They all nodded: their own sentiments.

They assumed the new positions.

"One walk to the left, one in the middle—where he probably is—one walk to the right. Begin."

The three went as a line, forward, toward the left of the dense, tall trees. Slowly, surely. They knew they had him; only a matter of time until he ran or shot or they saw and shot him. If he shot first, they'd be on him like stink on a skunk! These were cautious, eager, serious men.

Their first pass, walking and looking up into the trees for their "owl" came to naught. They re-formed into their "line" and started the middle pass, to go under the two trees, leaning.

Hardly had they begun when a muffled musket-shot rang out! It wasn't near, and Old Tom returned fire, yelling, "Over here!"

They all ran toward Old Tom, rifles at the ready. On a far rise, a man ran across a field, a musket displayed. Charles dashed for the hobbled horses but by the time he had even one of them separated from the rest and unhitched, the other lawmen were out of the woods and running toward the fleeing man.

Across the glade they ran, crossed the stream in bounds, maintained their speed through the sparse woods with their thorny thickets which tore at them but they paid no heed for their murderer was running on foot and by God they'd have him now! Their owl was flying, but owls don't fly long or fast; they knew they had him this time.

He was too fast; they were slow and tired. Charles brought up two horses but he wasn't sure they'd get this man: he seemed to know the countryside and where the deer trails led, as he surely followed them and fairly comfortably. At least he hadn't bothered to stop and re-load, then shoot again. Russell and Jared grabbed at the horses and the three mounted men now had the speed they needed; sure, now, and mounted: they'd get him!

Old Tom sat still in the saddle; his job now was to mark the flight of the murderer and give arm/hand signals to the riders and those who were still afoot. These men were accomplished hunters and drove deer like this, never failing.

Just when they thought they might have lost their prey, Jared spotted him going over the big rise. The lawmen forced their stallions up the steep grade, riding as trained cavalry after fleeing soldiers on a battlefield. At the extreme of the rise they held up, it not prudent to come careening across the highpoint of any hill with an armed felon on the other side; they dismounted and Jared cocked his new rifle as he judiciously peered over the top of the rise and watched the man—now exhausted from his long run—bent over, gasping for air, his musket on the ground and him in no condition at all to run anywhere else. The "murderer" looked up the rise, saw the posse, put his arms up over his head, turned a bit to one side and stood, waiting. An easy shot, now.

"I'll kill 'im, the son-of-a-bitch! Making us run our horses like that!"

"Wait, Jared; something is wrong here."

The rest of the group rode up, long-guns at the ready, anxious to get in on the mass-planned shoot.

"What did you say he was wearing?"

"Gonkin?"

"Yeah."

"Dark clothes."

"That look like dark clothes to you?"

The man at the bottom of the hill wore a white shirt and light pants. Russell motioned to his suspect to lie down and the man readily obliged, probably because he seemed so tired from his long run.

"You three, watch behind us; you two, take the sides. We'll go down and see this man who wears no dark clothing; he looks too familiar to me."

Down they went, rifles at the ready. His musket was on the ground, away from him, not loaded. Fired, but not now loaded; the man was lying face-down on the ground.

"Please do not hurt me!" he called. "I made a mistake but no one is hurt and please don't kill me; I have a wife and family to support!"

Russell poked the barrel of his rifle against the man's neck. "You turn over slowly. Draw a pistol or a knife an' I'll blast you!" He meant it, anger building because Russell knew what had just happened.

Painfully slowly, taking his time, the man turned over: Woodstock!

"You son-of-a-bitch; I should shoot you on general principles!"

"I didn't know you were there! You were riding on the road and I was in the woods. I saw a grouse and fired a shot at it; that's all I did, tried to shoot a grouse!"

Jared came up to them. "This grouse let our owl get away. Bet when we go back the mare is gone and so is he."

Russell spit. “Won’t take that bet! Horses, everyone! We’ll ride north; I want that owl!”

Russell waited until his horse was brought to him, Woodstock still lying on the ground. “You, I shall deal with another time; you’re a lucky man, Woodstock; count your blessings and say your Catholic prayers. This is one *more* reason I have to remember you. I still remember last year about your cousin, and won’t forget the part you played in that; you do the same here an’ I can’t get you for this, but some day...”

Woodstock nodded in agreement, from the ground.

“You live a long way from here, Squire Woodstock,” Jared said. “Why do you hunt grouse here?”

“Have to hunt them where they are and this is where they are: in the woods; plenty of heavy trees and brush for them here.”

“How is it we spoke with you on the road to Providence and you said nothing of going after grouse; you were going after you sons, as I recall. Is our owl one of them that you involve yourself in all this?”

“All my family are at home now. When I returned from Providence my wife reminded me we needed food for the evening meal, so I came along to where I knew the grouse would be. There are also turkeys in these woods.”

Russell poked his rifle-barrel into Woodstock’s throat. “Shut up.” His voice scared Woodstock.

Deputy Russell and Farmer Woodstock had a long-standing feud. Russell was no one with which to argue and he did have a long memory. This wouldn’t be the last meeting between them, but Captain Lyons seemed to have gotten away and Woodstock had just repaid him for that “handful of coins” Ashley had given his wife. Re-payments were open and given freely on the frontier...so were promises to get even—perhaps ahead, as well.

Sure enough, when the lawmen had gotten back to where they were looking up the leaning tree, the owl was gone and Jared did see scratches and rubs along the trunk. “He was up there.”

“And that damn Woodstock knew it! Distracted us!”

“Why didn’t you kill him then and there, as an accomplice!”

“His family is too powerful. They own most of the Rehobath land and part of Providence. The sheriff would have my hide stretched and drying on a rack if I touched one of his money-supporters. But there’ll be another time...there’s always another time for lawbreakers; they never learn. If his family weren’t so important in Rehobath I’d arrest him for what he did. As it stands, we’ll just have to wait until he does something more; then we’ll have him on a spit. Let’s chase our owl some more and maybe strip some feathers from his wings.”

“That mare won’t last; I saw her and she’s too little to run a long time. We’ll catch him on the long road.”

“If he’s running on it. This is either a talented man or a blessed one. And I wouldn’t be surprised to find an empty saddle on that mare when we find her.”

“Think he shooed her and stays in the woods?”

“Don’t quite know what to think, but we’ll have to chase his hoof-prints and boot-prints; he can ride her and before she drops go to hiding, or just leave her loose alone and hide in the fields. We’ll have to go slowly, check the hoof-prints to see if they waver, then hunt him over the whole day, hoping to find him before night.”

“He’ll be long gone.”

“We’ll follow that trail as far as we can. We caught up to him once...All we have are hoof-prints to follow, so, Jared, you look carefully at them and tell me if the mare is carrying him; then we’ll know how fast to ride. Our rested stallions should overtake his mare.”

He had to rest Bess. He had run her hard, pushed her, knew she would run her heart out for him if he wanted that; she was that kind of horse: she’d run until she dropped dead in her tracks. He didn’t want that. Joe would slow down when he was tired, and would balk at being driven, but she...she would ever give her all, until she fell dead. Yes, he was in a hurry, but there was a better way to do this. He smiled to himself. When they had gotten Bess, he had pointed out to Anna that Bess was not large enough to work or use on a long ride. Anna—Anna’s kind of wisdom—had responded with, “Good for you that you want a big, powerful horse. Find one and go feed it! This little one will eat weeds and go on in spirit when your big ones turn around and demand to eat before they go another step. How often would you work a big horse compared to what you must feed it if it were big and powerful? And your big, strong horse will bog down in mud...remember how the Knights had to have a week of sunshine after a day of rain before they would trust their big horses to run?” Anna’s wisdom. God, he missed that woman! Missed everything about her...everything. There’d never be another Anna. Even that heavenly night with Elspeth...God, that woman talked all the time! But she surely enjoyed being a woman, and she enjoyed using a man!

He could talk to Elspeth...she listened and had a similar story. The one thing about Anna was that she was fearful of his stories about Bren and the wise woman and Gair...she thought they were all witches who enchanted him and put bad thoughts into his mind. He wouldn’t argue against her; she always seemed so certain in everything she said...but his stories WERE real; he had lived them!

The only question she ever asked was if he had a story about a woman other than the old wise woman he had mentioned. Apparently she had some concern about women, but not old ones. When he said the only other woman who had been in his life before was his mother, that must have been the thing to say, as she had liked that answer and told him to please never tell her any more about the time he had been kidnapped or when he went north by himself, or that ship or canoe.

He never did tell her more, but those stories ran in and out of his thoughts like children at play. They were his stories, his losses, his nightmares. Those, she would not share with him...but those only.

At the next mail-relay station Ashley halted and—after some talk and too much exchanged coin—swapped Bess and ten silver sovereigns for a strong, young gelding.

"I need a runner!" he had told the post-operator. "I must get to Salem as soon as possible; my child lies ill there!"

Another lie for which he'd have to account to God when he arrived there...oh, well...maybe God would remember the reasoning behind this one and let it slip.

In mere moments his saddle was onto the new horse and he was away, running! The station-manager pocketed the sovereigns and guessed the mare could do four leagues fully rested, and that was all she was required to do on a daily basis when a post-rider took her, so the swap was a good one for him.

This time Ashley's horse was a gray and used to running. Another part of the disguise: a gray gelding instead of a chocolate mare. He had also changed into his damp white shirt and had orally changed his direction with the mail-station manager. If someone—the posse—asked about his destination, they'd hear "Salem" instead of Boston. *Maybe*, he thought to himself, *I'll be a spy after all.*

Back at Woodstock's farm, his wife had been worried when he left to chase after the boys, worried when he returned, saying they were fine, worried when she told him the same posse which had stopped him along the road had stopped there at his house as well and asked about that quiet Captain Lyons; worried when—after some thought—her husband snatched up a musket and rode off down the road at a direction he never used; worried when he was not soon to the house; and worried even now, at his telling of what had happened...Mister Woodstock spared his wife no details about events.

She asked, "What if they had killed you? In not recognizing you or in black anger? What would we all do then, without you? You have a big family to live for!"

"I didn't think Deputy Russell would kill me…not when he knew who I was."

"He could have shot you from afar or any of those others…they're all such a scruffy bunch…the man is handy with a gun, they say of him, as are they all, that trash!"

"That he could, but Deputy Russell likes to confront his victims, see them squirm up close. I relied on that. That same bunch killed my cousin in Rehobath last year for netting fish! I had a score to settle and these men are the only murderers around here! Whyever they hunt Lyons we may never know. But no matter what they say, and no matter that they currently are the law here, they are all liars and brutal killers. I had to do something."

"Mister Woodstock, you are an incredible man."

"I could use an incredible meal."

"I have something else just as incredible for you."

They both smiled. All the children were out of the house.

It was good to be back from the near-dead.

Incredibly good!

CHAPTER 19

Ashley had waited outside the outskirts of Boston before going all the way in, hoping darkness would shelter him in case anyone watched for him, regardless of the full moon and its light. After deciding Francis Lane was a Royalist and probably was familiar with the Frenchmen, he realized the plot to invade New England was huge and real, and many were involved—too many to just ride to Pennyweight's store and show everyone he was there. Imagine—in his lifetime—a country across the sea stood ready to invade and steal this land: unbelievable! Well, unbelievable until one realizes it was the same plan England used to snatch this place from France, who mapped it and already had—according to Bren—been discovered and mapped by the Norsemen…so more assault upon this land would only be another in a long line of many.

He had pushed this horse hard, but the animal didn't seem to mind, probably because all the mail-relay riders drove their mounts fast for three or four leagues, then changed them. Regardless, he wanted to rest the horse as he wasn't sure if the Providence posse would continue to chase him, and a rested mail-horse would rapidly outdistance their tired beasts. Ashley had gone a long way off the road, into an area where he could look down at it but still have a way out to run were he chased. These men were too good!

He thought he wasn't too far ahead of that team from Providence, and sure enough, only mere minutes after he had gotten into this place, the eight riders came cantering along, their horses frothed and wringing wet but still running at what seemed an easy rate for them. Damn! Even with his rested horse he'd probably have been caught! These men pushed their steeds to the maximum; who would do that but angry men. Just to see the horses from a distance, he knew they were being ridden into the ground and would never be the same after this run—if any lived to complete it, as they'd probably die running. Those lawmen would be walking soon, their horses founded or dead.

So they went past, and now he had time to spend. He re-arranged some brush and small limbs from trees, making sure no one could see him or the gray mail-horse up there. He wasn't at all familiar with this area, but on the outskirts of every road into a city was a blacksmith. They were needed—the horses of the sheriff's men would need the first they met. The posse would go there and the smith would either have horses for sale or would know where they could get fresh mounts. They wouldn't be paying for them: the city of Providence would foot that bill and never for a moment realize it was for nothing but anger and a seditious cause.

He sat there and watched, thinking of Anna, his heart's companion. So much had already happened…however could he tell her all of it? This thing, this investigation, this chase after spies in order to find addresses and write dates and reports led him on…consumed him, directed him…even excited him.

He must have dozed, for he suddenly realized it was night, and coming slowly toward him was a faint light…a dull glow…and then he saw the white, lacy dress of Anna. She was walking toward him, her arms reaching forward—to him. Then she was in front of him, holding him, leaning into him the way she ever did, whispering in his ear: "I want to be with you."

He heard himself say, "How?"

Then she whispered, "Don't die." And she was gone.

And he was awake and it was another day.

Much later—but before sunset—he saw the lawmen riding out from Boston, probably with their new horses. Maybe they had warned all Boston…maybe there would be roadblocks of sheriff's men with their eternal questions, maybe not. He waited a while longer, until the sun had set, then rode along.

The ride in to Boston again remained scenic. This time he approached the city from a route different than the one he normally used. The Blue Hills obscured the final rays of the sun's light—those which had gotten through the misty sky after all that rain—but he had noticed all the new buildings being constructed and the evening bustle of the outer city. Coming in at this time of the day, Boston lay dark and somber, a brooding hen cached with her chicks, protecting them by showing herself.

A good way into the city he began to see the lights from the ships, then those of the long, cargo-laden wharves, places where perishable goods forced laborers to load and unload regardless of the hour the sun or moon made, and not minding if it were raining, hot or snowing.

In the daylight he enjoyed watching the ships and boats in Boston's Harbour...his window in Pennyweight's store/home had always given him the best view of the Great Wharf and all the shops alongside until someone put tall buildings across the street and on the wharf itself. Without those, he could have watched the Frenchmen himself, from his room, and Elspeth's brother wouldn't have had to ever be involved.

Ashley liked the watercraft, all sizes and shapes—each for a different reason—liked to watch them doing their dance upon the waves, bobbing, moving up and down, those tied in the water swaying together, tilting to the wave-movement and the wind's breath as it endlessly arrived scented from other lands across the great sea or chilly from behind the Blue Hills, in an endless drive to touch everything it saw and move whatever it could with differing but unseen fingers of strength.

He rode to the stable Pennyweight used and turned that horse into an open stall, knowing there would be grain and hay waiting: that's how this stable was run, no worries about whose horse went where or whose horse got what, they were all permanent customers here in this private stable and no one but the usual renters came here with horses.

Then he went over to the back door of his mother's home and went in through the mud room and into the kitchen. His mother, in the kitchen with Ruth, saw him enter and rushed to him.

"There have been sheriff's men here, looking for you! They say you killed a notary in King's Town!"

"Oh, God! No! I never did that! I left that man alive and well, then took papers to Rufus for him. I never touched him, much less kill him! He was alive when I left there."

"Ashley, I believe you; their sheriff does not. You'll have to hide upstairs while..."

"He'll not hide anywhere," the voice of Mister Pennyweight called out as the man himself entered the room. "He's leaving right away!"

"Oh, my God, Mister Pennyweight, you'd have my son arrested?"

"No, wife." He hugged her for a second as he came up to his stepson. "I'm taking him out of here right now! I've spoken with the girls about this and we have a plan."

"A plan?"

"A plan to get him out of here in case he were foolish enough to come here at all. Ruthie, the clothes; Esther, the carriage."

Both daughters dashed away, preparing to help their big brother.

"Ashley, the sheriff's men say you killed a notary in King's Town. You look me straight in the eye and tell me otherwise. God will decide this right here and now."

"I tell you the truth and I swear in God's name: I never hurt or touched or killed that man, nor do I know anything about that. I liked him! We had business for Rufus Case to discuss and we spoke about London and then I went to Rufus with papers the notary had for him…then to Providence and I have just now returned from there I swear before God that this is the truth."

Pennyweight clapped him on the shoulder. "And I believe you! Ah, here's Ruthie."

Ruth had brought a long nightshirt, a bonnet, a pillow and knit booties.

"Take off your vest and shirt—and boots. Ruth will put them in a satchel for you, with some food. We're taking you to Granite City, to Lander's Stables, where you'll get a horse for Duxbury and let Rufus Case send you somewhere from there. Rufus wrote to us earlier and we received the dispatch from a special rider."

"Rufus wrote? Why do I have to take off my things?"

"To put on woman's clothes, with a pillow upon your stomach. You're to become your mother with child, headed for the surgeon."

"Oh, my merciful God!" Ashley's mother gasped. "You and the girls thought all this out? It will never work!"

"It's the only plan we think *will* work, especially at night. Change immediately, son; and let's be on our way. Hold your stomach with both hands, lean over and pull that bonnet down. Say nothing, but if asked, only groan. Be the best woman in labor you can, as your life and ours may ride on your performance."

Ashley changed his clothes, rolling up his trouser legs and pulling on the booties, nightshirt and bonnet. Esther returned with the carriage and then "assisted" the very obviously childbearing "mother" into it. He sat on the floor, bent over, a "pathetic piece of pathos," as the notary would have said.

Esther and Ruth got in, one on each side of him and Mister Pennyweight took the reins, driving out onto the street where immediately a pair of men from the sheriff' awaited them.

Pennyweight whispered to Esther, "Bend over Ashley and hitch up your dress so an ankle is exposed. Give these men something more to think about than Missis Pennyweight."

Esther grimaced but bent over her "mother," her dress by itself hiking almost to her knees. By then they had arrived at the roadblock of the sheriff's men.

"No time to stop, gentlemen; my wife is in labor and we take her to the surgeon!"

Ashley groaned a few times and Esther and Ruth replied, fussing over "her," talking rapidly to her, seemingly in an attempt to calm and soothe her before the child arrived, whispering also that "she" shouldn't speak or groan so loudly and that everything would be fine—which was the only thing Ashley didn't want to hear, as when someone says "Everything will be fine" it usually means: "I hope." Ruthie kept up a wailing cry, yelling at her father to hurry, that they had to get to the surgeon in Granite City: a pitiful scene, way overplayed, but probably not so well accomplished as one of those banned plays in England.

The sheriff's men—muskets ready—looked into the open carriage warily, saw Esther's bare legs and the rumps of both girls, remembered their prayer-meeting teachings about lust, and turned their attention quickly back to Pennyweight.

"Go along in God's name," one of them said, waving the carriage forward.

Pennyweight left as though he were in a great hurry—which he was. "I'm sorry to have to put you two through this," he said over his shoulder to his daughters. "Maybe we're right; maybe we're wrong. All I know is that if God didn't want your brother to escape, we'd have been found out and arrested then and there."

"I'd have fought them!" Ruthie volunteered.

"Oh, Lord..." Pennyweight sighed, holding his left arm as best as he could, then giving the reins to Esther and holding his left arm across his chest.

They drove to Granite City—down the seacoast road and turning to the right where the Merry Mount sign was displayed...Ashley looking warily at the deserted cabin and wondering how he ever got out of all that mess there.

Outside Lander's Stables he changed his disguise again and donned fresh clothing his mother had packed.

"I was afraid they'd see the stubble on your face, Missis Pennyweight," Pennyweight chuckled. "A close call, too close. There must be no more of these, you understand?"

"I certainly do. Are you in pain, Mister Pennyweight? Your face seems to grimace now and then."

"God puts nothing more on us than we can bear. Listen: Landers owes me money he'll never pay and has for two years, so we'll take some of that back in the rental of two horses."

"Two? Are you coming with me?"

"No, you're alone on this trip but we can't judge the quality of these nags Landers has, so you'll ride one and lead one. Ride them hard and switch off often. Get to Case's store and have Rufus aid you; he shall, as he wrote that in his letter to us."

"Rufus wrote to you?"

"Yes, almost daily. He first asked me if I would accept written explanations from him; he said he was afraid we might have the wrong idea of the service you were providing for him and has assured us everything you do is legal and acceptable to the assistant governor of Plimouth."

"Rufus' highly placed man he wouldn't tell me about."

"When I wrote back to Rufus and told him I would, he then began almost-daily notes to me, telling me you were writing to him and that you were well. He also implied the work you do is important; I believe him, but I have to ask you that myself." He grimaced again, holding his chest.

"Are you all right?"

"The meal your mother made tonight…I ate too fast and too much."

"You may believe that what I do is important—important to this entire settlement."

"Then we have a need to get you quickly and safely on your way." They got out of the carriage, Pennyweight looking in pain and holding on to the carriage for a while. "Esther, go knock on Squire Landers' door."

He said to Ashley, "Case was my competition in Plimouth, a tough businessman who put me to shame when it came to making big money until I moved to Boston. I didn't like him…respected him, but didn't like him. That's all over, now."

The two of them went over to Lander's door; his lamp on the second floor of his establishment had been lit after Ester pounded so hard upon his door. Pennyweight put an arm around Ashley's shoulders. "You and I have never really been close. That's my fault, not yours. I expected more from you than you were willing to give…no, don't speak: just listen. You've done some foolish things and told some wild stories. I tell you I still don't believe them, but I've come to learn that wild things—like this, tonight—do happen…and perhaps you told the truth more than I thought. Regardless, I do think on you as a son, and you have your sisters to thank for that. You take care of yourself and keep in touch. I shall contact an attorney-at-law on the morrow and discuss all this—secretly, of course; I promise. Perhaps in some small way you can be helped on that murder charge. Ashley: get the horses and ride swiftly. Rufus says he has a good plan to keep you safe and I believe him, but he won't tell me what it is. Take this purse—no, TAKE IT! Wherever you go you'll need coin."

Ashley had never before had help from his family. In fact, his family had railed against him, refused to believe him, called him everything openly except the word "liar"—which was really what they thought he was as a teenager, and held that only the Church or God could or would assist him in getting older and/or wiser. He had been "allowed" to stay at home—or return to it; he had been "permitted" to eat and sleep there without contributing to the household or store. Mister Pennyweight had provided everything for him and in truth he had returned nothing to the man, hardly acknowledging him in his own home. Ashley had left this home several times for several reasons, tried to tell his mother and she refused to listen to the truth: "his truth" was the way she put it. So long as he had stayed home and attended prayer-meetings with them (their one insistence) he was welcome. When he decided to go off on his own, she let him: cried for days, but let him. His mother, early on, had decided two things and stuck with them: one, she had to look out for herself, as life had taught her nobody else would; two, if she allowed her son to disrupt her life and the life of her new husband, she would be the loser, and that was the one thing which she could not let happen. The daughter of Irish parents, she was herself born in England and raised there; she above all others knew what a muddy path she trod in attempting to be "English." "Everything" had to be foresworn: her deceased parents, her former religion, old friends, relatives, voice-accent, even her thinking. To be "accepted" into England's even "lowest classes" she had to be one of them: so she was. She faced everything, got through everything. Got smart and didn't show it; hid whatever money she could; refused to allow life to frustrate her; wouldn't be drawn in by others. She had been refused a pension when her husband—a carpenter at the shipyard for the Crown—had died during his work there. She had been told she'd receive a pension if she apprenticed her son away...but rejected that out of hand, as at that time he was her only anchor and love in the world, and she refused to part with him. She had lived from day to day in London with a demanding, spoiled child; she had bounced from house to house to wherever she could live with her youngster, and finally realized the Puritans had a place for her in the New World as an indentured servant (for seven years). Why not the New World? The old one was treating her worse than a servant and not feeding her!

So she came to Plimouth and literally worked and cooked and kept a house so well that Mister Pennyweight did the absolute unexpected: requested she marry him BEFORE her time as an indentured servant was over. That she did and never looked back. Her son had begun to run away on a regular basis; she then had two daughters. She was cold to her son at times, but times had been cold to her and now she had just begun to enjoy her new life. She told her daughters these were the best years in her life, and they were the best daughters in the entire world. She never bragged on her son.

Landers was an easy man to pry from bed when there was money awaiting him; he was—after all: a businessman.

They rented the horses in the fashion Pennyweight had described: no cost, but a great reduction in the money owed him (Landers was initially disturbed at the arrangement but realized it was the best he'd get and he didn't really want to re-pay an old debt he thought forgotten: his debt to Pennyweight now discharged) then Landers turned to Ashley.

"Swear before God you'll take good care of these horses, stable them in Plimouth, and have them swiftly returned to me…or die trying!" The businessman's oath.

Ashley smiled. "I thus swear, and will do just that."

Landers nodded, then went back inside his home/office/stable.

Ashley was on his way again.

Pennyweight watched his stepson ride away, happy he had gotten him away from Boston but wondering in his heart if he had done the right thing. His career as a shop owner and his reputation as a religious man rested with the acts he presented…and who might discover them.

He felt badly—not sad, but quite ill, and had been this way since Boston and the sheriff's roadblock, hours ago. His heart had been pounding and now seemed to be worse; her had a shortness of breath which was becoming alarming; and the pain across his left chest and down his left arm gave him grim concern. He had held on to his chest and left arm most of this trip…Esther did a first-rate job of driving the carriage and he was proud of his eldest daughter for that and many other reasons.

Deep down, he felt very ill—gravely ill; very scared, thought he was about to die. Prayed even while he stood there…watching that boy who had turned into a man but all his life still had trouble. It all seemed to be enveloping Pennyweight, smothering him, pulling the very life from him. He felt the sweat all over himself, felt himself weakening, felt glad he had gotten Ashley away from Granite City and Boston…just felt weak and suddenly very tired. God, so tired.

He felt his heart pound, felt real pain, grabbed at his left arm, holding his right arm against his chest all the while.

"Father? What is it?"

Couldn't help it: he let himself fold to the ground.

"Father? Father? FATHER?" Screams. He no longer cared, but he wondered why they would be yelling like that.

They cradled their father in their arms: Landers came back outside and watched in amazement.

"Get him into the carriage! YOU! Help us!"

They put Pennyweight into the carriage; he was soaked with sweat and not responding to their shouts or all the lifting and dropping.

Esther somehow guided the hackney to the surgeon the family used and visited on a regular basis. Ruthie just sat there, crying.

Esther didn't know how she could get her father into the surgeon's house...but it probably wouldn't be necessary once she got there: her father already appeared dead.

CHAPTER 20

Darkness. The horses stumbling, they were so worn out from the long, fast run. Ashley sleepy in the saddle and only waiting to get to Rufus' store, as there was no rest in Boston after the Providence run…and run it had been, ahead of that posse of eight armed and vengeful men. He still wondered about Woodstock.

At the stable, Rufus told him, "Go in the tack room; we'll talk there! It was hushed but direct."

"Too tired to move."

"Go there or you'll sleep tonight in the Plimouth Stockade!"

That woke him.

"I'll get you some food and water; Bess is fine in a stall; there's everything in there for her."

"It isn't Bess. I had to sell her to a relay-station outside Providence to get a gelding there for the run to Boston, and I left him there; rented these two in Granite City and they have to be returned there. I need Bess back; please send someone to get her…oh, take the gelding from my father's stable in Boston and swap him back; I don't care about the cost…"

"Ashley, stop! Too much information outside here; you MUST get inside!"

Rufus pushed him through the stable, into the doored tack-room and closed that door. Ashley seemed to collapse on a chair.

"Why would you run Bess so hard you'd have to leave her for another mount?"

"Very long story; everything is written for you, except that I traded Bess and I'd like someone to get her back for me; don't know if the sheriff of Providence will come here; they went to Boston and Mister Pennyweight smuggled me out and got me horses from Lander's Stables in Granite City."

"Across from where he has a store on co-ownership; I know Landers. Why the sheriff of Providence?" Rufus bolted the tack-room door.

"Will you do it?"

"Calm down. Yes, I'll send Michael to return your horses and get Bess. Relax, Ashley; this is not just a tack-room, I had it made as a retreat if ever there were a fire here or...whatever. There's another way out, hidden from the front of the store."

"Why?"

"Why is there another way? In case of fire or hostile's attack."

"No; why all this secrecy? What about the Plimouth Stockade?"

"Our large friend is dead."

"Who? The one I went to see? The notary?"

"The same; killed by someone, there in his house."

"Oh, no..."

"I have not been there to look, but one of the sheriff's men is a friend, and he told me what he saw."

"Which was?"

"Death by a knife...along the side of the neck and across the throat, apparently by someone who knew how to use it. I asked how the room looked and he said everything was in place, seemingly no struggle or fight, and more assumed than apparent was that the man had just been working with inks, as colors of inks were all over his hands and had just been wiped, but not washed off."

"So you suppose someone went there, had papers of some sort prepared, then, in friendship or anger got close enough to him to do him in?"

Rufus nodded. "A terrible and deceitful way to go...the man was so old he'd have died in his bed in not too many years anyway...this is criminal and was not necessary. You and I know it was probably the Frenchmen who did it...maybe it was just a coincidence or maybe they used his skills and got forged papers and killed him to end their trail."

"I lost contact with them because they left Boston too early and on stolen horses rather than with the coach they had rented for a week or more...they could have gone to the notary's first, on their way. God. No coincidence with them around; that's what they do: murder. Everything around here is fine until they show up, then the boy dies, I'm shot, two men die in Merry Mount and now our friend the notary is killed. So since the Frenchmen are here, they must be here for a very specific reason, and Roland got in their way, but the notary?"

"Did a job for them they didn't want known. Changed their names on paper, whatever. Good thing you got my travel-papers when you did..."

"Travel papers! They went there for travel-papers. They must no longer be the Smith brothers."

"That was their name? The Smith brothers? I think I remember you writing that."

"And after he gave them the papers they went over to him to pay him and knifed him instead."

"They had to know where he lived..."

"That's the truth! I've lived around here twenty years and I never saw that part of King's Town before...they had to have local help...maybe someone from Plimouth, someone who knew what the notary did and where he lived...someone like Miles Standish. What bothers me is what could anyone want from all the places they visit that would be valuable enough for all these killings? I can see killing to steal, or coming here as paid assassins, but why leave a trail of murdered men...and the boy? It has to be more than drawing of fortifications...although they do that everywhere they go...has to be something they're searching for or someone...and if they find it they'll leave and never return...otherwise why allow the authorities to know they're here in the first place?"

"Seems like the people they killed were in their way...the boy may have surprised them and they just reacted by killing him...and the notary because he had done a job no one wanted known..."

"And their real task was to go places, get drawings of, whatever, but also..."

"The drawings are incidental to their purpose."

"But why wait until the end, after they go several places and just before Providence...wouldn't they want to have their travel-papers ready right away? Why not him first?"

"Because it *is* the end...they leave from Providence after they do that job, and they—in addition, have received new travel-papers. Maybe they didn't really need them, or thought on a whim to go to him as they were already traveling south. Maybe they knew him, where he was."

"Then that's it, Rufus...the whole trip is pre-planned for these men. They have a timetable and a map. They arrive and know where they'll be every day, and when they'll leave. They go around, getting something, then stay within their schedule and now they're headed to New Amsterdam..."

"Where, be assured, there is plenty of money..."

"And then England, on a ship which—although it stops in Bedford, then returns right away to London. Why kill the child? I can understand the notary. They could just as easily told the boy to go away and he would have..."

"Fear, anger, just for the sake of it..."

"Something they would do in their own country...they feel that safe here."

"Ashley, you must be very cautious..."

"Don't I know! And we never mentioned killing Roland because they wanted to."

"Who would just kill a child?"

"Roland is seen by them, watching them on the wharf as they do something...something we don't know about. These are men who probably have been in someone's war and are used to killing. Killing to them means something different than it does to us: they kill Roland just because that's what they do...the way they tried to do with me...for no reason than they set the fire...just...something they do. Roland is there and they see him; they kill him instead of sending him away. They saw me in Merry Mount and tried to kill me for the same reason: because I was there."

"They tried really good, but missed you. The fat man made their documents—and may have made others for them; we don't know how many times they've been here..."

"They kill HIM for no other reason than that's what they do: kill. Blood lust. They enjoy it."

"Then, others will die."

"I guess they will...I don't know how to stop them; in actual fact they almost stopped ME! I know what I'd like to do to these monsters...we don't know how many in Providence they killed."

"No, Ashley; you're just reacting to all the deaths and your own attack. Don't become one of them by doing or thinking the way they do; you're above all that."

"I've never carried a skinning knife on me before; always had one in the saddlebag, but never carried it as I do now. If I get close enough..."

"Stop it! That's idle and foolish talk and un-Christian! You can't become one of them—that's impossible for you, with your upbringing."

Ashley frowned but did stop speaking. Rufus pulled up a chair. "You carry a skinning knife?"

"Yes."

"Good leather?"

"Bought it here; you tell me if it's good."

"Three years ago, now, as I remember."

"Yes; before Anna...she didn't like me to carry it."

"Er...I have something...uh..."

"You're never at a loss for words, Rufus."

"Now, I don't condone you carrying a skinning knife, all right? It's far too easy to get cut badly by one of them if you carry it and play with it."

"I know that; the edge can cut you as you pull it."

"But the broad edge of those needs a heavy leather, and it's bulky to carry."

"I carry it anyway; prefer it to the long knife."

"No, no…that's not what I'm meaning to say…not that you shouldn't carry it, just that it's inconvenient to carry such a knife, looks bulky to everyone, and they all know you have one. But…"

"But?"

"But I have a vest I've made…and a fabric I found to line a hidden pocket so a person may carry one of those in safety, be searched by the sheriff, and usually the knife will not be found."

"Really?"

"My own invention. Presently, it's not practical, as those who use skinning knives do not wear vests, and those who carry knives do not use broad-bladed ones. But someday…oh! Here's the best part: you're left-handed."

Ashley stared at the wordy Rufus. "And?"

"Almost everyone in the world is right-handed. Pistols and clubs are always carried under or around the left arm. My 'pocket' puts the knife by your right shoulder, where very few think to search. Not a coat, but a lightweight vest, easy to wear, gives some warmth when it's cool, and people think nothing of it—it's just a vest. Here, I'll get it for you."

He reached into a drawer in the wall and pulled out an abbreviated-style of vest, which Ashley tried on. "Fits nicely; made for me?"

"Hahaha…made for ME! But we're about the same size, although I must admit it recently has become a bit tight for me; that's why it was in the drawer. I suppose you'll need other clothes as well…I can't send you anywhere in pants with holes and shirts with worn cuffs. Whatever would people say?"

"Send me where?"

"Away from here! Somewhere…maybe New Hampshire or…London?"

"I have been thinking London. My greatest fear is that the Frenchmen are a full day or more ahead of me again; those men don't just sit around; they move! It's a wonder they sleep at night, time is so important to them and they go to so many places."

"They caught a ship from Providence to there."

"True. To London; it's in my reports. Excelsior Ship Lines—I talked to them in Providence and the Frenchmen should already have left there, but they go first to New Amsterdam and Bedford, so it'll take extra time at sea."

"Then you'll go to London?"

"Happy to, but I'd have to go soon to get ahead of their ship so I could see them land and follow them from there; but I have no travel-papers."

"I was only thinking to get you away from here, not to have you keep following them. Those are bad men and better left alone once they leave here. Let someone else in London follow them. In London..."

"London is a big place and even if I see them they won't see me with all the people and buildings...not like all these open spaces where you can see half a league away."

"I worry about you; I promised your family..."

"I have to go! Feel like it and I can't stay hidden here."

Rufus reached up and pulled on a cord above his head.

"What's that?"

"When I do that it rings a bell for Michael in the store; or if I'm in the store, it rings in the stable. He knows then I need him or he has something else to do, someone is arriving or leaving so he can get a horse ready. He's in the store now, and will bring some food for you."

"You live like a baron here."

Rufus smiled. "We all do what we can. Ashley...be especially careful, will you? The Frenchmen may go to London on a ship, but then to another country, as I assume they went to the fat man to get travel-papers from him; the sheriff said there was too much ink for just one or two sets of papers; whatever he did, he did a lot of it. Ink was all over his hands and around him. So you may see the Frenchmen dock, and then you may see them leave on another ship bound to France or somewhere. Oh, Ashley, do you remember seeing a man and his two sons driving an ox when you went to see the fat man?"

"Yes, a farmer younger than me with two barefoot boys and an ox pulling a hay-cart. Passed them on the road outside his house."

"They told the sheriff you were the only one on the road besides them that afternoon; the only stranger they saw all month out there...he wants to talk to you, imprison you."

"What? Imprison me? Why?"

"Ashley..."

"Everything's fine, Rufus; I'll go talk to him, then after that return here and go from here."

"Not so fine...the sheriff's man says you'll be arrested for that murder, as there is so much evidence against you."

"How can that be?"

"Afraid it is. You're the only one seen there. No other suspects. He wants this cleared up fast, and you're the one he wants to pin it on; he needs a suspect; that's the only thing he does, so he has to make it look like he does 'something' for the people."

"We know the Frenchmen did that…the sheriff won't believe me?"

"Ashley…the job of sheriff is a political one. There's a murder and if he doesn't arrest someone right away, the tongues start wagging that he doesn't either know his job or won't do it. But if he gets someone right away—even the wrong someone—people stop hounding him and maybe the person he arrested gets cleared, but by then the community has relaxed about the killing or the real killer is caught. Either way, you could easily be imprisoned a long time, and just as easily hanged."

"Whatever shall I do? What CAN I do?"

"That's why we're in this room. You've got to hide or go somewhere other than Boston. I know an Indian chief; he'll take you in. I already spoke with him."

"Back with the Indians? I'd rather be chasing the Frenchmen to London!"

"You probably couldn't get there ahead of them anyway."

"Rufus, you're not listening. Their ship went to New Amsterdam, THEN Bedford; then it goes to London. If I catch a ship out of Plimouth, I might make it to London before them."

"To do what there? To report to whom?"

"To do what you paid me to do: observe and report. Only. Don't you want to know what ship they leave on? Or where they go in Dockside?"

"How do you know that's their plan?"

"I'm learning to be a spy."

"God's blood! I've gotten you deeper and deeper into this!"

"I have to leave here anyway and don't want to go to an Indian village. I was raised in Dockside, London, and know where to hide and probably still have boyhood friends there. I'll watch for the ship, *City of Leeds* and will see what they do once they're in London."

"You'll just observe and report? Not involve yourself in skinning them? Seriously?"

"Just follow; that's all. Follow, write a report and send it to you; meanwhile, you find me a better place to hide than some village in the woods. I've thought about New Amsterdam."

"You're thinking too much these days…all right; I'll see if we can send you to London."

"Who's 'we'?"

"I. I'll see if I can send you to London."

"You will have to ask yourself?"

"Michael is never here when I need him."

"Who will pay for all this? Not you, as you've no extra money: you put everything into the store."

"All your expenses will be paid—I'll have the purse tomorrow."

"From whom?"

"Not your concern. The fat man..."

"Why do you keep calling him that? He's a man like you and me and now dead, but in need of having his name said. Even the Woods-People speak kindly of their dead for a full year."

"Walter Foster."

"Thank you. I saw that name on your travel-papers."

"He...he has relatives...who will pay for any retribution to him...even if all you do is find out where his killer has gone. Just do that and they will pay out of a private fund they have."

"They will send an assassin."

"Not your concern."

"A minute ago it was 'us'; now it's 'relatives'? Who will pay?"

"Just know that relatives will pay but I shall handle the money and all the information-passing."

"You're beginning to sound like a spy yourself."

"Don't say that, even poking fun! The relatives will pay; I will funnel the funds to you; you send me the information and I shall handle everything else."

"I have no travel-papers."

Rufus sighed. "I thought on that. Use mine. I have planned for this past year to go to London in the late season...so...you take my papers; everything is in order. We're not the same age, but the start of that beard you have makes you look older."

"I'll shave it off if that's what it does for me! What else do you know about Walter Foster?"

"Aren't you too tired for all this?"

"Just talk, as you do that best and seem to know everything."

"Somehow he lost two fingers."

"How is that? What do you mean?"

"Not common knowledge, but he had two fingers cut off him before he was slain. The sheriff's man told me. There was so much blood from the neck that they didn't notice the fingers...only after a surgeon looked at him."

"So they *did* do it: they killed him! But why cut off two fingers? Oh! I know!"

"*You* know?"

"A demonstration; they cut off his fingers to make him do something…to demonstrate what they would do if he didn't comply. One of the Frenchmen said the fire at the store was a 'demonstration.'"

"The fire at your father's store? He said it was a demonstration? He *told* you they did it?"

"Said it was a demonstration, but I can't remember much more of what he said…I lost some memory when he shot me."

"You're lucky you didn't lose your life."

"Right. Which two fingers?"

"Ummmmm…The left hand, small finger, and I think the same on the other."

"See? A demonstration of what they'd do if he didn't do something for them with all that ink and those seals."

"Those fiends!"

"I keep telling you they're not nice people."

"Ghastly! Who would do that? Sick men!"

"Driven men…needing something he wouldn't give up at first. I've got to search his house."

"No…search his house? Whatever for? Anything there of value was taken by the murderers and what would you find? Nothing. Besides, you can't go there and the sheriff has a guard there. Impossible for you to do that; why would you want to?"

"There's something there…a piece of the puzzle."

"Nothing left there but an empty house and you don't want to be caught in it—they'd kill you on sight if they found you there. Foolish move; besides which, you must leave for London—you said."

"I want to go there…stand where they stood…look around."

"Well, you can't! And what about the sheriff of Providence?"

"He was chasing me with seven men, all on horseback and all armed with those new French flintlocks Miles Standish was talking about a couple months ago."

"Why was he chasing you and how do you know they had French flintlocks? Those are not allowed to be exported; France keeps those for herself."

"I saw 'em. Looked through the branches at them and saw them again when they passed me on the road. Different silhouette than a musket and plenty powerful; shoots instantly, instead of waiting for the spark to catch and jump or the powder to catch. The wave of the future in long-guns, Rufus; you should get some to sell; people would go wild over them...and those damn French again! They have everything!"

"Their country is old enough and rich enough and big enough *to* have everything. Is this where I ask you why the sheriff and his men were chasing you?"

"It's all written, but I followed the Frenchmen there and got the addresses. A blacksmith who owns a combination stable, tavern and boarding house was working with the Frenchmen and wanted to lock me in a room there."

"Merciful Heavens!"

"I got away...it rained..."

"Stormed here three days and nights."

"Same rainstorm. I started out the third morning and the posse came after me. I tried to hide in a tree..."

"With Bess?"

"Very funny. Those men wanted to *kill* me, not arrest me! They were trained better than the Plimouth militia, walking back and forth and searching so well; I just knew they'd find me, they were so thorough."

"I'll see the assistant governor and he'll contact Providence's governor and we'll find out what happened and why."

"What happened is that Squire Woodstock who sheltered me from the storm came to my aid, fired at the posse and they hightailed it after him. You'll have to get Woodstock out of gaol, if he still lives; if his family still lives."

"They are that bad there?"

"They were to *me*!"

"God in Heaven! They have that power in Providence to chase and kill?"

"You yourself said Providence was full of criminals."

"Yes, I did. All those who dispute God's teachings go there. But I didn't mean the whole community was full of criminals! Just that criminals go there, it's so liberal in its religious teachings and politics."

"Well, not all are criminals, as Squire Woodstock proved that to me; and not all dispute God's teachings—as Woodstock's family is Catholic and they saved my life twice."

"You truly met a Catholic? I don't think I ever have."

"Save it. There's bad men in every religion and everywhere; but there's a bunch of Royalists in Providence...and Salem also."

"I got your letters and we're acting on that information you already sent us."

"Who is 'we'?"

"Well, you'll find out in London. Now I'll go see what's keeping Michael and the food, and you get some rest in this safe-room. The escape door is there: pull this lever and shut it behind you if you have to run."

Rufus left, peering cautiously out the tack-room door before he opened it all the way, then closing it quickly so no one outside could see in. Ashley reached to lock it and Michael was there with a covered tray of food and a pitcher of water.

Some things you do because you have to do them…you're not forced to nor really want to, but you know they have to be done: like dirty dishes in the sink have to someday be washed or tossed out; but somehow, some way, some time, you know they'll get washed. Same as having to do some other things. Just the same. They just sit there and you know deep down that no one else is going to ride up on a white charger and do them, and they really need to be done…so you simply go ahead and do them. That's why: no other reason.

Ashley tried to sleep: couldn't. Stared at the ceiling. Talked out loud to himself, just to hear words that he might understand what he was thinking. "Sometimes I think I'm looking in the wrong direction. Like I see red in the sky and expect the sun to come up and it's not the sun at all but a forest-fire a league away. I don't know; I can't explain it. I've been chasing these men, watched two of them die, caused Elspeth's brother to be killed and maybe Woodstock…what would these men be doing without me chasing after them? They wouldn't have killed Roland because he wouldn't have been there; the five would still be alive and going to Boston, Salem, Merry Mount and Providence; no fire would have been set to destroy Mister Pennyweight's surplus goods…they killed the notary but not because of me: that may not have been their mission but I didn't have anything to do with that and am blamed for it all! He just got in their way, somehow.

"They come in, do their drawings, visit places, only stayed a week and now they're leaving—maybe already left. They have to be spies…going along the coast, getting cannon-emplacements and making maps and visiting people. Has to be for an invasion fairly soon; there's no real defenses in New England; no one cared to buy cannon or point what they have and there aren't enough cannon-trained soldiers here in the whole colony to shoot them anyway.

"The entire place lies open to invasion. Oh, people might hide in a local fort or in the woods…an invading army would expect that. But there would be no real defense if ships cannonaded the towns, then released marines onto New England's coast.

"Why would they kill the notary? Maybe he knew them...could/would identify them before they got their drawings to Europe. Probably that was it. Some seedy European who had done business with the notary years ago, heard he was here, came over to steal his papers and seals, cut his fingers when he refused to do what they said, maybe forced him then to notarize a paper, then they did him in to silence him forever. Everyone needs travel-papers these days to get aboard English ships and land in other countries...if I can get into that house I might find out what country they go to...well, London, as they are on the ship, but where after that, and when? I have to look; I have to get to London, also. Only can do one thing at a time and I then lose the other. Maybe more pieces of this puzzle are at the notary's house but maybe the puzzle itself is going to assemble aboard *City of Leeds*. I have to go to London; the Frenchmen make puzzles everywhere they go."

Rufus returned some two hours later and woke him. "The price of success!"

"What does that mean?"

"It means you've been so successful that you're being sent to London to tail the Frenchies, even longer. You're the only one with any experience and you have to get away from here anyway. Put on your good clothes; I just checked the tide-tables and *The Regal Prince* will sail in the next two to three hours. We'll have to get you to Plimouth and aboard her."

"I use your papers?"

"*The Regal Prince* is a government ship; the assistant governor of this colony appointed me to a governmental committee, so you can take my papers and ride her to London with no other documents than my appointment-letter and the travel-papers I give you. We'll have to go now, to get you there. Better this way; the sheriff will never find you if I can get you aboard. I'm older than you by a decade, but that stubble on your face and the darkness will help. Don't shave off that beard!"

Rufus had a new traveling-bag already packed for him, razor included for arrival on the mainland and new clothes for him to wear. The two hitched-up a carriage and Rufus took the reins.

"Stay low on the floor; put that blanket over you to beak up any silhouette, and hold on tightly; I've got to more than move along as I don't know the specific time the ship will leave." He flipped the reins and the big, hackney mare pulled, moving steadily and getting into her pace for the trip. Seemed like she already knew the importance of this all, and intended to take them wherever it would be at the fastest pace.

"On the tide." From the floor.

"On the tide as the master of the ship so says. Sometimes they drift out a ways—like that one I had to be rowed to when I saw Per...and they hoist the sails there, just for room to maneuver when the wind is up or down. You stay concealed and I'll get us there as fast as this mare will take us, and this one's fast: faster alone than with two together. If we miss *The Regal Prince* you'll have to return and hide four days before another ship leaves."

"I thought of something I don't like."

"What's that?"

"The notary in King's Town, killed on Saturday."

"Yes?"

Ashley waited a moment, thinking, then went on. "Last Saturday the militia meeting and practice was supposed to be held in King's Town."

"So? Was it held there? You didn't attend."

"Michael told me Miles cancelled all practice until a new captain is chosen, probably only another week, but last Saturday there was no practice at all and *that* Saturday they all would have been in the roads and fields throughout King's Town all day, different groups doing different things at the same time—concurrently, Miles called it—seeing whomever was riding the roads, seeing the Frenchmen!"

"It couldn't be Standish...bringing in those Frenchies to kill the notary..."

"We don't know yet, only suspect. I'm just wondering..."

"That bastard! That little, conceited, shrimp bastard!"

"You left out 'red-headed'!"

"I'll tell the colonel!"

"You don't know if that new English colonel is in on this all; he's from London, I heard. One of Cromwell's soldiers the Lord Protector sends here to train us in the art of English fighting, Cromwell's way."

"Cromwell's way is to use cannon to wipe out the enemy before his men go to fight them; the Scots say that is not fighting, but slaughter. Not many like Cromwell or his way."

"Lord Protector Cromwell owns England now, with the King dead."

"Ashley, what's the reasoning for that English colonel in the red coat to be up Standish's arse all the time?"

"He's here—I was told when I was a captain—to advise Miles of the new laws Cromwell imposes and to show the colors...that red coat is Cromwell's latest invention for the Army. He decided the Swede's Army looked good in their colors, so he's had red coats made for everyone in the Army and he trains them all in pike, sword and musket; they're replacing the matchlocks."

"All? Every soldier gets all that training?"

"Every one. They also get religious training, rough and tumble, they have to walk...'drill,' I think they said...There's an iron discipline, not like the militia. You look the wrong way in Cromwell's Army and they flog you."

"Merciful Heavens! Who would want to join that?"

"They have good food now, not the slop Charles the King sent them, and they all are armed, every one. They didn't all have shootable weapons, years ago."

"Who will he invade next, with that 'shootable' army he's already savaged a defeated Ireland. How much more blood can he spill there?"

"All that is Catholic. He despises Catholics and the pope. I heard he will go to Scotland to win that...we'll see about that one. The Scots won't take kindly to an English invasion."

"What in blue blazes could our Walter have done to upset Cromwell that he was allowed to be killed, and then the blame shifted to you? Those bastards!"

"So the Frenchmen are spies, and they are killers, and they may or may not be working for or with Standish and the Colonel...what have we uncovered?"

"A garbage pail, it stinks so bad! Ashley, we have to turn around, get you out of here!"

"Why? We're almost to Plimouth dock!"

"Too much death and underhanded dealings. I can't let you go to London after these men...that's suicide for you!"

"I can't stay here with people thinking I killed the notary and maybe others—that's what the law does: they get a suspect and throw all their unsolved crimes at him, and if he's found guilty of one, he's judged guilty of them all, so they clear their files of all the unsolved crimes at an innocent man's expense. The sheriff looks good and the community breathes a collective sigh of relief. I need to get away and stay away, I guess. I can't live on the frontier or with the Woods-People; Bren tried that, didn't like it. I have to do this. I have to find out what all is happening so I can understand it, put reason to it. Then I'll see what I can do, where I can go."

"Are you sure? I can still get you away from here; we've several hours before a full search for you begins and I know most of the roads where the sheriff's men will patrol and block."

"No. London. That gets me away and puts me back where I grew up. I'll find old friends there, but I'll still write to you—but not daily."

They rode in silence a short time, then, seeing no roadblocks or people along the streets, Rufus ventured a question: "Aside from what you told me, how did you find Providence? I've always wanted to go there, maybe set up a store there."

"I found it with ragged, stoney walls and cheerless talk, as in New Hampshire."

"I presumed more from there, the way it's said to grow."

"Oh, there is more…fortunes being made by some—like Lane. A great river to the ocean and well inland—like the Thames—bringing in people daily. I found a nest of spies and Royalists and lawmen who wished to be assassins…and good farmers and new businesses."

"Cromwell's influence extends its arms across the Atlantic, then…business breeds business, even in remote portions of England's holdings."

They made it to Plimouth Dock with time to spare and without incident, encountering no roadblocks or stoppages or sheriff's men at all; the sun coming up, pushing ahead of it a sky with orange-colored clouds shaped in a "V"; a beautiful sight to behold, and Ashley thought this might be a sign from God that things were well in Heaven, spilling over onto Earth; certainly things this morning were good for him, for here he was, escaping from the clutches of New England's long-range law while maintaining his lead in ships and is need—his desire—to further follow the Frenchmen and discover their secrets.

"All right to get out?"

"Yes, I don't see anyone but those on the ship and hawser-handlers."

Ashley unwound himself from his cramped position on the floor, tossing back the horse-blanket and standing, then grabbing his bag and starting to get out.

"Ashley…these men you follow are professionals. They know what they want and how to get it, plus they seem to have unlimited help."

"So do I."

"Promise me that you shall be careful, that I may write that to your mother."

"I promise I shall be careful, but cannot promise someone else will not take that carefulness from me, and you needn't tell my mother anything, hear?"

"Don't joke; this is serious."

"Not a joke. I was careful in Merry Mount and look what happened. How does one promise to be careful when another promises to end that carefulness? Don't suddenly be my mother, Rufus. I'll take care, all right?"

"Don't die. God, don't die there."

"Thank you for your support."

"I mean it! Don't die! If you do, I won't invite you to the Thanksgiving meal."

"Then, how could I promise otherwise? I promise I shall be careful and I won't die."

"Sometimes I don't know whether to believe you or not."

"When I come back you shall now I kept my promise."

"And if you don't come back?"

"Then I am either dead, in prison, or in the arms of a beautiful woman...and in any of these instances, I won't care to come back."

The credentials Rufus provided him had Ashley on board the ship before he thought to turn and wave a goodbye.

CHAPTER 21

The English sentry stepped sideward a pace, blocking any entry to the King's tent.

"Aside, sentry; I'm here on the King's business!"

"My Lord, my gracious King prays. I am to let no one in whilst he does so."

"I have news for the King! Need I tell him his sentry blocked the way of his tutor?"

"My Lord Tutor, the King himself said to my face, 'I will pray three times a day; I have been told this in a dream. Twice with the Scottish Bishop and once with the English Bishop. At these times when they enter, you will lower my standard to the height of your head. Then, I do no business of the Army, just the business of Our Lord and Our God. When the Bishops leave, raise again my standard, for then I do the business of the Army.'"

"But surely, King's Guard, you would let *me* in."

"My Lord Tutor, a recent day, a messenger arrived here with what we thought was news of extreme importance to us all, and I let him pass."

"When General Fairfax threatened to quit the English Army and leave them waiting without a Commander, south of us?"

"Yes, my Lord. The messenger had ridden all the way from there and I allowed him to enter during a prayer-hour."

"So if you let *him* in, you can let *me* in! My news is that General Fairfax, in accordance with his vow to King Charles the First, *has* quit the English Army; a paper to that effect has been published for all to read and now there is no one qualified to lead the Army in England!"

"My Lord Tutor, when the messenger went inside, I heard the King scream, 'Ahhhh…what deadly news is this that interrupts me so!' The messenger swooned on the spot in fear, and I—because I had allowed him to enter—wet my pantaloons and wailed in agony to hear the terrible death I'd have because I allowed invasion of the King's prayer."

"But you're still live."

"I live; the messenger died in there: never recovered of the swoon. So I say this, my Lord Tutor: I must bar entrance to the King's Chamber and this other guard will as well: this Scot who stands beside you and has sworn to the King will also do the same, on the words of the King. There is nothing else we may do. After the dead messenger was removed, my Lord King said this to our faces: 'Unless there is a fire which is destroying us or the English Army comes over yon hill, your King is not to be disturbed in prayer.'"

"This is new, that he prays with Bishops."

"My Lord King takes upon himself the weight of the Army. He prays for food for us, he says, and a victory over the English."

"That King Charles or his Army would require such prayers is a sadness. He might be better off praying that Cromwell's forces have eaten their horses and now have none to pull their cannon."

CHAPTER 22

Not since he had been eighteen had Ashley Lyons been aboard a ship on the high seas. This was no modified caravel—the type which had carried him to Hudson's Bay from the Debatable Coast of the Carolinas—this was a 46-gun English ship-of-the-line, a frigate whose change in length, beam and sail-plan from previous English ships made her faster than most ships of any country and far more dangerous to other ships as her rigging and equipment had been improved and she could maneuver better, out-sail, and outfight whatever she found in the Atlantic. Way above him, sailors were laying out on the yards, un-snugging. The ship was more than ready to leave; he actually had made it just in time.

Rufus' papers had gotten Ashley a berth aboard as a courier of official documents for the colony commission in London—in Rufus' name—and the two colonists had caught *The Regal Prince* as she readied to leave Plimouth Harbour. It hadn't been four hours since Rufus started his rush to get Ashley onto this ship, that Ashley was across the gang and escorted to a small cabin by a lower officer of the ship.

"When I was young, it took a fortnight and two for this trip to England."

"We'll almost halve that, Squire Case, and we go further than 'England,' as we sail up to the northern waters and go into the Thames. Your colonist settlers left from southern England. *The Regal Prince* is a fast ship and will get us anywhere we go quicker than almost any ship in the world except those with more sails."

"Then this ship would be faster than a French ship I know about which already has left Providence?"

"This frigate can out-sail, outmaneuver and run before higher seas than any French ships. They are changing to this model! Your Providence ship may have a day or two on us, but we'll be in Dockside before any Frenchie enters the river! At least a day before her!"

Ashley's shipboard cabin—the one Rufus was to occupy—was but a tiny room hardly larger than a closet in Mister Pennyweight's house, containing two cots—one above the other—and a slatted door which he supposed permitted the necessary light during the day, as it was at the bottom of a short flight of steps which led to the main deck, and therefore allowed air-circulation. He shuddered to think of how two men could function in this "room" at the same time.

"A bit sparse for a gentleman, but high privacy and comfort for a lower officer in England's Navy," he was told.

Ashley stowed the gear he had with him, looking through it and sorting it, not for any reason but to do something as everything here was going to be done for him regardless of how or what he wanted. "Putting away clothes" was not something Ashley usually did (Anna or his mother would have told anyone that), but this was a lot different from his usual experiences and in truth he was nervous about this entire trip, the hastily made plan, the excitement, the worry, the chase after spies to what was now a foreign land to him. He usually just went out and did what he did and wasn't nervous about anything—took things as they came and dealt with them; but all this was different. Things were coming at him from different points of the compass. He couldn't trust Miles, the sheriffs in at least two towns and probably three were looking for him, the notary was dead and they all thought he was the killer; he had sent Elspeth's brother to his untimely death...the Frenchmen kept trying to kill him, shoot him, burn him, cut him...Boston had become a trap and Plimouth was no better. Providence was too new and cunning: it had men who played games to get money and showed no loyalty to anyone. Why not London? Why not?

A beautiful dawn. The orange-colored clouds before the sunrise turned into white and held up a blue sky. At the cabin in Duxbury the trees were so tall and thick that it was an hour after sunrise before they actually saw the sun there, but here on the sea there was a light spreading everywhere, long before the sun came into view. Daylight before daytime: a wonder of the ocean.

On his trip to Hudson's Bay, Ashley had been able to move about the ship as he cared, when he wanted. That crew was friendly enough, never speaking to him, tho'; but there were no restrictions placed upon him and he wandered the decks as he felt, day or night. On *The Regal Prince*, he was told he could not go deck-side during the day at any time. He was permitted to be there after the workday was over and all through the night, but never during the daytime. But this was a blessing in disguise, as then all the crew was available at once to speak with, and few at night had any assigned duties.

As Ashley had left Plimouth and boarded this ship he had seen a man wearing a silver belt-buckle. Anna had given him a silver belt-buckle on their wedding night and he had put it away for safekeeping, then forgotten about it and left it in the cabin in Duxbury. Remembering this put him into anguish—that he could have cared so little for her precious gift on their blessed day that he would leave it behind. Saddened him to no end; brought tears to his eyes; increased the already-dark mood he was in. Had to do something about that.

He took his writing portfolio, sat quickly, daubed ink on the quill and wrote a letter—a note—to be sent in the post-dispatch:

> *Rufus, please be so kind as to have someone look in the clothing-closet of my former home in Duxbury—the cabin—there to locate for me my silver belt-buckle. Anna gave that to me after our wedding. Ashley.*

Heavy sigh. "I tried, Anna…I tried."

The Regal Prince was a picture of beauty, running before the wind, her sails wide and puffed, a butterfly upon the sea, all canvas laid out and in use: mizzens straining with topgallants and royals billowed, spanker laid aside and the mains full as they could be, stays'il and jibs tight and wood masts creaking under the strain, their courses taking the inner wind and tugging shrouds and ratlines all the way to the platforms and gaff. This was as good as it could get for any seaman, being part of a fast ship and her knowing it, responding to the wind as a woman to a lover, holding it close, using it, making it part of her: causing excitement and danger, thrills and release, speed and desire.

The first night aboard he fell asleep in the lower cot in his "room" as he'd been so tired he'd have slept about anywhere. When he dreamed, he dreamed of Anna, became desolate knowing that even in his dream she was gone. Then Elspeth excited him in his dreams…just the thought of her so many leagues away from him made him shiver for her, her touch, her naked body waiting for him, wanting to be combined with his…There was pleasure, but no relief.

The second night he fell asleep sitting on the deck—to be awakened in the morning by a kick and a voice which told him to go below. The third night was a restless one…waking, dozing, moving about. This time he felt he had to accomplish sleep but was awakened by shouts and the scurry of men past his cabin door. He peered out, then when the passage of men cleared went out and up the small set of stairs to the ship's open deck, where a voice yelled at him, "Get below and stay there!"

He backed down quickly, aided by the now-pitching ship. A storm had come upon them, apparently rapidly and possibly without warning. The wooden ship's great sails had to be furled fast lest they lose them; others had to be opened and aligned; and in general, the entire crew was out there and preparing for a heavy rain and great blow. Ashley wondered if this would be his fate: lost at sea with those of a hundred countries who had dared the deep waters and were now deep below them.

He left the door to his cabin tied open. Not long after, a ship's officer—one of those few friendly enough to him—came by. "No alarm; we're fine. Just a quick piece of weather we've now gone through. No damage. Sent us in the right direction. Good training for the men, actually; hard to find those training-storms: something to be concerned with without worrying the ship will tear apart and sink. Have a pleasant sleep."

And he was gone.

"A pleasant sleep!" Ha! Ship still tossing and rain pouring. Wide awake. "Have a pleasant sleep" indeed!

He couldn't sleep the remainder of that night, just lay there and thought: wondered for a while if he should write a poem about all this. He had written Anna a poem one time—before they were married. She had read it with a puzzled look.

"Is it that bad?" he had asked.

"Not that it's bad...I would never say that about your work...it's just that I don't understand what you're trying to say."

"Then it's bad."

"Never say your poetry's bad," she had told him. "I'd rather close my eyes to a sunset than say it was bad. I only said I didn't understand it. Tell me about it."

Anna knew how to approach things. She knew how to walk way out on thin ice, how to milk a cranky cow, how to make him feel really good and boost his spirits even when he knew he shouldn't respond that way...that's the way she was: caring, compassionate, charitable...a woman caring for plants which would produce blooms so short-lasting that even in the dark they never closed. He never would—never could—understand the reasoning she used.

One time he had brought home a dressed-out deer and she said, "I know God gave us dominion over the animals, but I'm not convinced that meant we can kill and eat them."

"Then we'll have to kill and eat your flowers, because I don't know what we'll eat if not this meat, and it's a sin to just throw it away."

She shrugged: the fight was already lost. "We'll have the meat, as the creature is already dead and we. alive, must have something...but I'll speak with Elder Otis about that."

She was hard to convince, but her concern rattled the way he had thought. *Suppose*, he wondered, *if the wild animals who weren't in the Garden of Eden weren't included in Man's domination? Would it then be a sin to kill those?* He'd have to see Elder Otis about that. He'd have to see Elder Otis before Anna did...but later he forgot all about that.

She didn't.

Elder Otis—the pragmatist—told her all animals—whether they were present in the Garden of Eden or not were presumed to be included in the domination. It was God's way of showing man was part of God and above the animal, then must man eat them to propagate in God's image and prepare the earth for Christ Jesus. She wasn't happy about that explanation but she accepted it; but she didn't volunteer that information to her husband. Let him worry and wonder. His mother said he was a "willful child": let him find out for himself—it'd stay with him longer...unless he asked her. She smiled to herself over that knowledge. It was fun, keeping that big, strong husband of hers a little off-balance about the meat he brought home...almost as if it were stolen and sinful to get or keep or eat it. One more piece of information she had that he didn't.

Sometimes he just wandered the ship aimlessly at night, staring almost sightlessly across the water. Always a black sea. In the daylight there was sometimes a green sea, sometimes blue, sometimes blue-black...always with whitecaps. The Ever-Sea: constant, churning, full of life but barren at the top. A place of wonder, beauty, fear and awe. You just don't—can't—realize it until you're out there: out on it. Then you know. Then you wonder. Then you feel fear at the starkness and detachment of it. The Ever-Sea. Looking at it each night he became lost in his own world, wracked with thought, never feeling the wind or spray, never hearing the sounds of the sea or the noises of the crew or the creatures of the night. Gone. Gone away. Detached. Not present. Not expecting nor wanting anything to happen...just staring without realizing. There but not there.

Aboard ship you live for the night. Day work is done; the darkness gives you rest; there is an escape from the whole world and daytime work. The sailors at night sang songs of their lives and the sea. They loved—Ashley could tell easily—their lives and their adventures. The songs told of sadness, leaving families ashore, wives, women, children...going of to the sea they loved equally well but always with misgivings.

Sad men. Lonesome men. Men who loved and left, ever happy to return and pick up the broken pieces left behind on land. Glad at sea; glad at home on land. Lost at sea; lost ashore. Men who had traveled so far, so long, they only knew traveling while they waited not to travel.

Men who chose the frightening sea to rid themselves of the confines of land: sailors. Just sailors. Ashley thought they were the toughest breed of man he'd ever met.

There was a chill off the water at this time of night which went all the way into one's bones. Damp, but not so damp as Duxbury; cold, but not so cold as Duxbury. Just a feeling from the dampness and the water, probably because there was so much of it...getting in your head, getting in your bones, getting in your life. Rufus' vest didn't much keep it out. Something like the reason he was going to London: couldn't keep that out of his mind either...leaving everything and everyone he'd known for the past twenty years and going across a wide ocean with someone else's identity and reasons...trying to help himself recover from Anna's death and both babies more than find some Frenchmen. Just moving...just keep moving...maybe nothing would touch him if he just kept moving and he'd move through everything and come out the other side without a scratch. Wondered then what was on the other side...what would happen if he couldn't find the Frenchmen and failed utterly in his quest—but that couldn't happen either! He HAD to find them; he HAD to beat the murder-accusation back in King's Town; he HAD to get information to Rufus and whomever it was who had started this arrow flying.

And then, thinking of the arrow he remembered the fight between the Anakapi and the enemy tribe in their wooden vests. Twenty years ago...still haunted by those memories...still frightened of the dark because of those caves...still afraid of deep wells like the one he had gone into for Bren. Just still frightened.

He didn't like the dark: everything was random then, waiting. Too many tales about the dark,. people hiding, children frightened, the worst things seemed to happen in the dark. And on the sea...the dark became worse because all things imaginable could be there, from a pirate ship ready to broadside and board to monsters of the deep, reaching up to grasp the ship in tentacles or claws and either eat it or—worse—drag it below the turbulent waters to drown and then eat everyone aboard.

Night on the ocean is not quiet. The dark seems to intensify the sounds, and the sounds are all their own. If the night is otherwise totally silent, the ship's bow, crashing through the water sends its noises all the way to mid-deck; and the creaking masts, spars and hull broadcast weird sounds. If there is wind, the sheets snap and flap, the sea rushes past…even the inhabitants of the water seem to create their own harmonics and send them through the heavy night air to frighten the listener.

But the night is good for thinking, and on a ship's deck upon the sea during the night is a good place to think. He sat on a coil of rope, playing back in his memory the past two weeks…couldn't let it go, had to stay with it, eat it, drink it, sleep with it, think about it all the time. Worse than a wife; more like a demon inside him, eating at him, forcing thoughts. It drove Anna from his mind and his caution from his senses. Needed to stay thorough, also; had to learn to be a spy, had to change his clothes once he got to London and go to different places each time he went out. Set no pattern for anyone to notice him. Had to remember it all, cover all his tracks, be more as an Anakapi slipping silently through the forest, bending but not breaking twigs. Had to build a system he could use at a later time. Needed to complete everything, stay thorough, get it all and write it for Rufus. Seemed he was standing on one side of a river, looking over to the other side and hoping he could find a bridge to take him over there. Had to be a bridge somewhere; he just hadn't found it yet, hadn't looked in the right place. There was always a bridge and someone always had been there ahead of you. Perhaps this ship was such a bridge.

He slept, but it was a troubled sleep…only a few hours, then a couple hours of strange dreams…drifting in and out…a semi-sleep he was able to remember. Bren. Bren standing there, his words being said but him not moving his lips: "Huzza! Pour le pays sauvage!" Then the caves…a series of tunnels high enough for one of those dwarf mounted-riders with those long pikes and wide enough to let their carts pass through side by side…"The Woods-People kill carelessly"…"I thought no one would care after all these years, but King James has a long memory"…hoping that so long as he walked he wouldn't freeze to death walking, wondering all the while if he were too asleep already to wake or too frozen to thaw…"The woods never change, just become a bit more familiar."…"Long life to you!"…Threatened from different directions. Strange, interesting, familiar, frightening, ugly, terrifying dreams…dreams from twenty years before, in that land under the land.

Every morning on the ship when he was in his cabin he would wake when the crew dashed past his louvered door and up that short set of steps, scrambling onto the work-deck to turn out for the morning work-details, not so much from their talk at that time—as they were strangely silent, these running men—but from the noise generated through that scrambling. Everyone other than the cook was on deck in the day, and everyone on deck worked—no one didn't—assigned a job or given one to keep them busy or busier, doing whatever was necessary daily, and additionally if the master or circumstances required. Monotonous work, the same, day after day, month after month. Work for work's sake. The kind of life a Puritan could understand and embrace. The entire community working for the simple sense of working, to fill the day only.

Night was different. Everyone had worked all day, so after the evening meal everyone who went to the deck rested, relaxed—other than those who had drawn 2-4 hour shifts for watch, steering or whatever—and enjoyed their life at sea.

Ashley asked a sailor how deep the ocean was at this point and was told, "Doesn't matter, so long as it's deep enough to pass the skeg of this ship! Anything deeper than your height will let you drown, and only a drunken sailor thinks the sea isn't deep at all." Lots of bitterness and philosophy there; no answers, tho'.

The next night changed their routine.

Sunset that evening was not the usual sight. Heavy, dark clouds filled the horizon behind them, blocking out the usual, beautiful way the sun had of retiring. Everyone aboard the ship knew it was a mean storm, hoped it wasn't coming toward them, prayed for safety as so far the passage had been uneventful and rapid.

They all turned in early to get as much sleep as possible before they were called to deck; lookouts were doubled and posted on the dog-watches to pay particular attention to any storm movements. A couple hours later, when the mainsails began to creak and the royals turned, they knew the storm was more than "coming": it was upon them.

The master of the ship was told immediately and he turned out the crew to prepare the ship for a hard blow and maybe worse.

It started as a squall, became worse. Became heavier. They turned against the weather-beam to run with it, a bit off course but the concern now was not the course but the safety of the ship.

Ashley heard them going up the steps, not so noisy as in the mornings, but noisy enough to give a concern to him. He heard the shouting from the main and master's decks, knew the men were going aloft in the dark with rain falling ahead of a gusty wind. He was glad he didn't have to watch them go up there—glad most of all he wasn't one of them going to the high rigging to reef the topsails and furl the mains...take in line, re-set it, shift the direction of the sails...how did these men know what to do? And if they were to fall...? To fall to the deck would be quite bad enough, but to drop into the sea to drown as you tried to get up to the surface or—worse yet—to finally get up to the rain-soaked air and battering waves, yourself broken by the fall or even only bruised, then to see your ship fade fast away before the wind, leaving you there...God! Too much anguish to even speculate about. Whyever did these sailors do what they did? Well...they looked for adventure and legitimate work and a different life but got terrorized by old sailors and young officers and squandered by captains. He had a taste of that as a cabin-boy out of Boston. A short voyage was all Ashley needed of THAT treatment!

The ship was now pitching, rolling, plunging...still seeming to respond to the wheel (the ships these days had "wheels"—unlike the steering of the *Mayflower* or *Lilac*) going fast, going heavily into the waters, shuddering at times. Frightening. The sounds now were only of the wind and the noises from that dreadful creaking and moaning of the masts and their trappings. No more shouts; no more deck sounds, just the rain hitting them in front of the wind, the dreadful pounding of the rain.

It was probably less than an hour, but then it was all over. The storm had run screeching past, the terror of a storm at sea had vanished, blown itself away literally. Then Ashley slept. The sea was still choppy, but they ran under close sail for the remainder of the night, a light rain teasing them, continuing for another hour, then no longer there. Came around to the original course and moved along, all relieved.

That next night, the last before they would make up into the North Sea, Ashley was on deck, speaking occasionally with one of the lesser officers—some mate or something: he couldn't understand ship's titles or designations. The sailor seemed upset and as they were well away from everybody else, spoke out briefly about that last storm.

"We lost a seaman, a boy, really, new to the ship and told never to climb the lines and didn't; then last night an officer panicked and ordered him topside and in the wind and rain he fell—into the water. Shouldn't have ever been sent aloft; terrible mistake. None of it will ever be written anywhere: they'll say that during a heavy storm a seaman became unaccountable. The Officer will have his pay docked—volunteered on paper to pay for the price of a funeral at home for the boy—and he'll have to do extra duties the remainder of the voyage, but none of that will be written either. They protect each other. His extra duties will be listed as voluntary and he'll get a better position on another ship when we reach London."

Ashley stayed on deck that night, thinking of the way the boy who fell had died and thinking of what he must do in London. Worrying again. Just worrying. the return to London was doing it and to hear that sailor-boy had died in the worst way—and so carelessly—hadn't helped either. And nothing could be done about that.

Standing on deck by a rail later that night, the cynical sailor who had told him about the "depth" of the sea wandered over, one of those new "pipes" for tobacco in his hand. Ashley's adopted father smoked a reed pipe which—in his language was called "tobacco"; the French had re-named it, and later the leaves he had smoked were replaced by the leaves the English called "tobacco." In only a few centuries the European had corrupted everything the Algonkin society had forged for lifetimes.

"How long do you think I've been a sailor?"

A partial moon lighting up the deck.

Bored: "Five years."

"Fifteen! As long at sea as my life was on land before I came to the sea. I never expected to be a sailor; I expected to plow land, plant beans, tend oxen, dig wells. Instead, I am grabbed one day and thrown aboard a ship. Fifteen and the toy of the crew! I cried; I pleaded; made no difference. We sailed and I sailed with them. Then came the night and they would use me. I resisted, so they laughed and pointed to the water. Go! Jump in! Leave us to find another with a tight arse. Feed the fish!

"Let me tell you I cried. I wanted to jump in, to drown, anything to get away from those beasts with pricks. I felt as a virgin must at a gang-rape, for that was what it was. Then I knew it wasn't just the water or the men that frightened me, but the comment about feeding the fish. That, I didn't like.

"So I stayed, completed the voyage. Almost a year. Then we got back to home port and I left the ship, headed home forever, never to go again near the water. My father had died in the coal mine and my mother—with no son to assist her and no other family—had been faced with whoredom to support herself, and killed herself. So I went back to the ship and found my old job waiting, but a new boy had taken my place with the crew, one who seemed to enjoy his nights at sea.

"So, here I am, fourteen years later, still sailing and never leaving the ship because I have no place to go. Do you have a home, sir?"

"No...not any longer."

"Then I know how you must feel and you know how I feel...just homeless men, always at sea, even on the land. Saint Elmo, pray for us both."

He offered a pipe and tobacco, which Ashley promptly but courteously refused.

The sailor lit his pipe while Ashley waited, wanting to leave but feeling he'd upset the man further if he just walked away from him.

"I'll feed the fish in the end. They'll have me after all. Now, all I do is wait, but now I'm the one who gets the fresh arse first."

Then Ashley left.

Sitting now on the deck—early in the morning—frightened to think; frightened not to think—to plan. Remembering a story told earlier by one of the crew: "I shipped to Odessa on the Black Sea one time. We could go to any tavern at dockside, so I went in one and a foreign-looking gent who talked English spoke to me. I asked what they had there for breakfast. 'Boiled beets,' he says. 'an' if you're here for dinnertime it's the same thing.'"

"I wouldn't want to live there," a sailor responded. "At least the beets here have molasses on 'em!"

The whole group laughed. Molasses was a staple of the Navy. Get some spoiled or salty food and pour molasses over it to get it down. Then chase it with the only other staple: grog—Portuguese rum.

False dawn comes early on the sea…long before the sun rises there is light. Then that light seems to fade and another arrives: false dawn and then dawn. Like a man thinks: almost gets a solution but doesn't quite—then he does. There's things that rattle around in a person's head…memories, usually of bad times. People seldom remember the good times—the quiet times—until they're reminded by someone…but they sure as lief recall the bad ones.

Sitting, thinking, remembering, trying to get together the puzzle of the Frenchmen without knowing what the finished one looked like, what it would look like to someone else…just wondering: and then the bad times returned. Anna and the unborn baby, their first child dead—his son—the boy, Roland, his tiny throat cut from under his ear to under his mouth. Ashley knew from militia-training why the cut was placed like that: it severed the great blood vessel to the brain and not only killed a person rapidly but almost immediately stopped him from doing any final thing: reacting, trying to get away, call out, any sort of aggressive move. Elspeth angry, that love affair probably ended. The attack in Merry Mount, the notary dead—that blame shifted to him…the thoughts all seemed to strike together in his mind, faster and faster they came, all together and yet all separate. Still a puzzle—all the pieces but no start—just all the scattered pieces of awfulness.

Everything started when the Frenchmen arrived. Too many coincidences. The five arrived in Boston and the boy died; two in Merry Mount died—but not by coincidence, but co-incidental. There WAS a plan, a thing they were doing; he could see that as they moved around, but hadn't an idea of an ending. What were they doing? Why was the boy killed? Why the notary? Everyone in Boston could have seen them yet they pick a boy to kill; why? Why the notary? He had gone there also, gotten the papers for Rufus, So if the Frenchmen wanted false papers, why KILL the man when he obviously was delighted to do things like that, and from all the ink Rufus said was around, they must have gotten papers. He and the boy were innocents: they had to be. Why would the Frenchmen just enter a colony and begin to kill "stray" people?

Were they that stupid? Or were they here to kill the notary, got frightened and killed the boy. That was more like it, but there was another side, another angle, another matter...if they were here only for the notary, they'd be gone. But they didn't kill him first; first they went around Plimouth, then Boston, then Salem and Merry Mount; then it was King's Town and Providence. That was the pattern. Drawing maps, meeting people, killing a man, going all the way along the coast...for what?

Why have five men? Why five? No spy in his right mind would call attention to himself, lest attention to himself with four companions! So he's not a spy. May be spying, but not a spy. May be gathering information for someone, but not a spy; probably not an assassin either. No hired killer works with four people around him...so, not a spy, not an assassin, but they kill. Maybe the leader didn't set out to kill, but directed them killed as incidental to what they did, and his companions killed them. Who would do that? It was all very sad...people with so much hate or willingness to kill to line their pockets or just to see the blood...so much death. God, so much death. Ashley gave his head a slight shake and it brought him out of his reverie. The sea had gotten rougher as they had left the mainland shoals behind them and were now out into the area where the cold Atlantic kissed the waters above the Spanish stream, a new battering of that tide assailed the ship, pushing and tilting it at the same time.

A confusion upon the foredeck happened and for no other reason than boredom, Ashley cautiously made his way forward until he was near a ladder which attached the main deck to where the ship's master and his crew of officers directed the wheel.

"He won't sail with me again!" he said loudly.

Then there was a short silence.

"Keep him below and out of my sight!"

"Don't you have him on my deck again!" Same voice.

"I don't care! Throw him overboard or throw him in chains...not on my ship ever again!"

Apparently the master was upset with a crewmember or one of the high-ranking officers, most likely an officer. Only officers directed, gave orders.

"Oh, my!" Ashley said aloud. Then thinking: *Why were the child and the notary killed? Because the Frenchman directed it, probably in anger, just as this ship-master would have a man thrown into chains or overboard. Then those four men with the Frenchman were his bodyguards or servants—although servants don't take upon themselves the responsibility of riding a man's horse or shooting someone in the back of the head. So they were his bodyguards...but who had bodyguards? Rich men. But these men were not rich: they rented horses and had to return them...stayed in cheap lodgings...no, not rich. No one else had bodyguards but royalty—and there were no present royalty in England but they were "everywhere" in Europe, and the way these men were traveling was not in the style of just anyone...so the leader—the Frenchman—had English-speaking bodyguards and probably was minor European royalty...sent here to...map? They'd send a map-maker alone for that. Kill? They'd send a lone assassin and no one would see him. Couldn't be an older man...had to be a young one, untrained but angry. Yeah...someone with a title who'd have bodyguards and think this mission was a lark. Lord Protector Cromwell had banished—exiled—Charles' family but Charles did have a young son...an heir to the throne. Oh, God! Could THAT be what was happening? Royalty here to meet certain Royalists, to get notarized information-documents to do something, go somewhere—then silenced the notary to halt the flow of that information along to anyone else? Killed Roland simply because he was there and shouldn't have been looking at a King's son? Because the man was angry—like the ship's master—at that time?*

But any English royalty would already have access to the New England coastline maps drawn years ago...so...not English royalty: some young Royal from some country who wanted to gain information, move around, see what is here, how this coast could be taken, then perhaps return to France or Spain or wherever and tell a relative that information. Just someone—five—wandering around, gathering and taking messages to people. No pattern because there was none: that was the puzzle: the pieces didn't fit together because they were being made here. Royalty traveling "sans rosa" as Rufus once said: in disguise. Some young European Lord who wanted to be a spy, a killer, an informant...God help us: God help me!

They were out of the North Sea and into the Thames before sunup, the tide carrying them in. The friendly ship's officer—awake early—stopped to chat with Ashley.

"They're talking about a new Navigation Act put forth, stopping all but English vessels from bringing goods into England."

"Didn't King Charles do that?"

"For a while, but this one is worse: bad for the world and stupid, as all other countries will then do the same thing to the English, to hurt us...and that will. You know as we stand here right now, today, we are on the brink of war with Holland's Provinces? We got fresh dispatches from a passing ship as we came into the river."

"I wasn't aware of that."

"I know more than most; getting around from port to port and hearing things from passengers and ships who hail us...war looks inevitable. A new magistrate-general is due to be elected very soon in the Netherlands, and if it is that young DeWatt...You know how rash youth is; he's only twenty-five; what a child for so high a position!"

"Then it seems the world will have war again?"

"So long as I have lived, it has seemed thus. Did you know Lord Protector Cromwell had defeated the Irish?"

"No...not at all."

"The last of May but he has kept his victory a secret in his war-plans. He has gone now to Scotland with sixteen thousand to take the place of Fairfax—who resigned. Another Charles wants to be King of England."

"Don't they all! Charles is there in Scotland?"

"Apparently has been for a while. They made him King there; well, he was—by law—King here when his father died, but Cromwell challenged that and Charles didn't stay around to argue. He left for Ireland and gathered a few soldiers there; now he's in Scotland, but not with Irish troops: Scots, all."

In his thoughts, Ashley remembered his Irish friend, Brendan Splaine, who had told him about the disgraceful and miserable ways England had treated its island neighbor, wantonly killing the Irish only because they embraced the Catholic pope and his religion—the self-same religion and position as pope all England accepted as her own a century before. So it wasn't "religion" England fought for, but domination of Ireland and all other states She could rule. The

Puritan government going into Ireland to take over was almost a joke, as two years previously the Presbyterians were ousted from Parliament (they had themselves abolished the Church of England in 1643) and England currently had no particular state religion to follow. The Puritans destroyed Irish religion to bring Puritan "business" to Ireland, not Protestantism. Charles of Scotland was more a Catholic than a Protestant, and it was he who now fought Cromwell to see whose religion England was to follow. Who could keep up with all that?

Ashley made a face at all the history. "We're out of the ocean; why are so many sailors up in the topsails?"

"A ship cannot sail without a directing wind, so if the mainsails face east and the wind is from the south, we can't move well on our course. We keep the main sheets spread, but turn the topsails to the wind, and our ship spanks along, waiting for the wind or the master to alter her direction."

"And the days there is no wind?"

"We get out in the boats and row, pulling the ship toward a heavy cloud, as there we'll find wind again. Have to go: England awaits."

CHAPTER 23

London was fabulous! London was a fairy tale! London was a gigantic city of tall buildings' spires, domes and towers. The Thames was laden with ships from all over the world…caravels, galleons, frigita…with varying styles of sails and differing numbers of masts. Ships in seemingly all sizes and from all countries, and not just the great ocean-going craft, but small boats, private sailers, independent luggers, barks, those of multiple decks and single ones. King Henry the Fifth's triple-thickness clinker-built had long since sailed into the Hamble River and that style was long gone, giving way to faster, sail-packed vessels. Regardless of any naval restrictions, there were all here and welcome.

Fishing ships all the way from the New Found Land Banks and Iceland were here; cattle and sheep in herds of thousands were sent here by ship and then their products removed the same way. Mined coal and copper, seasonings and spices, salt made from sea-water, eggs, chickens and turnips…all things which could be taken by watercraft were found at this place.

It didn't seem as if the food supply of this great port could ever dwindle, but so many people lived here and more arrived daily that as the food disappeared, prices rose. Good for some; bad for others.

The new-business companies had their own ships and boats, decorated in advertising and some carrying minstrels for sweet harmony to lure people to their products. The Queen herself—when she lived here in London—had a barge she frequented on this Thames.

And there were rowboats with people, people on the docks, people hanging out of windows, bustling on the streets and in and out of businesses: people seemingly everywhere. Ashley couldn't remember so many people when he lived here, and trades-people all over as well. Dockside alone had more buildings crammed together than Ashley had ever at once seen or could recall: shops of all sizes, styles and reasons for being…bakeries, corner barber/

surgeon offices, sellers of all things and the most amount of tiny stores possible to use whatever space was available.

There were pens where sheep and cattle were loaded or unloaded and held on a temporary basis, tin shops, piles of coal, cloth-makers, wool-fashioners, tailors, a place which cast bronze and anchors, sailing supplies, tack and leather-goods, even an iron-works with a blacksmith's hut attached was present. And this was just the arrival-point for the traveler. London herself lay outstretched, beckoning, sending her siren-call and expecting an answer.

And the houses. When he'd left here, the tallest house he could remember was probably three stories—similar to the one Mister Pennyweight had built in Boston, with the merchandise on the ground level, living-space for the family on the second, and sleeping quarters on the third. All the merchant's houses here were now three and four-story; mostly all new and usually whitewashed, with real windows of glass—not just a hole in the wall which was covered during rain and sealed for the winter. There were some gentry-houses also, along the riverbank and a few on Old Thames Lane.

Houses of great men—merchants, mostly: the new aristocracy—towered ten and twelve stories' high, their advertisement banners flapping in display; hulking monoliths of stone and wood with spiked towers, tin roofs, and dozens of windows these buildings were…the triple commodities of gold, wool and wheat maintained the peak of the world's business community and this all was expressed in the houses. Other commodities and products were important, but secondary. The world knew what it wanted, and London was happy to accept it or ship it through its great port.

Ashley Lyons smiled wider and longer than ever before. Here had been his old home. He had all he could do—just staring at what he could immediately see of the sights of his old hometown—and as he did, tears leaked away from his eyes, disappearing as puddles on a dry, dirt road. His London. Home again.

The Regal Prince had arrived at the mouth of the Thames during the previous evening, but had to wait until high tide commenced, as the Thames had never been a deep-water port. The Thames was the Thames…a tidal-flow within a country; a great, liquid worm which gathered its mass and strength from the North Sea, devouring portions of London and eating halfway across England before finally succumbing to the heightening land. Yes, the Roman fleet had come here—and all others since, from every country which traded with this island-empire—but the long, additional passage once in the river and the difficult wind-maneuvering once upon it, aggravated at the end of a storm-tossed sea-passage and added more time to it.

The Regal Prince came up to her pre-selected dock-space and warped in, and while this was about, the few passengers and their baggage were escorted to the main deck and held in readiness for departure there. The gangs went out, a pair, and as the passengers were signaled to disembark, crates and cargo began moving dockside. This captain was true to both passengers and freight.

Plenty of lights on the docks, here at night; more so than in Boston, where a carelessly hung lantern scarcely provided no visual cornucopia for the worker there. These workers could readily move cargo around the clock. Dockside workers knew what to do and when, when it came to shipping and receiving. This place WAS the world.

Before leaving his week-long home, Ashley shaved off the ugly and itchy beard he had grown; another small change in his disguise. Once ashore he thought he'd locate a barber and have his hair cut to a London-style as well (what hair was left after Matthew and Ruthie and each removed some). Proud of himself that he was so involved in their "spy-disguise" routine; looking forward to being "un-noticed" in London.

They had berthed west of Old Depford, and to the east lay the old home of King Henry's Dockyard, where Ashley's father had worked. The whole area had changed: wharves, piers, brick replacing wood, pens for animals, cranes and harness for cargo...lots more business than when Ashley as a child had been here. Ships from all over the world came and went from here regardless that it was arguably the most difficult port to reach—to take on or off-load cargo.

He left the ship's area, looked for where the passage-sellers had three booths and offices, and way down on the street-side, located the Excelsior Ship Lines sign: the same boasting sign as in Providence (We go to China, the Indies...etc.) What braggarts these people were! Inside, a clerk with nothing to do laughed when he was asked when *City of Leeds* from New Amsterdam would arrive.

"When she gets here, *if* she gets here."

"There is no date when she might arrive?"

"Tides, storms, cargo-readiness, pirates, sea monsters...do you know how difficult it is to cross the Atlantic Ocean? The trip back is easier than the one over there, but a laden ship runs low in the water and...I wouldn't want to be a sailor!" He reached over and grabbed a piece of paper with figures on it, then pushed it across his desk at Ashley. "This is a list of high tides for every day this month. *City of Leeds*, if she arrives, will be in on one of these...or maybe next month. There's a tuppence charge for this."

Ashley took the list and responded with coin. "Seems there's a charge for everything in this city."

"You're right there! We've had a grain shortage; the newly elected mayor wants paid constables at night instead of the free volunteers we now have; the shipyard says it will replace all the wooden buildings with brick…and Lord Protector Cromwell has decided he wants to pay his Army!" He shook his head. "In my day, we were in the Army to eat! Now they want to be paid, also!"

"Time's are changing."

"They certainly are!"

"Do you know what *City of Leeds* looks like? Amount of masts, whatever?"

"She's a converted French man-of-war, tired and creaky. That's why her owner was able to but her: she's old, but with a galley-style bottom so she can handle weight. I don't remember what she looks like…know her owner but don't care about the ship."

"You don't know what she looks like but you work here?"

"I'm only here until a better opportunity comes along."

"Who's the owner? Of *City of Leeds*?"

"Older man from the Baltic…Leipins…Squire Leipins; lives somewhere here in London. Only have met him…a tall, thin, handsome man with lots of hair; don't really know him other than to recognize him when I see him here."

Ashley thanked the agent and left…looking for a rooming house from where he could see the exit out of the shipyard…then finding one and getting a room with a window placed so he could sit inside and watch those who left the Dockside Yard. At first, the owner of the rooming house wouldn't even acknowledge to his new guest that he even HAD a room available which faced Dockside, but so soon as his new guest told him he'd pay "extra" for such a room, he suddenly remembered he had just the room which was requested, with exactly that view, wax-lights included (not simply wicks left in oil) which could be lit from the downstairs fireplace.

Funny how money can change a man's memory.

Ashley was also told a daily meal came with the room: "Green cheese with onion tonight; buttermilk and clear water." Yeah…that was a "meal" all right. He'd find a tavern for his food; Rufus had given him coin for that. Ashley had hoped to eat "wheaten bread," a very fashionable tho' expensive bread, creamy-yellow in color. Less expensive breads were darker; "black bread" was cheap—a mixture of wheat or rye and oats; but the usual "horse-cornbread" those in poverty knew was made with beans, peas and oats.

He paid double for the room: worth it for a good view of the gate at Dockside. (Glass windows were the fashion here; in Boston, his attic-room window had been covered with waxed paper in the winter and left uncovered during the summer.)

There was so much additional space in his small furnished room, much more to begin with than his berth aboard *The Regal Prince*. He could put three of those "cabins" into his little upstairs room in Boston; this rented room was almost the size of his home in Duxbury...and not actually the size to which Ashley was lately accustomed: he could have put his entire cabin in Duxbury into the "great room" of the notary. Incredible!

There was—in this room, of all things—a mirror. He was startled to see his defined reflection: how he had grown thin, gaunt, sallow of cheek. His clothing seemed to hang on him as the notary's had: the shoulders of his shirt falling down past his slanting shoulders and the worn sleeves dropped past his wrists. "If my mother could see me now she'd say I was wearing my brother's shirt!" Knowing he had no brother, but that was the kind of thing his mother said.

At last his hair had somewhat grown out—or he was more used to it—from where Matthew's powder had burned it, but the "salt and pepper" look was now more pronounced. He seemed forty-two instead of thirty-two. *Good*, he thought. *Another piece of the disguise and I better match Rufus' age*. But his eyes were sad and the lids had begun to drop over them; his cheeks were sunken as well as being pale: not the image he expected nor wanted. Glad that Anna couldn't see him...or maybe she could: who knew.

After he had married Anna, his mother said to him: "Trying to find the right wife is like looking for a green horse. You've never seen one; no one around you has seen one; all you can do to get one is paint one yourself. Now that you're married, do the things your wife expects you to do and you'll someday find a green horse right in front of you, all your own."

His eyes teared. Anna was a green horse and they loved each other as much in death as they had in life.

Couldn't stay inside. The past week he'd spent most of his nights on deck and had gotten used to sleeping days, so he had fallen asleep in his rented room and woke in the evening, so then he quietly went out of the rooming house to just stand, smell, look, listen, think: appreciate the night sounds and smells, other noises of Dockside he hadn't heard in twenty years: the old noises he remembered but couldn't remember, just knew they were there. The area was still awake...seemed funny to think a community which worked all day might still be awake or enjoy at all the nighttime—as the colonists went to bed with the darkness and rose to the sun—but here in Dockside there were people awake and active. The hackney-coaches were still busy, the horses plodding through manure and urine-coated streets, the wooden coaches making the creaking sounds similar to those he'd heard on the ship and the wheels of the coaches clattered over the cobblestones where there was no manure to muffle them; the sounds of the hoofs of the great horses thundered in his ears, taking up the night-silence. Other rental-coaches and carriages stood waiting, their drivers scanning for fares, yelling back and forth at each other. Then he realized why there was so much movement: the churches!

In Plimouth, every man's house was "a church." Here, there were great, stone edifices dedicated to religious meeting, talk, mystery and movement. These people in Dockside didn't use their homes for prayer-meetings; they went to a church. Now... it was true that all the churches were not specifically for "people": most of those who had them built had done so out of religious piety, and for themselves and families, rather than the populace. But as they were there, their families and the neighbors attended the churches to pray for the original owners...and a fashion of "attending church" started. Then the religious movement itself began to build churches for its lower-class followers.

Ashley wondered why people would attend a "church," as he'd always been taught in prayer-meetings that God walked with you and heard everything you said and watched everything you did: it wouldn't be necessary to "go" somewhere for God's presence, as He was inside you, around you, YOU were "religion": personified. In every person, God breathed.

Nearer the river Dockside had changed in several ways since Ashley was a child: an attempt to straighten the streets and form more of a grid out of them had been attempted and fairly well received. Old houses—shacks—had been replaced by mostly one, but several two-story homes; the width of the newly planned and developed streets seemed expanded; and the place—still dreary and "riverside"—was cleaner, the houses brighter with paints, the trash along the streets less, the laundry not so noticeable on ropes as it had been: just laid on the ground. New business was in the area and causing the old suburb to remake itself into the Puritan's idea of a city.

No tree seemed to have a chance here: what wouldn't be cut for fireplace logs or used as mulch on those purple flowers would be splintered by wedges and turned into kindling-chips; the underground roots covered over with cobblestones so not a twig could spring up between them.

Dockside's inhabitants were in mostly drab and tired clothing: no silver-buckled shoes or belts here, as in Plimouth. These were the new class of

England: a working class which was fast replacing peasants and indentured and forced labor.

By London's standards, East London was the place where the poorly constructed and "short" (one or two-story houses) were built; and the "poorly constructed" extended to the roads as well.

Dockside was a tumble of small, dirty alleys and some cobbled and partially cobbled streets without gutters, wide areas which allowed outside storage, and small houses, most of them seemingly recently built. Some of the streets were filthy with horse-manure and almost void of air, congesting any who attempted to breathe whilst sallying upon them. A tired man in traveling-clothes, Ashley Lyons, restless with his long strides, tramped about, trying to see everything around him as he paced along, his head turning from side to side in observation. He stalked the streets of Dockside as he combed the Indian trails in the Blue Hills: relentlessly and with purpose.

Workers and their families lived here, labored here, died here. Seeing the place from a different perspective, Ashley wondered how his parents could have lasted here for the several years they had called this place "home." White Place was his old street name, and both it and the house in which Ashley had been raised until the age of nine were still there, seeming the same as twenty-three years previously, purple crocus still blooming. And if that "shack" had been for a carpenter and his family "good housing" (as his mother had told him) then where would they have gone from there, to go into housing even worse, after his father died and they had to move from that "expensive place."

Coming home was always sweet and sad at the same time. Probably everyone felt the same when they saw a former house and home...it didn't make them want to stay; it didn't make them want to go...It was just a tear-filled time of mixed memories and wishes to have done things differently. He also wished he could have brought Anna here; Anna would understand: she was good at that. At Anna's funeral, one of the men of the community had taken Ashley aside to tell him "It's God's choice; you are what God wants you to be. You are born and raised in His blessing and you die at His pleasure. When God sends for you, there is nothing to halt that call."

Those should have been comforting words, they were meant as such: words to heal, but Ashley had taken them wrongly—as he did so often—and barked at the man: "That, sir, is a Calvinist attitude! We should believe prayer and good works influence God's choices! What you say smacks of Calvin predestination as the cause of a person's life!"

Oh…he was good in anger; good at rebuttal: the Pligrime Elders had taught him well.

Remembering that, Ashley now felt sorrow at his unforgivable display of anger. It was just that all these churches...all these people who went to them…none of that was necessary because you carried God in your heart and He carried you in His. Why didn't they understand that?

He missed the safety of those prayer-meetings in Plimouth with Anna…those were the good days and good times they always hoped to see but didn't know they were living.

London was exciting but Plimouth…he missed Plimouth.

Single again; alone again. Waking several times each night thinking Anna was there, then missing her all over again. Wishing she were there, praying for her immortal soul. Lonely. Tired. Sad. Aching for her. Had the child lived…had the first one lived…just so alone.

Anna had said a child completed them; she then had reason to live and enjoy. She lost the first child and never talked about it after the funeral—just insisted she'd have another. Maybe God would give her back the same one in a different body. Wanted a child for them both, so they could become "a real family." Ashley felt the same: he could re-live his childhood with a son or daughter, telling them he tales he had learned, teaching them the ways of the woods and the Algonkin Woods-People. He could do things with and for a child…those things he had wanted his dad to do with him. Things he felt cheated from doing with his dad when that man died; things he never even knew about until he was already grown; things he'd make up as his child grew. Wanted to give to his child what he didn't have as a child. Child-image-healing for the adult, based on missing things. Not for the child, really…for him.

Another thing he missed in Dockside was the birds. Oh, there was the occasional sparrow here and there, but in Plimouth, great flocks of birds flew overhead while others filled the leas and swales, stuffing themselves on ripe seeds there and in roadside meadows. At home in Plimouth he'd soon be seeing the long "V"s of geese from La Lavrador and overhead, different colors of ducks, their little wings beating so hard they ever seemed frightened in their passing.

Maybe the bird migration bypassed London. If it did, what a shame, as seeing those huge flocks of birds ever gave Ashley a thrill…for he knew they were going to a known land far away where they could be safe and warm. Wasn't that what everyone wanted? To be safe and warm?

There were no taverns here at Dockside Ashley could find; he imagined there wasn't enough money to support them and the close-knit religious community would violently protest any being built. Taverns needed to be able to rely on local business, not intermittent and wild foreign seamen. This was a neighborhood which cared for its own: churches gave soup daily to the old or infirm; people knew each other, worked or had worked with each other; a place where the nighttime fire patrol dragged drunken sailors to carts and wheeled them to their ships: that kind of a neighborhood.

He noticed there was a church now, in his old neighborhood in Dockside. There never had been one when he lived here; people used their homes or the homes of friends to hold prayer-meetings. Some of them had maintained that distance from a formal religion with a church, calling themselves "Quakers" and holding on to the old ways of the religion: before churches. (The churches with their interiors dark in stained wood and worked stone, reflecting for the masses the love of and for Jesus in their cross-shaped and forward-focus, inviting in all those followers to sit and pray in unison and participate in the Glory of God in "His" house.) Sad...but these churches used weren't built because "people" wanted to worship in them; they were constructed by the wealthy for themselves, to show their feeling for God to the aristocracy. The poor loved those empty places of God, as they felt His presence in them and why not? They certainly were large enough to allow God and Jesus to arrive and abide within them, and expensive enough as well. Churches allowed the poor to visit the home of God and give themselves the chance to see how they might spend eternity, praying forever for their creator within His church on high.

But with the country caught up in Puritan Protestantism, and with that fast becoming "official," "organized," "efficient," "encompassing" and "inclusive," the Protestant Churches took their bearings from the spires of the Catholic Churches and another service-organization emerged: an official structure of harboring those who labored within for the Glory of God and to the service of man through the Protestant Church," the Ministre (Minister).

Ashley walked again around his old home, a tiny place with the remnants of a flower garden and two windows a lot dirtier than when his mother cleaned them. White Place was cobbled rudely and all the vacant areas were home to gardens of some sort, mostly vegetables that he could recognize—maybe some herbs. Anna grew herbs and used them daily. Ashley smiled to himself that there were square leagues of meadows in Plimouth's areas not under cultivation; whatever would these people here with their little, cramped gardens think if they saw all that wasted land?

Diagonally across the street from his old place was a house where he had played as a child. The winter he was five years old he had met Mary-Lou Lightbody, a girl almost his age. Somehow her mother and his were friendly, and with each child an only one, the mothers must have reasoned the children could enjoy play together and the mothers could each watch the other's child to get themselves some time alone. Mary-Lou was a few months older than Ashley, and while their mothers drank tea or chatted or socialized as mothers do, the children spent playtime together, not knowing about "play" except what they had seen at home. They then decided the only game was "Mother and Father," and Ashley still remembered the time he told is mother when he grew up he would marry Mary-Lou. (All this at ages 5 and 6.) To this day he also remembered how his mother laughed at him, and the shame he felt but didn't know why and still did not. The things people remember. Then, he was six and his father died; the tea-parties ended, so did the marriage plans with a girl whose face and hair color he today couldn't recall—remembered only that she had been a lot taller than he. But he remembered her name, and looked across at the house where she had lived...went there on a whim—just for something to do: old times, perhaps. Initially wouldn't let himself knock on the door, but then he did.

No, no Lightbody family...no one by that name around here either...no, they hadn't been there when these people rented the house—only about two years ago—they didn't know anybody around who might have either been here longer or could have known that family. They were renters who had moved in to work the docks after Lord Protector Cromwell increased shipping. "All the old people," Ashley was told, "are dead or gone."

So much for childhood sweethearts in the light of adult years. A pathetic gesture on his part and he knew it, looking for a six-year-old girl twenty-seven years after he had left her, a "girl" now thirty-three. In remembering his time with her he also remembered the boys here were mean, always hitting him and throwing stones at him and making the fool of him. His mother always comforted him, trying to get him through the rough times. After a particularly bad teasing and beating he had gone again to his mother with that age-old question: "How can I get back at them?" His mother, tears in her eyes, answered her personal philosophy: "Outlive them. God will punish."

"Outlive them"...he remembered the words now. The only way his mother had to deal with terror: outlive it. She had; now he had to.

The next morning in London—he had slept during the night—he woke to a cock's crow...a rooster! Someone had a rooster in a city of a half-million people! The center of English civilization (and a place where the poor starved to death) and someone dared to have a rooster! He wondered how long that bird would last before somebody put him into a pot, or if these city-people minded that clarion call at dawn and throughout the day. Maybe they didn't; maybe whoever had it enjoyed the wake-up call or the idea of a farm animal inside a city whose cry was sometimes echoed by bells from towers and churches.

He was paying for "room and board," but with that first meal he became bored of the board, used his coin to purchase food elsewhere after that. Fried sausages with bread and gravy and wine had sounded good to the ear, but it wasn't his ear which had to digest it: his mouth found the sausage revolting, hardly cooked and gristly; the bread was horse-corn; the wine was warm and bitter (too much vinegar had been used to cut it), the gravy sticky and repulsive with all the lumps and poor taste. Good food improperly cooked was better than that which was served: poor food improperly cooked.

Signs on businesses were everywhere...signs of the times, as Protector Cromwell encouraged small business and money-movement. There may not have been a tavern he could locate, but there was a victualer's with a "Beef, Pork & Tender Lamb" sign, signs for "Laudanium for pain," "bees for honey," "Beef Tea," gayly colored "Sojourn Inn," "Roman Inn: meals provided," "Christian Inn: Pilgrimes Welcome," "Ostel," "Rose Inn," "Crown Inn," "Limetree Lodge and Inn: rest in comfort for God's Children," "Stonemason," "Goldsmith"...they went on and on. Some of the places denoting "cooked food" instead of the usual cold-sliced or just puddings or stews. And there were signs for day-laborers, artificers, bricklayers, domestic servants, machine-installers (cloth and wool) crop planters and harvesters...signs of all sizes and denotations Ashley never knew existed. The elders of Plimouth hardly allowed "a" sign...holding that they all knew who sold what and when, and God needed no sign to tell Him either!

The fashionable word was "cury": to indicate the food was cooked, not raw or blended.

One shop had a sign: "Perfumed Soaps For Ladies & the Gentry." Hmmmmm...the word "gentry" included those ladies born to royalty or riches, so perhaps in London there was a distinction in the word "ladies" Ashley didn't understand.

In the stores were more people than he had ever seen at one time, more than he remembered were here: carters, boatmen, broom-peddlers, beggars, pot-menders, basket-women, those riding and walking, standing and hawking;

along the river were crowds of people in and out of flat-bottomed boats, and canoe-like boats jammed along the water's edge. London was a great shipping port, a greater "user" port—with all the people here. He could see the roofs of the grain-market in Southwark: everyone in London knew or knew about the Southwark area. If you didn't have a business of your own, or didn't "fit in" to London, you had to live or work in Southwark; not that the experience was bad: far from it, it was merely "different." Everyone in London "worked"; those in Southwark "worked harder."

In Southwark—by the bridge—which still charged annual tolls upon passed-over merchandise that the crown could benefit; well, now it was the community which benefited, with Lord Protector Cromwell taking most of that for his Army—was the Clink area, itself a poor community with whores regulated by the bishop and a mass of foreigners. To its east—along the Thames—was Guildable Manor, another business/trading, prosperous district bordering Saint Olaf's (Olave's) Church on Tooley. Saint Olave's placement was within a great shipbuilding center and a regional woolen-cloth production-quarter and within this sprung ancillary industries including leatherwork, dying and soap-boiling—each an important and influencing business which influenced London with their products. To the west of the Clink were theaters and a large development of houses along the river.

Turning his sight north of the Thames, way off was Saint Paul's Church—a hundred meters or more high, dominating any view to the northwest. Mare than a half-million people crowded these streets and London's others...a gigantic workforce causing the new brick housing to be commonplace and having old, now unused, stores sub-divided into single-room housing. Here was Shipside Place; there was Olde Swan Place; going along Thames Way was Saint Clement's in the distance. More signs: for silk, pottery, glass...and there: King Henry's Dockyard at Depford, where his father had worked and died.

Way over was London Bridge: not seeming at all "bridge-like" because the foundation was so strong and wide and the bridge itself so inviting in its view, it had become completely packed with all sorts of homes and businesses placed upon it...becoming a tower of buildings which included five great houses, each towering thirty-three meters or more above the street level and literally dozens of other-use shops, businesses and stores. A community within a community, a way to use land which wasn't land in a land-poor place. A "bridge" which gave the impression it was a solid, single building, but at ground-level a street remained constantly in use, more really now a tunnel for most of its distance, as the buildings covered the majority of it.

And he noticed, looking toward the bridge, there were the cobblestones his mother had told him about...the ones laid for the Army too many years ago for anyone here to remember seeing it done...put in because the Romans had such stones laid for passage of their wagons and horses and foot-soldiers. Then the London gentry wanted to drive on dry roads, so the stones were placed all over the city to end the deep and continuing mud.

And after all the walking and looking...yes, there was a tavern and alehouse. Those English businesses were everywhere, after all.

His trepidation on arriving mellowed into a comfortable routine by the third day. It had rained off and on the previous two days and threatened even more rain by the third day, but he still had plenty of time before *City of Leeds* arrived. Ashley slept, ate, made rounds of the boat-docks and watched the activity in the shipyard, chatting with the same people every day, getting a feel for the society, letting London's sheer size become easier on him, going around by hackney-carriage and re-learning, remembering the streets and directions. The carriage-wheels making sounds all their own...jangling harness, metals, whip-snaps, creaking leather, straining wood, the bumping and noisy sounds as the ironclad wheels careened from cobblestone to cobblestone, sounds previously natural to him were now unfamiliar and strange.

Cheapside Avenue was even more grand than he remembered, with its five and six-story homes along that processional way. He could see New Palace Yard, with Westminster Hall and the Abby, and across from that the Great Conduit and the Clock Tower. And above them all, glaring down at London from its own hill, the Tower of London. There, through the initial order of King Henry, the Eighth, was kept the minted pound of silver specific for defining all of London's money. It had been scrupulously weighed and the weights were given names: a "pound" was equal to twenty shillings or two hundred pence. England's "pound"—based on her silver—was truly a joke to most of Europe's countries and monarchs, who saw gold (in France, for instance, gold was about six times more valuable than silver) as THE metal most known and accepted.

His city; no longer "his city." Before, this was all he knew; now, no longer a part of it for a score of years—now just another interested spectator and here on business, ready to leave whenever possible. London had become a distant, unwanted familiarity.

He felt badly for the horses which were out in every weather. The drivers could choose to work or not; their horses couldn't. He had gotten the same hackney-carriage twice in two days, and told the driver he'd probably see him on the morrow. The driver responded with, "You know what they say: 'God smiles when we say we'll do something tomorrow.'"

That was encouraging.

One morning he watched the fog form...something like Feldar's Misty Shades but denser and all-inclusive. Frightening, that image, beginning fuzzy and extending everywhere at once: the ghost of London.

On a whim—after he had again checked to see if *City of Leeds* was in or expected—he hired a different hackney-coach and told the driver to show him the city's sights. They went past most of what he'd already seen, then took in Gresham's Royal Exchange, the Plazza in Coventgarden and Saint Paul's, and went slowly through the grain market. The hackney driver was an independent sort—typical, Ashley found, of the newest men within this latest craze of "business." When Ashley had said (on recommendation from Rufus), "I'd like to see the Royal Exchange," the driver had responded, "There's nothing there for you, m'Lord; I'll show you Goldsmith Row: those are the most fair houses and shops within London."

Ashley insisted on seeing the exchange and there truly realized there was not much "to see": it was the working-place of businessmen and nothing present but a great building and hundreds of people, seemingly milling about.

Cromwell's influence was everywhere in London; he and the Puritans had welcomed in business of all kinds. The hackney-drivers were trying to get individual licenses and be free of the big livery companies; women were all over the streets, working as shop-clerks and cleaners; the "person" was becoming more important than the job he did. Trade-wars had begun, with "sales." Import/export companies flourished. The Age of Trade had started and London was the hub of that wheel; markets in London were everywhere.

In Dockside an old commodity received new life: coal. Marco Polo said the Chinese dug black stones from mountains and burned them. The Romans used it all over their world. By the year a.D. 1200, England and Scotland mined and sold coal, taking it from shallow pits that chased the coal veins. King Edward the First of England banned the use of coal, saying it aggravated the populace and was an inefficient fuel (he apparently never burned the alternative sod or peat). He imposed the death-penalty on those in England who used coal, but smiths continued to use it, cutlery-makers embraced it, those who could, used it regardless. Finally, the use of coal in the making of bricks and smelting brought coal back into common use, mainly as the new "chimney" now drew away those nauseating and deadly fumes coal gave off. Production methods of business made coal cheaper and better to use than the already-dwindling supply of wood in England.

In Dockside, the iron-works relished in its use of coal, pouring out soot into every neighbor's daily life. And coal by the long-ton was sent by boat and barge to all who could buy it. In many places, soot blackened the houses and streets, causing them to look gritty, grimey and greasy; the price a city paid for its now-legal embrace of coal and business.

Those three days of rain while he was waiting for *City of Leeds* dampened Ashley's spirits as well as his clothing. Couldn't just stay in that rented room and no ship was docking so he used even more of the money Rufus and his stepfather had pressed upon him to go looking.

Such horses there were here: the hackneys, drawing coaches of people, plunged their great forms through the streets and through the rain; some coaches were splattered with mud to their door-handles: in, obviously from outside the city, perhaps as far away as other cities. London was a giant wasp's nest, everyone contributing to its growth and upkeep, carriages and coaches coming in as fast as they went out, laden each way with some commodity—even if it were only human. Protector Cromwell had fueled the fire of commerce and London was a torch for small business. Nothing existed which was not sold or bought, traded or requested.

The coach Ashley was in this day reeked of some kind of perfume, but was far better in smell than the one he had used the previous day, which held musky odors of sweat and mildew, maybe cheap clothing or old harness. He breathed it all in, thinking neither Anna nor his mother had used something like this but he had heard of women who had—did—daily use perfume. What must a woman like that—one who used that French perfume—look and act like? Anna never used any scent, although when she gardened, that smell was upon her. That odor...here in the coach...was almost intoxicating and sensual to him; perhaps one day he'd meet a woman who wore scents like this.

The days he was able he wandered around his old portion of the city...looking and asking after people and places he had known up to the age of twelve. Almost everything was still here...some of the families, tho', had moved away but some remained: a tribute to the economy of the city and its constant growth. But the boyhood friends he had were gone; not a one could he find and the two flats he visited told him the same thing: "Gone years ago." Well, it had been twenty years: a lifetime for some. He hoped they had gone to a better life than the one Dockside presented: he had.

He looked carefully at some of those people on the streets: war-crippled or diseased beggars, people to whom the cost of salt was more important than which favorite should be King—for that was the undertone in conversations:

the people lacked and needed a King, but were frightened at the same time to think they'd soon have another.

This hackney-driver stopped in front of a place where there was music, noise and the drinking of alcoholic beverages allowed: one of those despicable places the elders of Plimouth told about in their three-times-a-week-and-twice-on-Sundays "messages." A place of alcoholic depravity and harlots waiting for the Devil to appear and for God to smite them all dead. This was actually such a place! What a tale to tell if he ever got back to Boston...but...damnation, the music sounded so good and the voices from the open door seemed so happy, it might be a shame to have God wreck this all.

"'Ere we are," the driver called down to him. "You said you'd like to go somewhere different today, an' this place is all that!"

"What place is this?"

"The Bear's Den! An ale-'ouse; they do bear-baitin' at certain times 'ere."

Anna would skin him alive if she ever thought he entered an alehouse! She obviously never had entered one herself but she had a great deal of animosity toward them, and taverns; perhaps her former husband frequented them. And his mother would have something to say about this as well—even that he had "stopped" in front of one, to say nothing of going inside one! But he got out of the coach, paid the driver and went in, regardless...waiting for the lightning bolt from God or an angel's touch to halt him before he went further.

The place was fairly large, long, but only as wide as hewn beams would allow it; a long serving-bar ran down one whole side and two men—the tavern-owner and the bar-man—stood behind that, speaking with the few customers at the bar. The music came from beyond an open side door, and people were wandering in and out, going from table to table and back and forth to the bar. He looked around quickly, then settled into a chair by itself, along the wall. The barman came over to ask his pleasure and—ignorant of any other answer—Ashley said, "An ale...nothing dark; something light in color." Rufus had said that once; a good thing he had remembered it.

Well...no barmaid; no tavern wench; nothing so far for either Anna or his mother to be upset about...er...maybe the ale.

The loud music halted and it seemed someone was now playing a stringed instrument; he got up and went to the side door. Ashley had never before seen the instrument which was being played, and never had seen the sight of several half-drunk customers trying to sing along with the music while several more clapped and yelled at them, all making fools of themselves but not caring.

The barman brought his ale and Ashley stood, rooted to the spot. There was a small amphitheater with bench-seating and a makeshift stage. Behind him, several more patrons of the place pushed past him, getting seats near the stage; the place was starting to fill with people: brushing past him, speaking loudly, yelling to others...certainly a place of great commotion, suddenly. That music stopped and the musician left the small stage to appreciative yells. From seemingly nowhere stepped a man with a violin, and as he stood upon the slight stage, the din of voices abruptly lowered without a voice commanding it. The music from the violin sparkled, danced, wove a magical pattern in everyone's mind. Ashley had never heard nor seen a violin played and his senses soared with the tune: rising, falling, moving and filling his ears as it filled the air. He was overtaken by the music's romance and wished Anna were here to listen to it as well. It went on several minutes, then halted abruptly and the audience seemed to hold its collective breath as the musician left the stage...then they all yelled, screamed and beat upon their seats and tables in appreciation. The walls of the alehouse weren't thick enough to repel the vibration of the crowd in their appreciation, but there had never been a complaint from anyone who heard it. An extraordinary experience for a colonist from a land where music was meant only for God's ear and came sparingly from an "approved source."

"It's his latest work!" a voice beside Ashley said. "He tries them out here before he performs them for the gentry. Isn't he marvelous! Doesn't his music sing?"

Ashley agreed: it did.

He went back inside, the barman stopping as he came by with a tray of full mugs, holding out a hand for payment of the—as yet touched—ale.

"Did you like him?" he asked, and Ashley responded with a "Yes, very much."

"He played for the King and Queen and gives concerts now for charity as he won't play for that Cromwell. The Queen herself used to come her to watch the bears."

Ashley paid and the barman left; the chair Ashley had previously used was still vacant, so he sat again, looking around and holding his mug of ale: a picture of Puritan distaste.

There was a man at one of the small tables, drinking from a cup and with an empty cup on the table in front of him. He was a sooty-color, a dark and seemingly angry man, talking to himself aloud and sometimes raising his voice above normal limits. He carried a bag of tools of some sort, in what seemed to be a sailcloth bag. Ashley had owned a pair of sailcloth trousers one time—

here in London. They took all a six-year-old boy could put them through, never tore, hardly stained, never lost their original color. His mother used to say they were "awful...miserable to make" and she said he'd not get another pair so long as she had to make them—which, of course, he didn't, as they moved from house to house a lot and eventually left London after that. Her new position as Mister Pennyweight's indentured servant didn't allow her time to make "tough" pants for her son; he received lightweight, "easy to sew" trousers after that. Pennyweight imported ready-made clothing and so she eventually used those, but they wore out so fast and stained easily. Then Pennyweight had married Ashley's mother and Ashley had all the "imported" clothing he needed—which was considerable, as he grew weed-like and rapid over the following years.

Anna was good at mending clothes for him: she sewed, cleaned, found time to plant, tend and harvest a vegetable garden and an herb garden (from seeds Mister Pennyweight had given her). Pennyweight liked Anna also; she had that effect upon men...they seemed to rush to her aid and do things for her which she never requested and they wouldn't do for their own wives.

(He thought it was her petite size and scrubbed face which did it.) She didn't reciprocate, tho'...and when she married Ashley she seemed to turn off that "charming" effect.

Maybe Elspeth had some of that. Ashley HAD written that poem for her—and seriously meant it to please her—and he DID think about her far too often...but he had—it all came back to him—unwittingly sent her brother to his unfortunate young death and however could either of them get over something that disastrous.

The sooty-man ended up drinking his large mug of ale while he mumbled and yelled and otherwise disturbed everyone around him; then he left and Ashley was both glad he had gone—as he drew a lot of attention his way—and disappointed because the man had taken away Ashley's disturbing thoughts...and now they returned.

Deep down, Ashley knew he shouldn't have come to London, shouldn't have attempted to be a spy. These men he followed, waited for, were professional men and they had allies and friends and houses to go to plus a destination. He had no friends here, nor places to hide; he was just—to them—"a colonist." No business being here at all! This was a man's job and Rufus had sent a boy. If he had a wish right now, what would it be? Just to get away from here alive. Maybe to start all over and never involve himself in all this mess. Perhaps to stay in Duxbury at the cabin and feed Anna's cat. What frail and mindless wishes! Perhaps to have God strike down all these spies so he could just walk away, free and happy. Yes. Just to be able to walk away free and happy...but he knew that wouldn't happen.

There was something in all this...nothing was random. The crimes they did telling him something, leading him somewhere, drawing him into them. People he spoke with were being murdered. Murdered! How many times had he heard that: the elders of Plimouth made that all very clear. If you killed someone who was trying to kill you because you were a soldier or a sheriff or it was your duty, that was not murder in the eyes of God. To kill an Indian who stole was sending a message to others not to steal, not murdering. Only if someone killed a person for personal reasons or revenge or pleasure was it murder. And murder was one of God's Commandments: "Thou shalt not murder!" These spies from France didn't just "kill," they "murdered"! It couldn't be for personal revenge and they wouldn't need to travel so far to enact murder for pleasure; the only thing left was money. The boy had none; the notary probably had plenty, but according to Rufus, they took nothing from his house. They murdered without a reason...Or a reason which wasn't apparent. Who knew what the notary had done in the past—the old man was so rich and had come so far to be in King's Town. Who knew whom he might have offended in his past, whom he might have run from. These Frenchmen—Royalists or royals themselves—might be a killing-squad come to settle old debts from a time when the notary lived in England or wherever. Probably. One leader and four men from Europe who had been trained in the war to kill, or kill on command. Soldiers turned murderers. God save us.

By now, the Bear's Den had a lot of people in it, but they just seemed to be wandering about, going in and out to the amphitheater and stage rather than just sitting and drinking, He tried to understand the movement of the crowd, then realized they were mostly going out the side door to the stage-area, carrying their mugs of ale. He sipped at his drink—tasted it, really—a vile and bitter brew unfit for consumption; the elders were right. Noticed a man waving at him, motioning him to come to the side door, so, hesitantly, he went there; the barroom was emptying fast, people pushed past him into the outside amphitheater. The man who had waved disappeared into the crowd and Ashley then thought he either was waving at someone else or he wanted everyone out here for a reason. Maybe the violinist would play again.

Ale was being served outside here also, from a window cut into the building. Anna might have liked this: an enclosed patio of chairs and tables for comfort and pleasure, surrounded by a tall wall, containing a stage for entertainment.

What wasn't there to like—except the vile ale. No stuffy air out here, just a private enclosure. Then he heard the dogs. Two or three, perhaps, barking, whining, yapping as hounds do, eager and ready to hunt. He never had owned a dog, but people in Plimouth he knew had some and those dogs made these sounds as they were ready to hunt. In Plimouth, he had heard their barks as they cornered wild pigs.

Next to the stage was an open area covered in sand, and the alehouse patrons cheered as a man carrying a chain walked to the middle of that sand to attach that chain to a short post, then he tightened it and ran to a small shed-looking building and raised its door. Out came a bear, chained now to the post, and the man quickly snubbed the chain to pull the bear closer to the post in the ground; the bear nor had about a three-meter movement-area, all on the sand.

The man then cautiously approached the bear, who was trying to get off the chain and not attack the man—but the man then threw something in the bear's face. Looked like sand…or pepper. Yes, pepper! The bear sneezed, shook its head, backed up, drooled. blew snot from its nose…definitely pepper. The audience was hushed.

Then the man stepped toward the bear with a whip and started to whip the bear, drawing s small amount of blood as the lash cut the bear's face and the blood flipped from the whip onto the customers who had crowded as closely as they dared. They screamed and laughed, but didn't leave their places.

The man then grabbed a long stick—looked like a lance—and began to poke the bear, who—now very angry—snarled at the man…and the man dropped the pole and ran into the crowd as someone else let loose a dog, who dashed for the bear.

The sight was gruesome. Ashley, shocked, stood to look in disgust, but with some curiosity. All around him, men shouted, placed wagers, literally jumped up and down, screaming. The dog went for the bear's nose, but the bear swiped him away—probably had his claws cut short or removed as he drew no blood from the dog tho' with claws he'd have disemboweled him—but he instead only managed to toss the dog from him. The dog swung around, growling and snapping. froth flying and growls from both animals the only thing heard, now that the crowd was so involved in watching. Another slam by the bear and yet another…the dog bowled over and rolling but back on its feet and after the bear again, darting in after the bear's snout and then stomach…but the bear turned, swinging its froth-strewn and bloody face under the dog and obviously biting it, slowing it down enough that the bear was able to smack the dog with a paw and flipped it over, the dog yelping continually in pain and fear. As the dog rolled, the bear again bit into its stomach, gutting the dog and spraying the nearest patrons with its blood, sending them back into the crowd, a mass, now, of exuberant but bloody watchers.

The crowd stopped cheering. Suddenly, two other growling dogs ran to the bear, grabbing different portions of it, one on the nose, the other taking an ear. Now the bear screamed, backing up, trying to dislodge the dogs as they held on, squirting blood about, spit and gore slinging with their tossed-about movements. The bear managed to throw off the dogs, the chain hampering its movements but the bear fighting for its life and showing that. He backed away for just a moment and the audience saw a piece of the bear's cheek and nose were gone; its ear hung by a bloody piece of flesh. The dogs jumped in again, the bear at the end of his chain, screaming and striking, trying as hard as he could to ward-away the would-be killers, biting as he could, using strikes instead of claws to protect himself.

Now blood was spurting all over the animals and the sand, reaching the closer patrons and making masks of their faces. The dogs had opened some of the large blood vessels and out the bear's blood flew, pink haze in and around the rolling, twisting animals. A dog backed away for an instant, a leg missing. Then it dove back wobbly into the fray, a whirl of bloody motion and impending death.

In the near end, the bear and both dogs were so mortally wounded that they all died upon the sand, no real winner of this contest for those who waged bets or cheered an opponent; certainly not a winner for the animals who had just fought and died for the grisly spectacle. A short-lived fight broke out when a man called that the bear had died after the dogs, so he had won...there initially had been a few cheers, but overall the audience went for more of the dark ale for which this alehouse was famous and no bets were paid; then the establishment became filled with talk and movement. Another successful event for the owner of the business.

The last time Ashley had seen a black bear he was in the Carolina, in a swamp. This day he couldn't express in words nor gesture his contempt toward the people who would use animals in that manner...of for those who egged on, cheering the animals themselves. Contemptible! No one in all of Plimouth would even think of a thing like that. The Pilgrimes loved their dogs and all animals, as they were God's creations as well, and they enjoyed the sight of wild animals as a part of Nature; although they'd use a dog to help them locate an opossom or fox, and deer and rabbit had to be killed for food, no one would consider such a blood-sport as he had just witnessed. And he'd been told the

QUEEN came here to see this? They couldn't have been telling the truth…although the man who said it seemed very proud of that.

He sat down the mug, still with most of its contents, thinking one would have to be drunk to enjoy that spectacle, and went outside, getting into one of the several hackney-coaches waiting. Before the driver started the horse in motion he looked in the small cutaway which served as a window to speak with his fare. "How was the bear-baiting?"

"I didn't enjoy it."

"Finally I've heard that response! Everyone else says they liked it or some such. I'm against it, hurting those animals."

"Then why do you have your coach here, outside the alehouse?"

"Best place for business on a Sunday night."

"It's Sunday?"

"Has been all day. You didn't attend a church service?"

"No…I didn't know what day it was."

"Bear-baiting is mostly on Sundays…the religious committee says it will put a stop to it."

"Hope they do."

"Never have seen one of those performances but I hear they're hideous to watch."

"Count your blessings; they're beyond gruesome."

"The Queen herself attended these shows a couple years back."

"I don't think so."

"The truth; I swear it by God, Jesus and the saints! There always are gentry here on Sunday evenings. The Puritans tried to stop it, but I don't think they can."

"Only the Puritans? Not the Baptists?"

"Only the Puritans; they're the only ones capable of doing anything political…England is run by them and their taxes, London especially. Where is it you want to go?"

"Dockside."

They went along to Dockside, Ashley vowing to himself that he'd not let another hackney-driver take him to a place of entertainment such as that again, Also, he didn't need to be doing this sort of thing…This "entertainment of the Queen." He needed to stay by the Port and wait/watch for *City of Leeds*.

That night—late—there was more rain, splashing harshly, making him aware that even in the darkness there was life outside, as trees and plants must smile steadily with the steady splattering of that liquid which nourished them;

and people were still in the streets, trying to dodge the raindrops while maintaining their lives and pursuits, hoping to do such in a drier place, On the morrow their new work-week would begin. Tonight, Ashley thought about Anna.

One time when Anna was carrying their son and fraught with swollen ankles and all-over pains, he was obliged to go for some time with the militia, chasing and ultimately capturing a band of outlaws who had ravaged a small community outside Plimouth and needed to be brought to either justice or death—whichever happened first. This was his first overnight time away from Anna since their marriage, and as the militia hunted down their quarry as skunks stalk for eggs in a grassy birds-nest, he took time to open a fast note to his beloved:

> *My Anna,*
>
> *You are ever with me. I beg of you to stay well whilst we are apart and not indulge in the night airs. That I have not written before this is my worst sin, but this trail has been one fraught with difficulty and it has taken all my skill to maintain our pursuit. Be assured of all my love for you and our child; I weep without you and am drained of any emotion but the urge to return quickly to you. We shall soon bring these cutpurses to task, and I shall be home as quickly as Joe will run. My love to Mother, whom I know cares for you almost as much as I try. Not much longer, my constant companion in Life, and I shall be home. Your love guides me as the North Star and maintains as hot as the sun. I send you a kiss with this letter; catch it quickly and press it to your moist lips, and thereto sate my fondest dream. Soon, I hope to be with you that we may whisper sweet secrets to each other.*
>
> *Your Ashley*

The next morning in Dockside could only be described by Anna…at least what words Ashley remembered Anna might say of it. She'd stand there, leaning against him in that way she had, the sun coming up slowly behind yellow-tinged clouds, and say: "It's a pretty morning, gentle and clean." This was her kind of morning—as gentle and clean as she. But in this morning in London, there in the dawn—instead of pine trees—were the sturdy, sharp spires of local churches.

From the veranda of the rooming house he could just see the tops of some of the houses on London Bridge. London's bridge. Not the original one, as that was a bit upstream and ancient, made originally of stones lain one by one in the days of the Roman occupation but washed away over the years through the stern tidal-flow. London's present bridge updated and outclassed the Roman one: it too was stone, but this one used piers of stone and timber to withstand the river and allow the bridge-supports a dry foundation, thus anchoring this bridge within the river Thames.

Completed almost four hundred years previously, shops and houses were immediately built upon it (cleared land being scarce and a need for a communal setting still within the minds and hearts of "castle folk") and a great style of "gate" to keep out any warring factions was installed (and used as a "toll bridge" to merchants, with the meager tolls mostly going to the King) giving to those who went over the bridge a sort of "tunnel-effect": over the water but under the buildings; a strange sensation, probably more a bizarre effect Ashley experienced as a child when his parents had taken him across/through it.

The houses and businesses upon the bridge were taller than most of the buildings on the land—save the churches. These, with their great, pointy spires defined the skyline of this city. And within the bridge a whole culture grew, building, remodeling, expanding, sub-dividing the dwellings which took shape upon it. Crime was present here, so there were patrols at night by night-watchmen, but through the years—as the pay was nil and the benefits scanty—those men who watched were now mostly old or infirm and only now watched for fires, not ever-present scoundrels.

Without the King to inspire or thank them, who among the young would walk the bridge at night, alone?

To the northwest was Westminster...Formerly a twin city to London but now co-joined, leaving Southwark—across the river—"lonesome." The only way to and from Southwark seemed by the bridge of London, but that wasn't so: "travelers" would use the bridge but Londoners aware of the thieves and rascals there preferred to cross the river by boat (ferry, company boat or personal one) rather than go through "the tunnel of London Bridge" and attempt to dodge all the hawkers and sellers and pickpockets there.

Southwark was a grouping of businesses more than houses and great churches, although around the Globe Theater the multiple-family houses went as high as seven stories, a few roofs taller than the steeple on the Globe.

The west end of Southwark was forest with half-timbered cottages in stone and wood, whitewashed and daubed, their outside timbers coated with tar to preserve them and the most populated area wasn't an eighth the size of the city across the Thames with its spires and towers and cathedrals. England was a country of farms; London was a densely packed hodgepodge of buildings for every use, their inhabitants knowing this was the greatest and grandest place in all of England.

So...a weekend of wandering over, amusement attained, searching satisfied, prior attempts to reclaim any former friends completed, visiting old haunts accomplished, Ashley Lyons settled in to wait and watch for the arrival of the now-overdue *City of Leeds*.

CHAPTER 24

Aboard *City of Leeds*, Johnathan also waited patiently to arrive in London, becoming almost melancholy. He was often in melancholia: his mother had told him for years to stop living in the past and go forward to the future. No matter: he didn't care to. He longed only for a return to his old house with the servants and his father coming to visit.

True, Spain was always at war during his life; some part of Spain constantly fought some country or another. France had recently ended one fight; Portugal maintained pressure to break away from Spain's control; Italy gestured; England roared; Catalonia was in outright revolt. But his home in Spain was always safe, quiet and filled with good memories. Now he was headed to his brother's old home…how nice that would be. Maybe.

As he played alone in his youth, Johnathan had thoughts which took him away from reality. He was in a room but his mind could slip away: he pictured himself a troll, lurking under bridges, waiting for passers-by to be grabbed and frightened by him, then to realize they were being eaten piece by piece; he left their eyes until last so they could see themselves being gobbled.

He was a gryfalcon—the largest and most powerful of the class—bigger than any of his father's birds, perched upon a leather gauntlet, waiting to be released to climb high, soar, dive fast, strike brutally and fatally upon a dove, devour the bloody meat, tearing at it, enjoying the utter savagery of the deed.

He was a wolf from the mountains, patrolling the lowlands in search of a young lamb or shoat that he could tear apart. Then he saw a boy. He pounced upon him, teeth ripping and blood spurting…smelling the blood, tasting it—salty and sweet all at the same time—eating the child, savoring that thought, then tasting the boy as he devoured him while the boy screamed. He felt wonderful. He warmed himself at the bonfire of death.

There were women in his life, but no girls around him.

Knives fascinated him as a child: knives cut things, did things his hands and fingers couldn't do. He began to dwell upon knives and how to use them: how they entered the flesh the way the long nails of the troll, the talons of the gryfalcon, the teeth of the wolf did...but the knife was smoother, cleaner, faster, easier, deeper. Then he began to think he could be a knife. He wanted to be right there, watching, doing, touching, wanted to see the fear in a child, see the blood spurt, make the knife-cut with himself—by himself—taste the blood, delight in the excitement, the desire, the release of emotions as he—the knife—entered a closed body and exposed it to the world: laid it open for all to see, its first and only glimpse of another world before it ran out of blood and energy and life and withered in shock and pain and helplessness. Wanted to watch it happen, see the blade enter, experience the shudder of the body, feel the tension of the impact and marvel that such a creation could be so carved and affected and devastated so easily. Drooled at the thoughts he had. Eager, ready, waiting. Couldn't tear himself away; wanted to do it right now, to anyone—no, not "anyone": someone young, whose firm flesh would respond so well, whose muscles were elastic and would make their body jump and writhe in agony; someone small, who couldn't fight back effectively...but that was the ultimate pleasure in it all...that the strike would come so fast and the effect be so gory that as they wanted to fight back, they couldn't: the ultimate, glamorous sight—an opened young body in surprise and pain and fear, blood and life spilling out, unstoppably.

He tried that one time, on a cat some local family kept. Johnathan had gotten hold of a large knife—he wanted a large one so the sheer weight and size of it would do the job with ease—but the exact thing he admired about the huge blade (it was formally a knife attached to a military firearm) literally slowed its effect: the size was readily seen and too easily identified, even by a cat, and the weight and heft slowed its strike such that the honed blade only pushed at the skin instead of entering it, and the cat sprang away, spitting, snarling, claws out and back arched and tail straight and eyes wide, frightening Johnathan so much that he never did that again.

The lesson was taught and learned: he needed a smaller, sharper, lighter knife, and upon whatever he would use it had to be completely passive: tied. No more claws, teeth, fear, surprise, uncertainty. He required a soft-skinned, clawless, passive...female. A girl. A little girl. A tied-up, little girl with a bound mouth and uncovered flesh. That, then, was his dream, his desire: a little girl to cut.

He was young, then, and realized he'd have to wait to be older and bigger to accomplish that; when he grew up, he received a rush of feelings he couldn't explain and no one in the rancho could or would explain those to him. But always—now—he wanted a helpless girl—to kill.

Slowly.

In wonder, he watched the bulls and stallions breed. Finally tried to imitate them but had no respondent until he managed to get a ewe to stand, then others, and other breeds. He had been shown by animals and used animals. Still no little girl in his life.

He tried a boy: a substitute for a girl. He tried himself in the boy: a substitute for the knife. No blood, but what his body spit out was quite enough: another substitute, but enough of one to accept it thoroughly. All this time he was growing, aging, moving away from being a child and becoming a man.

Tried a man and accepted it. Stayed with men. Didn't carry a knife anymore: had its substitute with him all the time. Didn't bother with girls; used men. Used Luke; stole Luke from Geoffry.

Geoffry: a large, bulldog-looking brute of a man with big hands. There had been another man in Johnathan's circle of friends who had hands like that; ham-handed, he was called. Geoffry was ham-handed.

And he had a stare. Didn't move his eyes around much, just looked ahead—probably from Army training—but the look in Geoffry's eyes…not the look of a dead man, not hardly the look of most living, either: a defiant look, or a dismissive one—like he was there but he wasn't thinking about it and didn't care whether you saw or not. A look not interested enough to show any animation in either his eyes or his face. Just there: watching, waiting. That kind of a look. It came to Johnathan: "disingenuous." A look of false appearance, for beneath it all, Geoffry knew it all, saw it all, knew that he was good…very good at what he did.

Geoffry was the son of one of King Charles the First's advisors. Charles had brought him to Spain when he went to woo King Phillip of Spain's daughter and his advisor had found wooing of his own, getting produced a boy he insisted—in the Catholic world of the Spaniards—be named "Geoffry," after his father. (Charles fully intended to marry Philip's daughter, but in the months he was there realized he could not become the Catholic they wanted of him—that he bring back that religion to England—and he found a girl he desired while he was in Spain more than Phillip's daughter; he didn't marry her, but maintained her as a mistress and did want his children from her: he was a good father regardless that he then went to France for his Queen.) Geoffry was raised in the English compound set aside for Phillip's relatives from other countries, growing up alongside—when he ventured out of the casa—Johnathan. They were fast friends, old friends; then they were separated as their fathers moved on with their lives and Geoffry went to England while Johnathan stayed in Spain. Geoffry acquired a position in the Army but couldn't ever be an officer and never rose very high in the ranks. When he was able, Geoffry left the Army with Matthew and lived in London's dark civilization. Several years later—at Johnathan's naval demonstration on the Thames (attempting to raise public interest to get his father returned as King of England) Geoffry again joined him and the small band of friends came together.

The circle was complete. Johnathan had his substitutes, plus now he had Geoffry as a substitute for what he had wanted to be: a wielder of knives which opened people and drained their spent energy, soul and life from them in seconds. Now Johnathan was a complete man: a man who had his substitutes to do all his cravings, who was able to jump into the idea of Geoffry, be Geoffry for a moment, experience the lust of Geoffry. Never had to worry about that cat. No claws, no teeth, no fear. Just send Geoffry. Johnathan, the man who could substitute reality and enjoy it better than the real thing.

When he achieved his teen-age, Johnathan discovered the intrigues of politics. He had always known his father was a King, and just as always knew who and what he was: a bastard son. But the details of his position were fascinating, and the one to teach him those details was Walter Foster, accountant to the King, treasurer of the King's personal wealth (the wealth he collected and kept from Henrietta Maria—the Queen) and paymaster for the King's Army. It was Walter who suggested to Charles I that he invest his personal monies, place it where it earned more, put it away from everyone's prying eyes and scandalous talk, take it from the country and make it private, have it grow as a weed, keeping up with the rising costs of everything, accumulating ever more wealth. And Foster accomplished all that for Charles I: made him rich and happy with his own fortune; allowed him to be openly hostile to anyone—for he had the funds to pay the Army to win any battle, and this allowed him peace of mind that he could go anywhere, anytime, and there—for cost—would a cousin or in-law or some country's King who would welcome him were he to flee England. The money he had put aside—Walter had secretly put aside—would do that for him. And Charles was about as hostile and reckless as he could be, because he had the collateral to back him in anything he said or did. Until he need it for England's civil war...and then it was gone.

Now Walter Foster was gone. It hadn't given him the satisfaction he'd hoped to receive...killing that Foster...but in telling Charles II, Johnathan would be the hero, avenging their father for that wicked deed Foster did to their father.

Johnathan loved Charles, but—after all—HE was the elder brother, the first child of their father, and only a poor choice of good women had caused their present condition. HE should be the King; Charles the Second was born after him and Johnathan's first name was "Charles" also: "Carlos" meant Charles in Portugal, where his mother had been born and raised before she came to King Phillip's castle in employment, where Charles I had met and seduced her, then set her up as a mistress for his child, where she then named her son "Carlos Johnathan Acores."

Johnathan thought he'd ask Charles II some day if they might share the title of King, perhaps even "act" as King for a while, if Charles were away...and maybe Charles would die, and THEN Johnathan would BE the King. Wasn't THAT a thought: perhaps Charles II might die!

CHAPTER 25

Ashley decided to do the watching by himself this time...no more sending a boy to do what he should; no more "eating someone else's food." In Plimouth there was a saying, "you ate someone else's food"—not said nor taken lightly. He had heard it only in Plimouth, but he imagined it was elsewhere within the Puritan community. What it meant was not what it said—and it had nothing to do with food. It figuratively meant you had gotten someone to do some work in your place and YOU took the credit for that work—or perhaps someone had written something and you said you wrote it, to get money or praise. The Puritans were a stubborn, strict society; they lived by the King James version of the Bible (the one so revised that witches could be tortured and slain because of it) and did everything it said to do and didn't do everything it said they couldn't. One could elaborate on the Bible's presentation: for instance, one could quote it and apply it to a pertinent subject or event, but one couldn't say he made up those words. If you took credit for something like that, you deprived the author: you "ate his food." (It didn't apply to feeding the poor, as that was simple Christian charity and a necessity of life at times.) The Puritans were critical but proud and honest, and they believed completely in hard work and individual credit through God. To "eat someone else's food"—to steal it—was unacceptable, anathema to their beliefs; a person had to do things by himself (friends or relatives assisting occasionally didn't count nor did—for instance—helping someone build a barn or structure or doing a community task). You had to make your own way in the world, start your own business or somehow receive a recurring income. To steal: to eat some else's food was a sin of Biblical proportion.

It took five full days, but in came *City of Leeds* on a high tide and Ashley happened to be by the wharf, watching as the old ship warped in. Nothing planned on his part—actually was caught by surprise as he'd been impatiently waiting as the long-overdue, now-converted freighter was turned and had been talking to someone rather than observing the names on the ships.

Looked at the ship's name in some surprise: painted in gold lettering: *City of Leeds*. Very impressive for a sad-looking old vessel, but...it had just crossed the Atlantic Ocean for its umpteenth time, loaded with freight and passengers, went through the same storms *The Regal Prince* had encountered and intended this crossing many more times, so even if the ship looked and sounded creaky and sad, this French ship had been well built.

It was suddenly exciting to be this close to these spies: dangerous but exciting. All he needed now was to follow their hackney coach to know their London address. Rufus could take it from there; his job was almost over. Just see the address, write it, and he could leave...unless they changed their address, went somewhere else a day or so afterward, used this city as they used New England cities—bumping around in and leaving; that would require some more following. Perhaps they would go from here to France...well, he wouldn't go to France—the one thing he wouldn't do—but he'd watch and mark their ship. So this probably wasn't the end of this following, this chase. But maybe he could today see the faces of the murderers.

Across the gang walked Johnathan, Geoffry and Luke, attempting to watch the area but trying not to have their heads seen as turning as they sought out the store-clerk. Following Johnathan's lead, they went immediately to a hackney-coach (of which there were 2500 in London) and Johnathan got in as quickly as he could, moving to one of the small windows to observe. He had watched everyone at the docking area, seen only workers he dismissed in his mind, but continued—as did the others—to scan for anyone who might be only watching and not working...although he knew from past experience the best watchers were unobservable in their actions and took on menial jobs just to be at events. Thus far, none of them had seen anyone suspicious.

Out the rear window of the coach, Jonathan saw Ashley. Johnathan had gotten into the coach first, Geoffry standing outside to speak with the driver and observe as he did that, Luke following Johnathan into the coach. Luke normally got into coaches first, to be certain no one—no assassin—was in there nor was there a viper on the seat, waiting for an unsuspecting bottom to strike—altogether too often the case between the choices in ridding the world of someone.

Johnathan looked toward he thought he would wait to watch someone, and there he was: the store-clerk/colonist/spy from Cromwell in that ridiculous vest and shirt of white. What an oaf! Didn't even bother to hide that white flag under a coat; just stood there by the tree and watched, like that child on Boston's big wharf—making a spectacle of himself by simply watching constantly. Well, let him have a good look, because soon that look would be all he had, and very soon the end of this game would be over and that clerk dead.

"Do you see him?"

"Yes; yes. There he is, not dead; not wounded, all alone as usual. I told you we'd have to see him first but it seems we've done it simultaneously. No matter: he'll take a coach after us and we'll be watching and waiting."

Luke called to Geoffry, out the open door: "Now, Geoffry; we've found him! Now we can leave before he becomes suspicious."

Geoffry slid in quickly. "I tol' the driver t' get movin', an' you'd tell 'im where t' go. So you saw 'im? Our little bird has flown across the ocean. I want t' 'ave a look so's I can pick 'im out when I'm outside the 'ouse. Ah...I see 'im...right dumb-lookin' oaf, out in view. 'E'll be a prime piece o' candy an' I'll make 'im 'oller about Matthew...right after you finish with 'im, Johnathan."

"All the worry we've had, Johnathan, and Matthew and Mark dead, all because of this colonist. We'll end his little game and get along—as you say—to our place in history."

"Driver!" Johnathan called through the trap. "Go along to Holiday Street and I'll direct you from there." He turned to his companions: "Brother Charles says to use the old house here for a place to stay. The caretaker-family has left, but their father remains in a third-floor room; he acts as caretaker and has no income, so Charles looks the other way whilst he sells furniture from the upstairs only, to eat and keep the place warm and livable. We shall have all the downstairs, where my father lived for a while."

They headed west. Ashley chose a hackney-coach as well, told the driver to follow the previous driver's coach but at a distance so they wouldn't be noticed. He dropped a gold coin into the driver's hand and got his attention and loyalty, and the man could have made a top-rate spy himself, as the pursuit was accomplished that well: Ashley's driver went a couple times along parallel streets so he wouldn't be seen as closely following.

The sky was gray, with billowing clouds scattering across it. Looked like it had already rained; looked like it would rain more. A perfect day for this work.

Off Shipside Place, along Thames Street, past the London Bridge. Not far—too far to walk fast and carry a large chest of clothing, tho'. Couple more streets and they turned on Pudding Lane, then to a side road off that. Ashley would never have found the house. Way behind it, to the northwest, was Saint Paul's Church, a hundred meters or more high, dominating any view in that direction.

Saint Paul's Church and Saint Paul's School To Teach Grammar. What a story lay there: under the present Puritan policy, no longer could people say paternosters in public or attend Mass and give liberal alms. Saint Paul's had often held public assemblies and produced fairs, but pickpockets and lawyers—integrating themselves throughout the years—began to keep people away. Then the Protestants brought further reform and made "merriment" a bad thing, and caused drunkenness, prostitution and gambling to be arrestable experiences. Old-Faith Clergy were hanged for preaching and the local Parson grew in favor. Protestant Clergy could have wives and were paid regularly. And Saint Paul's School—which had forced Latin and education values and in the re-formation banned cock-fighting and disputing the honor of Saint Bartholomew's School—had bowed to the Free School of Saint Anthony's, on Threadneedle Street.

The place where Johnathan's coach stopped was an old, large house, three stories high within the embrace of several similar along this alleyway. Ashley's coach took another road and the driver halted well beyond where the Frenchmen's coach had stopped. "Will you get out, sir?"

"No…just wanted to see where they went; just go back to Dockside, please." He marked the place in his mind, noting the street names and the church dome in the distance on his paper.

In his room at the lodging house he again wrote to Rufus—another short letter he tried to send on a daily basis to keep his friend and benefactor informed, included the street and a description of the house, told him he'd go back there to get the numbered address. Most of the houses had no numbers assigned, or the owners would just decide what number they liked and display that, but the "better" homes had numbers such that they could be located readily. Numbered houses were becoming more necessary than fashionable in this huge city.

Ashley also wanted Rufus to know there still were three men, no more having been added and none met them at the ship—all of which he felt was important, as it seemed this was only another stopover for them and they'd go along from here. The spy-part was becoming natural.

He waited a bit, then took a carriage back to the area where Holiday Street was located, and at a nearby corner spotted a tavern; told the driver to let him off there. That was almost the perfect place for someone to go, Ashley thought; no one would wonder at a lone man going to a tavern. So he went inside for a bit, to mingle with the folk there, use up some time until dark, think how he'd approach the house to get the address, and to calm down his nerves for a while—he was sure he was almost seen by them this morning.

He saw there were signs for "beer": beer being a fairly new drink and "lighter" than ale, Rufus had told him. (He didn't care to wonder how Rufus in a Puritan colony knew all these things about ales and beer.)

The tavern seemed full of tired men in work-clothes, sitting, mostly. The ones at the bear-baiting place had wandered all about, but these men sat, although a few were standing at the long bar. There were barmaids at this place, causing some excitement within him as he realized THIS was "the" kind of place about which he had heard so much scandal. He almost left right away, as he'd never been inside "this kind" of tavern. There were woman customers in the Bear's Den, but not barmaids, and "everyone" knew what "barmaids" did! One of Lord Protector Cromwell's "progressive" businesses, he thought; just another way to take money from the already-poor and send a portion of it in taxes to Parliament.

Then he saw a few of the customers putting their hands "on" the barmaid's legs—and a few other parts. Yup! This was one of the debauched taverns he'd heard about. The "maid" would go up to a table of men, stand beside each to ask his order, then receive a groping hand on her legs, hips, buttocks or breasts. The women seemed to take it in stride, speaking to each man, getting felt, moving on to the next after taking a call for some drink or eat, then—usually laughing—would leave that table and return later with several cups or mugs of drinks—and get the same physical treatment all over again.

That was abusive...maybe the "maids" were slipped coins in exchange for the groping, and maybe they weren't, but just the idea of that "touching" was obnoxious. Anna would have rushed over there, screaming at the men and telling the woman to flee! Maybe he should, too, but wasn't at all sure about what would happen after that, so he didn't.

He stayed standing at the bar rather than moving to a table, as that was where the "maids" worked—and it apparently was "work" to them. He took a sip of the beer he'd ordered: warm, sticky, with a miserable aftertaste. How anybody actually enjoyed this was beyond him. Well...maybe he could nurse that along, sip at it, leave some in the cup. He heard a couple of whistles and looked around. Some of the customers were drinking from cups with built-in whistles and when they wanted more—of whatever it was—they'd blow into the handle of the mug and it would make a whistling sound to draw the attention of the barmaid. He wondered what genius thought that up, but then as he heard the whistles more and more, coming from all around the room and saw the re-fills, he knew it wasn't "genius"; it was the "commercial advertising" Mister Pennyweight talked about. Make something—anything—fun or a game, and you'd get repeat sales. That's why he gave sweets to the children in his store: not to be nice to them—although he was—but to get them to always remember him and the way they were treated in his store—and they'd always want to "repay" those treats, so when they grew up they'd be customers for life, as would their children and families. The whistle-cup was a splendid idea! If things worked out he'd buy one and take it to the Massa-adchu-ess-et for Rufus to make and for Mister Pennyweight to sell. If things worked out.

He listened closely to the talk of the Londoners and remembered some of the accents from his youth. If ever he had to speak with one of the Smith brothers he'd use an accent similar to a London one. In actual fact, he could not believe that only twenty years ago he was a "wharf rat" on those very docks he now watched, with his father a ship's carpenter and working in almost the same area off Dockside as the ships now used, talking just like many of these men in the tavern.

He had briefly visited his old home and the house in which they lived while waiting to be bonded to Plimouth—he couldn't remember the two others. Not much had changed but the people and newly added buildings. There was so much to think about...so much had happened in this past month...the grief, the sorrow, the loneliness, the emptiness...all was still there, festering. With a deliberate effort Ashley recaptured the frame of mind he must maintain to watch, follow and plan his scouting for Rufus.

He didn't want to drink any more beer and didn't appreciate seeing the reaching hands all over the women tray-carriers, so he left the nearly full mug—which was almost instantly snatched by a nearby man—and went outside.

By now it was dusk, although the air remained warm, moist and warm. Usually by this time it had cooled off or at least had begun to cool, but for some reason, not thus far tonight. Maybe there'd be fog. Fog in London was different from fog in Plimouth, in two ways. Some evenings in Plimouth the fog—heavy fog—would form at the level of the ground, and as one walked, he could look down and see—for instance—his knees, but below that, only fog. "Ground fog" they called it in Plimouth. Then—in an hour or so—the fog would move up to a person's waist, and go no higher.

The other kind of fog in Plimouth was a general fog, off the water and everywhere at once, thicker in the low areas but still someone within it could see into it, walk through it, not ever so heavy as the ground fog.

It must have been the closeness of the buildings in London, or the heat from so many people and homes, for when the fog began there—as he remembered it as being a child—it filled the streets and made it difficult to see except up close. Ashley could hardly remember London fog; he only could think of Plimouth's fog…and Anna. Anna would see the fog from the cabin doorway and say things like, "God's blanket of quiet falls around us," or, "The plants needed rain but God sent it else where, as they needed it more, so He gives these plants fog, for it is dew."

Anna would have loved to see London fog.

Lonesome.

Longing for something.

Anna.

Always Anna.

He started walking down the street, toward the alleyway and the road where the old house the French spies had gone into was nestled-in among others of its ilk. The alleyway he entered smelled of cat-spray, similar to the mud-mat at the cabin door in Duxbury. Brimstone. What an ass that landlord was, but what troubles he caused by being so. All the past few weeks had been unwound by him and his craziness…well, maybe the witch's curse. People bring themselves to the table; the food doesn't just leap into them. More Plimouth retrospect.

Dark. Soon it would be night—dead night. The streets were empty of trades-people here; no broom-peddlers or men with post and baskets. He looked around for one of those volunteer night-watchmen, but probably it wasn't late enough for them. Well, Holiday Street was a fashionable place at one time, with its two and three-story houses and their high, arched and spiral roofs and their walls of stone and gardens and trees. A fashionable street in its day Anna would have liked. Ashley sighed. He didn't want to stay here long; too many fashionable people plus some fashionable assassin-spies might see him and decide to do something about him. All he wanted was the house number so he could report that to Rufus.

Nothing was happening here. All the houses were dark, the street dark except for the lamp at the corner tavern; that tavern was still full of those groping men and misused women victims. No more sense in staying on this street; he'd get the number, then his job was done; up to Rufus to do more. Just get the house-number, locate a hackney-coach, leave here, go home. All over. Amen.

But no matter how he named it, the search for the Frenchmen was no puzzle, no game. These were serious, deadly men using everything: money, power, trickery, oppression, threats, anguish…maybe more; things he didn't know about, maybe things he shouldn't know about…bad things.

Anyway this was over. The only thing he needed now was the number and description of the house where the Frenchmen went…and there it was right in front of him: 85.

That's the way it is: the moment you think you have it right, saw it all or heard all that could be said, something changes such that everything changes. And then all you know and thought isn't enough. And it was never enough. Things change right in front of you and without your knowing why. And you can't change them back. All the "damnations" don't help a bit.

A little, fashionable alleyway off Pudding. An alley, almost, it was so small and short with just a few old houses embraced in gardens of flowers and tall herbs and hedges telling of things a hundred years ago, with an old surfaced road of broken cobblestones and rocks—as if it were made in a time before masons and never improved: one of the roads laid before the gentry realized cobblestones were "the" pavement they wanted for their carriages.

And their houses? Good, old houses. Probably expensive and elegant in their time, groaning now from age, a mix of two and three-story homes, houses bigger than any in Plimouth and a couple larger than the mansion of the fat man (then in his mind he corrected that to: "Squire Foster, the notary"). Slanted houses with steep, pitched, slate roofs, old and cold-looking, as if they were watchtowers for the Romans and London build around them. Homes for the previously rich, sheltered and grouped. These people all knew each other, probably were related. A whole street of wealthy families. Sad homes now: the entire street reeked of bygone days and long-gone people…almost deserted today.

"Don't turn around!" With the command came a jab in the back.

"I 'ave a pistol at your kidney an' I'm a better shot than Matthew was. That 'ouse you're watchin'…go ahead in there an' don't think this is a matchlock so you'll 'ave a few seconds t' run, 'cause this is a new Frenchie flintlock: fires instantly; no waitin'." He gave a little, smirky laugh and poked harder.

"Go on, go on…I'll jus' rap your 'ead an' drag you if I mus'."

They went to the door and Johnathan was there, pistol in hand. Yes, not a matchlock: one of the new French flintlocks which fired immediately; he had heard about those from Captain Standish.

Johnathan waved them inside, stepping back as Ashley came in.

"Be so good as to join us, Mister Lucky Clerk…how you do get away from us, and how we do keep running into you."

Luke stepped in from the dark hallway, into the room with them, armed as well with a flintlock pistol—obviously had been watching the rear of the house while Geoffry was out front. Well…these men were thorough; no doubt about that.

"Tie him securely, you two; hands behind the back. Take off those farmer-boots in case he has a stray knife hidden and pat his pockets. Mmmmmm…gag him and put him in that bedroom until I come back; I'm late already, but getting this one makes up for ant embarrassment I may suffer."

They tied his hands, "rope" taken from the drapery pull-cords.

"Before you put him in that bedroom, stand him over there, at that table."

The two followers stood Ashley by the table as Johnathan followed them, seeming to glide across the floor, very happy.

"Turn him around; back to the table. Put his right hand there on the surface."

Ashley suddenly felt sick about all this…He had made a dumb move in this game, an ignorant, dim-witted mistake! He very effectively had allowed himself to vanish from New England and now he would vanish from London. Forever. All this he thought in an instant, including wondering if this were God's revenge for him being such a dumb spy who had gotten Elspeth's brother killed—as he now would be. It didn't really matter, there wasn't much left of Ashley Lyons anyway…no wife, no children, no close friends, no father…no one would miss him that much anyway, certainly not his mother, who always seemed angry at him, and most assuredly not the storekeeper who aspired to be a Lord: Pennyweight, with his Puritan talk and actions. No one would miss him at all; why not have it over and done with—perhaps then he'd be with Anna for ever.

Luke stood in front of him, a stained-tooth smile mocking his prisoner.

Johnathan came around behind him. "Luke, you on one side and Geoffry on the other. Hold him securely."

He turned to Ashley. "Are you a stupid man?"

His hand was so fast Ashley never saw it coming: Slap!

"You act like one!" Slap! The second across his face.

"Who are you? Why are you here?"

"You sound English," Ashley ventured, his face still hot and stinging.

"Why should I not be English?"

"You're not French?"

"Not since I've been born." He had a smile that never left his lips, the kind a hangman presents as he approaches with the noose, not especially wanting to do what it was he had to do, but glad it soon would be over: that kind of smile: scary.

"None of you are French?"

"'Ere, now; we're no frogs!"

"Please, Geoffry…remember, mother is in France and may marry there."

"I'm sorry, Johnathan."

"Because we accept the pope does not mean we are Catholic; the world is large enough for two religions."

Really seeing Johnathan for the first time and at a closeness he never thought would ever happen, the man did have the look of a Britton; he was darker, tho', and probably that was the Spanish or Scot in him…who knew with anyone how their features would turn out as an adult.

His stare was that of a schoolboy—his age not much more—perhaps the impression of a schoolteacher chiding his students; and there was no other expression in his face. He was decidedly in command and in control; and he was certain of that. No doubt; no surprise; no fear.

Once, at age fourteen, Ashley had broken a vase in Mister Pennyweight's store while he had customers there. This was that face Pennyweight presented while the customer was there: a mask, but you knew behind it was all sorts of hell waiting. Johnathan's face told Ashley that his life was now over: done. Right here and right now was all he had left. No one could mis-read that face. That face could be on a Roman coin, it was that chiseled.

"You don't need to know who I am for what you will do to me."

"Ahhhh…we have a dialog, now. Who told you we were French?"

No answer.

"I believe it's time we became serious, you and I. Time you tell me why you're here. I already know you are Rufus Case."

"I'm not Rufus Case."

"Come now…your identity papers in your pockets and all the documents from the ship show your name."

"I stole those. When I was in Plimouth."

Johnathan sighed heavily. "And I thought you would be honest with me."

"I am! I know you've caught me and you'll kill me. That was the chance I took. But I know the real Rufus Case is an older man and has nothing to do with me; I just stole his identity papers to make the trip here."

"To follow us you stole someone's papers?"

"Yes. I had the opportunity, wanted to come here, stole his papers; he's older than me: look yourself to see if I'm in my thirties and not forties."

"'E's lyin'!"

"Are you, clerk? Are you lying to us?"

"No I'm not! I'm not Rufus Case and I don't want you to hurt that man because you think we are related. I wanted to follow you to London so I stole his papers at the dock and told him he must have left them at home, so he left and I boarded the ship and came here."

"This is all easily uncovered; you don't have to lie."

"I know that. Rufus is a store owner in the Plimouth colony; he didn't realize I stole his papers. Kill me, but promise you won't hurt Rufus; he's completely innocent of my reasons to follow you."

"Ah…'reasons.' Plural. Kindly present the reasons but first tell me your name."

"My name is Al Gonkin."

"YOU are Al Gonkin? From Providence?"

"And only Squire Lane could have told you that! Is he one of your men?"

Johnathan laughed. He had a scratchy-kind of laugh, like he was trying to have fun but it wasn't happening.

"I KNEW he was a Royalist!"

Whap! The slap across the face came from nowhere! Johnathan had fast hands; he probably was a very good swordsman.

"You Puritans conspired against my father, and you use the word 'Royalist' as if it were a curse! Dichotomy. See, Geoffry, two opposing opinions."

"The King refused my mother a pension when my father died aboard the King's ship, and drove my mother and me to Plimouth so we could eat and live as indentured servants! If the word is a curse, it's against you, not your father!"

"So that is the way of it and that is who you are: a Londoner injured by some ignorant insurance clerk who now has a grudge against all royalty. Listen to me: the King had nothing to do with your insurance claim; it was some hateful little man in the insurance office, not the King! You're not Rufus Case and now you would have me believe you are Al Gonkin. Really. How you do lie. Francis Lane told me that name meant 'Indian.' You would do well to consider a different line of work and a more believable name. You act as a spy and I thought you were one, but you don't sound like one."

"I'm not."

"You see, Geoffry, how necessary it is to have a story before you are captured? Same question, clerk; and I'm getting tired of your juvenile answers. Why do you follow us? To what end?"

"You killed the boy and the notary. Both people I knew, and you set that shed afire."

"Ahhh...the demonstration. Apparently it did no good; what was I thinking that I imagined a colonist would understand a warning. Why do you follow us?"

"I wanted to find out who you were because I've been blamed for the notary's death."

"You? Blamed for Foster's death?" Johnathan really laughed then, almost uncontrollably for a few seconds.

"Whyever would anyone blame *you*?"

"I was seen on the road and you weren't."

"Fortunes of war, what, Geoffry?"

"Aye."

"And you were friendly with Foster?"

"Yes, I was. I was a courier of papers Foster used."

"Small truths. So you have no idea of why we went there? Why we killed Foster? Why even we were in the colony?"

"No."

"Why don't I believe you? You sent that boy to watch us, on the wharf, long before we did in Walter."

"Yes...To my grievous fault, I did send that boy."

"Why?"

"I was trying to get a job in a Boston store, saw you five and I thought I could get money from you—steal from you. He was only to watch where you went, if you went on a ship."

"You lie." A declaration. "One man steal from five?"

"The boy you killed was the brother of the woman I wanted to marry and I needed money for her...so..."

"Ah. A non-sequitur; you still lie. The boy said you were a stranger."

"There were plans for me to wed his sister he knew nothing about."

"Ah...a family connection. Quite the usual for intrigue. And Walter Foster? Another relative or one to be?"

"No...I had met him but once...I was sent to get papers from him and he said I might deliver documents for him. I did, with one."

"Connections, connections. What would we do without them; how do we live with them. Now you are connected to me, and I cannot have that. There can be no knowledge that the King's brother begs colonists for credit."

"The King's brother gets money from New England?"

"Money for the King, to *be* the King. Money from his loyal subjects; money to restore the rightful King to England, to the English throne."

"We threw off his father."

"How mean is your tongue! You are using the collective 'we' to mean you Puritans. You call yourselves 'saints' but your religious ways have put England back into serfdom! Do you not see it? Before Cromwell there were no taxes on the poor. No tariffs on trade. No laws about what a man might say or with whom a man might dally. No particular religion forced upon a citizen. No laws to halt free speech or assembly; a Catholic will be imprisoned if he says a prayer in public! This is your idea of a free society? You in the colony have no idea what has happened here in England! We cry out for our King to return, and instead have religious fanatics running England's Parliament, putting taxes on everything, even the deed of swearing!"

"I don't believe you."

"Then you are more the fool than you look. This country is doomed under the Puritans. Believe me; I lived in Spain and saw what the Catholics must endure. The Puritans want exactly the same, but without priests. At least the Catholics foster charity; these Puritans say a man should care for himself and not require charity, so the Puritans would kill off the poor and become a State of rich men...ready to be overwhelmed by a foreign country whose Army believes they fight for the rights of the individual man, that the world will someday be free through their efforts. Cromwell kills England as we remember Her; he must be ousted and the King restored."

"You didn't have to kill a child and an old man to do that."

"Apparently I did, as I did. And speaking of killing, you killed two of my good men: Matthew and Mark."

"No, I didn't!"

"No? They just died?"

"The big man..."

"Mathew."

"He rode up on my horse and had a pistol pointed at me. I ran toward my horse and waved my arms; the horse spooked, reared, threw off the big man and when he hit the ground he discharged the pistol into himself."

"In matter of fact that was exactly what we thought happened, but not with you frightening the horse. Regardless, you caused his death. He told me he shot you."

"He did, but couldn't have had a ball loaded."

"Another thing we mused. And Mark?"

"I wanted to watch the house so I went into the barn and started to go up the ladder when I heard someone snoring. The ladder creaked, he woke up, saw me and ran toward me...I guess he forgot there was an open stairwell because he fell—onto that hayfork. I didn't do that to him!"

"You didn't finish him off by sticking the fork into him? The truth!"

"In God's name I never touched that man nor the hayfork. He fell on it all on his own."

Johnathan moved behind Ashley. All the while, Geoffry had been holding Ashley's right arm and Luke his left; Ashley's hands bound. Ashley's feet were also tied, but Johnathan had him standing there, propped up by Geoffry and Luke and the table.

"Why do you follow us?" Johnathan hefted the pistol for weight.

Ashley prayed silently, knowing something would happen. *Oh, my God, don't take me now. I have so much to do for you on earth and in this life. Make me your avenger of blood that I may do on earth that which you will do in Heaven: send these men to Hell.*

"You are a very dangerous Puritan, very dangerous. *No* one but a fool or a zealot would do what you have done...but you are no fool, so what am I to think? I think you are too dangerous to stay alive."

"One thing I will say: I have no shame in what I have done in this assignment. The bitterness I found and foul doings were never in my power to do, and God alone will judge what has happened."

"Put a gag in his mouth; I want to hear no more from this man who killed our comrades and would kill us as well. Put his right hand on the table and hold it there."

Johnathan uncocked the pistol and made it safe to handle. He held it by the barrel, swung it back and struck Ashley's hand as tho' he wielded a hammer!

Ashley cried out, his yells muffled by the gag. Luke grinned as he heard bones break.

"A little pain and agony to remind you of what I go through daily, remembering my big man and my close friend."

Leaning over, Johnathan again swung the pistol butt, and the impact on Ashley's head seemed as if it would break him into a million pieces. This snake didn't just rattle, he struck!

"Seemingly endless resistance. He has a fire within him...I see it burn. A pity he could not be with us instead of against us."

"We wouldn't have needed him."

"Of course not, Lukey...you're twice the man this colonist is."

Johnathan sighed. "Now we have him, whatever shall we do with him? We can't kill him here; I can't have this house and the caretaker involved in any scandal."

"We'll toss 'im off the bridge after I knife 'im. I knows a place wha' s gettin' repaired an' no one is there...high up. I'll knife 'im an' over 'e'll go."

"You'll not be seen carrying him there? It's a way off and you'll have to use a coach."

"Naw...jus' two ol' mates in the night, proppin' up a drunken pal...Luke an' me 'ill take 'im an' give 'im a right proper sendoff. We'll fill 'is pockets wi' sand an' 'e'll go right t' the bottom."

"Be very careful of the night watchmen. They scan those houses on the bridge..."

"Johnathan," Geoffry cut in. "I knows a flat up there, bein' repaired. No winda, jus' a 'ole in the wall. No one will suspect; no one will see; no one will know. We'll carry 'im between us, an' 'e'll be gone from 'ere."

"So, I suppose you've been there already!"

"Awwwww, Lukey...Johnathan will tell you a warrior chooses 'is own goun' t' fight, an' I looks aroun' wi' that in min'."

"Indeed, Geoffry, had you not looked around we'd have no place to dump this Puritan. You've both done very well and I'm proud of you. Our colonist still sleeps?"

"He's totally unconscious, Johnathan; that slug to the head was a good one."

"Don't rely on it. Put him out that window and knife him...then I'll rest easy. Again, no one watching! Be extra careful about that!"

"We hear you, Johnathan."

"Aye...I'll make sure we're alone up there."

"That's a great relief, Geoffry...you'll be rewarded for all this. The world cannot yet be told I beg money for Charles."

"Coo...I do it for you, Johnathan...we're ol' mates from years ago, almos' brothers."

"All very true, Geoffry...and I have every confidence in your ability."

"Then we'll take him now?"

"No, Luke; let Geoffry have his fun and after I leave you go hire a hackney-coach and take the Puritan to his new home. Be sure the driver thinks he's inebriated and hiding from the Puritan-sheriff so he won't be suspicious of what you do. Pay him extra."

"I'll tell him our friend passed out from strong drink and we're taking him home to his bridge-flat...and we'll get out on the bridge and carry him from there. It'll all be done by the time you return."

"A watchman might 'ear the splash."

"Yes, but no one will see you two because you shall have gone across to Southwark and when the fun settles, then returned without notice. Walk back; a long way, but no witnesses in drivers."

"Southwark…I loves Southwark, Johnathan…all them 'ores…"

"Patience, patience, dear man…France and her delicacies await. Oh! Shove those identity papers into his pocket; we don't need anyone finding them around here. Let the sheriff deal with them when the time comes."

"And when that time comes, we'll be far away from here."

"Won't 'e be surprised when 'e wakes up t' see the fishes!"

They all laughed.

"I would!"

It had taken Luke some time to locate a hackney-coach in that area, but he had, and the extra he paid in advance brought the horse-drawn vehicle to outside the Holiday Street house. He went back inside, looking for the caretaker while knowing he was on the third floor while they stayed there, got Geoffry, and the two carried the still unconscious Ashley to the coach, then loaded him inside while a non-curious driver (he had seen things like this before: friends helping a passed-out man home) paid more attention to his horse than his fares.

The trip in the coach was fairly rapid: they weren't that far from the bridge to begin with, but it was too far to carry him that distance. Few people were on the streets this late; Johnathan was right about that; they had waited just long enough for the majority of people to be gone from where they went. Luke had slung his jacket over his shoulder, shoving an arm into it and pulling it around him. Even summer nights in London could be chilly and this was too late in the summer, almost autumn. New England had spoiled him or the weather had changed; he wasn't sure which, but the night air bothered him now and it hadn't in all the decade he was in the Army, lying on the ground at nights with no blanket or coat, just a short jacket and oversize pants for warmth.

"The Puritan" had never awakened from the blow Johnathan administered; Luke was sure he never would again regain consciousness. The man could now be considered dead; all they needed was to dispose of the body.

Just before they entered onto the bridge they saw a few people—most likely a family—in a small park beside the river. An open carriage with a horse stood waiting at the park's entrance.

No night watchmen on the bridge at this point: too perilous for them to be out alone on London streets after dark; bad enough they had to patrol inside, out of the weather but still targets for those who preyed in the night. Geoffry had the coach halted and Luke again paid the driver, dismissing him and his hope he'd get the fare back beyond Puddingside. Soon as he left, Luke helped Geoffry hold their unconscious Puritan: they each grabbed an arm and put it over their shoulders, propping Ashley between them, and after they again looked around carefully, they made for the nearest stairway. It would be several flights up, and Luke didn't enjoy dragging this man in the public's view, even if it were nighttime and few if any should be around.

They went up the stairs slowly and cautiously.

"It's difficult to carry him like this."

"We're almost there. We used the coach t' get 'im 'ere, so wha's the trouble?"

"I'm taller than you, so I have to take more of his weight! If I had the body of Matthew..."

"Coo...you wouldn't want that now! Jus' ben' over a bit...you know how t' ben' over, don't you?"

"Now that's mean of you to say that! Did I say anything about what you did to this colonist while I was out getting the hackney?"

"Nawwww...yer a bit o' all right, Lukey...You're my candy but this one's jus' some excitement for me. I'd carry this one myself but we're so close now." Geoffry stopped, seeing two men in the semi-darkness of the third-floor landing.

"'Ere! Wha's this? Buggerin'? You'd better run!"

The men grabbed at their previously removed trousers and did run, Geoffry laughing softly but long as they disappeared into the darkness of that level.

"This is so risky...why couldn't we have just dropped him in the river outside?"

"You didn't see the people outside? Coo! Jus' do it this way an' things'll be well. Com' on...another four lifts an' we're there."

They carried their burden steadily upward, to the level Geoffry wanted and where the empty room was waiting. As they entered the door-less room—slight light from outside coming in—there were voices in the hallway, coming toward them.

"More damn people 'ere at night than in the damn day!"

"This is *your* choice of a secret place, remember?"

Get 'im t' the winda an' drop 'im there! We'll wait for 'em t' go by."

The "window" Geoffry was going to use had been a "window," but now was just an empty space in the wall. The window itself had been removed and eventually a new one would be installed; the masons were still working here, empty bags and piles of sand cluttering the floor for they were re-plastering and ready to lay a new flooring.

They more dragged than carried Ashley to the window and gratefully dropped him, feeling at the same time piles of sand, lime and stone-dust on the floor: mason's supplies they couldn't bag and carry away after their day-work was done. Luke's foot hit something else and he heard a startled cry: there was someone else in this room!

Geoffry heard it also and his knife flashed into his hand. The small amount of moonlight through the open wall didn't light up the room but it gave an "almost light" to them.

"We'll leave!" a voice called from the shadows.

"We didn't know anyone lived here," a woman's voice said.

"We're going right now," said the first voice. "We're sorry we stayed here and we'll leave."

Two long shadows rose from the floor, and three small ones. A family without a home had been sleeping here this night (and probably others) and were now awake.

Ashley was awake also. Consciousness was returning slowly as he had been carried up the stairs, but being jolted as he was thrown onto the pile of sand on the floor brought him back to the land of the living. He couldn't feel much of anything but pain from his crushed right hand, but his left was into something cool and slick, some form of sand. He squeezed his fingers and gathered a fistful, trying to come fully awake…he knew he had missed a lot—like—why he was here and where "here" was, but he remembered the Frenchmen, now Englishmen.

"Com' on; get along!" Geoffry urged softly as he could so no others would hear. He was very startled at the idea of several people in the "empty" room with him; Johnathan would be angry at this: he had promised Johnathan the room would be empty and tossing the clark out the window would never be witnessed; now an entire family had seen them. This room had been totally vacant when he'd used it those times, but he'd been away from here too long and relied too much on memory without first seeing this place. Now there were strangers here, but they probably were homeless peasants and already frightened. They would run and not tell anyone; he'd just give them reason to run, and run from London forever!

"Stay 'ere whilst I chase this gang down the corridor."

Out they went, homeless couple, children and Geoffry: a mother hen shooing her chicks.

Ashley's hand reached out for some sort of tool or weapon but found only piles of lime, sand and stone-dust.

Luke bent over him. "Still asleep, Puritan? Not much longer and you'll sleep forever."

Ashley's hand clutched as much of the lime as possible, then he flung it toward where he imagined Luke's eyes might be!

"Ahhhhhgggg..." A muffled surprise.

Ashley tried to stand; couldn't use his right hand; terrible pains in his head and hand coursing through him.

Luke, blinded, staggered away from what he thought was a dead man, suddenly unable to see and instantly frightened.

All of this had been too much for Luke: the "supervision" by former-lover Geoffry, Johnathan sending him like a servant after the coach and made to assist Geoffry when Luke's present position was as a lover of Jonhathan, the darkness here he feared so much, the surprise attack upon his eyes, the deed he was about to do, the family of witnesses... He spun around to get away from the dangerous Puritan and go toward Geoffry, but instead stepped out the open space in the wall where the window had been.

When the Roman Bridge across the Thames was built (stone by stone), small boats would sometimes smack into the pillars holding the span, almost wrecking the entire bridge and causing local history to remember that. So in the planning of the present London Bridge, oval areas called "piles" were filled with stones and placed around each bridge-support such that any ship would be halted by them before it could strike a bridge-support and topple/destroy the bridge. Most of these oval areas were filled with large, angular rocks. Geoffry was wrong about the "window" being placed over the river; it was over a "pier": a "starling of rocks."

Luke fell without a sound, close to twenty long-yards, his eyes totally shut, his arms widespread—as in the Catholic symbol—his mouth in the shape of a "O."

The rocks which were placed to stop large ships from damaging the bridge stopped Luke also. Thankfully, no damage was done to the London Bridge.

CHAPTER 26

It was a struggle to stand, but he used his knees as braces and forced himself up, holding on to his leg with his good hand, clasping the injured one to his chest—still in pain. Pushed himself up, wobbling; hardly could keep his balance, dizzy, finally standing and the dizziness passing.

They had put on his boots; hadn't tied them very well and they'd probably flop, but they were still on his feet and he might be able to walk with them, perhaps run.

On his feet now, still a bit woozy but gathering his bearings. Had to get away from here…where? Where was he and which way should he go?

The voices had come from behind him, so Ashley used the dim moonlight to see a sort of hallway beyond the removed door, and went to there as fast as he could.

He was on the bridge; he knew that. And from the height he had seen briefly out the hole in the wall he was very high, so he had to get down to the walkway of the bridge.

When he lived in Dockside, his mother had taken him often across this bridge, in and out of the shops, even to some of the Flats where her friends lived, so he had some kind of an idea where he could be and how he'd get out, down, wherever.

He found a stairwell and went down, fast as his loosely tied boots, sore hand and head would let him, floppy-sounds made by his boots but him not now caring. Speed was the thing here…but after he had left the sand-room there was only blackness, so he had to run with caution or he'd do what Luke and Mark did. Yes, he knew—remembered—their names: those names he'd always remember.

Down he went, staggering, winding, picking up speed on the stairs, being careful at a landing and the start of a new set of stairs, going in the same direction on each level but trying to shift his escape, making noise with his boots but not caring: had to get away, HAD to!

On a level where there was pale moonshine he turned, then running down that long hall, down another stairway, finally coming to where he thought was the bridge Road. Behind him he thought he heard running footsteps. Geoffry!

He ran out onto the bridge full tilt, using all his energy—precious little—to get away. There were night-lights here, not many, but spaced so he could tell the direction and see the obstacles. On he ran, frantic now, no night-watchmen nor people anywhere around. The time for caution was over and he had to get all the way across this long bridge...a great distance for one so sore and tired and frightened.

About where the bridge ended there was a cobbled crossroads. Overhead—he knew without looking up—was where the pikes were onto which the traitor's heads were placed that all could see and know English justice was attained and here was a good object-lesson for any who might try to subvert England. There were so many hanged here in Southwark a hundred years ago that portable gallows drawn by horses had to be made to go from street to street, taking those arrested and dispatching them on the gibbet several at a time.

Now he knew where he was!

There had to be someone out: some hackney-driver looking for a fare, some drinker returning from a tavern cascading between the buildings, some pair of lovers seeking place after place to linger in lust, some night watchman appointed by the Mayor, ANY one!

He ran regardless of his partially tied and floppy boots and the sounds they echoed all through the tunnel of humanity and out onto the vastness of Southwark, ran knowing Geoffry was behind him, right behind him probably, ready to shoot or knife or snatch him and fling him to the cobblestones.

He felt ashamed of himself, running this way; no self-respecting militiaman, especially a former captain of militia, should be so cowardly as to fly pell-mell into strange landscape when the situation is one-on-one, and even if it meant a fast getaway in order to set up an ambush, it just wouldn't be done!

But Geoffry had the upper hand and he felt this wasn't a runaway in fear, only a tactic to equal the sides, not having a pistol as Geoffry. With one of those, he could meet that knife-murderer face-to-face at least with an equal chance.

So it was done: he'd convinced himself within a matter of seconds that the running was not cowardice but a tactic and he'd deal with the anguish of his actions later; right now he only had to stay alive...and he realized that was probably what Peter was thinking when he denied Jesus those times.

His instinct told him to turn right, to get away in the shadows, going along the waterfront toward the houses, but he disregarded that message, feeling instead that Geoffry might think the same. More lights, brighter now; now he would be recognized by Geoffry at a distance. He ran forward, then turned onto a left-bearing alley between two streets. He paused a moment, dropping onto his knees and peering around a corner where he had just been. No one there; thank God!

There was no other way afoot to get across the Thames anywhere around here, but there also was no good reason to do that. Safety in Southwark was just as welcome as safety in Dockside, so he moved quickly and quietly down the alley, seeing a tiny light ahead.

The light was coming from a candle in a room, spilling through an open doorway where someone stood. Ashley froze: could this be a trap?

Two seconds his heart pounded, then, he had no choice; he had to decide.

He moved forward, walking, getting ready to pass the open door: cautious, careful, ready to run, fight, yell, whatever.

Something white in the doorway.

A man in white? Was that possible?

No…he got closer. A woman in white, a woman wearing a white dress or robe…a robe.

"Good evening."

She knew he was there; the darkness hadn't hidden him. Perhaps Geoffry could see as well as this woman.

"Good evening," he responded.

"Dark out there."

He drew closer. A woman alone. No Geoffry.

"Yes…dark."

"Would you like to come in out of the darkness?"

"No, thank you."

He was almost past her now.

"I can do anything."

What was the answer to that? What did she mean?

"No one else on the street is up so late. Only me. Why don't you come in and you can tell me why you're out so late?" She smiled…a lovely smile; an enticing, enchanting smile. Even in the darkness she lit up his hopes. *Have to get off this street; Geoffry will see me at any moment!* Inside her room would be safe—away from Geoffry.

"Er…that would be nice. If we went inside would you shut your door?"

"Of course, silly...that's what doors are for: to be opened and shut."

She backed into the room and Ashley looked quickly behind him, then looked fast as he could for a trap as he entered the room.

She immediately closed the door.

"Have you a window? Does the candlelight shine outside?"

"No..." she almost purred like Anna's cat. "No window; only the rich girls have windows. I'm lucky to have a door; some don't. Some only have blankets." She reached up and pulled down a drape, so when it fell it completely covered the doorway.

"Now there's no light that can be seen outside. No light at all; I've looked. Why don't you want anyone to see a light?"

"A man is following me."

"Oh. A night watchman?"

"No...I'm not a criminal or an arsonist; I was attacked earlier by three men...and they beat me..."

"Oh, that's awful! I see your hand is injured."

"I'm...I got away from them but I'm still being followed by one of them, so that's why I asked if the door could be shut and if the light would shine outside. I don't want him to know I'm here."

"Well, I certainly don't want him in here, either!"

His eyes were more accustomed to the candlelight now, and he could see her. He tried to keep his eyes from staring at her. In the light from the candle it seemed she had red hair.

"My name is Margaret."

"Er...I'm Ashley...Ashley Lyons."

"It's very nice to meet you, Ashley Lyons. Do you live nearby?"

"I'm staying at a room in Dockside..." He let the rest fall away from the conversation; she didn't need to hear it all.

Margaret was pretty but damaged-looking, with red hair that should have been combed and a shy sadness in her eyes. Her smile was gentle but lacked any gayety. Even tho' she was thin, her face wore wrinkles. Probably in her early twenties, he guessed, and wearing what appeared to be more nightclothes than day-wear. Yes...she had on only a nightshirt!

He thought how pretty she'd be with a real smile, and at the same time feared her husband would suddenly burst into this room to yell at her and eject Ashley in an embarrassing situation. Embarrassing and dangerous, with the right husband, especially as Geoffry stalked the dark streets outside, his knife and pistol ready to be used.

"Are…are we alone?"

"Of course."

"You have no husband here?"

"None anywhere."

He sighed inwardly, looking around the room at the same time. The candle gave orientation to the room but not much else. The door had a heavy cloth across it, and this seemed not at all like a house, but just a single room. Just this one room he could see, and not that large. A bed up against the width of the room across from him. There was a thick but small, oval rug by the door.

"This is…not a house?"

"No…just a single room. I pay rent for it."

"Well, it's a lovely room…I'm intruding here."

"No! I've been…lonesome…all evening. Please stay, even if all we do is talk."

"I'd like that. I haven't 'just talked' to a woman in a long while." Talk. If she'd just talk with him for a while…let him rest and maybe that assassin would go away. It wasn't that he wanted a woman, just that he wanted to BE with someone…a friend, not someone like that cynical sailor aboard *The Regal Prince*.

"So that's what we shall do: talk. You pull the chair close to the bed and sit on it; I'll sit on the bed and we shall talk."

"I'm not interrupting anything?"

"No…not at all."

Then she smiled a real smile at him…and the world disappeared for a flash while he wondered what that meant.

The chair was already beside the bed, at the head of it. She moved some cheap, flimsy female clothing which had been tossed across the chair, and a pair of worn shoes probably re-soled as Ashley's boots had been. No jewelry. Anna had made her own jewelry of shells and rawhide and polished stones, much as the Algonkin made wampum. No ocean-side here, to find those shells; no rawhide either.

He gladly sat and she drifted onto the bed, close to him.

She sat there, picking at a spot in the blanket, waiting perhaps for the right time or when she could put together the right question. Wearing out that blanket in the meantime, picking at it.

There was that elfin smile again.

"The things people say when they remain quiet."

Her hair had been pinned up, probably for sleep, but now she slipped out the pin and shook her hair, a waterfall of red hair cascading past her shoulders. Anna's hair had been short.

As he saw her hair fall down it excited him more than he'd ever been with Anna. Anna was a friend and quiet: a sweet wife in all respects. This indecently clad woman in front of him was Sin and Circe, excitement and desire, a dreamer's wish and a man's woman. What he wanted right then and there was beyond all thought of a Puritan whose religion had forbidden even Christmas!

"Stop laughing at my hair! I try to keep it straight, like an English girl should, but it has curls and kinks and makes me look untidy."

She changed the subject right away: "Are you from London? You said you stayed at Dockside."

"Used to live there a long time ago. A man in uniform came to where my mother and I were living and told my mother my dad had died on one of the ships in the harbor. I was six. Ever since then, I've wondered what it would have been like to stay here in London with my mum and dad. We had to go to the Plimouth colony as indentured servants, but now we are no longer such and I'm here on a visit, staying at Dockside, near where I lived when I was a child."

"I'm glad for you that's all behind you, all that sorrow. I had to leave my country to get work, and ended up here, not really working but working harder than I ever thought possible. Are you married?"

This girl got right to the point. Well...we said we'd "talk."

"I was...my wife died in childbirth fifty-eight or fifty-nine days ago...the time just seems to slide by on me now..."

"And you're just here to visit?"

"Here on business...important business."

"Does it have anything to do with your sore hand."

"That wasn't part of the business; they—the men I told you about—did that earlier tonight."

"A business rival?"

"Definitely a rival."

"Do you still love your wife? Most men do not count the days their wife has been gone when they die."

"Of course! Just because she's gone does not mean I don't love her."

"Do you love her this very minute?"

"I'll always love her, but this very minute I'm setting aside for us."

She smiled, and he was back with Anna. That smile...that smile...God, how he missed that smile.

She had perfect lips on a perfect face, a pouty mouth that said nothing but told him volumes, and a look from her eyes which made him understand she wanted whatever he could give and she'd give even more back. Then she noticed his right hand against his chest—the hand was swollen and in that swelling mis-shapen and just the sight of it let her know it had bones broken.

"Your hand..."

"They did that...they knocked me unconscious...hardly could move it before but now I can't move it at all and it hurts dreadfully."

"Looks broken."

"Feels broken."

"I had a broken finger once: someone shut it in a door. I know how that must feel...and I know how to put a bandage on it. Take off your shirt." She went to a drawer in her dressing table and took out a roll of bandaging-cloth, then brought it over to her improvised sink, washed his hand—poking every portion of it, making him groan in pain until she felt she knew just where the breaks were, then applied the bandage securely.

"Take this off in the morning and re-wrap it, understand? Or I'll do that if you're still here."

"Will you still be here in the morning? You seem as a Guardian Angel, doing good things and leaving."

"I'm no angel, but of course I'll be here in the morning; I live here, silly."

"Then maybe you can do that in the morning." It was a statement with a question wrapped inside it and she unwrapped it.

"That was exactly what I was thinking."

"I want to pay you."

She smiled one of those elfin smiles...the kind when someone knows more than you do and is not letting you in on the secret—knowing, of course, you're going to find out for yourself really soon anyway: that kind of smile. "Not now."

"If you hadn't been outside...he'd probably have found me."

"You're safe in here; don't worry."

The woman was all smiles and tenderness; she made his heart melt and his pulse pound.

She guided him back to the bed, where they were before, and he sat on the chair; then she reached down and pulled her nightshirt over her head. He knew he shouldn't look...but there was so much to see!

"Stand up."

Still a girl in her looks, with red-haired, green-eyed innocence, an oval face presenting a smattering of freckles, nipples the size of the thimble his mother used to use. He sat there, salivating. She was carefully beautiful—on the verge of being a raving beauty but hadn't yet made the transition because of her poverty: she didn't have quite the "look" beautiful women wear so well and easy. Beyond that, she was immensely attractive, even in the light of wicks in wax.

It didn't look as though she had any hair below her belly, then he realized it was there, but so light a red color it hardly appeared, and it seemed as though it were cut, the way the grass at the Meeting Hall in Plimouth was sythed short; she had to have cut it...which was another wonder to him, as Anna never did that and she had heavy, dark hair there.

Completely nude. What dream was this? Did he ever have to wake? Was he dead and in Heaven?

Completely...totally, stark naked. Even Anna didn't do that, and Elspeth did it only in bed. This girl was now standing in front of him!

"Come on, stand up; only your hand is hurt."

She rapidly undid his trousers and let them fall to the floor.

Then she leaned into him, beside him, seemingly to comfort him (or herself) as he had stood; smiled as their eyes met and parted while she moved to put her lips on his ear and with a light, moist breath whispered, "I need you." Then she gave him a brief kiss on his lips, warm and tingling—asking for something not expressed but desired: a hope, a promise to be fulfilled, a question in itself left unspoken. Kisses were now fashionable in London, and "everyone" was doing them.

She reached down and held him...Ashley suddenly lost every memory he'd ever had when she did that...then, as though she had thought about it and reached a decision, she showed a faint smile, opened her lips, and bent down. Anna had never, never—no one had ever done that to him! Actually, Anna had told him on their wedding night that her mother had told her how that night must be, and what she must do for her husband. This part wasn't ever mentioned and Ashley wasn't that interested in the talk between Anna and her mother...and he was interested even less when Anna continued to talk and not act. But they had gotten through that like good Puritans and had intimate moments as often as possible after that.

Margaret was intimate, but it was for longer than "moments"! He wondered not when, but IF she would stop...hoping she wouldn't!

Not only had no one done that to him before, but he hadn't ever HEARD of that being done!

He closed his eyes and the pleasure soared, heightening the sensation and tumbling it throughout his body. Suddenly, Margaret was the only and most desirable woman in the world, and every other thought in his mind fled unashamed. She was instantly his entire world and all he ever wanted from it.

Then she said, "Sit on that chair…I like it best that way."

She eased him onto the chair, holding his bandaged hand outstretched.

She sat on him, muzzling noses and wriggling herself as she sat there.

His world spun…whatever she was doing was better than anything else anyone had done with him. He was panting, thrilled, exhausted, exhilarated all at once.

She cleaned them both with a damp cloth, all the while pressing an ample breast against him, then pushed him toward the bed; and when he was in it she pulled off his boots, stockings and trousers. As she tugged at his long stockings, pieces of paper fell from them, but it wasn't paper she wanted so she left them on the floor.

Ashley knew he looked as though he could use one of those Roman baths his mother used to kid him about when he was a child: "You're so dirty a Roman bath wouldn't get you clean!" He had wondered at the time what a Roman bath was anyway…must really be old by now; maybe no water in them.

He had bruises everywhere! And he hurt everywhere. They must have kicked and punched him while he was unconscious. "Bastards!" as Rufus would say.

Margaret pulled two pillows from under the bed, tossing them one on the other, beside him; then she jumped in, pushing him aside and settling her bottom atop them. "This way is good, also." She pulled at him until he was on her, with the pillows raising them both.

It was good, also, as he quickly found out.

He let her lead the lovemaking, actually glad of it as she went places and did things Anna never had done. Happy, wriggling around, grabbing at each other, playing…he inched his left hand toward a very personal part of her and she didn't push it away as Anna had done.

Anna made "happy love": Elspeth was submissive and delighted; this…this was different from anything but better than anything before. It didn't take long, but she refused to end it, just going on and on, drawing him in, giving him experience and pleasure, even concern with the way she writhed and acted. Then they were quiet, but still locked together.

Anna used to say that Ashley liked the game of "peek, pinch and poke." Margaret didn't play that game, nor any other Ashley knew or could think of.

No rules in THIS game...just beautiful, wonderful experiments and excitements.

It was comfortable with Anna, almost embarrassing with Elspeth, but this...this was joy and delight, exploration and invitation, primitive exuberance. At the end they just kissed again, holding each other, her skin warm and sweaty. If he had thought Anna knew it all and Elspeth had more to teach, Margaret was a surprise! She moved in all directions, doing everything: positions a Puritan never would think to do or think about at all, just dismiss those thoughts as un-saintly. She was no prude, no Puritan, no...anyone Ashley had known. And to his amazement, she seemed to enjoy it as much as he, smiling and purring and making sounds of delight as she opened new doors and raised the level of his awareness with a woman. She made them one with her closeness: bonded them.

So joined, he briefly wondered if this could go on, would happen every time with her, might remain so thrilling for all their lives...if, even, she would consider being with him all her life and his. He was on her, under her, beside her, around her...things he hadn't thought to do ever before—ever! When he finally ran out of strength she continued—until he fell asleep, then she did as well.

He woke on a fluffy cloud with an angel beside him...but no wings or halo or robe, just towseled red hair and lots of warm flesh. He hoped Heaven smelled so good—and looked so fine! She must have had the mattress stuffed recently as it felt better than any he'd ever been on...and the pale-skinned Margaret slept—still as pretty as her Irish face could let her be—circled beside him, nude and still very enticing. She woke as he started again, smiled that knowing smile and went along with the actions for the few moments it took. She was used to that.

His tender and bruised body—from the beating he had taken with Johnathan and his men—was now aggravated from all these antics and activities and movements, but the instant they stopped he wanted to start all over again and tried; she laughed, sounding like ice tinkling in a cup, and he stopped. It wouldn't have happened anyway...what was that old saw about lightning?

She wasn't shy about letting him see her body, in or out of the bed. Her breasts were full, rounded, inviting...crying out to be held or suckled. Anna's were not so large, but the milk for the baby swelled them almost to this size. He lost himself—looking at those breasts—until he saw another thing he wanted to see even more.

Anna always seemed to be hesitant and she wouldn't walk around nude, but would let him see her like that in bed. Elspeth was a tease, permissive in bed but covered herself as often as she could. This was absolutely crazy: he was comparing these three women as if he were choosing meat at the butcher's! Had it gotten to that? No wonder the Puritan men kept themselves from women until marriage and stayed with that one woman from then on. To know these differing styles of lovemaking was information well beyond their need, and made him wonder who might be next and what new things they might do. Extremely un-Puritan thoughts!

Again, he woke in happiness…the lumps in the mattress and odd smells discarded. Margaret was there, still asleep and even prettier in the low glow from the single and shortened wick-candle. Outside, it must be dawn. Late. He'd overslept, probably. People would be on the streets now and it would be light enough to be recognized by Geoffry. He prayed Geoffry wouldn't be waiting outside and all the throbbing and soreness in his hand came back to stay with him.

Looked at Margaret again, feeling he'd like to do one last snuggle with her, be inside her again, wanted to touch her all over, smell her, taste her…do the entire night again. What a night that was! He'd done things to and with a complete stranger that married Anna would not have allowed him: embarrassing things…but nice, delicious, tasty things; candy to a sweets-starved man.

He shook his head slightly to try to rid himself of the thoughts and feelings. She'd be perfect for Boston…a young, savvy and beautiful girl who gave herself to him with abandon…with no questions or promises or anything withheld. What a perfect wife she would be; what a life he—they—could lead!

Margaret had broad hips; she could have children easily; that was a secret he'd been told one time by an old man, before Ashley married. "Marry a woman with broad hips and she'll have easy childbirths." Anna was so little…that's why she had lost the baby and died…and probably why the child died as well: her little frame didn't allow for the room babies needed to develop—the surgeon told him—his mother had said the same thing, that Anna shouldn't try to have children; she said she told Anna that herself.

Wouldn't that be wonderful…to have his own children with Margaret and be able to tell them about his adventures when he was twelve, then at fifteen. His own children. Anna tried; God help her she tried; she must have loved him more than life itself to try to have children for him: what a wonderful woman and wife; he loved her dearly and always would…she was faithful to her death, her memory would ever be with him as the perfect wife.

Two of her children gone, Anna gone; maybe Margaret would give him children. His mother would like that also: the youthful mother who was at least ten years older than she admitted on paper.

Being with Margaret was a lot like being with Anna and Elspeth together; hours of repairing his soul just now accomplished. Not as in redemption: Margaret buying back or getting it back—but more in recapturing it from where it had gone when Anna and the baby died...perhaps a salvation.

However it was, he was glad it was back with him, buoying him back from the bottom and letting him breathe on the top. An almost-religious experience with Margaret; what a night of star-studded and moon-shone wonders he had experienced!

In great surprise, as he rose he saw another woman, seemingly nude also but wrapped in a blanket and asleep on a thin pallet atop the oval rug on the floor by the door, the pallet and her blocking the door from being opened.

Margaret moved beside him. "That's Velma."

"Who?" Still the owl.

"Velma, my roommate. We live here together but whoever gets the bed, the other has to sleep on the pallet on the floor."

"Where was she last night?"

"Out working. She goes to taverns and I stay here."

He dressed quickly, faster than he'd expected he would because Velma lay there, ready to wake or awake already. Margaret pulled on a robe, but didn't hold it together.

"I'm almost at a loss as to what to say...your roommate came in and got her sleeping arrangements and I never heard her; never heard the lock on the door open."

"There is no lock on the door—the landlord won't permit it; that's why one of us sleeps next to it: to know if someone tries to get in."

"No lock...?" He had thought differently—that Geoffry was locked outside and would make a commotion were he to try the door.

She reached across at him, snuggled up against him, the robe wide open, and kissed him long and lusciously. "A girl can always use some coin."

"Oh!" He reached into his vest. "Don't be frightened, I have a skinning-knife I must get."

Margaret backed up against the bed and Velma sat up and grabbed at the door handle.

"No...only to cut the stitching on my boot! I carry extra coins in my boots...Rufus had these boots made for me, called 'Traveler's Boots'—they have extra-thick soles and sewn-in coin-pockets so if you are robbed, not all your money is taken." He cut one and pulled out two gold sovereigns, handing them to the still-uncertain Margaret.

Then he put away the knife in the secret pocket of the vest which also was designed by Rufus the Inventor. Velma walked to the now-empty bed, tugging the pallet after her, pushing it under the bed and not now seeming to care that the scare was over. Then she curled into the still-warm and damp blanket he and Margaret had just left.

Velma had a straight body, everything there and in place, but not the hips of Margaret, tho' more curves than Elspeth. Poor Elspeth: wanting a man so badly she threw herself at one—and almost caught him like a fish on a hook. Velma seemed to be able to have any man she wanted. Maybe the difference between them...only in attitude...although Velma was no "thin as a rail" woman by any means.

Ashley hugged Margaret, his thoughts racing. "I'd like to take you away from here."

"Tell me more."

"I must finish some business I have started...but when I leave London I'd like..."

"Leave London? You'll leave London?"

"I live in New England: Boston."

"Where is that?"

"Boston? Across the Atlantic Ocean in the new colony..."

"Across the ocean?" Her repetitions were getting aggravating.

"In North Virginia...New England."

"Virginia?" From Velma. "I've heard of Virginia. Savages and a plague there!"

"This is way north of Virginia...quite some different place." He wished he had just told Margaret alone or had simply carried her off with him after he came back here for her.

"What do you do there?" Velma was still questioning.

"Presently...not very much. I was a captain of militia..." He let that "incident" slide away.

"Then you're rich." Not a question.

"Not especially rich..." The words trailed like a duck trying to fly off a short pond.

From Margaret: "But you've given me gold coins and you want to take me there to live; you'd have to be rich for that or you want me to work for you."

"No work...it would be an easy life, a good life, better than this one for you, but right now I'm not rich." He sensed he was losing her.

"I have a letter of credit...plenty for us to get good passage on a ship to Boston and there I'll get whatever it takes to make you happy."

"But we'll marry here first?"

"Yes," he said, playfully...rubbing her and wanting to use the bed again. "I'll need new clothes and then to see the banker. Then I'll return and we'll plan."

Margaret hung on him again, beginning to cry. "I believe you're telling me the truth...but men change their minds when they leave here. This isn't the first marriage-proposal I've received, and Velma also...Men say they want wives but all they want is free fun."

"When I get back I'll take you and Velma with me to New England..."

"Not ME!" Velma called. "I'll have the whole bedroom to myself when she leaves!"

Margaret frowned, almost scowled: disappointed over what Velma had said and willing to let her know.

He began to laugh at the antics of the two women but Margaret's kiss halted that. He held her tightly again, touching her all over, under the robe, then draining her lips once more in a greedy kiss. "Margaret...I wouldn't take you to a place where you'd be poor...I can make a good life for you there."

"And you'll marry me before we go? So everyone here will see me married and a proper woman?"

A man in love will say anything, but not so quickly as a man in lust; and so it was said: "Yes...we'll be married here and return to New England as husband and wife, and all your friends can see you're a proper lady and we'll enjoy life there."

"Coo! You wouldn't really do that would you, Red? Marry and go to Boston? Leave us here?"

"If he showed me that he could and would do all the things for me he says he will...I might. Not much 'ere...night after night the same...thing. Could be a nice life as a proper lady...an' you'd come to visit me and maybe live with us, Velma."

Ashley suddenly realized he was in over his head and couldn't swim. "I...I should be going along...I have a banker I must see."

"A banker...I like the sound of that."

"He'll never be back!" Velma called, rolling over and turning her bare back on the two by the door.

"After the banker you'll be back here for me? Here?"

"Yes…I promise I will. You took me in, bandaged my hand…"

"How *is* your hand? I'd forgotten that's how it started."

"Better…still swollen, but it doesn't hurt until I move it; not as bad as last night."

"And you'll be back?" The robe opened again—maybe with a bit of a twist on her part—and she clung to him, alternately hugging and kissing.

He melted completely and she knew it.

"Stay for breakfast. I'll get you what I had yesterday: eggs, bread and tea. The tea is from China…some place far away from here, but it's a good drink."

"Yes, I know about that Chinese tea."

"I'll have that, Red," Velma called.

"After what I had last night, I have no appetite for food."

Velma turned over in bed. "Marry that one!"

A smile played gently across Margaret's lips and here eyes were bright with a joyful look. This was her happy face, and it embraced his as much as had her arms the night before. She tied the cloth belt on the robe, reached up and briefly kissed him again. Ashley looked with indecency at the swell of her breasts, hoping to see the dark spots he had longed to see on Anna. Gulped. Beginning to get waves of emotion and unclean thoughts again.

"I'm gone for the breakfast!" She tossed back the drape on the door and out she went, fast and happy.

Ashley turned to Velma. "Where is she going?"

"Old Mary's…she cooks for everyone here. Cheaper than we could and a whole lot easier. She's only around the corner; lives in one of these rooms. You'd think Mary would be a fat woman, eating all the leftovers she makes, but there aren't usually enough left over for her to eat. She'll feed us before she feeds herself."

She looked straight at him: "Are you really going to marry her?"

"Yes, I am." Definite now. Glad of it. Happy.

"That gold coin will help us a lot. We have to buy our meals, but there's onion stew tonight and we like that. The old woman—Mary—who cooks, does it for everybody in this building." Ashley didn't ask, but the "old" woman was thirty-six. Life on the streets aged one rapidly; Mary was glad to be "only" a cook, as she had been involved in other professions prior to that.

Velma sat up in the bed, smiling. "When I go over for the food I always say something like, 'That wasn't the missing cat, was it?'"

Both laughed at that.

"Or I'll say, 'Whatever happened to that old parrot Billy lost?'"

Ashley was still smiling. "There is an old saw which says, 'A rarity for a man is a good wife.'"

"Then it will be the same for a woman to get a good husband...you'll both be rare!" She laughed, happy for the two of them. Ashley realized that below that tough surface, Velma herself was a rare prize. She wasn't the nightshirt-kind of girl Margaret was...Velma was "right there," always aware, always concerned, always nude at home.

Yes, she had that blanket she put off and on, but right now she was sitting up in bed and not covered by it; either the warmth inside this room or whatever she was thinking seemed to govern that. She was definitely an exciting woman Then he thought, *I wonder if she does that to entice me on purpose? So if I get excited by her, then Margaret will be jealous and not marry me.* That was probably her reason, he figured: make sure I love Margaret enough that I won't think or look at another woman while she's not around, one who's already naked and ready in bed; one who teases me and tempts me...without Margaret here, a stray word or touch by me will be told to Margaret and I shall lose her.

"I feel badly that you had to sleep on the floor last night."

"We take turns; it's all right. It's really the only way we have of knowing if someone wants to get in here—we're not allowed to put a lock on the door, so the landlord can come in when he wants to sneak a peek at us. Thus far, it's worked out. If Margaret leaves, I'll have to find some other girl to live here in her place; she's a sweet girl: you take care of her, hear?"

"Are there other of your friends here besides old Mary?"

Velma had turned around and now was sitting without the blanket wrapped anywhere around her—talking, interested like an old friend. Breasts bared, magnificently naked and showing it.

"There's about a dozen of us here in this apartment...men and woman. We watch out for each other as best as we can."

Velma had long hair also, long and dark; she moved around in the bed, gathering her hair, then giving it a twist the way Margaret did, piling her hair atop her head the way he saw Margaret do and somehow pinning it there: a comfortable mess, untidy but not taking a thing from this woman. Her eyes looked dark; her cheekbones were high; altogether an attractive woman in any country, he wondered why she wasn't already married, then thought she might be, or was but perhaps her husband had died or gone away: perhaps into the Army, so she stayed with Margaret for company.

She must be a fine woman also, to be so brave without a husband present. His mother was like that, after his father died. Velma was lucky she had no children. Ashley remembered that his mother was almost six years a widow in Dockside before they moved to Plimouth and she never re-married all that while and never relied on a man during that time, either. A truly remarkable woman, and Velma must be the same. Actually, without Margaret, he'd be thinking about Velma—that naked and beautiful woman who was beginning to entice him—he felt that.

Velma seemed closer to his age and decidedly a person who created conversation; she'd be a prize in the Massa-adchu-ess-et. And her being naked all the time they were talking added to his excitement. He hoped Margaret would return soon.

The door was ajar, letting in sunlight. Ashley looked around. All these women had in the world was in this room…and it wasn't much. Beside the door was a small table; several of those square horseshoe-nails had been pounded into the wall to hand articles. What he had mistaken last night for a painting on a wall was now revealed as a towel, hanging there to dry. A high-backed chair was by the wooden bed and one similar a few feet away but with so many clothes of all colors piled upon it they nearly hid it. There was something like a brazier in the corner, but it had blankets folded over it; he hoped they didn't use coal inside this tiny room: the fumes would overcome them during the night.

In the far corner—a few foot-lengths away—was a mound of what seemed to be either dirty bedding and dirty clothing or just a pile of fabrics; he imagined it was clean but knew it wasn't.

And there were odds and ends scattered about: two girl's treasures of a decade or more, there to behold and be sorry for. Nothing here worth anything except to the person who lived here and used it; certainly nothing worth being stolen by the landlord or a visitor.

The room was bigger last night; maybe it was the promise and the life inside it which made it that way. Right now it was a tiny room, about the size Anna wanted the mud-room to be. And Velma with her smooth skin and Margaret—that wonderful, sparkling, happy girl who loved life so much she shared it with everyone she met—stayed within it, living their lives and giving out as much pleasure as they could to passers-by. *Margaret*, he thought, *you fill my heart*.

Margaret had changed his way of thinking. Why in Heaven's Name was he chasing those spies when he could have this little piece of hot flesh all the time with him, hanging on him, looking with those big, understanding eyes—open and exciting, eager to please him—and wanting at the most to be "a proper lady." Rufus would choke when he saw her...Ashley's sisters would be so envious they might go somewhere to be married just to get away from her because she was so beautiful and vibrant; men in Boston would turn when they saw her, watching her move into and out of their sight, weeping as she left that they no longer had a glance of her; Puritan men would cover their eyes when they caught sight of her, holding up their carried-around Bibles to ward-away the shameful thoughts they'd have. Margaret would be the wonder of the colony...yes, and no woman there would speak to her or have anything to do with her, the crones! He'd have to just show her off and take her to New Amsterdam, where beautiful women were appreciated and adored.

This was it! He was finished as a spy! His final written report to Rufus would be posted, then he'd get Margaret, plan a wedding, marry her and return to Boston. Rufus or Mister Pennyweight would get him started somewhere—probably in New Amsterdam in that new job...New Amsterdam or New Netherland, upstream. And—oh—the notary was no longer around to give him financial and business advice and his killers still lived nearby. Rufus had said the notary was rich; he could have asked him how to be rich had those Frenchmen—Englishmen assassins and spies not killed him. The thought of the notary's death angered him and brought him back to reality.

All right. First things first as his mother said. Clothes, the bank, write and post letters to Rufus, the wedding, then the trip to Boston and his new life in the Dutch colony. The notary was still dead, but if those letters of credit Ashley carried were his, then there was plenty of money he'd no longer need, to give Ashley and Margaret a head-start in the New World.

He guessed he really was in love with this girl...and she'd probably be able to give him children so he could tell them all about Gair and Bren and all the adventure stories about the Lavrador he had piled up in his brain, waiting to be told and appreciated. That's what he wanted with Anna: children. Poor Anna...God, poor Anna. He said a silent prayer for her, as he'd been told that prayers for the dead were especially needed and gave blessings to both the departed and the person who prayed them. He surely needed blessings now...getting ready to wed and start a family...maybe several children, like those "stepping stones" of Farmer Woodstock's...Margaret seemed young enough for several. Several to care for him as he aged, fuss over him the way his sisters fussed over their father, take care of him if he were ill, pray for him when he died. He'd have as many children as he could...he'd work hard and make Margaret rich and a proper lady with lots of children. Ashley Lyons was the happiest he'd ever been in his life. Now he knew what he really wanted to say to Margaret and do with her: just what he had thought and told her.

"HEY! WAKE UP!" Velma got up our off the bed and came right over to him, right in front of him, still with no clothes on.

"What?"

"You really must be tired; you seemed to fall asleep standing there and I wasn't sure if you were going to fall or ever wake."

"I'm sorry…I was just thinking."

Velma: naked and right there, a fingertip away. She was very attractive up close, but hard-looking in her face. He thought she could stare down the Devil.

"Tell me," she demanded, "if you are already married!"

"I am not. I was…My wife passed away in childbirth just fifty-eight or fifty-nine—I think—days ago…The time shifts on me in my head; it still hurts from that hit…"

"Thank you for your honesty. If you had said she just died, I'd have had reservations about you. Many men tell us that—'Oh, my wife just died.'—Ha! You must have loved her with all your heart to recall the number of days she has been gone. However could Red—Margaret—a stranger, replace her?"

"No one can replace Anna…but Margaret and I have our own calendar; it started last night and I shall count the days of our lives together as closely as I've counted the days I've been apart from Anna and our babies."

"You had babies?"

"Died; with Anna, now."

Velma smiled and put her hand against his chest. "Then you have my blessing. I feel I'm giving away my daughter, but you're the only one I've met who could make me feel like this. She's only four years younger than me, but we've been together in this room a little over a year."

"What's her age?" he whispered, thinking of Pennyweight and his mother.

"Nineteen," she mouthed back. "She hasn't been doing this very long…I started when I was nine. She's like my little sister."

Velma: a bluntly pretty face which didn't show all her emotions. Ashley didn't know whether she meant what she said, as she held that steady gaze and almost defied him with her eyes. Graceful legs, almost perfect to look at but he couldn't keep focused upon her legs alone…too much stuff above them. Had to force himself to turn away.

A temptress! Velma the tempting temptress. Oh, God! Too late: he had already become excited!

Velma knew why he turned and almost laughed aloud. Yeah…she knew what men wanted and how they showed that wanting.

His present love returned to the room carrying a tray of food. "Mary says the dog is good today, Velma!" She put down the tray and clung to Ashley a few seconds, kissing him with several quick kisses: happy.

Velma began to eat—still naked as a shorn lamb and the door open. He pulled his gaze from her to concentrate on Margaret. "I can't eat; it's late. I have to get new clothes and find the banker."

More smiles. "You can't leave yet; I have to change the bandage."

What a woman!

She re-wrapped the bandage, frowning at the old one as it was pulled off and the swollen, broken hand was again exposed. "I told Mary about us; she sent bread, jam and cheese: she's so happy for me! I have a flowered dress I can wear on the ship." She was aglow with happiness and it was easily passed along.

To take this beautiful young woman to another place, another land, another life, another time...he owed her that. To free her from this room, this stalled life, this desperate, daily struggle for survival—the two of them, but Velma seemed used to it—just to get her away, get her free, free with him so the two of them could be as one, and that one happy forever...his mind held her in his memory: how pretty and willing and...talented! God! Talented! How was it she could burst into his life and heart and soul like that? Heavenly sent: he knew it. Anna wouldn't care—probably had a hand in sending this girl to him like his mother ever tried: but Anna knew he needed someone just like this: youthful, happy, willing, experimental with her favors.

"I can't stay to eat; I must go."

"You'll be back?"

"This day I shall find someone who will marry us; then we'll take the ship to Boston for our wedding present."

"You freeze my heart when you talk like that."

He kissed her lightly. "Then, tonight, I shall warm it up."

Velma, sitting cross-legged on the bed, facing them both and still "sans vetements"—called: "Stay and rub my feet until I fall asleep...Only a few moments, I'm that tired."

He paused as if considering Velma's proposal...what a chance!

Margaret's tinkling laughter brought him quickly out of that fantasy: "She says that to all the men who hang around here, to make them leave. They do, too! No man wants to rub a woman's feet." She laughed again and kissed him passionately, exciting him even more.

He forced himself from her—duty to all stronger than duty to self (the militiaman's swear and the Puritan way) and looked out the doorway, then stepped through, pausing to glance around to see if Geoffry were there. Satisfied there were no spies outside he turned back to the waiting Margaret: "You don't have to worry about naming the children…the first boy will be Brenden Splaine Lyons and the first girl Bran-Wen Margaret Lyons."

"Decent of you to tell her," Velma called.

"I hadn't thought of children at all…" Margaret's face paled.

"We can think of other names once we're together—before the other children come; we'll have plenty of time in the New World."

"He's planned a busy life for you, Red!"

Margaret just stood, blank-faced, staring.

"I need clothes and to see the banker; I'll be back as soon as I can—oh, and to find someone to marry us! The banker can tell me where to go." He grabbed Margaret again and gave her a robust kiss.

"I'll tell you what Bren told me: 'Hang on, you're going for the ride of your life!'"

She almost didn't say it but had to: "Bran-Wen?"

"The daughter of the Irish King!"

"Oh…that Bran-Wen."

CHAPTER 27

Once outside the door, Ashley returned to his militia-training and instantly became on guard. His eyes searched for any further sign of Geoffry and he waited for the hairs on the back of his neck to prickle if he were to see him, the way they did when he located that smuggler that time. But all his looking found no one suspicious, so he then looked all behind him to be sure he'd remember where to return for Margaret—that would be a major blunder: not being able to locate this room again.

Margaret's room was one of several...apparently an old store or storehouse formerly here and vacated, then individual rooms built inside it, some opening onto the street and some down a tiny alley in the center, with rooms on each side off that. Margaret had a door which opened onto the street—a plus for the women's work; most other rooms had doors which opened into a hallway down the center of the old building. Convenient if you wanted to live in a tiny room with many other people around. For all his talents and understanding, Ashley Lyons never at all realized the "occupation" these women in their tiny rooms pursued and plied. Probably just as well.

He found a hackney-driver (a coach with a pair—more expensive than a coach and one) and told him he had the previous night been assaulted by a highwayman who stole his clothes and left him these rags, but he had kept a gold sovereign in his mouth during the holdup and now could pay for the ride to a clothier's shop in the Banking District...the closest one to the Tremont Banking Center, Federated Banks, Limited.

He needn't have made up the story: the sovereign spoke volumes to the hackney driver. Ashley got into the coach, feeling safer than usual and prouder of himself than in a long time. Inside the coach he somewhat relaxed. His hand still hurt terribly, his head pounded; bruised flesh and sore ribs and kidneys sent out their own signals of pain as well. Inside the moving coach he was bumped around even more, the cobblestones taking their toll on the iron-clad wheels, moving all the time with the surface of the road, up, down, sideways. Damn! Like that feather bed but without the reason for the movement!

All the beating he'd received from those savages pretending to be gentlemen spilled out, reminding him just how mean and dangerous they really were. And underlying everything now was a pledge to a stranger that he would marry her and take her to Boston! Right. To show her off to Elspeth? Just what he didn't want to do. Damnation!

And where on God's green earth would he find a place to settle her? Not in Plimouth and probably not now in Boston…maybe he WOULD have to go to New Amsterdam or New Netherland and work for his stepfather.

"Hi, everyone…I'm home and here's my latest wife, a young, Irish redhead I found on a London street and went to bed with, then promised her I'd marry her and make her a proper lady…oh, and by the way, she expects that I'm rich!" There was no mouse for that owl!

Actually, though, the moment he saw Margaret in that doorway he'd fallen in love with her. Young, tender, vivacious with an innocence—real or imagined—portrayed all the time. Who couldn't help but love her? Well…Elspeth.

But Elspeth held a different kind of love…she was all woman: strong, demanding, knowing what she wanted, claiming an innocence but unable to present it properly—the way Margaret did. Elspeth was calculating. She planned her moves and went forward to her destination. Too much woman for him, probably. Way over his head, way beyond his awareness. Better to stay with Margaret. Yeah…and explain THAT one to Anna! God!

Margaret was no innocent; she was a Londoner and supposedly aware of life's events while Elspeth had done life's events and put them aside. No…Margaret was no innocent—the way she used her body; she seemed…anxious…for him, radiating an innocent love which entered his heart and made him feel happy and excited—all at once. She seemed glad to be with him: that excited him even more. He wanted her now—in this coach!

They rode along and he tried to imagine what he should write to Rufus, to let him know he was finished with spying and was returning to Boston with his new bride. Some kind of explanation was in order. He thought: *Being a spy is more a way of thinking than an actual doing…one must think and do rather than study what to do and attempt to imitate someone else's behavior. To understand and penetrate the connections and happenings and to be able to list them in an order and assemble all that to see actions and results is true spying. At age thirty-two, I believe I have become a whole man, knowing now what it is to HAVE to become stealthy and frightened and angry. I have outgrown Miles Standish in these few weeks and feel a confidence about my actions. Yes.* Sounded good in his thoughts. He'd write that later, and about Margaret as well...in another letter. He had to quit the spy-business first; this ride, though, he wanted to just be able to relax and recall pleasantly the quiet and sentimental moments of the previous night.

There was no time to relax.

The coach stopped and Ashley was in a portion of London he hadn't before seen: street after street of busy businesses, tall buildings, crowded walkways, side-by side coaches and carriages, people everywhere and not begging or looking sad or hawking trade-goods: determined in their step and going somewhere to do something. The driver had known exactly the right haberdasher, and it was on the street—easily walked—where the bank was located. Ashley was impressed by the haberdasher's sign:

Regal Haberdashery Former Tailor to the King Notions & Gentlemen's Clothing & Footwear

That was the kind of sign Mister Pennyweight should have, and once in Boston he'd tell his stepfather that the old "Penny's" sign wasn't a proper one for elite trade. Finally he was seeing the "real" London!

Before he left the coach Ashley looked at the letters of credit he had carried so long in his stockings. Good thing he still had them; good thing Rufus had thought of that. One to leave at a lodging house, another for clothing and incidentals. He hadn't used the first for where he stayed at Dockside: they never had one of those presented and didn't know how to use it, so he just paid in gold.

He and the coachman thanked each other and he went inside the clothing store. A clerk popped out at him as he entered, halting any further movement into the store.

"May I assist you?" Probably wondering how such an ill-dressed and dirty person with a bandaged hand could ever dare to enter such an establishment.

"I've been assailed by a highwayman and given these dreadful garments; I have a letter of credit and I'd like to purchase a suit of clothes and other articles of clothing from you." There! Probably the haughtiest speech he'd made in all London.

He was certain the clerk sneered at him, and took the wrinkled and dirty letter of credit with two fingers from him, holding it as tho' it were far too filthy for him to even touch.

"Please be seated; I shall carry this to the bookkeeper. Thank you, sir."

Ashley sat, a comfortable leather chair. The store smelled like leather and wool…the kind of smell similar to old money…no: kidding: clothes. Maybe incense or something.

"A suit of clothes": it sounded almost regal to say it. Rufus Case was the kind of man for whom business suits were sewn: he had a wide set of shoulders which filled out a coat and let it fall straight. Ashley had shoulders with the kind of slope and long torso which makes tailors cry as they attempt to take up and let down fabric to make up for his "droop."

It took a few minutes, but the next clerk who approached him almost slithered toward him, holding his hands in a wringing fashion, a person different from the two-fingered man.

"My dear sir, Regal's is crestfallen at your misfortune. Whatever we can do to assist you, rest assured it shall be done. We spare no effort here for our clientele, and intend to please you in any clothing matter."

He bowed. Really.

Well, that wasn't what Ashley wanted for Penny's, but it surely helped THIS sale!

"A suit of clothes that I may this afternoon visit my banker and not feel ashamed, shoes and stockings; whatever. Oh! Where may I find a bathing facility?"

The clerk just nodded his head. "For our extraordinary customers such as yourself, a bathing facility is just next door. There is a barber there as well, and someone to care for your injured hand. Please, let us rapidly take measurements; then we'll escort you there, and when you are finished, perhaps your fitting and alteration can begin. We'll have you dressed again as a gentleman in short order."

Ashley blinked his eyes. "Thank you." He wondered how much that letter of credit could be, with this kind of service. And he had another as well! Oh, yeah…he and Margaret could get back to Boston all right…maybe to anywhere in the world—on Excelsior Ship Lines, of course.

A clerk told him he'd take him to the baths, and there gave Ashley a heavy robe to wear after he removed his clothes; then the man left. Ashley undressed, smelling each of his clothes he shoved into a bag. Most of them reeked of smoke and sweat, horse-manure and hay, longtime wear. He'd take them all with him when he left here, smelly or not: some day he'd need to use them again.

So…the scented bath and the fresh undergarments and the fittings went well and rapidly, just as promised. He had asked for pen and paper, that he could write an accounting "for the sheriff," but of course jotted down his adventure for Rufus, complete with the Holiday Street address. He wanted Rufus—at least—to be aware he'd be arriving with Margaret; "someone" had to know and be friendly toward them; couldn't keep dodging the law with her at his side, explaining nothing to her. If Margaret were disappointed in her first visit to New England, how could he expect her to stay and enjoy it there?

Then he began to write the events of the previous two days. From what Johnathan had said, Providence was a nest of Loyalists to any King, probably Salem as well. And Matthew had told him the man in the stable also wanted the King to return. From the story Johnathan told, it was the Royalists against the Puritans—the Civil War still being fought at a secret level—and the Loyalists/Royalists stuck together while the Puritans watched out for business, each for himself. If this were a game, Rufus would win, but Rufus had to be warned that he was in this game; it was real, and it was deadly.

He was sure Johnathan couldn't have known he was followed from Dockside: Ashley's driver had taken more precautions than usual. There were three of them, though, so one could have watched all the time out the rear window of the coach to see if anyone followed. Still…his driver had been more than thorough and no one—the way he followed—should have been able to…he paused: the coachman! Not that any of the three had seen him, but the driver of the hackney-coach probably told the other driver he had followed his coach and been paid handsomely for that! That must have been it. Those drivers all knew each other; one would tell the other right away. Then the coachman would have returned to his fare to tell him and get money for that information. What was the phrase Rufus used about information: "Those who had it knew; those who didn't, worried." That was what had allowed these assassins to do all the things they did: information. They collected it as he did, probably not the way he did either, but with their widespread network of information-gatherers, the spies were way ahead oh what happened, why it happened, and what would happen.

That's why Geoffry was waiting for him: he knew Ashley was in London, following the coach and most probably would return to watch because he had done just that in Merry Mount. Well, those days were over! New ones with Margaret lay ahead—way ahead. No more spying; he liked the new clothing and having salesmen cater to him. New Amsterdam would be the best for them both: he and Margaret—and their children. Easy from there to visit Plimouth and Boston.

The way these spies played this game—and it was a game to them because Johnathan had likened it to a game of chess—he was a loser from the start; he was a novice player in an on-going, professional chess-match. And he didn't know how to spend money, also: the way he had thrown-around gold coins had drawn attention to himself. Well…to Blazes with Johnathan! Someone else could deal with him; someone from London. Ashley had a new life now, a new wife to be, a new suit of clothes and a new look for his new job in New Amsterdam. The next time—if there were one—he did spy-work, he'd know not to get too close, not to spend so much money, not to be alone, not to be captured. Damn! He was SO glad he had gotten away!

Well, enough about spies. There was nothing strange or magic about them: just ordinary men within a spider's web of information-gathering and secrets. HE wondered what secrets the notary had, that it was necessary for him to die. Probably to even an old score from England, as the notary had done nothing wrong in Plimouth. Ashley had to clear up that business also; it would be hard to return to a normal life as a wanted murderer.

So…To Hell with them all! (the Witch's curse). Let someone else watch the spies as they gathered their little secrets, drew their drawings, met people…They could keep London also, with its ale and beer and bear-baiting and knife-wielding thugs! He was headed back to Boston with a new bride, maybe go somewhere distant and run a business for old Pennyweight or Rufus.

That in itself was excitement enough for him.

He and Margaret wouldn't be able to visit Plimouth for a while…years…but Mister Pennyweight had told him he could live in New Amsterdam and be a buyer/seller/transporter for goods arriving from ports which refused to serve Boston. The Dutch had access to teas and coffees, diamonds and gold: items shipped from places who would war on England, given the chance.

The strength in New Amsterdam lay within its banking methods and trade agreements. The Hollanders had treaties with almost every country in the world, so their sea-going merchant fleet could go anywhere, carry anything, sail anytime. And…insurance! Every cargo could be insured against piracy, hurricanes or the plague. The Dutch could assure all receivers they would get their goods or the money it cost to purchase them: neither shipper nor receiver could lose on a Dutch ship. Boston rejected their ships and Pennyweight figured a buyer living in New Amsterdam could access "interesting" commodities while getting rich sending them overland to Boston stores. THAT was the way Ashley would live out this murder accusation: go to New

Amsterdam as a buyer/seller of imported goods and use Pennyweight and Rufus and others as his outlets. He'd soon be rich and Margaret could be happy as a proper lady in a new city with all the clothes (in the daytime) and a big-enough house for all the children. Perfect! Just perfect! No more single rooms for her.

And she could have Velma visit any time she wanted...Ashley smiled at the thoughts he was having...wondering if Velma would still walk around naked then. Damnation, these were good thoughts! He could taste Margaret in his imagination, smell the powder she had used, touch her in every portion of her body—as he had the previous night. "There's not a King's finger of me you haven't had your tongue on," she had told him when he woke for her third time.

Happy. So glad it was going this way and this well. Bren would be proud of him...Brendan Splaine, his big Irish friend who had gone north with him so many years ago. He'd name his first son "Brendan Splaine Lyons" and his first daughter "Bran-Wen"—Brendan's daughter's name, after the Irish King.

Just that thought was enough to send Ashley into paradise. The spying was over; the worry about Espeth was through; the trouble concerning the notary would be worked out somehow or forgotten; and he'd soon be rich and married to a woman who enjoyed nude lovemaking! Then he REALLY smiled! God was good to him. He had completed his mission for Rufus and detached himself from the still-desirable Elspeth (whom—he assumed—would pitch a fit when she found out he almost had a child-bride: a redhead who oozed feminine charms and smelled sweeter than a Duxbury meadow in August).

Ruthie would be happy for him. Ruthie was the "good" sister, younger, but she looked up to her big brother the way little sisters are supposed to. Yeah, he loved her also...and Esther as well. But Esther took a lot of getting used to and a lot more love than he was willing to give her.

She was the "pet" and everyone knew it. Old Pennyweight doted on her, sending around the world for dolls and clothing she wanted. Ruthie was an afterthought, he guessed...loved but not really expected to be born. A part of the family but not the reason for it as Esther had been. Yeah...and HE should have been that reason—as firstborn—but all of those times he left home, and the refusals to do any work for his stepfather, and the secrets he kept—still—and all that had happened...certainly he was no longer the family pet and never had been. Of course.

Well...he'd been places no human alive had been, received the secret to speak the Algonkin language, met strange and frightening beings and challenged and fought two Bear-Gods. Not bad for a boy between the ages of twelve and eighteen at those times. But the treasure was lost, the gold only iron pyrite, the seashell horn returned, the chest given back to Gair—wherever he was, as he never had returned from the caves in all these years—and Ashley had resumed living at his parents' home to settle gradually into the Puritan spirit and the ways of the colony. That's the way life was: highs and lows, money and poverty, feasting and starvation, good women and bad ones And thinking of the bad ones gave him an even bigger...smile.

CHAPTER 28

"You took some time; I was forced to break the fast without you. Where is Luke?"

"You ain't gonna like this, Johnathan."

"I'll be the judge of that."

"'E got away."

"No he didn't!" Johnathan had an evil stare, seldom seen.

"I came back to tell you…'e pushed Luke out the winda an' ran away."

"And you stood there and let him? You were there whilst he accomplished what he did? You let my Lukey go out a window?"

"Naw…I was shooin' some trash-people what was there, watchin' us wi' 'im…in the room…the clark seemed knocked out…we dumped 'im by the winda an' I went t' chase off some people what was lying there in the dark so's they wouldn't see us shove 'im out…I said I shoulda used my knife…"

"Stop!" Long pause. "So you did. You did say you should have used your knife here and I forbade it—and still do! This man has gotten away from us in Boston, Merry Mount, Providence, and now here…we apparently missed him in Salem! Four times, now, and three of you are dead and he seems to want to accomplish our deaths as well."

"I'll go back an' see if I can fin' where 'e's gone to…I wanted t' tell you what's been 'appenin'."

"I think going back is a fool's errand, but go…this time, kill him if he's in front of the Lord High Sheriff himself!" Understand?"

"I understan' an' I will." It wasn't only an agreement with Johnathan: it was a promise. The clark needed to be killed; he had caused far too much trouble and death and had upset Johnathan…a man who did not take upset in his life lightly. Matthew, Mark and Luke were martyrs for the Cause, but this man, this storeclark whoever he was, had to die.

Geoffry went back to the bridge, up to the top, where they had been, looking again at places where the clark could have run or hidden or waited. He re-traced in his mind where he had run, then did the whole episode over again, going down the stairs, out onto the bridge, all the way along—where he heard him running—seeking the man or someone who might have seen him.

Afternoon in Southwark.

At the end of the bridge was the great intersection, then the flat-houses began on one side and businesses—going wide open now in the daylight—on the other. He decided to go this time to the street-level and wander around where the clark might have run.

A few public carriages went by as Geoffry continued to walk and look and think. Where could a man running go? He had heard him running...did he go that fast and far that he was completely outside London right now? Was he that scared? Nawwww...not his clark...not this one. He was here, somewhere. Here.

There were several people sitting on stools, eating, in one of the ally ways where there were a lot of open doors. Geoffry hadn't eaten, so he was drawn toward them; they seemed a fair lot, chatting away and happy enough. Hmmmm...mostly women; a few old men. This wasn't a public eating-place; it had to be a private group...then he realized that the women were street-whores...and they would have been available last night for someone who was running off London's Bridge.

He went over to speak with them, maybe to eat something, an atypically friendly smile pasted on his face.

CHAPTER 29

It had taken several hours, but the haberdasher and his tailor had done all they had promised: a different-appearing man from the one who had walked into their establishment now walked out. Everyone was happy. Tired, but happy. Even the two-fingered clerk had rebounded: he called for a light carriage to take "Squire Case" to the bank: a mere foot-walk, but they'd not have their customer "walk" anywhere! A gentleman just didn't walk when he could ride, and…the shoes were new.

In that first hour after entering the store, Ashley was clean, shaven, had his hand attended properly—with the advice to see a physician or surgeon about that as soon as possible: the barber who replaced the bandage told him several bones seemed broken. After that, it was a flurry of clothing and fast alterations and food placed in front of him to devour. The store initially threw away the vest Rufus had made and given him, but Ashley managed to have it retrieved (as a keepsake, don't you know; made by a dear friend for me only). He realized he DID look like a colonist when wearing it, but that's what he was and the vest meant more to him than the other clothes—but also he wore a jacket over it.

For all the rush, the clothes fit well. The shirt was stiff: he had never felt a shirt so stiff yet soft. Mister Pennyweight should get some of these for resale. "Cotton from Egypt," the clerk had said about the shirt without being asked. "Starched. Our newest line in men's shirts. We hope you return often as you'd like; we give you the best available—of everything."

Ashley thanked him, feeling as if this were the dream and Anna the reality. He felt differently. Now he was looking forward, not "in the past" as Rufus told him he did. No more spies; no more worries about being chased by Geoffry. Hope. Expectation. Happiness. Margaret. In that order.

As the store had fed him while he waited, he was once again refreshed and thinking about his red-headed Margaret but he was required to turn his attention to the bank. However, THIS time when Margaret saw him he'd look "clean"...and that thought pleased him.

At the Federated Bank, his attire was a door-opener! "Yes, Squire Case; Yes, Mister Case; This way, please, good sir; Squire Case, we're delighted to welcome you, sir..." It was as if he owned the bank and these people worked for him. He didn't like to see them humbled—especially as he was not Squire Case—but that was the way they were in London: still acting as though the King lived down the street and gentry were royalty.

He was shown into a large office—larger than his entire cabin in Duxbury had been—a room paneled in dark wood with a large glassed window to the street (barred). A middle-aged man dressed even finer than Ashley sat behind a large dark-wood desk, and he stood as Ashley entered.

The banker was wearing a tailored Business-suit (Ashley could now understand most of the clothing terms after hearing them all day) of some wool blend. Whomever he was, he looked the part he was playing and seemed to be more at ease in his suit and manners than Ashley was or ever could be. Even with his new suit, Ashley was simply a dressed farmer from the colony. The banker had a reddish tinge to his hair, but Ashley had heard earlier that day that some men in London had begun to use the styles of France and were placing "color" in their hair. Regardless, the man looked trim, healthy and happy, and his teeth were white and "all there." Ashley's tongue automatically touched his broken teeth and empty spaces in his mouth where teeth had been and were now gone forever. For all the chalk his mother had told him to use on his teeth to keep them white, they still were not the whiteness of the banker's. Anna had told him that babies take the teeth from their mother's mouth, which was why mothers of many children had few or none. But that was no reason for his teeth to be so bad.

"Sit down...please sit down. Can I offer you a drink of any kind? There is tea, coffee or Sherry, whichever you'd enjoy; whatever you'd like."

Ashley thanked him, declined any drink (he'd had three cups of tea earlier and felt it already), and did sit, in an overstuffed chair in front of the banker's desk. (The notary should have had this desk; he needed the size...well, he HAD needed it.)

"Please tell me your name."

"Rufus Case. I gave my letter of credit and travel-papers to the man out front."

The banker smiled on of those thin-lipped smiles...the kind lawyers have when they ask you a question and already know the answer. "Yes...I understand you are Rufus Case, but I require your real name to let this go further."

"If it's proof you need..."

"See here! I happen to know you are not Rufus Case, and I'll ask you politely again: what is your name!"

Well...this was a big difference from the way he'd been treated all day...the banker sat there, his head slightly tilted as if attempting to hear words yet unspoken, staring, waiting for a name.

"In all honesty I am not Rufus Case; I'm a friend of his: Ashley Lyons, from Duxbury, the Massa-adchu-ess-et."

"There! How easy was that!"

The man sounded like Johnathan: someone who knew it all and made another person wiggle like a worm on a fishing hook. Well, as Elspeth had said, "In for a pence, in for a pound." So now he was in.

"I know you're not Rufus; he is my brother-in-law and has written me about your coming here, but I had to challenge you for I wasn't sure if you were Lyons or someone had robbed your papers...you're late in arriving here; I expected you more than a week ago. You play a dangerous game, here in London. I'm delighted to finally meet you, Captain Lyons..." He reached out his hand in friendship. "Rufus has written all sorts of good things about you, and wrote that you might be wearing that—er—ugly vest he made. He had that on the last time he was here; I'm astonished he parted with it."

Ashley almost laughed out loud. "He's outgrown it and it has a secret compartment..."

"Yes, for a knife. I heard all about it. I'm sure it's a necessity in the colony..."

"And two other, smaller, pockets to hide coins. He also put pockets on my boots for coins."

"Mister Practical...ever thinking how he can hide-away coin. Rufus couldn't be a banker, he can't stand loaning-away his fortune." The banker smiled and rose to come around his desk to Ashley. "It's my extreme pleasure, Captain Lyons...there is hardly a letter Rufus sends me that does not mention your name and deeds...and your travels. I feel I already know you. Please tell me what has been happening with you here in London."

If Rufus had ten years on Ashley, this banker had twenty. Another tall, thin man, a bit shorter than Ashley who in every way looked and acted the part of an English banker. As Ashley told his story about the Frenchmen he followed who had turned English, the banker's gaze was steady and interested. He didn't interrupt, but seemed shocked and with a graphite pencil jotted a few notes on his desk-pad. He heard about Ashley's travels, the deaths in Boston, King's Town and Merry Mount, Lane trying to put him into a room in Providence, the posse-chase out of Providence, and his trials at the House on Holiday, and on London's Bridge. He finally ended, the banker having to sit: it took so long to tell, explaining about Margaret—including the part where she sheltered him and bandaged his hand…but "neglected" to mention the escapades of the night and meeting the nude Velma. To say further would have been ungallant of him.

Tea being served signaled Ashley that it was late in the afternoon and he wanted to get back to Margaret as soon as he could. The banking business was finally over and Ashley wanted to return to Margaret as soon as possible and locate someone who would marry them. He'd been assured that there would be enough credit for him to marry Margaret and sail with her to Boston "in a decent manner"—as it was put. Ashley figured "decent" to this banker was "very good" to him.

All the information he had uncovered would be recorded and sent to Rufus, but the banker would also pass it along to Lord Protector Cromwell's staff here in London, so they could act upon it. Arrests would occur. His "spying" was over.

Ashley said his goodbyes and got a carriage—no coach was needed on such a fine day, a day when he no longer was required to hide inside a hackney-coach—and set the driver to go over the bridge, hoping once he got there he'd remember where Margaret lived. He didn't know what to bring her—he hadn't yet found the Marrying Minister—so he had the carriage stop where a woman was selling flowers by the side of a street, bought a grand bouquet, and went along, hoping in his heart that Anna wouldn't mind. Anna had grown her own flowers; he'd never gotten a "bought" bouquet of flowers for his wife. Poor Anna…had she lived, not a bit of any of this would have happened.

People are hung up in the past…at least Ashley Lyons was, what with all which had happened to and with him and all happenings afterward. Everything was because of the past; the present was here and the future would be. Hard to think about, that what happened would continue to shape your life and future…wouldn't ever go away, kept gnawing at you every time you tried to make a decision or go down some path or make a plan.

The only way to get away is to go away—and never return. Sure, you carry your past with you like a knapsack on your back or that roll of fat above the beltline, but if you go far enough, long enough, with someone you care about...well...the past is still there but you don't think that much about it and it doesn't pester you that much either. You've outrun it, even if it's still in the race.

That's what he wanted to do with Anna: get away from the caves and the north and "those people" with whom he had dealt...not that some of them weren't good in their hearts or true friends...just that the old memories haunted him every day and night until he met Anna. Then SHE became his past, because all he thought about was her.

Then it seemed to him that it was Elspeth who was his future and would lead him from his past; Elspeth of the curly locks, the tin body, the woman who looked like a girl. She took him away but his stupidness in thinking he could tell her the truth after just meeting her and not suffer for it did him in. "Always tell the truth," he had been told...so he did to his mother and she prayed for him, not wholly believing what he told her, thinking him demented. He told the truth to Bren and Bren died a lingering death. He told the truth to Anna and she slunk away, too frightened to deal with his past. He had told the truth of his past to Elspeth but couldn't bring himself to tell her what he did to her brother. "God," he prayed aloud, "please give Elspeth a good husband and a long life of happiness...You know she deserves it."

He hadn't ever prayed for Bren—all those years ago—and he wondered for a moment or two if prayers today would make up for prayers which should have been said years—decades—ago, then guessed there were no "makeup prayers"...if you should have prayed and didn't, it was far too late now, except to say you were sorry. Never too late to say you're sorry if you're still alive...so he closed his eyes to the traffic of London and said aloud, "God, I'm truly sorry for all my sins and omissions of prayer; and please guide and protect my loved ones, especially the soul of Brendan Splaine, my wonderful wife, Anna, my father, my two children You have, and all those friends and relatives I have who are now in Your Land of Glory. I love them all and pray that You do so, also. Amen."

And now to get Margaret. While he was waiting for the clothing at the haberdashers, Ashley had the urge to pen a poem for Margaret as well. He wrote:

Margaret at nineteen:
As gentle as the Moon; as heated as the sun.
Sweet music heard in these ears alone.
Blind love feasts upon her laughter and song.

The carriage driver halted on the main street by the intersection in Southwark, beyond the London Bridge; there were too many people in a crowd to get past them, into the alleyway where Margaret's room was situated. Ashley told the driver to swing around but wait for him, and went into the crowd, pushing his way through the gathered people. Far too many persons for just a weekday in the Clink. The throng was thick—worse than he expected a usual day here might be; there had to be several-dozen people, probably most of them residents here or shopkeepers.

The bell in the clock-tower at Saint Olaf's was chiming: a hollow, sad sound which everyone could (and was supposed to) hear, that they knew when the evening gatherings would begin and that the faithful could be gently reminded to show up on time and perhaps with more than just a pence; perhaps they might bring a new convert or one who had fallen away from the Faith.

Many of the citizens of Southwark felt the big churches were more than symbols of Religion: they seemed as Catholic reminders and wanters of coin. Could it really be true that they were "Houses of God"? If so, then He was not—as their new ministers told them—"everywhere at once, seeing, hearing, knowing it all." Did they truly need to be in attendance inside a church instead of their own home? Hadn't the Puritan Faith told them every person carried God within him?

Then, why were the churches necessary?

Ashley almost got to Margaret's room when he was halted by a watchman.

"No further, sir: Sheriff's business."

"I just want to get through to that room."

"That's where the sheriff's business is! No one can enter."

"See here, Watchman, the woman I'm about to marry is in that room and I SHALL go in there, regardless!"

"Awwww...sir...there's no one in there for a respectable gentleman such as yourself. All that's in that room is two dead whores, cut up an' bloody. Probably wouldn't do what a customer paid 'em to do."

The left-handed punch to the watchman's jaw seemed to come from nowhere! The watchman was on the ground before people in the crowd realized Ashley had hit him. And as fast, Ashley pushed through the few in the inner ring of people, going over to the doorway of Margaret's room...where he had left his future and his heart...and the nineteen-year-old girl he wanted to marry and take to the New World.

Margaret was there, on the floor, still in her white nightdress, but that covering was now mostly dark from the spill of now-drying blood. Velma—

still nude in the bed; blood everywhere on and around her; her throat cut and her beautiful body stabbed several times. A great, bloody mess, the entire room.

"Here, there!" a voice called. "You can't be there! Go back or I'll have to detain you!"

Ashley never heard the voice: he was remembering last night and this morning...all the promises made to and for her...were no longer any good. All the happiness and caring and planning for the future was forever gone, drizzled out upon that red-stained floor. He wouldn't ever take her to the Massa-adchu-ess-et nor to New Amsterdam or Rufus' store.

Velma had several stab-wounds in her breasts and shoulders which looked like she had fought too long and lost too hard. He recognized the way Velma's throat had been cut: Geoffry!

Then he looked at Margaret. From a distance—from the doorway—it appeared as if she were smiling, but a closer look was hideous: poor, pale Margaret, still a beauty with all that had happened. Everyone who knew her would miss her. The "smile" was a bled-out slice carved by Geoffry's knife...the same kind of cut, the same place she had been cut as Elspeth's brother, and just the way the cut on the notary had been described to him: started under the left ear and slid down and across the throat, taking with it the great blood-vessel to the brain and all the close ones of the head and upper body.

It couldn't have hurt too long: the amount of blood-loss was too much to have let her stay alive in suffering for very long. That Royalist Bastard, Geoffry! That was his cut!

Ashley knew there was only one chance he'd get; had to strike like a woods-rattler and do it right the first time; the second time there would be a man alerted and responding. Had to do it fast, without thinking; just cut whomever opened the door and smash past him—leave him to bleed out—to get the second man, wherever he would be. No reason for this but pure hate, maybe revenge—the avenger of blood the scribe who penned the Bible wrote about; maybe just hate; probably hate. He'd had a lot of that experience in hating building up recently. There was an old story along the frontier—a legend now, as it was almost as old as Ashley—about a settler whose wife was kidnapped by a local Indian and taken to his village. The settler loaded two muskets and took his long-bladed knife, found and watched the village until he knew where his wife was being held, then he readied his muskets, slipped into the village—making the dogs bark as he knew they would—stabbed the first

Indian coming out of the wikawam where his wife was being kept, dashed inside and saw her there: nude and bound on a blanket. He shot her dead with the first musket and before he could feel the arrows and knives slicing into him, killed himself with the second musket, putting a ball up through his chin and into his brain. He was determined she'd never have to be an Indian's slave, and couldn't—wouldn't—live without her. After that, the owner of the Indian village sent a messenger to Captain Standish that his people would leave that land forever, as the white man had too much honor and the Indian clan could not stand that kind of hate. Stealing women was an everyday occurrence; the English didn't understand.

This, too, was about honor and hate…mostly hate.

If Geoffry were allowed to get away with this, it would be God's work. If he failed, it would be God's plan. Either way he had to try. Ashley had spent weeks hunting this devil; now he would confront him and kill him—if he could be killed…And who can kill the Devil?

Ashley knew he could never be what people wanted him to be (like his mother or Mister Pennyweight), and probably couldn't be what he'd like to be…so there he was: being himself and not admiring it. Why not kill and be killed. All his life he had run away…from home, from family, jobs, security, society, religion, himself. Now it was different. This meant something. This pond was full of fish; who cared if he broke the dam.

No guilt, just action. His soul was vacant.

Rough hands grabbed him and rudely pulled him from the doorway. The crowd was yelling because he had struck the Watchman—a man of several decades and admired by many. The sheriff's men who moved Ashley were talking to him but he wasn't paying attention to them. He had to leave, and leave now. He did. While people were speaking to him, trying to hold him, yelling at others to help them catch him, with a deadly purpose in mind he shook them all away and left.

Ashley pushed someone from him, someone who had chased after him; got back to the carriage he had hired and didn't have to tell the driver anything at all, for he had turned-around the vehicle previously and now just whipped the horse forward regardless of the crowd—which parted fast before the fleeing carriage, yelling and calling to them both to stop in the law's name, and for God's sake. The two watchmen who were holding on to the carriage let go fast, shaking their heads; they knew they couldn't have arrested nor detained the gent anyway, but were more than willing to try. He'd be the focus for the sheriff, not them; men dressed that way he had too much political advantage to be held at murder scenes anyway…but they had enough of a description to tell the sheriff, so, no matter: let the rabbit run; he'd come back to the clover patch.

Beyond the bridge, Ashley yelled to the driver: "South Pudding! Stop when you get there!"

The tide was going out on this game and if he didn't get there right now, he'd be on a cold, rocky beach instead of in warm water. Had to be done. Now. Nothing else to do but this; had to be done.

He had the feeling of being very alive, that he could now do whatever he wanted to do, but not Margaret or Velma—left there unclad with so many people around yet completely alone, never again to see, hear, talk, feel…two young, friendly, happy women no longer alive. He shuddered, seeming to wake.

The noise of the hackney-horse, its hoof-strikes ringing against the old cobblestones of an ancient Roman town, the leather of the seat emitting creaking sounds as he was jostled back and forth inside the light carriage, his swollen hand throbbing with every pulse of blood—the thing causing that discomfort never again to be felt by Margaret or Velma…he was all things at once: miserable that she/they were dead, convinced that Geoffry did it, puzzled as to how or why it was done, and—strangely enough—happy that he lived, glad he was here, sad that Margaret was not and would never marry nor see Boston. He wanted to pray but he couldn't, had too many thoughts immediately upon him: what to do, how to do it, consciously removing from his mind anything at all beyond that meeting with Geoffry and Johnathan. Wanted to be angry but wasn't; wanted to cry but didn't. Just knew he needed to do something, and this was all he could think to do.

God with him he would survive; God not willing, he would fail. This was no longer a civilized city on an island fortress: it was a place where people bled and died and went away and never came back no matter what, and that was his plan for Geoffry: make him go away and never come back the way he had done to Margaret, Velma, the notary, and most probably Elspeth's brother, Roland.

It was only an instantaneous flash in his brain, but it drove him along his path, determined.

CHAPTER 30

He got out of the carriage, paid the driver too much in haste, and walked without a word down Holiday to the house where he had been taken prisoner and held, walked in through the unlocked front door, bold as Billy and down the front hallway, holding his skinning knife in his left hand and going to the room where Johnathan was staying. Hardly paused before he knocked, still holding the knife. Whomever opened this door was going to get it in the face, the throat, the heart—sliced the way Geoffry had done on all those people Ashley knew, and probably scores more over the years. Then he was going to cut off his fingers the way the notary had been brutalized, and everything else he could find to cut off this man…and maybe Johnathan, too! A bold strike: a strike of the owl! Bren would be proud of him.

He caught him there. Damn! The arm came around the left side of his head and circled under his chin, putting sudden, unexpected pressure on the big blood vessel at the side of his neck and in addition to scaring him just by being there, scared him because suddenly he seemed pinned, unable to get away, losing some motion, unable to use his right hand, thinking as it happened it was getting worse every second!

He moved, tried to jerk away, helplessly fought the arm, swung his small knife toward that hand and felt the point of a sharp knife jabbing into his neck, making blood drip onto his new clothes.

Then the knife appeared in front of his face and he heard a voice, loud in his ear: "You stop movin' or I'll kill you where you stand, clark!" Not a pleasant voice; not a pleasant thing to hear. He stopped trying—like it was helping anyway.

"I should kill you 'ere an' now, clark…but Johnathan wil' want t' do that by 'imself. You lie on the floor, now, an' I'm gonna tie your 'ands, an' if you move a finger I'll put this knife into yer kidney so fast you won't ever know it's there until you die." Not yelled: spoken. Didn't need to be yelled: the message got through.

"Drop tha' little penknife or use it now." It was dropped.

Ashley went onto the floor and before he realized what was happening, a noose was on his left wrist and then the right one and they were bound together; than a dirty-tasting and smelly rag was placed across his mouth and tied behind his head.

"I'm tyin' yer ankles t'gether also, clark; you won' run this time. You'll be able t' stand an' walk a bit, but no runnin'."

Ashley was trussed and pulled onto his feet, able to walk with small steps with the knife putting pressure in the kidney area of his right side.

"Yer better than most, but not so good as me."

Ashley was unsure of an answer to that, but couldn't speak anyway.

"Straight back; down the length o' the 'all...the door t' the far left o' this 'allway. We changed our room because o' you, an' a good thing it was. Clark, I'm so mad at you right now I could cut you inta little pieces an' feed 'em t' the cats out back, but I don't know whether t' do that or slap your back for bein' such a fool as t' return 'ere. Give me a reason t' cut you...you did it t' Matthew, didn't you! Tell me!"

Ashley shook his head to mean "no."

"You lyin' bugger...an' Mark? Them was well-traveled men, soldiers both, cold-killers an' war veterans. They'd never let the likes o' you 'appen t' them. 'Ow did you do Luke, at the bridge?"

Geoffry smiled, hardly like him, but Ashley could see a smile in the dim candlelight. "Why am I askin' questions when y' can't answer? Hahahahahahaha Why shouldn't I cut y' now, clark?"

"Because you don't want to have him bleed on my father's hall-runner and stain the new wallpaper, and because I want to talk to him first." The door to the far room had opened without the two of them realizing it and Johnathan stood there, pistol in hand. He had a cold voice, low, but threatening. This man meant what he said, under all that foppery he displayed. He had saved Ashley this time...but meant to kill him later.

They pushed him inside, then into a rear ante-room with a bed, a room without a window; worse than the room at Lane's in Providence. A low fire in the fireplace gave a sort of illumination. Enough for three men.

"Is he tied securely?"

"Yes, Johnathan."

"Will he get away this time?"

"No, Johnathan."

"Them I'll have you to thank or blame." An open threat.

Geoffry didn't respond to that, but pulled again at the rope on Ashley's wrists, finding it secure. Johnathan pulled off the gag from Ashley's mouth and Ashley sucked in great swallows of air...he never ordinarily breathed through his nose, and this gag had given him a fear of smothering. In another moment he had recovered his breath.

"Before you kill me, what country do you spy for?"

"What do you know about spying or what I have done?"

"I know you make maps and visit fortifications. It's only a frivolous question...could I have an answer? Spain? France?"

"The Dutch, of course."

"The Dutch?"

"Geoffry, is there an echo in this room?"

"Y'er funny, Johnathan, jus like wha' Matthew said." A partial smile on a half-open mouth, broken teeth and gaps exposed in the low light.

"You colonists are too far from the truth. Within this year England will be attacked by the Dutch fleet and what's left of the great English Navy will be destroyed. Then the Dutch will go inland along the Thames and take care of what is left of Cromwell's Army as they level London with their cannon. England has brought all this down upon Herself...that damned Cromwell and his laws and Acts! England shall be no more; then my half-brother will step in, become King as is his right, favor the Dutch with trade-ports, and world peace will drive commerce. Cromwell's boast to refuse foreign ships into English ports is a slap in the face to world trade. England's price for that shall be Her trade, and perhaps Her religion. The Dutch say the pope will be grateful to have England returned to his fold. His gratitude translates into gold, and therein lies our aims.

"Now...I have told you my secrets, you tell me yours. Who do you work for?"

"I was just asked to follow you and report where you went."

"Geoffry would like to cut some parts off you...you tell me the truth!"

"That IS the truth! Someone in Plimouth asked someone to ask me to follow you after you landed in Plimouth, and to write down those observations and mail them daily."

"Mail them to whom?"

"Just in care of a local mail-station, as I was not to know who did all this. You were seen getting off a ship in Plimouth and someone there wanted to know where you went, and I could write, so I was asked to do this job."

"It can't be so simple as that. Are you working as a spy for Cromwell? You seemed to know London well enough for a colonist."

"I was born in Dockside and grew up there, moved to Plimouth and have recently lost a job…I needed the coin."

"What was your pay?"

"About a dozen gold sovereigns at first; more to be had later."

"And you always were alone? No one to help you?"

"I was always alone, just mailed my reports off daily."

"And you truly stole the travel-papers to get here?"

"I swear; those are not my papers and not my name."

"What a remarkable man you are...the child told us about the gold sovereigns, and the stableman. Yes…you are the clerk, all right…back from the dead several times. A damnable dangerous Puritan. I didn't know one existed outside Cromwell's group. Why do you pester me so? Kill my men and try to kill me if all you were paid to do was write about us and record our movements?"

"God's truth: I did not kill your men. The big man shot me but either missed or didn't have a ball loaded."

"I knew it! Tha's wh' 'e' use' t' do in tha Army! 'E'd wait t' load until 'e was ready! Yeah...tha's the truth an' it done 'im in."

"And Mark?"

"In the hayloft?"

"Yes."

"I told you all this before. He was asleep; I heard him snoring when I went up the stairs. He woke and came running at me and ran right off the loft floor."

"Onto the fork, or did you do that? Tell me the truth!"

"Onto the fork, I never touched it or him; then I left by the loft door."

"The one we found open, of course. My father, the King, said the Puritan zeal was the toughest the world had seen, similar to the Saracens…I seem to be running into that. And what about my Luke? On London Bridge?"

"He tried to throw me out an opening there and fell backward, I swear by God! I didn't push him or touch him."

"You have been the luckiest man I have ever met. You slid away from Francis, dogged me, picked off my men…Geoffry?"

"Yes, Johnathan?"

"Hand my pistol to me."

"Yes, Johnathan."

"You shouldn't be here, Puritan...you should be at one of you prayer-meetings…Mattins or Evensong…do you play chess, Puritan?"

"No."

"This entire effort has been—to me—a simple chess-game. The King protected, the Queen off observing, pawns in line for each side...only me—the white knight—able to move within the enemy force...strike, leap back intact with information and leaving death behind me in an empty space on the board. Now you—a pawn—seized power, became as a black bishop and smashed diagonally through white's defenses, taking pawns, forcing the white king to move aside, threatening even, the King; that is what you have done: you have threatened the King of Great Britain and Ireland."

"There is no King."

"Oh, yes there is. A King of heredity, already accepted by most of England and the only man worthy to be the King...but that rotten scoundrel Cromwell denies him entry and his throne. Oh, there is certainly a King; never forget that. But this game you and I play...it's a simple game, a simple style. Nothing complicated and all well-planned until you added complication; a move not expected because you were not a professional in a professional's game...and a professional would never move the way you did. But you did move, and three pawns were taken, others scattered in fear. Now it's time to end the destination and destruction of the black bishop, take him off the playing-board so the game may continue without his interference...because, Puritan, the game WILL continue, and all your little moves are no longer powerful."

"You said your father was a King; you are the son of Louie?"

"Louie? Louis of France? Hahahahahahahaha...am I speaking French to you? Wherever did you hear that?"

"Back in Plimouth, when you first came ashore they said you looked like Louie of France."

"Imbeciles! The present Louis isn't old enough to be my father; he's only twelve. *His* father was sickly and his mother too domineering to allow him to have bastards. It *is* true, however, that I am vaguely related to him but *am* the son of a King: King Charles the First of England, whom the farmer Cromwell executed in public."

"Why was the notary killed?"

"What is the matter with you? You're going to die and you're not asking to be spared or sending prayers?"

"If I am to die, at least tell me the answers."

"You are sturdy, Puritan; I like that in you. Still full of questions with a pistol in your face. Well...I imagine that's why you have come so far after me, to get your questions answered. You simply amaze me; such person you show! With a dozen of you I could spy for every country. Ha! He was killed to settle

an old score—for my father. That fat fool had looted the personal wealth of his King...took monies and jewels my father had placed into his safe-keeping, eloped to the colonies, had that mansion built and lived as a Duke there...but he forgot to hire bodyguards—not that it would have mattered much to my men, right, Geoffry?"

"Right, Johnathan."

"He didn't know I had heard what he did. He and I were very old friends and had regular correspondence. When my father tried to go to relatives in France, he became stranded without funds in Scotland, couldn't pay his Army and couldn't get a way to leave the island...Cromwell captured him there. With the money Foster stole from my father, the King would have been alive today and still the King of England. I owed it to my father to kill that despicable man, that thief of gold and jewels and my father's life!"

"How was Miles Standish involved?"

"Who is Miles Standish?"

"A Puritan captain of militia in Plimouth—the notary's area."

"In the colony? Never heard of that name. Why am I talking to you? Telling you all this? Why aren't you dead? You have been here twice; each time we have captured you. What drives you to do this? Where is your sense? Don't you understand you are not good enough to hurt us? Not smart enough, not devious enough, not strong enough...before, I called you a dangerous Puritan...now I call you a fool. Thing what happens to the fool when he no longer makes the King laugh."

He circled Ashley again and Ashley knew what was coming.

Sure enough, he anticipated the strike by the pistol butt and felt it instantly when it arrived. His body shut down like a candle without air. He again fell to the floor.

"Coo...did ya kill 'im?"

"No...whyever would I do that? And ruin your fun? I must go away to post these missives to Charles." Johnathan handed the pistol to Geoffry and put an arm around him. "My poor man...walking the streets all night, searching for this stupid Puritan and he walks in here unarmed and happy...ignorance is bliss."

"'E won't be so happy in a few, Johnathan."

"Who in God's name *is* this man? Why does he hurt us so? How many times do we have to kill him?"

"Only once, Johnathan...only once. Let me do it now."

"Not now; not yet. Soon."

"Johnathan, I don't want y' goin' soft..."

"Have no fear of that. What I do, I do for my brother and Scotland. But I must repeat: the Puritan's death cannot leave blood here; the body cannot be left here; and neither can you nor I can be seen with him. What I'm thinking is...get a dray and leave it at the back entrance..."

"Hahahaha...I know about back entrances..."

Johnathan smiled a polite smile. Geoffry's expertise at "back entrances" was beginning to tell on him...putting up with the sexual antics of this sodomist and killer was becoming more difficult for Johnathan to take. First it was Mark, then Luke...

"Geoffry?"

"Yes, Johnathan."

"I had some thoughts about this...when Luke died last night...on the bridge?"

"Yes, Johnathan?"

"When you said you went to shoo some people away...did you bugger one of them while Luke was with the colonist?"

No answer.

"Did you bugger the boy? In Boston?"

"Awwww...Johnathan...You don' like t' hear things like that..."

"Then I imagine you did. You always liked that."

"Well...I mus' confess I still do."

"And our big clerk?"

"I likes 'em small...but I takes 'em where I gets 'em."

Johnathan understood that. Once in Scotland, Geoffry would have to have "an accident." It would be a shame to lose him, but his appetite for buggering had surpassed rational bounds, and he had almost become as dangerous as the Puritan who presently miserated his life.

A boyhood friend and a perfect bodyguard, Geoffry had simply become so undesirable that his death required certainty. Besides, when Charles reigned as King of England, a beefeater would guard Johnathan with his life and not "disappear" at times when young boys were around. If Geoffry were to trifle with Charles' son, Johnathan would also get the axe.

Geoffry Texira, renamed Geoffry Smith when he joined His Majesty's Army, had been a dedicated soldier, but hadn't always done the right thing. On the battlefield was another story: he was a demon when young and relished any fight. But his obsession with male soldiers removed him from good graces when the fighting was over...put him into an Army prison where he easily toned his desire and polished his sexual greed. Once out of the prison he bumped around the seedy portions of England, taking his pleasures and killing them to prevent accusations—the accusations which initially imprisoned him. He was attending the spectacle on the Thames when Charles the Second protested as a way to get his father released from Cromwell's chains, and there met Johnathan, whom he had known in childhood from the Portuguese section of Spain—where Johnathan was raised. From then on they were inseparable. He was Johnathan's bodyguard and attack-dog; he assembled Johnathan's group and lent his last name and vicious manner to them. When asked about him by his family, Johnathan said of Geoffry: "Even the most dangerous man needs a friend."

"Go out now and rent a dray. Purchase a large rug so you can roll the Puritan inside. Begin rolling him into the rug; do your thing with the knife but don't let blood spatter onto the carpeting here...remember this was the King's house and still belongs to Charles and the family. The old man upstairs needs no upset in his life; he has been years as a caretaker here. Do the Puritan and take the body out in the dray; be sure you have removed all sign of us here. Then take the body out by some marsh or whatever and throw it there—keep the rug and throw that somewhere else—farther away. We cannot establish a link between the rug and the Puritan and us."

"The war may soon be over an' it won't matter."

"Why do you think thus?"

"Well...we got the pledges an' you 'ad them fixed up..."

"And if the war is not soon over it shall matter greatly. You did those two whores; the sheriff's already looking for a knife-murderer; we don't need to link this one with those."

"Now, Johnathan, that was strictly business. I was out all night, snoopin' aroun' askin' questions about the colonist..."

"And I hope no one remembers you and your questions."

"I don' think they will...so I asked 'er for some service wi' the min' t' get more information. She said she'd quit the business but 'er roommate would do it. So we went inside an' I tol' 'er I'd pay double if she'd lock the door so no more customers would come in, an' watch me whilst I did the one on the bed."

"Rather purple scenario, my man."

"I likes 'em where I gets 'em. The I tol' 'er t' stan' real near an' she did...an' I 'ad my fun, then went t' put on my clothes an' 'ad more fun wi' my knife. I knew enough t' take off my clothes whilst I cut 'em...no blood on the clothes an' I washed myself afterward. Tell me I'm smart about my business."

"Did you find out where he stayed?"

"Who?

"The Puritan. Did she tell you where he stayed?"

"Naw…She didn' know."

"Well, it's a good thing he came here to us or I'd be looking over my shoulder in Scotland for him."

"'E ain't no professional man, an' no Army man. 'E 'as no skills at all I can see; 'e's jus' a bloody bulldog, bitin' an' holdin' on."

"Yes…tenacious. A gambler who cannot quit, tho' he loses constantly. Could he truly be here only because of the boy and Walter? We know he's here now because of the whores. That may explain the reason he follows us so doggedly…he's some crazy colonist who wants revenge more than he wants life."

"We'll give 'im that! So, when yer brother—excuse me, Johnathan—when King Charles wins this next battle, there will be no more war, as Cromwell will be dead or captured, an' the Puritans will give up right away."

"You have the confidence of Noah, Geoffry…and the zeal of Moses. What a King you would make."

"Awwwww…Johnathan…I couldn't be no King…YOU could be; you're gentry. All I wan' t' do is be in yer service."

"Well-spoken, my good man. Wherever I go, whatever I do, you shall be with me, protecting me and having all the 'candy' you want. Now I must make ready to depart. You go for the dray and I shall watch our dangerous Puritan. Remember, the ship sails in less than four hours and I cannot miss that. If you do not return, I shall have to complete all our business by myself."

"I'll be back soon, Johnathan, I promise. I'm bloody tired now, 'aven't slept in a great while."

"Sleep after this is all over; you've earned it."

He returned in half the time Johnathan had remaining.

"I 'ave the dray an' one outside the back entrance, an' I got a large, cotton rug so if it gets…liquid…on it, it'll 'old the stain an' not drip."

"You could be a rug salesman, my man! You have done splendidly! I have enough time to reach the ship and in about two hours it will sail. You'll remember to give me enough time to get away to sea before you go outside with your…rug?"

"'Es."

"Excellent. I can't begin to tell you what all this means…once the true King is restored the entire country will be different. I'm very proud of you, Geoffry.

I was here, thinking again how funny it was to get all those pledges from the loving supporters of my father and Charles...those big parties we attended where I told them all we needed was a show of love, a note of allegiance that they had a certain amount of wealth and thus were well-enough off to do this, not to sign a notarized letter of credit, just an un-notarized one to show Charles and the Scottish Council that the King's supporters in the colony loved him so...they signed away their lives and homes and personal fortunes and businesses; then we got old Foster to notarize them, making them pledges of promise instead of letters of information."

He chuckled and Geoffry joined him. Their ruse for Charles had worked.

"But I must say, now that this is mostly over, I shall miss it all...the parties and food, the women's favors and their dallying, the life as a personage from a King, the usual ways of being treated as a baronet, the traveling from and to countries...even the lackluster life of the idler. This year alone I have attended pledge-gatherings if four countries and two colonies, raised enough credit to pay seventy-thousand soldiers enough for the entire summer, and exhausted myself in the process. How I go on, I do not know; and how much more I shall have to raise is in serious question. This has to be the end, for I am beaten to my knees and have not the strength to smile throughout one more party nor shake the hand of one more contributor. I never was an overweight person, yet my clothing drapes upon me as tho' I've lost several sizes. Do I really look so thin, Geoffry?"

"Naw, Johnathan; yer not so thin."

"My trousers tell me differently and my shirts look as if they were made for Charles and not me. God, I miss Spain and the foods and the gaiety and all the reasons one stays in mother Spain...I want so much to leave here and return there...I had so many clothes there...And my father was there at the very end...I will tell you something which tugs at my heart...A truth. It is public knowledge that my father was executed: hanged, But in truth I tell you...He was—by Cromwell—beheaded."

"Naw, not the King!"

"It pains me to say that...I'm having tears in my eyes because I even think about it...the people of England have never before witnessed the killing of a King, and this one was terribly done, with the axe-man holding up my father's head, splattering blood on all those around him, saying, 'This is the head of a traitor!' All knew he loved them and England, and that rotten scoundrel Cromwell goaded them into doing that."

"I never knew..."

"It was silenced after it happened; too gruesome for words."

"'E was a martyr, Johnathan…the 'ouse o' Lords had executions in it also an' the 'ouse o' Commons became the law. 'Olland recognizes your brother as the legitimate and only King of England an' so does Scotlan'. 'E'll win this battle wi' Cromwell. 'Is time will come."

"His is dangerous work, and he bears us all upon his shoulders." Johnathan sighed heavily. "I so much want to leave here…"

"Charles prob'ly feels the same way in Scotlan'."

"Touché! You stab my heart with your words! Of COURSE Charles has it worse than we here…you return me to reality; whatever would I do without my good man! Now I have these notarized credits in this satchel and the banker in Scotland will honor them and give Charles the credit he needs for the Army; and the jewels from our father will let me fit right with the Family, again. How wonderful it shall be to be a baronet once more, the known brother of the true King of Great Britain and Ireland…we have done good work here, Geoffry…Charles will see how I love him and the lengths to which I will go to help bring him to power. The jewels alone should buy an army of mercenaries…I'll help him onto the throne and life shall be better for us than it was when we were young."

"Those were years ago, Johnathan…an' you stayed in Spain an I was sent 'ere t' London. Years apart an' we're back t'gether."

"And so now we shall go to Scotland. Geoffry, I have just had a delicious thought: let us go back to Spain together as soon as Charles become England's King."

"I'd like that, Johnathan…I really would."

"And so we shall! To stay at the seaport of…"

"I think we've 'ad enough o' seaports, Johnathan."

They both laughed.

"Probably so. None so tiny as that one in Plimouth; none so busy as the one in Boston; none so dedicated to Charles as Providence and Salem. By God, Geoffry, we're going to have a great life! The weather, the wine, the woman…"

"The bulls, the bravado, the boys…"

"Old times shall return to us! Meanwhile, who would have thought that this colonist would come back to us?"

"Not me, Johnathan."

"Nor I."

"You were loved in Spain, Johnathan...the first child o' a King what was gonna marry the infanta. They didn't like it when yer father went t' France instead."

"He couldn't convert to Catholicism and give England to the pope...they didn't understand. I pray it is part of God's plan to make Charles King of England."

"If it is, it will only be done because o' you."

"Because of us all...those three comrades who gave their lives as well. All of us who love our King and long to see him returned as leader to this land. England needs Her King again; she suffers now; we all do. When he is crowned here, then, by God, England will again be a free land and the world's finest country!" Johnathan wept openly, daubing at his eyes with a tiny cloth.

Tears formed in Geoffry's eyes as well.

"God," Johnathan started and Geoffry joined in..."Bless the King!"

"So now I shall leave for Scotland. The ship sails in little over an hour. Do nothing with the clerk until at least then; give me time to get to sea; then if something goes wrong, the ship will not be stopped and the pledges and jewels of my father the King shall get to Charles on time."

"Nothin' will go wrong, Johnathan, but I'll wait like you said."

"Knock him on the head again with the pistol butt to be sure, then get him into the rug and do your way with the blade. Cover the cut to sop up the blood...use a large towel; he looks as though he has a lot of blood in him."

Geoffry laughed.

"Remember, we can't have blood here in this house...we'd lose our standing with the family when they found out and it's such a private place here."

"Then after all that I takes 'im out t' the dray an' moves 'im as far as possible before I dumps 'im in a bog...then the rug in another, an' on t' the northern 'ouse and then t' Scotlan' t' join you."

"Perfect! Just perfect, my good man, my boyhood chum...united with me again after all those years spent apart. Sino!"

"Fate."

Johnathan took his baggage and left the house, located a hackney-coach down the street whose driver was waiting for a fare by the corner tavern, had him return to get the luggage and then went along to Dockside Port and the *Edinburgh Princess*.

Safely inside the coach and relieved he was finally on his way top Scotland and Charles, the jewel-box wedged beside him on the seat, Johnathan wondered about Geoffry. The man was so friendly and knew his place, but so warped when it came to sexual encounters…Charles would have no place for him in Scotland, but who else could Johnathan trust as a bodyguard?

Geoffry had been raised in his youth within the English Compound in King Phillip's Spain, having Johnathan as a playmate—tho' Geoffry was older—for several years: eating the same food, playing the same games, listening to the same tutors and hoping for the same dreams.

The connection to Spain fell apart and Johnathan was taken away by his mother, across the border to Portugal, while Geoffry was sent with his dad and mum to London.

When—in 1639—Charles I imposed his religion upon Scotland and they rebelled, Geoffry, tho' young, joined the Army to aid the King he knew from childhood and stayed in the Army through King Charles' death in 1649. He had met Johnathan (after all those years apart) at the rally for the King upon the Thames, and had officially quit the Army to be with Johnathan and work for his King, then his King's issue: Charles II.

Geoffry had been there at Edgehill to hear his Monarch say to his troops, "…the foe is in sight…come life or death, your King will bear you company…In his grateful remembrance."

Impassioned words, and a win for Charles I.

In 1643, Geoffry was in Yorkshire to again join his King in fight—when the Queen was sent with the crown jewels to borrow money to pay the Army. Charles I loved his soldiers.

By one vote—one vote—King Charles the First lost his petition before a tribunal and was quickly executed. Geoffry cried aloud when he heard the news, endearing him yet more to Johnathan.

Yes, in the years before he'd joined the Army he'd been involved in nefarious things—and whilst he was with the Army as well—but originally he was a child, and children do stupid things for what they think are good reasons. And, yes, he'd been imprisoned briefly three times or more with involvements started by his knife, but each time he was released when his mother promised he'd be good or the witnesses against her boy had disappeared or died suddenly.

Geoffry didn't need to look for trouble: it came to him. But when it did he was quick and thorough as his father—a King's captain—who taught his son how to fight and solve any problems; and his mum was there for him. Geoffry's boundaries were blurred only by the love he had for his King and his loyalty to England.

To think this man rejected intense feelings because he was low-born and cruel would be wrong. He loved and respected his mother and father all his life. His mum loved him no matter what he did or was said that he did, went daily to bring him food when he was imprisoned and his father away with the Army. The woman hardly had food for herself, so little at times she had to beg help from some of the royal gamily (who did assist her), and she gave whatever coin she received to her son.

Some people who knew Geoffry wouldn't have anything to do with him, but they liked and respected his mother and her devotion to her only child; so they looked the other way when Geoffry was accused of killing people and sent—or returned from—prison; and they tried to help his mother exist without him: feeding her—and she'd take half the food to her son.

They really loved each other, that small family, and they loved their Kings.

There could never be a reason not to have Geoffry around, and Johnathan knew it.

Johnathan watched his baggage—such as it were—brought aboard *Edinburgh Princess*. He missed already the clothing-chest his mother had given him; he seemed so poor-looking without it. Well, not to worry: Mother and Charles awaited, with much better days.

CHAPTER 31

The coals in the fireplace had burned low and the air was damp in this room. Geoffry tossed on some sawdust and coal to bring back the fire and keep back the dampness, went outside to see if Johnathan had finally left and watched a moment as his bags were loaded into the coach and Johnathan was away, then returned to the bedroom.

"My first plan for the night is a good ride. Then we'll go along t' the marsh, Puritan." He undid his trousers but held them so they didn't fall to the floor.

He was tired and it took him longer than usual to complete his efforts…but the unconscious clark didn't stir as he was buggered and, completed and even more tired, Geoffry returned to the front bedroom.

He never had so much candy from so many people in so short a time…maybe it was his age or just that he was so sleepy. Yesterday he'd worked all day, that business with the damned Puritan and Luke last night; then he'd had to walk all night, more frightened to return here and tell Johnathan than anything else. He had heard that stumble-footed colonist run down the stairs and heard him several more times as he searched the bridge. Then the Puritan was "gone": vanished! Had made that same loop of stairways and businesses and houses, checking for unlocked doors, dark places, people who might look like the clark…even went to the end of the street and back, checking doors and alleyways.

He had even—against his better judgment—inquired of several people, including the night watchman he met. One of them—joking—had said, "Probably went inta some 'ore's room; there's a warren o' them there, off the main street."

At the time, he had dismissed that sarcastic fool's answer…then as the hours passed and it was that light so all the hiding places in and around the bridge could be seen as empty, he started to wonder if the watchman could be right…and it turned out he was.

Late in the morning, after he had spoken with Johnathan, Geoffry circled back and asked around, found some chubby girl standing outside who would speak with him, told him the Puritan he sought had been there at that room all the night, and, yes, his hand had been injured!

"How?" she had asked. He told her he didn't know, only that his friend's hand had been hurt and he was looking for him to take him to a surgeon.

Geoffry decided this was a girl who knew too much and thought as well that he could offer her any amount of money for some candy, then he'd never have to pay her. What a bargain! He asked her price and she begged off, telling him she was no longer in the business but her roommate—who was inside—was, and if he paid that price, he'd be cared-for right away. He told her he'd double that price if she'd go inside and watch while it happened (no problem as the girls weren't about to keep the coin regardless) and told her that's all she'd have to do: watch.

The rest became history for the sheriff of London.

So...he had seen Johnathan gone and had his candy; the whores were dead, the Puritan unconscious and either dead or close to it. He had the dray; he had the rug; he had the knife.

Geoffry sat in the big, cushioned chair of King Charles the First, in his old sitting-room, realizing now he was extremely tired and very sleepy. It didn't take half a minute before he was sound asleep in the chair...thoughts of what were to happen pleasurably forgotten right now.

CHAPTER 32

"Your pardon, King Charles."

"Speak."

"Our horsemen on the Olde Harbour Road stopped a courier to the English Army and we have his dispatch." He held it out.

Charles never moved from his chair nor extended his hand. "Am I to read this as a schoolboy or has someone else already seen this?"

"I have not seen it, my Lord, but have heard it comes from Protector Cromwell in Ireland."

"From Cromwell? Himself?"

"Yes, my King."

"And it says…?"

"I am unable to read, my King, but I am told it says Cromwell has beaten the Irish and comes now to Scotland with sixteen thousand to take charge of the English Army and fight us."

"We were twice his number, now we are less. Call General Leslie and my tutor, now!"

The guard left and Charles thought this through. News he had not expected—Ireland finally beaten and Cromwell arriving—but news he could weather, as Leslie's battle-plan was a strong one, the kind his father would have made…exactly the kind he, himself, was not capable of framing. Leslie was good. He thought beyond the battle, factoring-in the English Army's needs for re-supply, water, reinforcements and communication.

The English Army—once started as a fighting force—would have to move northeast, toward the North Sea and the Firth. They would be required to re-supply there at the sea; they must at this point be desperately in need of food, probably already eating their houses and ravaging the land for anything else to eat. Charles' own Army was almost the same until a short while ago.

So along the course toward the North Sea they probably would move; it didn't take a military specialist to understand the need of a great army for water, food and an escape-route. A league southeast of Dunbar was a plain between rolling hills and the North Sea. Cromwell would use this; it was a natural funnel to the open waters beyond, whereupon English ships would bring food and men.

Leslie's plan was to occupy the hills, mainly Doon Hill, and as the English Army poured onto the plain, sweep down from upon them in a semi-circle, attacking the English rear. Charles smiled to himself: "attacking the English rear" sounded like something his half-brother would say. He rapidly shook away that thought.

With Cromwell pinned against the waters of the Spott, Leslie could then cut him to pieces, force a surrender, win the entire war! God! He might very soon BE the King of Great Britain and Ireland! Not just in fanciful title, but in reality! Wouldn't his mother be proud of him then! Then he could bring her back from France, wed that Portuguese girl from Bragona, and live an easy life. He already had more than a dozen mistresses—none, of course, with him. But with Catherine as a wife he'd inherit a three-hundred-thousand-pound dowry and the naval bases of Tangier and Bombay. His personal finances would be assured for the rest of his life and the commerce between Portugal, their far-flung holdings, and England would increase England's economic standing in the world market. He would cancel the taxes those Puritan Merchant Committees put into force, sign treaties to bring more English trade to the Portuguese Colonies, and in general make the life of the English poor and working-class a much better one. Only a true King could or would do something like that; no farmer like Cromwell could think far-enough ahead to understand that the people of England were England's treasure, not her taxes.

Everything Charles wanted to do was for England. Cromwell was destroying the country from within, seeking taxes and other "charges" from the peasants—who could ill afford them—and imprisoning them just for being poor. The English "businessmen-class" hated the poor because the businesses were required to give money to the country to help support them, another thing the rotten scoundrel Cromwell made happen. When the pledges from the colonies arrived and were sent on to the Swiss, Cromwell would be attacked in London; England would return to her legitimate rule; and the people would again be safe. Their King—who returned the love the peasants gave him—would build England into a haven of love instead of the state of business it now was. This, he promised himself.

It was all Parliament's fault—this war. Parliament had written a grievance to his father, saying the Kings of England did not have absolute power when it came to choosing a state religion, and said the people of England had outgrown their dependence upon him and his appointed barons. What else could the King do, after this open slap in the face, but dissolve Parliament the way his father had. The King was the King; he had to rule and command; the country expected no less—and really more. So Parliament had to go. Then THEY started this war, replaced the country's religion, imposed unfair taxes upon everyone, established Cromwell as captain-general of the Army, and initiated the Civil War.

His father tried in sixteen-thirty to keep taxes from the poor, but Parliament—what a joke: "Parliament, the working-man's friend" they called themselves—levied taxes onto everyone! The King got the blame and Parliament got to spend the money the way THEY voted, not the way King Charles the First wanted to.

Charles the Second would fix all this.

His friend and tutor arrived, ahead of David Leslie.

"We've been together, what, six years?"

"Since you've been fourteen; yes, my Lord King."

"And you've tried to teach me how to do battle and my father the same. He had me with him at Edgehill, but I just can't seem to understand how to use troops successfully."

"You're an apt pupil and brilliant in other things, your Majesty. You know and love religion and the arts, and speak fluently three languages."

"But a King who cannot command an Army is a King who will lose his army—I heard that often enough. I have a final concern about this battle: I fear the winner shall become King, not I. Either Leslie or Cromwell."

"Neither can be King; only you, no matter what the outcome of all this. You have the only bloodline to the throne."

"Johnathan would argue that."

"Johnathan…Johnathan is a young man's folly, a disappointed man's frolic. You and I have been over this again and again."

"At least he is more fop than general or he'd be here now, in charge."

"This is why we use Leslie: Leslie is as brilliant at battle-plans as you are in other matters, but he cannot rise beyond being a soldier."

"I'm sorry I am a flawed King."

"My Lord, you are not a flawed King, you just don't have the stomach for killing. Your ancestors wielded swords, chopped opponents, dove into the very thick of things without realizing what would happen to their country where they to fall in battle. Charles, you *cannot* do that! We love you too much to have you fall to some stray arrow. What would happen to us all if—everyone—if you were killed? You *cannot* fight in this war! You *must* remain in overall command; who else can make decisions during or after the victory? We've had this discussion before; you *must not lead!* Let Leslie go out there and run with his men: when they return, you will be here to greet them and give purses for valor. No one faults you for being so loved that you people can't bear to lose you in battle. Much better, Lord, that you direct it all and be the one who watches what is happening. If Cromwell breaks, left, you will see that and reinforce right. If he fords the river, you can send troops to intercept him whilst being aware how to use your reserves. These things you can do well. We can't lose you—suppose Leslie is killed or wounded...without you in charge, the entire battle fails! Your country needs you; you inspire the people. Scotland, England and Ireland need you. We couldn't stand it if Cromwell were to kill another King."

Charles frowned. "Then I shall not take part in the fighting, but I shall be there to be part of the win; I will not disappoint my men in that."

"Thank you, my King. I had almost forgotten: the reason I arrived here so early is that we have heard again from Johnathan: he is returned to London and at you old home there, only for a day or two whilst he completes that business for you."

"I hate that word, 'business.'"

"He comes here soon, on a ship from London to Edinburgh; I have already sent a squadron of men with a mount for him, and an armed guard shall be detached from there to escort him and his...business...here. He writes he has an 'immense surprise' for you."

"Probably a new male lover. You said you sent 'a' mount for him? He is alone? No man-servant like last time?"

"Apparently alone; he writes thus."

"Good. That man was so crude."

"Johnathan is not at fault; he was not raised properly and appears to project that in his choice of friends."

Charles sighed. "Johnathan is an accident of my father's disappointment in Spain. Yes, blood-related, but not legitimate. This family has spent a lot on his education and he thinks he is royalty."

"The King—your father—made him a baronet."

"And Parliament cancelled that."

"Will you give it back?"

"If Johnathan arrives here with the pledges he promises *and* with my father's jewels, I'll make him an earl for life!"

"He loves you—as do we all."

"And I, him, when it comes down to it, the bastard...but having him around is like having the temperament of a terrier in a wolfhound: he has no limits and cannot be called off once he starts. He frightens us all."

"After you are King of England, my Lord, you will tame that hound."

"England. Right now, England is full of religious zealots who claim to speak directly to God and hold their own sainthood whilst living! They're insane! They infiltrated the Parliament and used political maneuvering to make my father look bad in the eyes of his people. The people wanted more Sheriffs and less crime, so my father appointed them from Parliament and they turned against him. Then the people thought the poor jobs the sheriffs' did was because the King appointed them, not because they were deceitful men in the first place! In order to run England and pay the debts and run the Navy—which Parliament refused to do—he had to order Parliament closed so the country could stay alive. Then the Puritans said he was a tyrant and ungodly. All the Bishops in Scotland complained he hadn't cared for Scotland, and they railed against him. It was like a paper house in a windstorm...nothing could stop it from ripping apart."

"Your father was a good man, a good husband, a good King, and a good Englishman; but all the religious zealots conspired against him and set up the farmer, Cromwell, so someone would look good in the eyes of the people. Then Cromwell did even worse than your father and he blamed his mistakes and failures on your father...and then..."

"Yes, I know the 'then' part: civil disobedience, civil war, and my father executed. All because those Puritans think they are more religious than the Catholics and don't require priests. They are ill-informed, sad people who believe Jesus will save them over God's plan. They forget Jesus is dead and only God will help. I pity them, but I fear them; their religious views border insanity."

"Your father gave his life to England. He brought great artists and painters to the country, ever believing it would benefit the people at large. Parliament did him wrong! He was winning the war with Spain and Parliament refused to give him money for the Army."

"Old news, old friend."

“England needs you now; they protest in the streets for you and your line must continue. The people pray for you, they demonstrate their love for you, they hate the farmer Cromwell; he saw his chance and he took it, has been lucky since. But that kind of luck runs out. As you say, when Johnathan gets here with the pledges of support, Europe will side with you.”

“All we need do now is win this battle. We barely stay alive out here, but the pledges Johnathan brings from our subjects in New England should quiet France and give us better support there.”

“They need England’s trade and are denied that by Cromwell. My cousins all across Europe can celebrate with me.”

“You’re the youngest King to do anything like this since Alexander. England has been tricked into accepting a religion which is not true in faith. The Puritans overtax and penalize for small infractions; they join the Catholics in finding and torturing witches…and court business from Countries who are our sworn enemies. My King, you *must* stop Cromwell: all of Europe hangs on your rule.”

“This, then, we try. The latest news is that Cromwell comes even now to lead his Army and engage us.”

“If he can get his Army to move…our spies say they have no food nor water and he loses men to desertion daily. His ships will have all the food they’ll need; the Army will fight or die, and I fear a man who sees food behind me and has to go through me to get to it.”

Charles clapped his teacher on the back. “That’s why you teach and David Leslie fights; Leslie would fight while you would flee.”

“There is no shame in fleeing when you gain an advantage…”

“And the advantage at Doon Hill is ours!”

“He brings another sixteen thousand.”

“Then we are equal: the desertions he lost and the men he brings equal our force of thirty thousand. Our great want is cavalry, as was my father’s.”

“The English are all blooded veterans; good Englishmen, all. Some your father led.”

“Why do we haggle, you and I? Leslie’s plan is a good one.”

“Remember Cromwell’s cannon? He wins battles with those.”

“We have cannon.”

“But Leslie will not get to use them offensively. If he does as he says and ‘sweeps down’ from Doon Hill and runs—literally—into English cannon along that half-a-league he must run his men…he has few horse and cannot use them to charge…”

"Let Leslie and the Kirk Commanders take care of that. We shall surround Cromwell."

"Yes, my King…you'll surround him with his back to the water—where no fighting can take place; and you'll give him a full field of fire for his cannon in any direction. Please, Charles, set up a defense…"

"Stop! The battle-plan is drawn. You think Leslie doesn't respect English cannon? He and I spoke about this and he says the cannon will be drawn by horses at that point and cannot be brought into play for hours; Cromwell will have no cannon in use when we attack. You yourself said Leslie was brilliant…we'll take Doon Hill on the morrow and wait. When Cromwell comes, he will be funneled into the plain with his front to the water and no bridge or ships."

"God, I pray that happens."

"Johnathan has sent more good news! He is on his way here with more than eighty thousand pounds in pledges *and* my father's jewel-box with *all* his jewels! More than enough to hire the Swiss *and* pay our Army!"

"Thank God for that!"

"Don't I know; I fully intended to send the credits to the Swiss, to launch an attack on lower England, but that would take some time, of which we have none. But another plan comes to my mind, all mine, not Leslie's. All summer long, the Marquess of Montrose had had his army and Scottish troops in the north of England, ready to invade and conquer. I'll use him as a diversion for Cromwell and as a flanking attack. He needs money and support and already is poised to fight. Better to use the funds for friends than mercenaries. This way we each strike at Cromwell."

"The Swiss are very good."

"Agreed, but they are far away and Montrose's splinter of men is already there. No more talk of battles. Johnathan's most recent letter to me says he has lost another man but is on his way aboard the *Edinburgh Princess* and arrives on the morrow's tide."

"Good news!"

"He has had to evade an entire group of Puritans—captured one, so he knows it is they."

"The man is a marvel! Fought them and captured one!"

"But he has lost another man of his group."

"Another lost? The Puritans must be relentless, and he heroic or extremely lucky."

"He shall tell me all tomorrow, when he gives me the pledges and jewels. I never knew my father had hidden-away such treasure...and Johnathan could have kept it for himself...so that goes a long way in bringing him back into the family. I myself will kiss him in public for that, and make him an earl!"

"Wonders never cease. Does he require any assistance? There are beefeaters in London..."

"No...he's already aboard the ship and will be in our port in the morning. Here, he is safe; and with the pledges, so will I be."

"Charles the Second, our religious Anglican Lord; and of Great Britain and Ireland and our hearts, King!"

King. It was good to be the King.

CHAPTER 33

Coming awake: groggy, like a dream-sleep where he knew something was going on but he couldn't put it all together nor could he wake. Engrossed in his own thoughts—almost seeming to be dreaming—his thoughts wandered: he was there with Bren when the beaver frightened him; then he was in the canoe with Bren, headed here. Somehow, Rufus was talking with them, there in the canoe. And he heard someone groan, and again. He seemed then to wake—and heard the groan once more, realizing this time it was his own voice, his own groan.

His throat dry, unable to breathe through his mouth and suffocating, his eyes bulging, his heart pounding, his mind a tremulousness mix of fear and the need for air and escape. At one point he literally exhausted all the air his nostrils could suck in without him realizing it and he swooned, his head throbbing, knowing in those brief seconds he would die of trying to breathe before he could ever escape the ropes. Lost the awareness he had for a short time—fainting in fear and exhaustion—then slowly recovering to find he had finally enough air through his nose and positioning himself on the floor to attempt to complete an escape.

So…awake and where? Oh, God! NOW he knew where! His wrists and ankles tied again; different room, same sad and sorry situation. He thought only an instant about the notary and the alliteration of "sad and sorry succinct situation" before he began to apply his mind to whatever he might—must—do.

This wasn't the opportunity for the "secret pocket with the knife" Rufus envisioned, because the knife was gone and tied this way he couldn't reach it anyway. There'd have to be a secret pocket at the tail of the vest, not on the shoulder. He'd tell Rufus if—yeah, if—he ever saw him.

The light in this room was almost non-existent, being but from the dying coals in the metal fire-bin. The rope was tight and Ashley had been shoved to the floor and for some reason his pants were down around his ankles—then he thought he knew that reason, having gone through that humiliation once before. Geoffry deserved a very special place and a very special way to die for that.

It wasn't a large room, only some tiny room off the main bedroom...who did things like that? Then he realized it was a child's room off the parents' bedroom and held a bed, a dresser with a pitcher and had a small fireplace with a metal fire-bin and fireplace utensils.

Beginning to feel better—if that meant he could ignore the pain from his head and the small amount of air his nose could capture. Ashley was a mouth-breather and enjoyed great gulps of air as he lived his life. Felt beaten: was beaten. Stiff, scared, his face and back sore—they must have kicked him until their feet swelled it felt so bad. Not satisfied with just capturing and trussing him, they felt obligated to strike, beat, injure him in several ways, in several places, just to take out their anger on him. These men—especially Geoffry—were beyond cruel: they were sadistic.

What a damnable fool he was to even attempt to watch these men or try to harm them for Margaret. Maybe he'd meet her in Heaven...but then...Anna would be there...God...what kind of a Heaven would THAT be?

He had tried to be hard: a hard man; someone who could/would hunt down and kill the murderer of Margaret and Velma, a revenger of blood for God. He thought at the time he could do it, but it was exactly like they said: he was a stupid, trussed-up man who was about to die painfully.

Anna was gone, Margaret was gone, Velma was gone, the boy and the notary and the three murderers. Soon he'd be gone as well. Tried to say the Lord's Prayer and say the name "Jesus," as Elder Otis had told him, out loud. Couldn't. Tied, arms behind him, felt on fire, sore, God, just awful. That Geoffry: eyes like a wild animal, a vicious animal, piercing and looking all around at once...determined. Devil eyes!

Ashley felt so badly: dizzy, sore, confused, frightened—all at once. Then he was more awake and it was just a throbbing in his head and hand which really woke him...and...remembering how much of an imbecile he had been, woke completely.

His hand was like a great lump of extremely painful flesh. He couldn't see it, but sure felt it, while questioning himself if the hand were really still there. There seemed to be some movement in the thumb and little finger; the rest of it was either not there or too damnable numb to feel. For an instant a thought flashed in him mind to be concerned about his hand, but his brain turned it off before he could get that into action: there were a few other—more important—things to think about.

This time, the headache he had experienced in Merry Mount was back, banging a drum while others pains were kicking his ribs, trying to pull him apart from the inside out. Damn! Why did it always have to be his hand and head these bastards hurt? He was nauseous and sore all at once, his hand throbbed, his neck felt wrenched, his arms seemed stretched…he lay in agony, feeling pain as never before, trying to get enough air into him just to live. Not the usual aches, like those from chopping wood or building a cabin. Not like a horse just kicked your leg and it still hurt…nothing so little as that. Dreadful pain. He feared he would vomit and choke to death on it, then he almost passed-out trying to get even more air through his nose.

His eyes were open but he closed them, squinting; his head pulled into his neck as he imagined a turtle would do…anything, any position to ease the pain; anything. Knew he shouldn't sleep, that he had no time to sleep, that if he slept he might never wake or wake as he was being killed, but he slept a while more, really a comfortable sleep, a short one, waking again, thinking the eyes of a lion watched him, then realizing they were two cooling coals in the fire-bin, ember-like and about as dead as he was.

He realized once more he was in pain…but it was lessening. They had hurt him, but he was still alive, he was still Ashley Lyons, he was going to get even, maybe ahead. This time his head pounded but he wasn't afraid he'd been shot, like the time Matthew had shot him; that gave him the incentive to move now, investigate what was happening, where he was, how he could get out of these ropes and away from here…how he could return and burn this damnable place down with its spies inside it. Oh, yeah, he was back. Piss on the pain: he had to get out of these ropes.

What would a spy do, wrapped up like this? Think spy. What was this room like? What was in it? Then his thoughts shied away and he wondered how long he'd been in here, how long he'd have before someone—Geoffry—came in and killed him. Unpleasantness. Decidedly unpleasantness.

Think!

Hard to move, almost couldn't maneuver.

Here he was again, he had been here before, but they removed the bindings to carry him to the London Bridge. He almost laughed out loud: same situation; was again going to be killed. He WAS a stupid man and now he'd die a stupid death and Anna would tell him throughout all Eternity how stupid he had been. Stupid, stupid, stupid!

Damn the pain in his head! No, he wasn't getting used to all the cracks on the head and wasn't getting used to these ropes. Didn't they know another way to hurt a person? Always tie him up, kick him senseless and leave him somewhere alone? Well, he couldn't get out of these ropes before until they took him to the bridge...and he didn't think Geoffry was about to repeat that move...so he'd have to get out of these by himself and pretty damnable fast!

Looked around as much as he could from his position on the floor. Coal burning low in the bin; coals covered by a screen so they couldn't snap an ember onto the floor or rug, but to heat up the screen to throw more heat into a damp room. End of summer and they needed a fire. Probably made by the landlord for each guest in every bedroom. Courtesy; damn fine of the landlord.

Still didn't help to know that. He couldn't burn off the ropes because the coal was inside that metal screen, the skinning knife was long gone; he felt just like he was sitting in a tureen which was filling with soup: you know what's going to happen beforehand but hope it doesn't, then it does. Then you start to drown. Damn! Had to get away from here!

He could see the vague outline of the doorway to the main bedroom of this apartment, so he was again in a bedroom. Last time he was here he was unconscious and never knew where he was...not until he put it all together in his mind. He was struck on the head—that hurt enough such that he knew that; he saw a fire-bin...maybe if he put his legs against the metal fire-bin...no, it would have to be his wrists. Freed ankles gave him little leverage against the two men with their pistols, knives and unbound hands.

His thoughts strayed an instant as he thought he had to urinate...then reality set in. Forget it! But the urination-thought cascaded into others. Here in a bedroom was a place to urinate, a chamber pot! Had to have a chamber pot here. Looked around in the dim light and saw one, under the bed. His mother—in Dockside—had said: "What does a rich man have over his bed that a poor man has under it? A can-o-pee." Thank God for mothers. Two ways to use a chamber pot.

He wriggled a bit, turning himself around as he realized he could move most of his body and although his legs were tied, he had some leeway with that rope there. His legs hit the side of the bed as he flexed them, and he scooted around, rubbing his cheek on the rug and glad he had a full day's growth of beard as the rug-burn would be mean on his face. Then the thought flashed in his head: *Doesn't matter if your face gets rug-burned, you'll be dead soon.* Not a comforting thought.

With some effort he concentrated and forced himself to move…ooooh…what a headache! His long legs reached, identified, and began the dragging-out process of the pot…and after several attempts he finally got it out from under the bed.

Well…there were a number of ways to break one of these…as most of them were solid, shallow and sturdy (another alliteration he realized: that notary!). He shuffled around until he had the pot against his left shoulder. (God, his hand hurt so much…those Royalist bastards!) He moved close to the pot, rolled his body up, them threw himself down, his left shoulder striking the pot. "OW!"

That hurt and did nothing useful; a small amount of noise…still no Geoffry; had to work faster and quieter. Maybe if he hit it with his head…yeah, that was a smart thought.

What. What could he use to break this thing? The pot was made of clay, with a brown glaze—probably made in a monastery, as many for the gentry were. There was a crude carving along the side: "God save Elizabeth, Queen of Bohemia." Ashley eyed it; clay would break.

He slithered around again, bringing his tied legs over the pot, measuring the distance, getting the proper range, lifting his legs and bringing them down: Bang!

Nothing. Nothing but noise. Johnathan and his pistol would soon be at the door.

Once more: bang! A small piece of the rim had chipped off. Damnation, this was a good pot!

He moved as quickly as he could, tied, achy, almost exhausted, hardly no breath, sore, head pounding, fingers numb, shoulder hurting, realizing he still had on his boots. NEXT time Rufus put a "pocket" for a knife somewhere, it should be in a boot; that "shoulder hideaway" wasn't too practical. Only for an instant did his mind register the thought: *How could I be so dumb as to let these people catch me twice?*

He maneuvered the broken piece of the pot into his left hand and manipulated it as he could to start sawing at the rope. It wasn't rope. Oh, it looked like rope, twisted and swirled and dyed as rope was…but it wasn't "rope." It was an imported piece of cloth which had been dipped in dying-liquid to give the appearance of rope and the strength for its use as a drapery-cord. He could thank the Dutch for importing that: good English cordage almost couldn't be cut!

Once the outside layer of the drapery-cord parted, the inside fell apart. FREE!

He quickly sliced the cords on his legs and—somewhat in wonder—pulled up his pants as he stood, and tied them around his waist.

Lost his balance and fell onto the floor—toward the fireplace. More noise, but only a muffled one.

This time, however, Geoffry, coming awake, heard it.

He had fallen asleep in the King's chair after all his exhaustion, and these three hours of sleep didn't completely revive him, but he was an old soldier and they wake fast; he was awake enough to grab the pistol in one hand and his knife in the other, and go cautiously to the ante-bedroom door, opening it slowly, letting in some light from the larger bedroom lamps and peering in, seeing Ashley by the fireplace and in the process of standing.

"'Ell-o, 'ell-o, wha' d' we 'ave 'ere? The man from the street is on 'is feet! Johnathan mus' 'ave not 'it you 'ard enough; mus' be losin' 'is touch...well...we'll see about that. I would never have thought some colonial Puritan could do anything like wha' you've done."

Geoffry laughed a short laugh, entering the room. Ashley tried to keep his hands behind his back.

"'Ere I am, soundin' like Johnathan. Them good manners really do rub off after a bit, don' you think, clark?"

The pistol was cocked and pointed.

A sudden tension—a dynamic—between killer and prey. Each knew what should happen next: the pistol should speak or the knife drink. Geoffry was as a bull guarding cows, ready to charge. Ashley seemed still tied, weaponless, defenseless, not a threat but a thing to be done-away with: resolved, removed.

Light in this room was meager; the embers gave little light against the overall darkness and what filtered in from the front room was scant. Geofry had placed a taper on the floor as he opened the door and the flickering of that as it sputtered in poor tallow was mostly the light they had. Geofry's talk was light and friendly, but his face in the candle-light broadcast a different message: there was no smile or friendliness, only a mask of bitter promise.

"That pistol isn't your choice of weapons, is it?" Ashley ventured. Bren had called that kind of talk "baiting"...telling someone something to get a response in an otherwise sticky situation.

"Nawww...I likes my knife. This is jus' t' see 'ow yer ropes are...then I'll use my knife on you. Coo! This's a fancy place; wouldn' want' t' use no pistol ball in 'ere, but I will if need be, so you remember tha'."

Geoffry came closer to him, almost up to him. Ashley could see his eyes, which looked small, but he knew all eyes were the same size and only the skin around them gave them the appearance of wide-eyed-wonder or pig-eyed-squintyness. Geoffry's were the latter, and his thick lips and wide nose made his eyes seem even smaller. What a work of art Geoffry was: a work of vicious, frightening art, the kind you remember from your nightmares and cross the road to get away from.

"You lie down like a good clark an' I'll go back t' my sleepin'...ain't nothin' like a good sleep after a piece o' candy. Hahahahaha 'ay, Putitan...did y' know them cute little 'ores over in Southwark? Hahahahahaha."

Ashley started to move, keeping his hands behind him.

"They was plumb ripe, them two. Buggered 'em both, then cut 'em...jus' like 'ore meat."

Ashley twisted around from just the thought of Geoffry killing Margaret.

"'Ere, m' god man; be a good sort. We all die. Even o' Geoffry will die an' go see 'is mum. This is somethin' you an' I mus' do; you understands, don' you?"

In his mind, Geoffry was back on the bed with Velma, having just stabbed her and then she slapped him; then he stabbed her—fast—about three times more and looked over at Margaret.

He saw the blank look on her face and knew he'd captured her soul with terror; she wouldn't move: when they looked at you like that they couldn't move; they were frozen in fear. She wouldn't yell or anything else, she was so completely and utterly stricken by the violation of the knife and all she could do was attempt a protest in her thoughts. Margaret wanted to scream but knew the closed and draped door would hold that inside, and even if it got out on the street it would either be dismissed or forgotten. Her eyes were wide and her mouth open to gasp the air she'd forgotten to breathe in. In her mind she thought that this couldn't be happening, but in her heart she knew it was, and it was about to happen to her. Didn't matter that her face was white with already-drained blood before the knife cut; didn't mean anything that she stood frozen in fear, She was a bystander, watching it all happen. This was a thing that happened top "other girls" but never could happen to her or Velma. The man, the knife, the blood...This was beyond a nightmare, beyond even her remembrances of the heads of the traitors on those posts at London Bridge. It was so real her mind halted. She couldn't think and was totally powerless as the knife did more than she felt or imagined it could. She still—as she fell—denied it was happening.

He hadn't really been watching that left hand; thought the colonist was right-handed and Johnathan had settled that hand with his pistol. A few of the men in the Army were left-handed, but they were literally whipped into using their right hands to service and fire the matchlocks and to slash with the saber. No left-handed man in the service of the (former) King dared present a picture other than complete uniformity to his leader.

"'Ere, now...don' be standin' on that rug...move over 'ere where I wan' you t' be." He motioned with the pistol and Ashley could sense there was no time left: this man was about to shoot him, no matter where he stood.

Ashley was standing between the fireplace and Geoffry, the fireplace poker was standing upright, alongside the fire-bin. He let Geoffry see him glance at the door behind Geoffry, Ashley thinking Johnathan would surely come in at any moment but had to chance it...yelled: "DON'T COME IN; HE'S GOT A PISTOL!"

Geoffry half-turned, not quite believing his prisoner.

Ashley had no fear, for there was not enough time to have it: just had to instantly understand and simultaneously respond: the sword's edge of life, when instant reaction is the correct solution and a pause or thought takes just long enough for the enemy to attack first. About the same amount of time you have when you see a trigger pressed on a musket and you have to throw yourself away from the oncoming ball: that little time.

It didn't take two seconds. Ashley grabbed the poker and lashed it across Geoffry's face: "Smack!"

The poker-strike got Geoffry's attention: a dull thud without him saying a word in response and he needn't have, for he was used to things like that in battle. By the time he could regain his firing-point with the pistol, tho', and re-align his target, the poker struck again, this time in a downward slam, atop his head: a heavy strike—a strike of the owl.

Geoffry let out a great sigh, blinked, and turned away from Ashley...but the pistol turned slower than he did, his coordination off, but this man was still tough and dangerous.

Ashley dodged to Geoffry's side and struck again with the poker—to the head. He heard a crack...Heard a moan...Geoffry started to wobble, then slump...Then fell to the floor, his head split open like a torn seam, blood staining the King's rug. Without wasting another second—as he thought Johnathan would come suddenly racing in—Ashley struck again: wham!

The skull split and...things...came out of it.

"That was for the boy in Boston!" Ashley heard himself talking aloud, realized Johnathan must have heard him also; grabbed the pistol and slipped to the door, crouched down the way the Plimouth militia had taught him when there was observation to be done and a foe nearby, and peeked around the door-jam…No one in that room at all. Immense relief!

He went quickly as he could to the bedroom door and locked it from the inside. Still no Johnathan.

Back to Geoffry's body on the floor.

The pistol was a good one, new and efficient: the pride of French weapons-makers. Cocked and ready to use, it was just what he wanted for the way he intended to use it. He set it on the floor and took up the poker again, standing over Geoffry.

"This is for doing to me what you did." Smash!

The head flew apart in pieces, like an overripe melon split by a knife. He reached into Geoffry's pockets and retrieved his purse and skinning-knife and without wasting any more time sliced Geoffry's neck from ear to ear: fitting justice long overdue and never felt, but vengeance.

So easy it was like he hadn't done it.

"That's for Margaret and Velma, you scum!"

Then he used Geoffry's knife and rapidly cut off each finger. "And that's for the notary!"

He wiped away some blood, using Geoffry's clothing, picked up the pistol, checked—as the militia had taught him to see if it were ready to fire—and pushed the muzzle between Geoffry's legs.

"For all those who were hurt by you…And those who couldn't fight back and those you hurt and killed over the years…And for being what you are." He pulled the trigger: Bang!

Standing up. "I think Bren would call this a particularly mean death." He loosened his trousers and used his urge to urinate—which had been put aside when the fun began—and urinated upon Geoffry. "Sorry, but the chamber-pot appears broken."

It took a solid minute before he relaxed the grimace from his expectation of death and looked around, still expecting Johnathan, then beginning to understand he wasn't there and maybe wouldn't be—surely wasn't right now about to shoot him. Then he began to breathe normally. He had put on the cloak of the avenger of blood and was content he had worn it well.

Then he began to feel tired—worn out with all the events. He about dragged himself out of the main bedroom into the hall, carefully looked about, then headed toward the front door of the house. An old man came down the stairs and over to him: "What was that noise?"

"What noise?"

"A large bang, like a musket-shot, but not so loud."

"I never heard it; it must have come from outside."

"It sounded as if it came from the King's bedroom, at the end of this hall."

"Ask Johnathan when he comes back."

"I shall. Who are you, good sir, that I may tell Johnathan you called?"

"Oh, I'll come back and tell Johnathan myself; you don't need to. Meanwhile, I seem to be ill and must be along. No one is in that apartment; I just left there. Go back upstairs, all right? I'll return in a few hours; you can tell Johnathan that for me. I'll return."

"I shall, sir; I hope your illness is brief and gentle upon you."

"Wonderful..." He started out the door. "Bye, bye."

Ashley felt awful...tired, sick, had to get out of there. He had spent all his energy and had no reserves; still, he was overjoyed Johnathan hadn't been there and at the same time frightened that he could be identified by the old man—who apparently was the caretaker. He staggered more than walked toward the tavern, hailed a passing coach, and asked to be taken to the Custom House on Lower Thames Street. There he got out, and after that coach was gone, caught another to Temple Church. From there, another to nearby the Federated Bank—which was his destination. He hoped the changes in drivers and left-off places would throw off any pursuers and inquiries about where he might have been or where he was going.

There was a small park down the street from the bank—a tiny corner-spot where a house might have sat and perhaps the owners or the city decided amidst the bustle of business there should still be a tiny place of vegetation and rest, so a dedicated Park was there placed. Ashley went there for the remainder of the night and early morning, sitting behind shrubs, way in back, chilly from the dampness.

He looked around to see if anyone watched and saw no one at all. Got down on his knees in prayer: *God in Heaven, I know I have done murder in Your eyes and shall pay with my immortal soul...I'll never see Anna in Paradise. But You know why I did it and only You will judge me. Please care for all those whom I love who are in Your care: Anna, the babies, my father...* He wept openly...*and Margaret and Velma and the boy, Roland. None of them asked to die and did so because I forced my way into their lives; and I hope You give me the reasoning for all this. Amen.*

He went under a spreading, short tree and sat, secure that no one from the street could see him here, wondering a short while what it might have been like to have Margaret with him…Margaret the lovely vixen who put a bandage on his hand and a hole in his heart. And thinking about the bandage he proceeded to pull it off, that anyone seeing him should not rapidly identify him with a bandaged hand. And that hurt.

He supposed—because she was raised in London—she wouldn't have liked the colony anyway…She had said she hated to leave her room, her friends, her London…God: London. He was born in London raised in London, left London, returned to London, almost killed three times in London, met and lost Margaret in London…Glad to soon leave London. London was his past. Now it was his past two times—provided he get out of it this time. Damn, he was sad about Margaret…But not leaving London!

Sore and sick, with a throbbing hand and a heavy heart he waited, dozed, longed for the bank to be opened; and when it did, he looked around once more, saw no one who seemed suspicious, and went inside, asking to see the banker and still using Rufus' name as his identification.

Another long wait. He fell asleep in the chair whilst he waited, to the embarrassment of the bank-employee who had seated him there—a tribute to the chair but a sight customers shouldn't ever see: a ragged and dirty man asleep in "their" bank!

Finally he got to speak with Rufus' brother-in-law.

"Lyons, you look awful! I'll send you to my physician immediately!"

"I…I don't feel well," was all Ashley could say, folding into another chair.

The banker left him there and sent an employee after his physician, expressing there was a very ill man at the bank and he might require hospitalization. The physician was busy—as most are on a normal basis—but said he'd get to the bank as soon as he could; meanwhile he'd arrange for someone to be there with a carriage to assist the ill man.

As they waited, the banker supplied coffee and sugar-cakes—the usual antidote for anything—and Ashley became somewhat revived from his lack of energy and the mental fright. Still in the banker's office, still ill and not understanding why.

Not much later, the sheriff arrived.

"My apologies for this inconvenient interruption." A phrase he must have practiced and used a lot. "I am seeking a man who was seen in connection with several slayings."

"Surely, Lord High Sheriff, you do not seek him here!"

"In actual fact, sir, I do. The gentleman sitting there seems to fit the description of the man who was seen in Southwark, where two...businesswomen...were brutally slain."

"Outlandish! Preposterous! Impossible! Not my brother-in-law, surely! The man is quite ill, as you may see, and has spent these past three days and nights either here in this bank or with me at my home. Certainly, Lord High Sheriff, Squire Case is not a suspect in any nefarious activity."

"Everyone is a suspect, your Lordship, until I say they are not a suspect. In this case...I think there's a little joke there: this 'case' and he's a 'Case'..."

They politely laughed.

"Pleased to meet you, Squire Case. Can you tell me of your movements over the past three days and nights? I need to know where you have been since your arrival in London...Squire Case. I haven't yet been to the Dockage, but I'm sure the record of your arrival—only three days, was it—will be there. Easy to get and understand, Squire Case."

"He's been here with me, and living at my home since he got off the ship...And I had a man get him from the ship, bring him here to the bank; we stayed together and went to my home together, where we dined and involved my family; then he stayed in a guestroom there and has been with me or around me every hour since: we are quite close and inseparable on these trips of his."

"Is that right, Squire Case? *Have* you been with his Lordship *all* the time you've been in London? *Never* anywhere else on your own? Like Thames Street? Covent Gardens? Lindsay House? None of these places? As I've had people—several people—tell me a tall man of your appearance was seen all around London Bridge and in a few shops as well."

"We visited a few shops and places together, Lord High Sheriff...always together; and as Squire Case is far more interesting in age and feature than I, I'm sure no one took notice of an older, bearded man with him. We walked a lot around the area...Haven't had a chance to go many places with all the business we've had to conduct...We're opening up more business sites in the colony and some in the Swedish colony far south of New Amsterdam, with Squire Case as my personal representative. Everything has been approved by Parliament and all necessary documents are signed. May I show you these, Lord High Sheriff?"

"You know, I'd like to see those documents you speak about. Do you have them here?"

"Indeed! I'll call a clark to fetch them." The banker gestured and a shirt-sleeved clerk almost ran to his desk.

"Bring all the papers we have worked on since Squire Case has been here."

The clerk ran away to a nearby desk, collected an armload of papers and returned with them.

"Here we are, Lord High Sheriff...from Parliament, from the Dutch East India Company, from Cape Royal...permission countersigned by Protector Cromwell himself...to enter trade in the Swede and Dutch Colonies, and permission granted by their colonial governors."

"Enough! I'm suspicious by nature, but no longer of Squire Case. Your pardon, Squire; it is only that the investigation is so important...several people have died and I shall not concern you with the details, but a manservant of our former King—God rest his soul—has been most brutally slain, and our informants kept mentioning a tall, oddly dressed stranger with a vest. Co-incidentally, the same description was given me by a watchman who was savagely attacked at the scene of a double murder in Southwark. Then, one of my men reported that same description of a man who would not leave the murder scene, then violently got away from there...and I have had other citizens report this same man in different coaches, public houses, different places and—I should say—not *only* over the past three days your brother-in-law has...been with you, as you say, but over the past *two weeks*! Very interesting situation. But...I'm a reasonable man and I know that things sometimes do not appear what they seem...but criminal things seem to happen together.

"People do bad things all the time, even good people. We expect the bad people to do bad things, but not the good ones. So when a good person does a bad thing, some people turn their heads and refuse to believe it happened. I know differently. I know good people do bad things sometimes...sometimes it's a mistake; sometimes they set out to do something bad. These are the people, sir, I delight in apprehending: the good ones who do bad intentionally.

"I can see my informants did their jobs by noticing you, Squire Case, but they could tell me no more and now his Lordship has cleared up any questions or suspicions I might have had. Will you be in London long, Squire Case?"

"Oh, yes!" the banker answered rapidly. Ashley sat there stunned, All that information about him...and all true. So much for HIM being a spy and not being noticed in this huge city!

"We have a lot of business to conduct," the banker went on, "and I suspect Squire Case shall be here a fortnight or two, as usual."

"Then you are here often, Squire Case?"

"That he is, Lord High Sheriff...every two or three years he arrives for an extended stay."

"In that...hahahaha...'case'...I shall leave you gentlemen to your efforts and go along to mine."

They all made their goodbyes and the sheriff left; the banker became serious. "I'm taking you now to someone who will get you out of London and on a ship to the colonies as soon as possible!"

"What?"

"Ashley, the egg is cracked; let's not let the yolk run out. The sheriff is as suspicious of you as he ever was and you're leaving London *now*, and getting onto one on my company's ships! He'll poke around and find something and return; I know him. He'll come back with men and warrants: they go away but they always make an action and come back with plenty of help so they can make arrests."

"Will you be in trouble?"

"Not if he can't find you; but I know about this man's tenacity: he seems now to have gone away but he'll have men watching this bank right now and he'll return here to arrest us both as suspects. Without you, I have my connections and will be well-treated. With you, we're both going to prison! Let's get out of here right now—out the back way!"

The banker rose and got Ashley up and moving toward the back of his office, where he pushed on the wall and a doorway opened. He got Ashley through that and pulled him along a narrow hallway. "I have a carriage out here and Justin has already been signaled to hitch the horse and meet us there. We'll go immediately to someone who can get you onto the ship, and then get me back inside the bank without the sheriff's men seeing me."

They stepped out through a sliding panel in the back wall, went through a narrow aisle to another door—which opened into a stable three buildings down from the bank. There, Justin the bank-worker had the already-hitched carriage.

"Down on the floor and this robe goes over us. You know where, Justin."

It was like a pre-practiced militia drill...the carriage went out at the far end of the stable—which extended behind all the buildings in that block of businesses—and at an angle so watchers wouldn't see anyone on the floor of it. Ashley was ill, but not yet so dull that he didn't wonder if this was the regular escape-route of the banker, and he and Justin weren't members of the group of men who fought both sides of the political ladder silently, gaining control from each without letting the other know about it.

"Lyons, you're still under my protection and there will be no record of your return to your colony, especially in Rufus' name. Tell my brother-in-law 'Hello' for me and tell him to postpone his visit here until I can calm down this whole situation. I'll have my physician meet you on the boat and it'll take you to the ship. Think you can walk a bit?"

"I'll certainly try…I'm hot all over and stiff; ache, dizzy and weak. Won't you be in trouble with the sheriff?"

"I'll tell him you were ill, which he knew, and went outside to vomit—then didn't return. If his men didn't notice you—that's their problem. I'm fairly well placed with Cromwell's administration—as you may have noticed—and the sheriff—one of the old King's men who are scheduled for replacement—will find it difficult to prove any compliance of my part, especially if he doesn't have you. He'll look like a fool to blame your involvement on me, and I'll just say I don't know where you are, which I won't, once we reach this boat."

"What about Rufus? Will he be arrested in North Plimouth?"

"Rufus has spent all the time you were gone with Captain Standish and Elder Otis, and others of their standing—you know them all—proving he never left the colony. He's already told them he was supposed to come here on business but had his travel-papers stolen, and has postponed his trip until he finds them. He's fine; perfect alibi there. Rufus is my business partner, but also my brother-in-law; he married my sister and when she died my wife and I took his children to raise as our own…they were little and didn't really understand…we've told them since what happened, and their father visits them every two or three years. My wife never could have any children, so it was the perfect arrangement for all of us. He's doing what he wanted, and I have a family.

"Captain Lyons, my sister was a bitch and everyone knew it. Our father spoiled her, her entire life; and when she met Rufus she assumed he'd do the same thing. When he didn't—when he began to work for the bank and travel without her, she found new interests and new men to indulge herself, and died of a disease from those indiscretions. All the family loves Rufus, and still does. When he visits here, it's the biggest event this family has. I, personally, would go to Hell itself for or with him.

"Rufus couldn't bear to stay here when my sister died…he bumped around from ship to ship, business to business until he discovered the fur-trade out of Plimouth colony and went there. Since then, he's visited us every two to three years…we expected him this year but the letter I received from him all about you the spies you chased, asked me to give you all the assistance I could, so

I have. You should have come to the bank right away, when you landed. Oh! Did you ever locate those spies?"

"Yes, I did."

"And…?"

"I stopped most of them but one got away."

"Not that Johnathan, I hope."

"Afraid so."

"Damn! He's repeatedly a thorn in our side…He represents the group which will fund Charles' return."

"I don't think he'll return to where his father was killed."

"With the Kings of England you never know; nothing about them surprises me anymore; they do what Kings do—which is what people never expect them to do. Well, enough about that. Bankers get nervous when they hear about spies."

"From now on they'll get *me* nervous, also."

"Once you're away from here you can revert to your old name and not worry…"

"I can't leave here!"

"What?"

"What have I done to Rufus? Rufus will be arrested in Plimouth because they think I am him!"

Ashley shook his head, seeming confused.

"Lyons, you're delirious. Once we get you to the ship…"

"I have to tell the sheriff Geoffry killed Margaret and Velma, and I killed Geoffry!"

"The Lord High Sheriff looks unkindly on killers."

"Not murder; he was going to kill *me*! I only escaped by beating him to death with a poker whilst he held a pistol, and then turned that pistol on him…"

"God in Heaven, man, you're out of you mind! I had no idea you were so ill! Justin, faster! Squire Lyons needs our assistance!"

"I'll tell the sheriff…"

"He wouldn't believe it; I know that suspicious functionary; he'd say you went there with a pistol, then beat and shot the man, or whatever. He'd turn around any story you told him! The man is out for glory and wants to arrest and hang those men who gave him status and reason for keeping his job. Your hanging would be a feather in his cap and another stone to step on. Also, if you're truthful—in prison you *would* be truthful—you would involve me and Rufus and all the business-community has struggled to do to save England from these usurpers to the throne. All of us would be tried and found guilty as accessories, get imprisoned at the least for life, and I do not relish telling a different tale to that appointed Royalist! You *cannot* talk further to that man!"

"You did this to me! All along…I've been used! You didn't care about me, only Johnathan…and you knew I could be killed but you thought me worthless, only useful!"

"No! I asked Rufus to have any suspicious men followed, and have that following reported. Written. No one ever thought you'd become personally involved in all this. Just watch and write: that was the assignment. But no! You had to do more! You went beyond what we asked or expected. Once we received your written reports 'real' spies were sent to follow and act on that information. In God's name, Lyons, I meant nothing to happen to you! I only wanted to see where those men went, not for you to get a child involved or yourself with those whores!"

Ashley struck him, weakly, taking all the effort he could muster, then falling back onto the floor of the carriage.

"Listen to me, Lyons…I know you're sick, in pain and confusion, but all I wanted—all any of us wanted—was to be able to discredit Acores, find out who his contacts in New England were, halt his movements in London, connect him to Charles and demean Charles' name. Only that! Not murder! All this to discredit Charles. Not your death; not anyone's death! You went too far!"

"I did all this to myself?"

"Lyons…I'm especially sorry to say that, but it truly is accurate. You did bring this down upon your head, as Sampson the temple."

"I didn't ask to get shot in the head!"

"And we didn't ask you to go beyond that. *Think* what you did…you sent that boy, you wouldn't leave Merry Mount when you could have, you pressured Johnathan Acores, became involved in the deaths of two of his men; you said yourself he was angry and upset, but you went *back* to that house…We've had men watching you here, Lyons; this was only supposed to be a political move, not a mass murder! We never in the world wanted anyone killed!"

"But *they* are the killers—the murderers! Don't you sit there and tell me I have done murder! I have acted as a revenger of blood!" Ashley slumped on the floor, unable and unwilling to speak further.

"Lyons, are you all right? You've gone quite pale, suddenly."

The banker shook Ashley's shoulder. "Oh. Oh, Lyons, you're not well at all."

CHAPTER 34

The sailing-boat belonging to the Federated Bank took on a physician to bolster the surgeon already aboard, then sailed immediately, headed out with the last of the tidal flow and a bright breeze to the North Sea. Ashley never knew at the time where he was or what was happening, had fallen into an unconscious state and was lifted aboard *Star of England*, there to be treated with the diagnosis of suffering from a dangerous infection, then received a sleeping potion for rest and the operations upon his hand.

In actual fact, for the next three days and nights it became touch and go for the Puritan colonist...and he slept the whole while. When he woke, the physician was there beside him.

"I'm alive...for how long?"

"It is my considered opinion, having tended the wound itself and afterward sewn you together, you have about thirty left."

Ashley went paler than he already was. "Thirty days or minutes?"

"*Years*, dear man, years! You'll have a complete recovery! I've cared for many people who were shot, stabbed or otherwise broken over the years and your case is one of the simple ones. Years, Rufus, years! Go back to the colony and send us more furs and that delightful maple syrup! Your brother-in-law told me the task you had taken upon yourself...finding and following the bastard brother of Charles and those spies around New England and London...told me the entire story, of how they shot you and tried afterwards to kill you and did kill several innocent bystanders...and told me you'd gotten into a few stickys with Himself the sheriff...I think I know the whole story, but what I don't, you can tell me when you've a mind. I won't tell anyone, unless you say I may."

"You've been with me since yesterday?"

"Been here with you three whole days and nights."

"Three?"

"You've had a bad infection...probably from breaks in your hand and the cuts on your head. Four of us have taken care of you...I had to operate on your hand so I gave you medicine to sleep—knew you'd require at least two days to recover from it; you made the third day by yourself and we had some concern, but you must have needed the rest and you got it. Sleep is the better healer for the body, usually. My nurse prayed for you, and it seems it got through to God, for here you are, awake and presumed well-enough to re-enter Life. I'm sorry about your hand; I'm afraid it will bother you for a long while. Two of us—the ship's doctor who is a fine surgeon—and I, worked on that, attempting to re-align the bones and get you good circulation the way that Italian physician has written about."

"Four of you?"

"Four in all. Your brother-in-law said to spare no expense in your recovery; it seems you are valuable to him—or the bank. Yes, two of us surgeons, a nurse and a barber...you've been our project for this week. We've had to keep you asleep most of the while, cutting on your hand and doing repairs...something like crochet-work I would imagine...hahahaha...but it seems we've gotten it as good as it shall get, although you won't be able to write with it for a while, and perhaps will always have a problem with it."

"I write with my left hand."

The physician at first looked astonished, then laughed loudly. "Wait until I tell everyone! Good thing we didn't know that three days ago!"

Crushed bone, displaced blood vessels, missing nerve endings, scars which he would wear for two decades or more. Entire pieces of flesh missing. The surgeons had done their best: they saved Ashley's life and hand. On the affected hand, parts would recover; some of the nerve-endings never re-join others, others would take years to re-form, replace. Some blood vessels were forever displaced. Still, a successful surgery was done, to repair a moment of increased violence and several pounds upon the head.

Ashley never had seen who struck him there at Johnathan's room. In his mind he knew it had to have been Johnathan who did this to his hand, but in his anger he blamed Geoffry...always would, just so he could stop hating him so much because he was very dead but Johnathan was away in style. That hate even Anna couldn't stop. After a while, a portion of Ashley Lyons would become Geoffry, just so he could stop hating him so deeply by identifying with him. It had taken thirty-two and a quarter years, but Ashley Lyons had learned to hate and hold that deep inside him.

"Case," the physician's voice came through him, "were you recently shot or shot at? The back of your head..."

"Shot at and missed, is my guess, or there was no ball loaded. Why?"

"Well, there's involvement there...where did it take place?"

"Merry Mount, outside Boston."

"Hmmmmmmm..."

"Why?"

"Looked like particles of French gunpowder imbedded in the skin—tattooed into it, not English powder."

"They all had those new French flintlocks."

"There! Knew it! Inferior gunpowder! Caused a weeping sore; no wonder you were so ill; could easily have killed you eventually had we not cleaned it. English gunpowder would have all burned; ignited and not lingered. Would have been a cleaner wound, not a festering one."

"Hooray for Johnathan's new pistols."

"Probably not even pistol powder; probably for cannon. Cheap powder."

"I don't know why he just didn't kill me with his knife the first time he grabbed me, but he did say he didn't want a stain on the rug."

"Well, I have a good idea about that; I worked several times with the sheriff—the previous sheriff, I hasten to add—in murders we suspected Geoffry did. This was before I went into private practice. His mother was well-known by the Royalists and they assisted her and him after his father died in some battle. He was a hero of a sort, I heard. Then the mother passed away. We thought Geoffry had killed so much, so many, that he seemed to require 'more' from the deaths. In Geoffry's case, he wanted humiliation of his victims. He would kill then, only after he buggered his victims, forced them to endure—say—a fate worse than death: fear and indignation and shame. Some women will kill themselves when a town is invaded in war, like those who killed themselves as the Mongols swept into Europe...because they knew the torture and rape they'd receive, then death, would be worst on them than the sin of suicide. Perhaps they'd get a reprimand from God, telling them they had sinned in their suicide; then perhaps He'd go easy on them; who knows. They felt they'd be killed horribly by the invaders anyway, so why wait. And it was just that sort of fear which Geoffry wanted to create. He must have thought—probably was certain, given what he did for so long—that he could kill anyone. The knife was only an instrument...he'd kill with his hands, but the knife made it easy and fun."

"He kept talking about 'candy.'"

"That was probably the physical sex he took: the rape, not the food. Geoffry took his pleasure with you—and probably everybody else—while you were unconscious; the bruising is still there: his trademark. He probably wanted one more go at you before he killed you, but you turned the table on him."

"You...you know about that?"

"Dear man...I've seen every inch of your body and a lot inside it, including between your toes. Just a normal examination for me, but I understand what happened. That's why you were kept alive, Rufus...to be used one final time before he killed you."

"I'm just now realizing that must have been what happened. Matthew wanted to shoot me—did shoot me. Mark would have stabbed me to death and tried...Luke wanted to dump me out a window atop London Bridge by himself while Geoffry was...somewhere else."

"Probably raping someone he found at the bridge and throwing *them* off it."

"Yes...damnable lucky for me. Geoffry was different because he would kill, but only on his terms. All the others tried to kill me right away."

"All behind you now—pardon the phrasing." He smiled. "A little physician-humor there."

"What kind of physician are you?"

"A physician is a surgeon with a University-study of the body. An old term; most people are treated by barbers and surgeons. Physicians are treaters of the rich and powerful."

"But you're treating *me*!"

"Ha! Then it goes to show you that I work for friendship instead of fame in this case! Ha! 'Case'! Quite good! I'll have to tell my wife about that...That I worked for friendship instead of fame. She'll never believe it!"

"You saved my life."

"You were about to give yours for the Cause. We—all—here, worked on and for you."

"We're on a ship?"

"All this time. This is an old dispatch-sailer converted by the bank for local travel and vacations. She's fast when the captain wants her to be, but I had him slow us down so I could work on you. Should have been in Plimouth a lot sooner—that's where you transfer from this to an ocean-crossing ship: *Parthia*, out of Blackpool. She'll take you to New Amsterdam, courtesy of the Federated Bank, and you can get back to Boston from there, I'm told."

"How do I pay for all this?"

"Already taken care off. Your brother-in-law spares no expense when it comes to you."

"Will you be in trouble for all this...do you know..."

"I think I know what happened. You've been following Royalists—'Cavaliers,' they call themselves—men who were attached to young Charles. Were you there on Holiday Street? When the manservant was killed? It was extremely brutal, I heard."

"That was Geoffry, there, not the caretaker."

"*That* was Geoffry Smith? The one who did this, that we just talked about? *You* killed Geoffry Smith? Astounding! Geoffry Smith has been a local ne'er-do-well suspected of killing several men and women, mostly street-people, and he has been imprisoned at least three times. A bad man...one of those knife-carriers and bullies...we knew, the business-people knew, that he was involved somehow in King Charles' restoration attempts...and he was there the night young Charles protested on the Thames, before his father took the ax. Nasty time, that."

"I heard that the King was hanged."

"So did most everyone else, but he was beheaded. We could never put together a pattern with Geoffry Smith, other than he might have been involved with Charles the Second. He's really the legitimate King, you know...Protector Cromwell and Parliament are in charge of the country, but Charles is the rightful King and everyone knows it. Scotland has just recognized him as such and made him their King. Geoffry was friends with young Johnathan since Spain, sometime: apparently raised there with him in the English community there. They must have gotten together for this pledge-business I heard about...pledges to restore the rightful King to England and make Charles the Second her King."

"So now we know the full story."

"Yes...Geoffry was part of the trash on London's streets that the former King allowed, the socialist-reformer that he was. King Charles seemed to like the poor for some reason. I say they all should be given work or sent away, but that's just me talking. Anyway, good riddance to bad rubbish, in Geoffry's case. And as for that 'rumor' about being involved in any murder at all, you and the sheriff can sat all you want, Squire Case, but the authorities of England will attribute that to the fact that you're somewhat of a socialist yourself, and a good Christian, and always try to help your fellow man. We all had a look at your travel-papers and letters of credit, Rufus. We're all very proud of you that one of our Londoners could survive in that forest of the colony to make himself into the mercantile dealer and fur trader you have become. You're as well-known—in the business-world of London—as Geoffry Smith was in her gutters, but not for the same reasons, I hasten to add. Would you care for a bit more anti-pain medication?"

"Will it put me to sleep?"

"Most likely."

"Then no. I want to be able to talk. The 'Johnathan Smith' Geoffry worked for…"

"Was Johnathan Acores. Some Portuguese bastard of our late-departed King…Lived very well as a baronet while Charles the First was alive, I understand. Went all over Europe in the King's name, trying to raise money for him, getting pledges, that sort of thing, don't you know."

"*That's* what he was doing: getting pledges! I didn't understand what he did, why he went to certain places and not others."

"Same as in Church: you write that you will donate a certain amount at a later time, say, when the harvest comes in or you're paid for something at a later date, and the Church relies upon that and can then promise to make their own payments because of the credit for the coin they know will later arrive from your signed pledge. They're used like letters of credit by some churches—so they can borrow money now and pay later, when the pledge-money comes in."

"Oh!"

"Yes?"

"Johnathan escaped to Charles with those!"

"Now *that* was a shame! Were I a swearing-man I'd certainly swear over that. And those to another damned 'Charles.' Whatever possesses the royalty to name their children 'Charles' escapes me. There's a half-dozen French 'Charles,' more than that in Naples, Spain, Sweden; now we have two!"

"But with the pledges he can win the war!"

"He's already lost!"

"What do you mean?"

"When we stopped in Hastings this morning, the news there was that the battle is already over! They're calling it 'The Battle of Doon Hill.' Seems three days ago Cromwell marched into Scotland, headed to Edinburgh and at Doon Hill was attacked—flanked—and lost a lot of men in the daylong fight: thousands. At nightfall they quit the field but Cromwell worked his men through the night whilst the Scots slept, brought up his cannon and fortified his position, then in the morning when the Scots charged again he cut Leslie's men to pieces, charged what was left, and won the war!"

"God in Heaven, it's already over? Did they get Charles?"

"No...he's still somewhere in Scotland...they elected him their King so they rally to him and thus far have protected him...spirited him out of the battlefield and away to safety, but Scotland is not the size of Ireland, and Cromwell will ferret him out. He was living in Holland's territory..."

"Holland! That's why Johnathan told me he was spying for the Dutch! Charles was hiding there!"

"Johnathan Acores *told you* he was spying for the Dutch?"

"Yes he did. He was going to kill me and I asked him who he was spying for and he said, 'Why, the Dutch, of course,' or something like that—like I knew all along...but I didn't believe him...but now know why: his half-brother was living there."

"Yes...and with some English support. All those Royals are related somehow...all have cousins or in-laws all over Europe."

"I've heard that but didn't understand it until now."

"Case, what you said about Charles and the Dutch is more than interesting; it's worthy news for Oliver."

"He said the Dutch Navy would attack England this year."

"Is that true? Case! Is that true?"

"Yes...that's what he said before he hit me with a pistol."

"My God, Rufus; you're a free man!"

"What?"

"When I tell Oliver Cromwell about all this and the Dutch Navy, he'll give you a complete pardon for anything! That information is priceless! A Godsend! Cromwell could *never* handle a naval attack without preparation; he's used all the men-of-war as troop-transport and horse-carriers and hasn't kept up the Fleet—let the Navy slide whilst he waged land-wars. When I tell him...he'll make me a viscount and will give you a general pardon! Oh, my God! Thank you, Jesus!"

Ashley smiled. "Put on the armor of the Lord, Jesus Christ..."

"And 'make not provision for the flesh, to fulfill the lusts thereof.' Paul knew how to turn a phrase, didn't he?"

"Words to live by, and I shall now try to live by them."

"Would you like to live in London again? You're going to have all your problems here erased, and the Lord High Sheriff may find himself out looking for a job."

"No...I should return to Boston...my family..."

"I don't know if the authorities there will accept England's Pardon for you—although they should—but it's a different setting there, not so civilized and all..."

"My family is there, and my life. You've all been very good to me and I thank you for that. If you ever need me in Boston or Plimouth, I'll work for you again or do whatever it is you need done...But to stay here...I apologize, but...I cannot trust people here."

"Well, according to your brother-in-law, that's why you left here in the first place, so...you're leaving again. Go with God and may His blessing be upon you."

CHAPTER 35

At the rail of the ocean-going-ship *Parthia*—now leaving England's Plimouth—Ashley watched the isle of his birth disappear across the water, becoming smaller and smaller as the briny solution of the great Atlantic again surrounded him. He said quietly: "And so to New Amsterdam," a variation of Saint Paul's statement, "And so to Rome"—where he was imprisoned and crucified.

Ashley thought back over the previous few weeks, wondering how it all could have happened. When he had arrived in Dockside he was so happy, returning there…there had been a vacant lot where the children of his youth played, a stunted-tree-strewn and overgrown place with tall grasses and dead leaves from countless autumns, and worn paths which ran past a tall stone everybody there climbed at one time or another (King of the Hill, don't you remember?) and the remains of an old carriage that all of them pretended had horses attached which pulled them around the neighborhood. This was his favorite place, a place where his mother would sit upon a blanket and wait patiently whilst he ran and chased and made the rounds of all the choice places there, then returning—running always—back to her for excitement and safety and love.

It was gone. Gone as his youth. A business-block rudely in its place, with its brick and stone and walls which blocked out the sunbeams and held in the morning fog and afternoon heat, and stopped any running and playing and acting the fool as children do in glee. The business community personified: out with the play and fun; in with rigid control and profit. He had blinked his eyes in the vain hope it would go away and the park return, but it didn't…so he did.

And one more thought re-played within his mind, there at the rail, with the ship *Parthia* leaving England in her wake…he remembered the bear-baiting at the tavern…seeing again as he did then those close-set eyes of the chained bear which looked more human than animal and appeared to see across the distance of that sandy place where it was chained and into his heart, into his soul, conveying a plea but refusing in pride to request it. He remembered then as now the eyes of the great bears of his youth...eye-contact always being so telling an experience for any of God's beings...but that chained bear's eyes told a story of fear and uncertainty without words so full of expressions and questions and calls for help...an old man's face inset upon that little bear, perhaps an old man's soul as well. The face of the bear being the kind of face which lets you know in a look that it has seen agony and tumult, simplicity and wonder; but screams at you in anger—the anger of courage and satisfaction and deliberations and well-used proficiency in facing and bringing death.

He felt sorrow for the bear; it wasn't right, what those men did in the guise of frolic and entertainment for pay. They must have filed-down the claws to stop those rippings and gnashings bears produce so well and easily, but it didn't matter: there was enough of each nail left to carve a bloody gash each time the paw connected with the dog; and the yapping bites of the trained canines couldn't match a single claw of this woods-beast as it chose its targets and dove that pointed-like head into the dogs, one by one, not flinching whilst they hung on its skin or tore at its ears or snapped for its nose, flinging warm blood and gore of all those involved around the ring of sand, pelting the nearest spectators who laughed at its mark. And one by one the dogs fell to one side, becoming piles of gut-opened intestines and shredded, bloody flesh and parts which quivered and shook and made pitiful sounds before they gave up the light of life. That was London at its best: the entertainment side of it—and Ashley didn't want nor need any more of that.

Reflections. Reflections upon a child's life gone forever, a man's poorly used, a country's life mis-spent for stupid reasons by its leaders due to the triple commodities of gold, wool and wheat: the maintaining columns of the business community of England. Yes, other things were important, but these drove the business coach and put coin into circulation for all the other niceties and oddities and necessities of "civilized" life. The gold allowed the country to use silver, and based its riches upon England's "silver pound"—which was a joke to most of Europe, who saw gold as THE metal known and accepted and to be treasured. In France—as an instance—gold was about six times more valuable than silver, so the wealth of England was but a pittance to Europe, though England never realized it.

CHAPTER 36

Parthia was aged and heavily laden, a weather-beaten ship with a weather-beaten crew. Her salt-softened hull squatted low in the water and her decks held too few crewmen to attend properly to her salt-crusted sails. She previously had belonged to the Dutch East India Company and had been purchased only to bring settlers and supplies to New Amsterdam and New Netherland (well north along Hudson's River). Several of the settlers had to take turns as crewmen in order to keep *Parthia* going along in just the right manner of a sailing ship; her master felt he could get enough help for the return trip from men who were sick of the small colony with it's "Indians" in New Amsterdam, and of Governor Stuyversant's high-handed policies which pitted Protestant against Protestant.

Peter Stuyversant had been appointed governor in 1647 and had immediately argued politics and religion with those already there in the governmental place: he didn't want the current governing board of the colony to have any power, and—as a Calvinist who disagreed fundamentally with most Protestant views on how a person might approach God or receive Salvation—wanted all the Puritans and Quakers out of Flushing. He developed the town of Long Island, made great strides in attracting settlers (only a thousand or so were there in 1650), and felt the colonists—in the fashion after England—and the ship's supplies (mostly timber and its products) should be the focus of the colony. New Amsterdam's people wanted diamonds and crafts to be the draw to their towns and cities...so the rift between Governor and settler grew.

If Ashley's trip to London on *The Regal Prince* had been a good one, encountering only two squalls and making excellent time in a fast ship, then this voyage was a bad one. There was rain most of the way over, squally weather with heavy winds which ripped apart two of the mainsails (which hadn't been roped for fast takedown) and tossed several topsails with their wood and lashings askew. Of course, the sails couldn't be properly repaired nor spars and top-timber replaced (especially as there was no ship's carpenter as what sober and competent carpenter would sign on to her—the owner relied upon the shipyard for repairs in dry-dock) so *Parthia* limped slowly along, her course mostly set by the winds and current which guided her and the poor attempts to steer her during the nights—those nights when stars could be seen.

The ocean's movements skewed *Parthia* southerly of her intended course as she drifted into the Spanish current, and it took all her master's skills plus the assistance of even more of the passengers (several women included—and not one complaint registered) to right her sheets and bring back her onto their course so they could again make for New Amsterdam. One of the crew told Ashley he thought for two days they'd end up in Delaware with the Swedish colony which had set up there, but the *Parthia's* master brought her about quite skillfully (when there was no storms) and only three days off their planned arrival-date they docked safely in New Amsterdam...water three feet deep in the hull, but perhaps that had added to the weight and stopped her from overturning.

This area had been discovered in 1524, then explored thoroughly along the great river in 1609 by Henry Hudson, an Englishman sailing for the Muscovy Company—who sought with other trades-people to find a northwest passage to China. Hudson sailed his ship, "Half Moon," up fifty leagues on this large and long river before accepting the truth of the local natives: this was not the route he sought. Regardless, half his crew were Dutch, and immediately upon his return there was a Dutch colonization begun there. Fort Nassau was built six years later.

New Netherland had no such "beginner's luck," as most of the colonists wanted to stay south, near what civilization they could find in this water-strewn and forested land. By 1640, settlers from New England and Virginia joined the few Dutch who attempted to bring order to "their" land—lower Manhattan being purchased by the Dutch in 1626—and the additional amount of Europeans was too grave an insult to the local Algonkin Nation, who from 1641 through 1645 attacked the settlements.

Eventually, the Dutch won through attrition: the Dutch town of New Amsterdam and its adopted settlers from else where became a world port. New Netherland—up the big river—was but a trading post with a church.

New Amsterdam was another Providence in size, but with a lot more action. European colonists were arriving with every ship, a large portion of them—forced by the governor's rule and rage—opined to go north along

Hudson's River to New Netherland. Ashley had been to New Netherland once with Brendan Splaine, coming back the big river from Mont Real Island and wearily stopping at the Dutch Reformed Church in a small, newly settled village just before they turned east and trudged along the Mohowauuk (Mohawk) Trail into Boston, and then along to Plimouth.

Ashley hefted the two bags of clothing and gear the physician had impressed upon him, and left *Parthia*. There, over by the entrance to where all the ships were docked, was the now-familiar "Excelsior Ship Lines" sign. God! These people WERE "everywhere"!

He went over to a nearby stable and spoke with the manager there: "I'd like to get a horse to go to Salem...do you rent or must I purchase one?"

"Salem? The Salem north of Boston? Take a ship!"

Ashley nodded. Better to say "Salem" than "Boston," just in case someone still sought him; but this man must know he just got off a ship—and he wasn't about to get on another. "Want to ride there."

"Then you'd do better to take the packet up to New Netherland and go straight across Massachusetts on that Indian Trail...it'll take you into Boston, then follow the signs to Salem from there. Get yourself an Indian guide at one of the Dutch churches up north...cost you less that way; otherwise you'll still have to hire a guide here for more coin, go north, then east to the Narragansett (shades of Francis Land and that posse) then you still have thirty leagues or so to go further north. The cost of the riverboat is nothing, compared to what you'll save on guide-fees alone, over getting one here. Not that I don't want your business...and if you really want a horse I'll sell you one—a good one—but that's the way I'd go—the way I *do* go—to get to Boston and back. Longer, but cheaper."

Ashley thanked him, and the "poor salesman" pointed out the packet, bobbing in the big river. This time, Ashley was no longer "Rufus Case," as he had left that identity in England. Once aboard the Baker's boat he had become "James Ellis"—taking the traveling-papers of the surgeon's assistant.

The packet—a small mail and passenger-carrier—was ready to make its weekly trip up north, having awaited the arrival and possible passengers from *Parthia*—so there wasn't much of a delay: they were outbound before dark.

At the site of the village where the Dutch Reformed Church had assisted Bren and Ashley twenty years previously, the packet stopped, dropped off its supplies and passenger James Ellis, then warped around and pushed back to New Amsterdam. It wasn't hard to—for gold coin—to locate and hire a guide. The Church knew a guide they trusted and who was one of their flock, provided a map—Rufus would be very interested in that, would copy it and sell those copies to arriving settlers and those of the Plimouth colony disappointed enough to go west—and a young, local native who knew no Algonkin but who had four times been across the renamed "Mohawk Trail" to Boston volunteered to be his guide.

Ashley remembered this trip…had done it twice already but wasn't about to do it this time alone. More than eighty leagues of forest path and wagon ruts leading to Boston. He looked at the trees…their leaves turning color. This was it: Saint Martin's summer: Indian summer.

Exactly twenty years before he had come across this very trail—before all the signs and wagon ruts—in ropes, dragged and prodded to move by six young Anakapi warriors who had just raided the outskirts of Plimouth, kidnapped by Lavrador Indians and taken far north to a strange place with magical people.

Heaving a great sigh, he came back to the present and told the guide he wanted to start immediately, that they could eat along the Trail. The guide responded by saying if Mister Ellis wanted to start right away he could, and the guide would catch up with him on the morrow, after he ate, packed, slept and broke the fast.

So that became the plan: the guide's plan, and Ashley accepted it.

They started that next morning, after careful preparation on the part of the guide, as he knew the moment he got his client to Salem he'd have to turn around and return immediately, watching for bad weather all the trip back—alone. The trip was essentially easy. Most of the way was well-defined from the wagons and oxen which had passed along it; at the river, there was a makeshift ferry. Yes, there were two routes available—upper and lower—but this one was the easier and most used.

Then…there was Boston. He paid the guide as requested and gave him more: the banker had been too generous with his purse and that generosity split out of Ashley's; he never saved money—it was created to be used, as man. There to be used and replaced. The guide balked at "leaving him short of Salem," but on the second: "I mean it: go." He left, happy he'd return fast with "winter money."

Home again. No fog, no bustling city, no Dutch spies. Intoxicating autumn foliage, rapids in the local rivers showing whitecaps, deer eating in the gardens.

Back in the Massachusetts colony (the Plimouth one being the Massa-adchu-ess-et—the local Indian name; Boston's colony chose to call it self "Massachusetts"). Back in the ugliness of a group of people who feared and hated witches. He remembered London when he had seen it as a child, compared to the size and glory of it now. What a difference! Why would any Londoner ever leave there? Why in God's name would they ever come HERE? Probably just to get away from all the royalty and busy-ness and to live a quieter life. Here, it was so quiet at times you could hear the mosquitos buzz.

On one hand, Ashley had felt as disappointed as Mara—who (in Ruth) had returned home empty; but also when Paul had taken ship and returned home again, home. He felt whole again, regardless.

So...London was behind him; that adventure over. The London of his past and his present. He was glad to return safely to the Massachusetts—the Blue Hills—but wondered what Plimouth had in store for him. Presently he was wanted for killing the notary, and Lord only knew what else those people had dreamed up! Seemed like Sheriffs everywhere arrested the first people they could find in any investigation! If ever he were found to be present when those in Merry Mount died, he'd be hanged for sure, for sure—as Bren would say. Bren: running all his adult life after arrowing and killing a tax-collector who had turned out his family into the cold and caused his only daughter (Bran-Wen) to die of consumption. Bren had said many times that the Arm of King James was long, and he had many eyes. Now Ashley was beginning to understand the two-decade-long career Bren achieved in dodging the English some twenty years before. And if escaping from Ireland and working as a French trapper in the Mont Real area and upon the Great Lakes for two long decades didn't keep the arm of England's law from him...however IN an English colony could Ashley ever avoid capture and execution?

He had no plan other than to go to his family in Boston and let them know he was alive and well, and ask about working for his step-father in New Amsterdam. Yes, he could have written to them, but also he needed to see them, and letters could be intercepted and used dammingly against him. Needed to see his family one more time. Finally, he and Mister Pennyweight were talking together, planning. New Amsterdam could be more than a getaway from Boston: it could be a new start to his life and perhaps he could make it mean something for once. Thus far, other than Anna, there was no meaning he had found. He didn't know why God created him, had several times saved his life, nor could he apply a reason for his current existence.

So...the guide had gotten him here quickly and safely, and he was now back home. The guide had been surprised when "Mister Ellis" said he could find his own way to Salem from here. Surprised and happy, the guide left immediately and Ashley readied himself for a nighttime arrival and long-range surveillance before entering the city.

The thought crossed his mind to go instead to Rufus, but Rufus' store would probably be watched as well; he didn't know what the sheriff would do about Rufus, and he had already involved Rufus in his trials in London, so it was probably better to stay away; why should he further involve him in more problems. He could watch Pennyweight's store to see who—if any—guarded it.

The time was now late; the fall sun would soon set. Ashley fed his horse and sat to wait for semi-darkness, and while waiting allowed himself to compose a poem:

And now my life is again my own; those against me overthrown.
My prayers to God upon my knees be answered well and give me ease.
And now New England is my home;
No more London; no more to roam.

Sitting there waiting for the night to hide him, watching for anyone, needing escape and relief, lingering in a forest of mostly pine with luxurious scents and only the sounds of the trees for company, thinking and wondering and saddened from all which had happened over the past month…maybe he had to start over, anew, somewhere else. Maybe that would hide the terrible times and Anna's and the baby's deaths. Start over somewhere else, where people didn't know him or try to arrest him and hang him. Bren tried that…he had come all the way across the ocean from Ireland to start over in a new land with a new people: the French. Still, England found him, frightened him, made him run even further until that running took him too far north and he was caught and died there. Because of running. So much for starting over.

Then he thought what he did—watching Johnathan and his men—might have had some real meaning…the physician said so. Might have—in the long run—saved England AND this New England from the Dutch—who would afterward lose to the Spanish or French, probably the French, as they were already here. After all the notary had said about the Peace Treaties signed and countries halting their wars, Ashley supposed the world was now at peace. Perhaps he had—through tracking those English/Dutch spies—helped to maintain that peace. But if God wanted this, God could have made it so. Even Elder Otis didn't know what God wanted or why. How foolish it was of him to even be concerned about it all.

Darkness arrived so Ashley rode his rested and fed horse toward Boston. Along the road were more people than he thought should be there…and he avoided some and turned off the road for others...then it dawned on him that the nighttime would be THE TIME the roads were watched the most...and his courage failed him. At an intersecting path he turned his horse to the south and struck out for North Plimouth and Rufus' store. At least Rufus had a safe room there, where he might be able to stay and hide.

CHAPTER 37

It was noon the next day before Ashley decided it was safe enough to approach Rufus' store. He waited until Michael had gone for lunch, then rode into the stable and pulled the rope Rufus had as communication between him and his stable-hand.

Rufus was there almost immediately.

"Returned is the traveler! Anyone know you're here? Tell me what happened!"

Ashley laughed—the first time in a long while. "Lots of things happened."

"You look fit. Travel must have helped."

"The fed me well in hospital."

"Hospital? You were in-hospital?"

"Later. I have to tell you: Miles was not part of the plot to kill the notary; the Frenchman himself told me."

"Well…I found that out."

"How?"

"The English colonel I talked with…he said he pushed Miles to pull back your commission because he thought that would give some spine to the volunteers, but a lot of them sided with you and haven't been attending meetings."

"That's a loss for everyone, especially with an invasion pending."

"What invasion? Did I miss something somewhere?"

"Tell you later; it might not happen. I'm sorry to hear they won't attend…I liked what the militia taught, even won my life on some of that training. I actually still do miss those weekly meetings."

"Another Lyon's tale! Listen: close and bolt this door. Go back through the getaway tunnel and see where you come out, just in case."

"Just in case what?"

"Good news and bad."

"Being?"

"Good news is that our dear, departed friend, Walter Foster, had an Indian woman living with him—somebody no one knew about."

"He didn't!"

"Hahahahahaha...yes, he did, that old panther! No one ever saw her in the house, but she was there when you were there."

"What good news is that? Another witness to put me to death!"

"No...this is a good witness! She had made the tea and went back upstairs to her room when you arrived, then watched you leave as her room faces the front of the house, and returned to talk with Foster—if that's what they did..."

"You dog! Don't speak badly of the dead!"

"Hahahahaha...anyway, Foster told her he was expecting visitors later that day or the next, and while she was later outside in the garden getting herbs, she saw several men on horses coming up toward the house. She slipped into the woods until they left—watched them go and then went in to see Foster, but found him dead: THEY killed him!"

"A witness for ME!"

"Wait...the sheriff won't accept her as a witness as he says she was living in sin with Foster, was far too close to him to be an objective witness, wasn't a baptized Christian, and didn't tell him right away—I think the 'right away' part bothered him the most. Anyway, he looks down his long nose on the Woods-People...but I believe the woman; she's traded here often and is a sharp trader, someone Foster would want around him...if it were a 'trader' he'd want."

"Stop it! Well...at least *you* are convinced."

"I always was."

"Rufus...with all of everything in that big house there must be something to prove...something. I have to search it."

"Seems to me I've heard that song before...you can't!"

"Have to! Have to look at what's left...something has to be there."

"Been more than a month; nothing's there. As a matter of fact, I'm going over to Foster's house myself, on the morrow; my friendly tax collector's going there to take an accounting of everything for the estate—although no one has found any relatives yet—and I'm going with him as a witness and concerned citizen, compliments of the county's administration. That means they'll pay me for it when the estate is liquidated."

"Take me with you!"

"Not even with a command from God! You stay here, man; you're in serious trouble!"

"Look at everything!"

"Don't worry; I shall. If I can find any reference to the Frenchmen, or whatever…I'll bring it here to you. We'll have a sheriff's man with us…but both he and the tax collector visit this store and I feed them."

"Rufus the humanitarian, feeding the poor."

"They're friends. Whatever I find, we'll all know about it and they won't question me. Not everyone is against you; you seemed to have gathered a few people who like you. They only want to try to find the names of relatives so Walter's belongings can be given to them…who knows, maybe his relatives will come here to live; looks like everyone else seems to be, with all the recent settlers moving in."

"Because of the war."

"War?"

"Cromwell defeated Charles in Scotland but people were leaving England in fear because of the war which was projected."

"I heard Oliver won the battle, but he lost more than half his army, and barely got through to get food from his supply ships, then he left there. Didn't sound to me like any 'war' he won!"

"However…more settlers mean more customers for your store."

"That's why I have it: for the pleasure of my customers."

"Well, Rufus…I'd return your travel-papers but there're no good now, me having used them so much; and if you haven't gotten the post I've sent, I'll fill you in on that."

"And the hospital story."

"I owe you for the letters of credit I used to buy clothes and pay the physician, and buy a funeral for the two girls Geoffry killed, and my return here…"

Case just stared. "Say that all again, slowly…and explain it all; but so far as the letters of credit, no repayment is necessary: I owe *you* monies…"

"I'll tell you everything later; have to get out the important stuff."

"Interrupt me all you want, but let me tell you I just got a letter from some London physician, investing in my business and telling me of places in London to send furs and 'local oddities such as maple syrup.'"

Ashley laughed. "That's the same physician who operated on my hand; he talked about liking maple syrup. Take him up on his offer; he means it."

"He just about made me rich overnight! There are letters of credit to me for furs, syrup and all the Indian merchandise I can send to him. All because of you!"

"It's an ill wind which blows no good to somebody."

"Oh! What about the Frenchmen!"

"They were English...but the leader got away with the pledges they had collected here, probably to Scotland; maybe Spain or the Netherlands."

"Pity. Anyway, your part in that is all over; I'll go through whatever documents I find tomorrow and tell you then...we'll probably be all day there, if we can do it in a day. Michael is here for the store and completely trustworthy. There's plenty of food here—hey, this is the store—and I'll get Michael to cook something, maybe his favorite: skunk."

"Thank you; you are ever kind."

"Stay out of sight, all right?"

"Yes."

"What thing important did you learn from your trip?"

"I learned I could breathe through my nose, when I had a rag pushed into my mouth."

"Well...that's important...I'll have to hear more about that. Funny how we can do things when we think we can't."

"Rufus, you said one time that there are things which will put wrinkles on your face, and harden your heart and make you think no one tells the truth anymore."

"I remember saying that to you. Did I not tell you the truth?"

"You held back some things when you hired me to do this work; not really important things, but without them I thought Miles was dirty, into all of this, and the assistant governor was a man who only wanted a job, not a name in history. He's the one behind all this, isn't he." Not a question.

"I..."

"I know: you were pledged to secrecy as was I, but I would have told *you*! You above all others I would have told. You have a habit of asking me what I learned from things; I now ask you the same."

Rufus pursed his lips, held them tight a few seconds.

"I've learned that politicians have their own time-schedules and, unlike us, do not wait upon the tide but go regardless. I've learned friendship is better than business, as I was promised an increase in business were I to send someone to complete your job and I did, but almost got you killed."

"Six times. I counted."

Rufus' eyes seemed to water. "I've learned that if I rely upon a man I should share everything with him, as a man and wife share, because that is the only—and correct—way to get along with another. And I've learned that to wound a friend hurts me more than it does him, and I'm sorry for not telling you the complete truth."

"Well, Rufus, I appreciate all that and I feel the same way. I'm sorry I turned down the job you offered about your fur trading because the one Mister Pennyweight wanted me to do has evaporated like snow on a dark roof."

"Then I shall make the offer again, with even more emphasis upon it, since my benefactor in London now wants so many furs."

"Then I shall take it, and when we're both ready we'll speak more about it. I no longer want to stay here; I want to go away somewhere for a while; I need thinking-time in peace."

"This job will take you to the Ohio."

"The French Ohio or the English Ohio? They are separate."

"The English. The south side of the great lake. I have to tell you though, the area is dangerous."

"More so than London?"

Rufus laughed. "Probably not more than London. Only Indians there."

"That over, we remain friends."

It was after dark the following day when Rufus got back from his inspection of the notary: Walter Foster. Ashley was waiting, and asked him about his findings.

"You won't believe this."

"What?"

"When we were looking through Foster's belongings we found a waxed letter."

"Probably the one he wanted me to take to Johnathan."

"You knew about the letter? The jewels?"

"Jewels? No. Nothing about jewels. Just that he had a waxed envelope he wanted me to give to Johnathan—of course I didn't know his name then. I didn't want to take it and he left it there."

"The sheriff's man let me read it—as a witness. It's addressed to one Carlos Johnathan Acores; another 'Charles.' He apparently was a son of our former King—a bastard son, but a son nonetheless. Too many of those damnable 'Charles'...you'd think we'd have had enough of them with the first one and his legitimate son; now there's some Portuguese Charles."

"Johnathan found a lot of support to make Charles the Second King of England...apparently a lot of our colonists want him as our King; you really think he'll get to do that? Be our King?"

"Not while Oliver Cromwell lives! He'll likely hang him also and banish his name from all England. Anyway, the letter said that Foster had seen a stranger watching his house and heard that the same man was asking questions after him of the neighbors and at your step-father's store in Plimouth. Foster wrote that he assumed it was information for Johnathan, and said he was sorry he took the monies and commodities from the King and hoped Johnathan could find it in his heart to forgive them, given that they had such a close relationship for so many years, and he'd return the jewels if that would make amends. Apparently it didn't."

"He had stolen Johnathan's jewels?"

"More likely the ones King Charles had...no wonder Foster could build such a house...I always wondered about that. Gold and commodities and jewels from King Charles—England herself! Probably sold the gold and commodities in New Amsterdam; they're big on that sort of thing there."

"Then the notary was just a thief?"

"Oh, I'm sure he was not 'just a thief'...he must have been high in King Charles' court and maybe his accountant. Anyway, it looks like he swiped all he could and ran when the Civil War broke out and Charles left England. Foster must have made trips here for years, getting the land, having the house built—I think it was Wyman Briggs who was the master carpenter on that one...he use to come in here a lot, then, a few years back. Wyman must have put in those stupid-looking windows that go to the floor."

"Doors. French doors."

"And the doors also. Must have brought all those doors and windows here—had them sent from England months before the house was finished. A small boy with some rocks could surely have some fun with those...anyway, the sheriff is checking to see when all that arrived and what dates the house was built and when Foster came here to stay...all those sheriff-things. Looks now like he planned his retirement from England years ago...but notaries are like that: they plan ahead. The sheriff wonders if Charles' family has a claim on the house and furnishings, as it was their gold and jewels he stole to have it built. Up to the elders to work that out."

"A nice home...a King could live there; it was better than the old, dirty apartment King Charles kept in London."

"He kept an apartment there? He had a damned castle!"

"I think he wanted a place away from the castle…where he could entertain…"

"Ohhh…I understand. Say no more."

"Notary Foster was a deliberate man…he must have known Johnathan would catch up with him…maybe a decade ago it was easier to get lost here; today, with couriers and roads and all the towns springing up and the new colonies…not so easy to hide. He had a good taste in tea: I had some."

"Damnation, yes! Now I've lost my source of tea and coffee! I'll have to find someone else to send those to me…you wouldn't consider a trip to China would you?"

Ashley held up his hands to stop that line of questions: "No!"

Rufus continued: "There's a lot more that was there."

"More jewels?"

"More information. Foster left a will which states his entire estate—if it is judged his—goes to some old Indian chief…Pork-something. That's why the sheriff wonders if he had any family in England."

"Porc-espine."

"That's it! Porc-espine! To him and his family. Who does that? Leaves his estate to Indians? Damnation, Lyons, we just moved them off this land and now they'll have a *house* there?"

"You read that will?"

"The tax collector found what he says is a legitimate will and a set of documents recently sealed that say since he has no living relatives—we'll see about that—and no wife or issue; he bequeaths everything he owned to Chief Porc-espine and his family, for the long-term relationship and association in business they shared. The tax collector says it all goes to the Indian, while the sheriff says it's up to a judge to sort it out. Makes no sense to me at all…Leaving all that to someone who can't enjoy it, won't live there and probably won't get it anyhow."

"Does make sense. He obviously had been waiting years for someone in England to catch up with him…whether it was for the jewels and gold or for something else we don't know about right now…but he has someone who worked on the Plimouth Dock watch every passenger off every ship, and when someone arrived who frightened him, he signed and sealed away all his possessions. He probably wanted them followed and their travels documented so someone had a story to give the sheriff about who killed him. *That's* why he hired me, not to follow spies; to watch these men go there and be a witness. Poor man, living in fear like that…staying in comfort but living in fear. No wonder he spent so much...couldn't take it with him and couldn't ship it ahead for him like he did here...so he probably tried to spend most of what he had, and all that was left over was the house and some of the King's jewels he either didn't want to spend or hadn't gotten around to doing that yet."

"How's an Indian going to use a house? The neighbors out there will torch it before that happens. Foolish bequest. That money could have gone to the poor."

"There will ever be the poor...one man's estate isn't ever going to change that."

"I suppose."

"Think about it, Rufus...if the tax collector has the house sold to an English buyer so the neighbors won't complain, and gives the profit to Chief Porc-espine and his family, that will make them wealthy enough to buy things here..."

Rufus broke in: "I get the implication! I should leave well-enough alone and just accept I have a rich customer! It'll be like the fat man is still there, buying things and investing in my business! His money, after all...hmmmmm...maybe I should ride out to see the good chief and take him some sugarcane...might take some pots and pans with me...get him used to coming here again." Rufus smiled. "I heard there will always be the poor...good thing I have a rich customer. He used to trade here a lot; probably getting too old to make the trip nowadays. There's a story about him...how he got his name."

"Rufus, there's a story about how *every* Indian got his name!"

"But this is a funny one! When he was young, he used to carry a lance, and years ago he stabbed the leg of a trader with it, who had—probably accidentally—spit on his leg during a trade for furs. The tribe changed his name to 'Porcupine'!"

"Porc-espine."

"His original name was...ummmm...similar to that...peace...?"

"Peage?"

"That's it! Peage. Used to be Peage and now he's Pork-epine."

"'Peage' means' 'power,' or 'strong-tasting'; 'powerfully strong.'"

"I forgot you speak Algonkin."

"I knew a Peage...was one of my adopted brothers. Common name for an uncommon people."

"Well, this Peage would certainly like to talk with you; you learned that talk a score of years ago as I remember and can still talk it; you'll do good in the Ohio."

"It was a gift; nothing I learned. Given to me."

"How long were you with those people, that you know their language? Do you know dialects like Miles Standish says he does? He knows—says he knows—seven dialects of the Indian-talk."

"Miles says what Miles says, but I know he is a good talker of Algonkin; probably he does know seven. I just know the Lavrador-talk, almost not understood around here except by the old men of the tribes. The Lavrador-ones were the original people and they probably all are long gone, now."

"How long were you with them?"

"Too long. So…someone will eventually buy the house and Chief Porc-espine will get the credit. I still wonder at that."

"I know why and I saved the best for the last."

"What best?"

"The sheriff's man asked around at the neighbor's houses out there, only three or four places besides Foster's, and he was told that Foster's maid was Porcupine's daughter."

"*That* explains it! But if you call the old chief that English name you'll probably get a lance in *your* leg!"

"Right. I'll try to remember 'Porc-es-pine.' The neighbor said she lived in one of the houses, so we went out there to speak with her…"

"Wait a minute! She is Foster's *maid*, and has a *house* of her own? An unmarried Algonkin woman?"

"Foster had a small house built for her at the edge of his property—about the size of your cabin in Duxbury, so she could live there when she wasn't at his house, working. Apparently—so she says—she didn't stay overnight with him: that's what the neighbor told us, that she'd see her walking home in the evening and back in the morning. Anyway, we went out and spoke to her."

"And?"

"She said she was there in the fat man's house when you came in, and she saw you leave and he was still alive. She's the one who made the tea you two had, and when you rode up to the door she unlocked it and told the fat man…"

"Please? The man had a name…"

"She told 'Foster'…can I get on?"

"It just bothers me to hear you call him that. He was a person, not a spectacle, regardless of his size, which was…sufficient."

"Right in the middle of my announcement you interrupt. Anyway…the Indian woman's name I cannot remember nor pronounce anyway, and apparently Foster couldn't either, so he called her 'Morning Star'—don't tell me the Algonkin for that, just listen!

"This Morning Star liked the sound of that name so she had her father change her name to that, however it's pronounced in their language. Anyway...stop salivating...I'm getting out the story. She said, after hesitating some while, the reason why she left the notary's house *after* you rode away..."

"*After*? After she saw me ride away? He was alive then? So the sheriff *does* believe me!"

"You just won't let me tell the whole story."

"Rufus, if you trade like you talk, no one will ever swap a thing!"

"She said she saw you ride away and began to fix the evening meal and she had a visit from her friend...whatever that means..."

"Oooooo...I know what *that* means! Anna used to say that every month."

"All right; now I know. I thought that's what that meant. She went every month for a week to her father's village...I guess going there every month reassured old Pork...Porc-espine, that his daughter wasn't in a family way. Apparently she did more for the notary than just being his housemaid."

"You dog! Speak well of the dead!"

"Ashley...the man gave her a job with meals, a room in his house, built her a house of her own nearby, let her be away a week every month...and left the family all his possessions. Can you think of one other reason for him doing that?"

"All I can think is that she has cleared me of that death."

"Well, not completely."

"What? Why 'not completely'?"

"True, she says she was in the house with the notary alive after you left, washed the teacups and made him a meal, and so it went until she was in the kitchen and her 'friend' arrived and she had to leave. By the way, we found a bloody rag in the dustbin of the kitchen so that seems to be a true story...and she says that as she was going across the field on her pony she saw three men on horseback..."

"Johnathan and his men!"

"At which point she had already left the notary's property and just went along to her father's village to her family."

"She had a pony also?"

"Do I get to finish this? She had carried away with her some food that was extra, after making sandwiches for Foster, probably so it wouldn't just sit there and spoil; he had a different woman from the village come prepare food for him and do the housework when Morning Star left for her week. So Morning Star left on her pony; she has a Welch pony with a saddle made just for her; Foster seemed to think of everything where she was concerned…"

"When you're rich and spending someone else's coin, I guess you do things like that….indulge yourself and others."

"Yup. He never could spend it all, I guess."

"So she went to her forest home for a few days, then returned to find him dead?"

"No. The neighbor we talked to went over that night to light the outside lights, went in calling Foster's name, and found him. She was totally shocked, thought it was an Indian raid, because of all the blood—or that Morning Star had done it; her husband rode fast to the high sheriff in Plimouth right away."

"And that very next day the farmer with the hay-wagon and two sons told the sheriff I was the only stranger he had seen on the road—even if it were a week's time-difference."

"Right. When we went today to the house—which had been locked by the sheriff, we saw several used wine and spirit's glasses…no teacups, so the sheriff's man told me he was satisfied that Morning Star was probably telling the truth, and men were there, drinking with Foster before they cut him and killed him."

"How awful…so I'm cleared of the murder."

"Not officially."

"Why? What does that mean?"

"There are some fine points of the law…"

"What points?"

"First, the sheriff wonders if an Indian can inherit English money; he personally doesn't think so. We'll have to get a finding on that from, maybe the governor, probably England."

"Really? The Lord High Sheriff doesn't know that?"

"He can't say definitely. And…"

"There's always an 'and.'"

"The sheriff is a good Christian and he says the Indian woman is not a Christian; therefore, she cannot give sworn testimony. She would have had to have been baptized a long time ago and show she's stayed within the limits of the Church…and being the lone woman in a house with an unmarried man…Ashley, they just won't believe her."

"Then, what do I do?"

"Stay hidden until we can work all this out. It's still up in the air whether single women can share an inheritance if a male relative is still alive…I imagine

Foster thought about this and that's why he left his estate to Chief Porc-espine *and* his daughter and family, with him being the head of the...well, not the 'house,' but...the head of the family...hoping some would be given to Morning Star. Damnedest thing I ever heard of...well...this whole mess, I mean, you included. I talked briefly with the assistant governor and he'll try to get a ruling on everything. Meanwhile..."

"Meanwhile I'm still accused of murder and Johnathan has gotten away."

"That's the way of it."

"What shall I do now?"

"Well, you can't go after Johnathan: he's too far away, mean and protected...and he has a purpose against the people. Someone will get him for something; he won't last, doing the game he does."

"Maybe we should send Chief Porc-espine after him."

They both laughed.

"He could put a lance in his leg!"

"Oh, I wanted to ask you: when that Geoffry-fellow you talked about had you, why didn't he kill you right away like he did that child on the wharf? You wrote a lot about that, but I never quite understood why you were left alive."

"Gee, Rufus, thanks for caring, I think. In truth, I've asked myself over and over about all that, but the ship's physician pretty-well explained that to me. He said Johnathan had been raised in a place by people who were rich enough that they didn't need to kill for themselves, and held interests in the things the rich enjoy, but not killing; so he was willing to have his man kill, but he himself wouldn't. He wasn't a soldier like the men he hired, but Geoffry...he was, and he enjoyed killing. The surgeon said Geoffry probably had killed so much that killing no longer excited him anymore. I remember his face when Johnathan was talking to me: pacific. Then when Johnathan told him to do something—like kill someone—his face changed: he was happy. Now that I'm thinking about it, when he saw me untied and standing he didn't just shoot me...he seemed to relish that he'd caught me, made up some rhyme about it. Must have thought I was more of a challenge to him than before...so he just wanted to keep me alive and torture me, then sodomize me: his ultimate thrill. I think he probably did that to the boy, instead of letting him go."

"What a beast."

"Killing no longer excited him; he was a man who had killed too often; I guess, gruesomely. Anyone who cuts throats in a certain manner—the physician told me—has done it too often; and Geoffry must have perfected his skill over the years. As he did that, he lost his taste for killing, rather would brutalize. Death to him was a release, not a punishment; he tried to get the most from everyone he killed before he killed them."

"Some sick bastard, to have the ritual you wrote about."

"The first time they got me I was unconscious. After I ran away I began feeling 'something' had happened to me, and I remember some sailor on a ship telling me the only happiness in his life was being the first in line to bugger the newest crewmember."

"Someone *told* you that?"

"Yes! After the second time they got me I felt the same…discomfort. I thought it was something he did as a habit before he killed: Geoffry's 'mark' he put on people to get a sense of extreme pleasure."

"Could have killed you but wanted more."

"Right."

"A very sick bastard. I return tomorrow to the notary's house with the tax collector and the sheriff's man…I'll speak with them tomorrow about all this, once more. Meanwhile, you stay in here with the door bolted and if you haven't already, see where the tunnel leads outside, just in case."

"Already have done that."

"Then…wait. Michael will bring you food."

"I'm already feeling like Johnathan, with people doing things for me."

"Please…"

He waited alone, wondering all night how in God's name could all this have happened. Felt as though he were stuck in a mudflat and couldn't move his feet, couldn't pull out or get away. No one in sight to signal, yell to, encourage or help him. Just…lost-ness. Wondered if by doing what he was doing, having done what he had done, if he weren't already just a hired killer like the men he followed—and killed—for he seemed to be doing the very same things they did, and men died because of him.

Bren had said, "You don't go into the water without getting wet: some of it goes on and into you."

Guess this was true: you play their game so you must use their rules. Their rules were not those of a Puritan, but some demon-possessed, lost soul. He thought a couple of seconds more, then said the name "Jesus" aloud, and recited the Lord's Prayer. Couldn't hurt…Elder Otis had said so.

He felt better—well-enough to sleep—afterward.

The wait that next day was long…after dark in the evening before Rufus showed up.

When he entered Ashley's room, he was as happy as ever Ashley had seen him.

"By God I *found* it!"

"What?

"The Indian woman's baptismal record! Morning Star was baptized by one of Plimouth's elders who is now dead, but the notary had all her documents in a big jar there, I suppose safe from fire. Birth certificate by a Plimouth barber, agreement from her father that she could work at Foster's house for pay—so she wasn't a whore or a kept-woman; she was a real housekeeper! He paid her through her father, monthly—all the receipts were there! The man was fastidious about keeping records. Oh…and a lot of old records from England…looks like Charles the First had a few people killed. Those are all going to the high sheriff and the governor."

"So the sheriff has accepted her testimony? About me being there while he was alive and Johnathan's group coming in?"

"*Has to*, now! The sheriff's man found those…and he's already taken them to the Lord High Sheriff. *Now* you're going to be cleared of that unpleasantness!"

"Thank God!"

"God and your persistence that 'something' had to be there in that house! It looked like your English assassins had rummaged through some papers and drawers, probably for money or items to steal; I guess they were in a hurry and didn't want attention drawn to that place or they'd have burned it like your stepfather's shed. Thank God for *that*!

"One more thing, Ashley."

"What more could there be?"

"I'm so late in returning here because I had to go see Elder Otis. He was there—years ago—when Morning Star was baptized, and has followed her life, especially because she's a converted Indian, but he was very concerned about her later being a single woman in an older man's house, so he saw her and asked her about that as often as he could. She came sometimes to his prayer-meetings."

"The man who was always too busy wasn't so busy he couldn't tend his flock."

"You're right: the man's a true saint. If Otis says something is true, you can believe it; the sheriff does."

"Elder Otis. God! He's saved my life twice this year!"

"Someone else saved it also."

"Well, of course…God and you, Rufus…and I…"

"Not me: a local trapper."

"A trapper? Saved my life?"

"Just like your friend Bren…a fur trapper who works for me. By itself, this wouldn't be much 'evidence'—as the sheriff's man says—especially as the trapper works for me and you and I are so close; but taken with all the rest…"

"What? What 'rest'?"

"You're going to love this: when the spies left Foster's place, they must have forgotten to water their horses there, because they stopped at Three Bridges to water them."

"They were seen there?"

"Better than that: they were *heard* there! The trapper who works locally for me was under one of the bridges when they came riding up and hid, because…well, because some furs are out of season, and trapping there is not supposed to happen, all right? Anyway, he saw a couple of them take the horses to the river and listened to them speak…one of them said, 'Why did Geoffry have to kill him? He had given us the papers and jewels and you were friends.' The other answered, 'To settle an old debt to my father; also, he knew us and I didn't trust him; who will miss him?'"

"Thank you, Jesus!"

"It seems these men we thought were accomplished spies were only new to the game. They made every error, from being seen by people to not killing you right away."

"Why, thank you, Rufus…I hope to God you never get to train any foreign spies that you tell them the right way to do it."

"I'm not sure that was a compliment. Anyway, the Indian woman…"

"Morning Star."

"Had a Bible bound in a golden leather Foster had given her and she swore upon it that he was impotent—had been for all the time she worked for him. All he ever did—she said—was to hold her and hug her and sometimes kiss her, and not much of that or for very long. She says Foster was a lonesome man. He also had gout, and that kept him from getting around much. Seems I owe Walter a rather large apology, as I ever thought him to be a rake and libertine."

"Tell him when you see him."

"*If* I see him; I've not led that choice a life, either."

"So it should still be possible…but now you're finished? Completed at the notary's?"

"There are still mountains of paper to catalog and arrange, but the tax collector had them all baled and took them to his office at the Great Hall. He'll complete them and give the pertinent ones to the assistant governor for prosecution of the spies and to correct some ideas about our late, departed King Charles."

"Amen."

"So be it. What did you learn over there in England that you can use here?"

"I learned I love Anna, but I can love another."

"A very deep subject."

"I learned the world is not so large that man cannot travel it in search of whatever it is he seeks."

"Something of value you can carry with you."

"I learned that killing doesn't make you feel good inside; and getting even isn't as good as it's told to be, even in the Bible."

"There's something to know."

"And I learned that coming home is the best feeling I can have."

"Then, London changed you."

"Why do you think that? How could it change me?"

"You're not the same man...harder, perhaps; smarter, maybe. You're not so fast with a joke or so wavering in an answer. You grew up there."

"Nothing left to joke about."

"Then you know how a man thinks. See, that's what I meant. When I asked you before about working for me in the fur trade, instead of questioning me about the fur trade you just said you'd do it. That was the decision of a man."

"And I wasn't a man when I was sent to London to do a job?"

"You weren't the man you are now. Accept it. I don't know if it's better or worse that you're harder; maybe for your own sake it is, but if Anna were still here..."

"Then Anna wouldn't have let me go to London."

"Touché! But you'll still do it? Go to the frontier and take trade-goods and bring back furs? If you're not interested..."

"I need to get away. The women I love seem to die."

"Not because of you!"

"Definitely because of me."

"There's probably already snow in the Ohio. Wouldn't you want to wait until spring? The best you could do would be to go to where Gerald is—the young man who works for me but discovered that big cache of furs—in New Swede Church, up the Delaware River."

"And miss a winter worse than this one coming will be? I was out there once, in the summer."

"In the Ohio? Over the mountains?"

"Not that far…the traders and surveyors were headed there, but we had a falling-out and I left them."

"By yourself? You must have been fairly young, then."

"Not twenty; old enough."

"I didn't know about that."

"Miles sent me there because I knew Algonkin, but the Woods-People don't talk that out there—over those mountains. I couldn't have been of much value to them…Besides, my traveling-companions wanted more from me that I was willing to give…And they tried to…Like Geoffry."

"Oh. So you came back alone? From the Ohio?"

"Had a lot of help with that; that's a story I don't want to talk about—one you wouldn't believe anyway."

"Well I believe that—that I wouldn't believe it. Maybe someday."

"I don't think so."

"With all that's happened to you, Ashley, how do you feel? Deep down, I mean."

"Well, it hurts; I'll tell you that. I don't know from day to day how to go on. I've never had a feeling like this before, and the funny thing is I don't want it but I'm afraid it'll go away also…and then I've lost it completely: another loss."

"You've learned more than most, a lot faster than most."

"The past to me is much closer than the future…"

"Hind-sight, it's called. What's behind us we see easily."

"I hadn't thought at all about Oliver Cromwell, just that he was the captain-general of the Army and won a lot of battles. You think more people are working to raise money to get back the King? The physician on the ship told me Cromwell could never be made King—the people wouldn't stand for it, even tho' he's won England for them."

"The people have always *had* England…Cromwell's only a man; men only live for a certain time. The Kingship is England, not the man."

"What then for us here in the colony when Cromwell dies?"

"What it's always been for the past score of years: redemption in a real land for some, money for others, a new life for all. No matter who is the King, or if we don't have one, taxes and laws remain. We won't change, and they won't, either."

They each smiled, commiserating the other.

"Do you suppose there'll be a tax on doors?"

"You're either the smartest or luckiest man I've ever met."

"Luckiest."

They each smiled again.

"Rufus?"

"Yes?"

"You remember my little friend, Gair?"

"The little gnome you dreamed up when you were taken by the Anakapi?"

"He gave me the Algonkin language...and I wonder if he gave me even more..."

"You're just damnable lucky! How can anyone give someone a language or any kind of luck?"

"I've always thought religion had a lot to do with it. You know...prayer?"

"God's love is everywhere, and His ear; and He has raised His hand to stop all that you went through. That's your luck: God's protection for a righteous man."

"Put on the armor of Lord Jesus Christ..."

"And make not provision for the flesh, to fulfill the lusts thereof."

"Words to live by, except that I haven't."

"Now, Ashley, you can go home."

"Home. What a nice word."

CHAPTER 38

The table was set as if it were for the annual Thanksgiving. Rufus had sent word to Boston by courier that Ashley was coming home a free man, and his mother had responded to that. He had missed the past three Thanksgiving meals at his mother's, having gone instead to Anna's parents' home for them. Anna's mother had told Anna: "Always wed in January, for that begins the coldest time and keeps your husband at home with you…and you have almost a year to learn, before you have to set the large table for the Thanksgiving." And probably after the first child is born.

So, this was the scene, and Ashley—the prodigal son—had returned.

Right after he arrived, his mother pulled him into a corner. "Your father had a heart-spell the night you left here dressed as me. He was a full week in Granite City, at the surgeon's, there. Now he is home but unable to work as he did before, takes two powders or more each day and has a specific food-list of what he can eat."

"Is he all right? Will he be all right?"

"He's frightened, but had had no more involvement since that night. God help me, but I actually wonder if seeing you will be better or worse for him."

"Perhaps I should leave."

"No…he knows already that you've arrived. The surgeon called it an erratic wandering of the heart…he said it might happen again in days or it could take years for it to return. He didn't think it would be fatal to him, but Mister Pennyweight is very cautious now, of what he does."

Lord, Ashley thought, *my actions have done this to this good man. What a poor son I have been. He thought he would die that night so he talked to me, put his arm around me, told me I would be the man of the house. He knew he had a heart-illness and thought he would die soon, so he told me what he really felt. I did this to him…all my escapades and adventures over the years, and my refusal to assist him in the store.*

His mother's voice interrupted his thoughts: "Remember Mary-Lou Lightbody?"

"Hmmmmm...from London? Yes! That was when I was five or six."

"Just those years. You and she played together...said you would marry each other."

"Yes." Embarrassed. Smiling. "Those were the good old days...Dad was alive..."

"Yes, good days, but a long time ago." She seemed to pause a moment, remembering that dry-board house in London, her ship's-carpenter-husband she adored, letting her son bring back to her some of those times which were good. Then she said, "I have heard from her a few times."

"You haven't! I looked for her when I was in Dockside and her house is still there but the family moved years ago."

"Isn't that a coincidence, you looking for her and me hearing from her!"

"How does she know you're here?"

"Well, when we moved from our home in Dockside, I wrote to her mother and after she passed away, Mary-Lou and I have been corresponding over the years. Not many letters, but at least yearly."

"What a pleasant story, Mum; I wish I could have seen her when I was there."

His mother was smiling. She was too happy. Now he got frightened.

"She's coming here."

"Here? To Boston?"

"Here, here. To here."

"Here? To this house?"

"Yes! Won't it be nice to have an old friend around? Mister Pennyweight says she can work in the store, perhaps even manage it, as she's done sales-work for her family's store in London and has such good references. They moved from Dockside after we did, and after a while her mother passed away and her father couldn't keep up the rent on such a big house as he'd gotten for their large family, so they had to move again.

"She never married...always kept house for her father and brothers, and when her brother got a store of his own, she worked there also, until her father passed on; then she lived for years with her eldest brother and his wife, working in the store and keeping his house, but the brother's wife started having children...I think six of them...so they ran out of rooms and asked if she'd move out...so she's coming here!"

Ashley just stared.

"She'll arrive soon; Mister Pennyweight already arranged her passage."

Pennyweight came into the kitchen, talking: "She didn't get an officer's cabin like someone we know!" He put an arm around Ashley.

His mother kept on, undaunted: "It'll be indentured service at first, but she'll be safe and comfortable here. And how often do you use your room anyway?"

"Apparently not enough to keep it. I really like that room..."

"Esther will be moving out soon, Missis Pennyweight," her husband volunteered.

"I was thinking Ashley could take that room, but it would work out better for Mary-lou, on the same floor with Ruthie...oh, that's a good idea, Mister Pennyweight. That's settled. Ashley, you can have your old room back; does that make you happy, dear?"

"Relieved. Er...wasn't Mary-Lou rather...not pretty?"

"Somewhat—as a child. She looked a lot like that rendering of Queen Mary your father had. But children hardly stay so plain and larger noses always seem to fit adult faces. And I'm sure she has a lot more hair than she used to; her mother had it shaved for lice at one point...girls get a lot prettier as they age; isn't that right, Mister Pennyweight?"

"If you are any indication of that, Missis Pennyweight, then she'll be a raving beauty, for you certainly are."

"You make me blush, sir. Ashley, you haven't seen Mary-Lou since you were six years old; won't it be nice to have someone your own age around? Someone you have known from London? I'm just so thrilled to have her coming here after all these years and letters back and forth...I could just swoon!"

Pennyweight leaned forward in the chair where he sat after he entered the kitchen. "As the King of Israel was passing by a wall, there cried from the wall a woman, saying unto him, 'Help me, O' King.' And he said, 'If the Lord do not help thee, whence shall I help thee?' Second Kings."

"Oh, stop, Mister Pennyweight!"

"The interpretation being, if the boy wants to get to know Mary-Lou, he will. Stop pushing her on him."

"Yes, you're right...I have work to do in the store; I'll leave you two to talk. But it *will* be good to have Mary-Lou here."

"The Lord killith and makith alive. He bringith down to the grave and bringith up. First Samuel. Thank the Lord she's gone, that matchmaker!"

They each laughed.

"You don't expect Mary-Lou before we eat, do you?"

"So you can eat and run? No, son; you can eat in peace for the next day or so. That was a good one, about your room...I had all I could do to keep from laughing out loud!"

"If the surgeon were here, he'd say you were cured!"

"Well, I have been, but don't tell your mother."

"Why did you agree to have Mary-Lou come here?"

"I need help in the store anyway, and that Elspeth volunteered, but I didn't accept her assistance; I'm leery of that girl...she's too good to be believed. You like her, tho'. Esther and Ruth are doing more than they normally would, and business will drop off soon, now, anyway, with winter approaching. It'll be good for your mother to have another woman around. Esther's making sounds like she's wanting to get married; tho'...she tells me nothing beyond that."

"You've always taken good care of her, and me, too. I thank you for that. I thought you liked Elspeth."

"I did when I thought you two would marry, but since, I get the feeling there is something other than friendship with your mother she wants...some personal desire; maybe just you."

"Well, I did something...stupid...that's why we no longer speak."

"Couldn't have been too stupid; she speaks well of you, always looking for you."

"She hasn't connected the dots yet. You're working in the store, still?"

"A small amount of time, more to tell Esther how and what to order; I have to rest in the afternoons."

"I heard you had some trouble the night I left..."

"Mostly over now."

Ashley leaned over and put an arm over his stepfather's shoulder. "A couple of things I would say, if you're up to them."

"I'm all ears, as the elephant said."

"First, I'm glad to see you again."

"Ha! You don't know how good it makes me feel to be able to *hear* you say that! I have a thing to tell you also."

"Mum said you weren't working so hard as you used to. Maybe there's some way I can help you."

"Ashley...the job we spoke of? In New Amsterdam? It's no longer there, son; I'm sorry. I just can't take on any more efforts right now."

"In that case, I'm thrilled to hear that...I...accepted another job from Rufus—don't blink your eyes at me: yes, I know he's your competitor, but this is a good, simple job for me: just looking at furs and shipping them directly to

London. There's a man already there in Rufus' pay—in New Amsterdam—who'll assist me."

"Then it's good for us both; I worried about you thinking you had a big job to go to when you returned…but not so good for your mother…she plans on having a new daughter-in-law."

"Lord…I was afraid of that. I'm getting out just in time. I see you've been reading…I've had some time to read also, lately…"

"That where you've been? Out reading for a month?" He smiled more of a grin, giving away that he knew where his stepson had been."

"In actual fact I have been to London."

"You haven't! Really? How did you find it? I haven't been there in about twenty-five years."

"Full of people, church spires, and hackney-coaches."

Pennyweight chuckled. "You didn't stow away to get there, did you?"

Ashley smiled widely. The inference from his stepfather was that he had been accused of doing exactly that—twenty years before: stowing away on a ship out of Plimouth Bay to London, when he was in fact kidnapped by the northern Woods-People and carried away there. "No…had a real officer's cabin each way."

Rufus wrote to me and told me not to worry. What a way to travel at sea for you: in an officer's cabin and meals served. Good on you! In *my* readings…in Kings'…it says, 'Thus saith the Lord…I have heard thy prayer. I have seen thy tears. Behold, I will heal thee…and will add unto thy days fifteen years.'"

"I had forgotten that; that's a good passage. Thank you; it's appropriate for you. Here's one which I have said a few times recently: 'Heal me, O Lord, and I shall be healed; save me and I shall be saved: for thou art my praise.' Elder Otis would want me to add the Lord's Prayer."

"Hahahahaha…how is old Otis? I haven't seen him in years. He's…let's see…older than me by…Lord, he's seventy-six, I think!"

"When I saw him last he was well, and Rufus has seen him just this week."

"Which reminds me, I have a communication for you, sent via Rufus, here, from Anna's parents."

"Truly?"

"There on my desk in my office; get it. If you have the time, sit and pen a response. They're good people and deserve a prompt answer."

Ashley got it and opened it in front of his stepfather. "An invitation to visit, dine and stay as long as I want."

"We'll miss you, but you should visit them; they miss their daughter and you can help make up for that."

"I will...but...right now I cannot...this job for Rufus..."

"I hope it's not like the other one."

"Does Mum know what I did?"

"No...she only knows you were away, working for Rufus Case. She'd have been over there in London if she knew!"

"This job is truly only getting a large supply of furs and shipping them—anyone could do it but Rufus says the ships 'lose' cargo and he wants me to stay with his trade-goods and deliver them to his man in person in New Swede Church..."

"The Delaware? In that Swedish community up there? I read about that."

"He said the furs were 'in the Ohio'; I expect we may have to load them from a Woods-People village somewhere in the forest."

"Then you'll go north, as the Swedes have the trade sewed up along the river itself...I've had furs out of there also, but the Indians have been pushed back and there's little trading going on with them now...maybe his man went inland to get the furs and couldn't bring them out by himself. That may be a disappointment for you, all walk and no fun."

"That's probably what it is, just an overland trip to a village. We'll see; I'll write to you if I can. And right now I should write to Anna's parents."

"The best time to do something is always now."

Ashley went into the office, re-read the invitation and wrote:

> *Beloved in-laws. I have been away on business, but now am in receipt of your most welcome letter and generous offer to visit you both. Thank you for writing, and for your invitation.*
>
> *I shall visit, tho' I cannot soon do this—but I shall notify you by post in advance of my arrival there. My life is different and difficult without Anna: unfulfilled.*
>
> *I shall try to write you as I can, from where I can. I leave Boston soon for a year or more in another inland colony. It ever will be remembered by me that you offered your kindness at a difficult time in my life. Loving favor is rather to be chosen than silver and gold.*
>
> *In the armor of the Lord Jesus Christ, Ashley.*

He took the letter to the kitchen, where his stepfather still sat.

"I'll post that in the morning for you."

"Thank you."

Ashley's mother came into the room and hugged her son.

The evening meal was perhaps the best he remembered eating, and he told his mother exactly that: she had once more outdone herself.

And—other than the cranberry sauce—the highpoint of the meal was a note delivered to and read by Pennyweight at the table: a practice he previously had refused.

"Ashley, this says Bess is back, and in the stable at Case's store. He writes that Michael went to get her; she hadn't been ridden because she's so small, and she's happy to be where she was before. I sense there's a story there, but perhaps it should wait until later this evening. Right now, we all want to hear about London; spare no detail!"

Leaving out the (best) and (worst) parts, Ashley told all he could recall about London, the bridge, the haberdasher, the spires of the churches and the banker. He reported on the churches and the sights he had seen in the hackney-coaches, and told as much travelogue as he felt comfortable to say, but he did admit: "There were a few other things I did for Rufus I cannot relate—business things and meeting some people."

Hardly had he finished speaking when the kitchen door opened and a man strode in.

"Sorry to interrupt your meal; I'm here for Ashley Lyons."

"You enter my home without knocking? Where are your manners, sir?"

"I said I was sorry, Squire Pennyweight; I wanted to find Mister Lyons and didn't think he'd be waiting for me if I paused to speak with you at your front door. I assume, sir, you're Mister Lyons; you seem as described. Sir, if you'll come with me?"

"Who, sir, are you?"

"I'm from the Lord High Sheriff's office in the Plimouth colony; I'd like to take you back there with me right away and all will be explained there."

"This is terrible!" Ashley's mother interrupted…"Bursting in here like that and arresting my son!"

"Madam, I have no warrant for anyone's arrest, but I am here officially, and he will come with me. Ashley Lyons, I ask politely, sir, if you would do that right now."

Ruth had slipped away from the table as he was speaking. No one really noticed her leaving.

Ashley stood, pushing back his chair. "I'm Ashley Lyons."

"Then, sir, if you'll come with me I'll explain everything as we go along to Plimouth. It's a longer ride than I'm used to; but we'll have changes of mounts at the relay-stations."

"You won't be going alone, Sheriff; I'll be going with you," Pennyweight interrupted.

"The only one leaving this room is Ashley!" Ruth's voice came from behind the sheriff's man's back. She stood there, not a tall woman, but with a rather large musket, cocked and ready, pointing it at the intruder.

"Ruth!"

"He leaves; you stay! You move; I shoot. *That's* official!"

"Ruth!"

"No, Mother; he's not taking my brother anywhere!"

"Oh, Lord," the sheriff's man groaned. "Don't shoot me! I'm not supposed to tell anyone: they wanted this a surprise. In my pocket are letters to Captain Lyons from the assistant governor of Plimouth colony and Captain Miles Standish. The first says that Ashley Lyons is officially cleared in the death of Walter Foster; and the assistant governor wants to thank him personally for his efforts in halting a plot to spy upon by foreign agents and a planned surprise-attack to England and New England by foreign countries. The second is self-explanatory, about the return of Captain Lyon's commission in the militia."

He reached timidly into a pocket, withdrawing a waxed letter. "This one is from Captain Standish and there's an attachment from Elder Otis which says the council of elders has investigated charges against you as a witch, found their allegation to be in error, and has returned your privileges to attend all meetings—prayer or otherwise—and indulge in commerce in Plimouth colony, immediately; the year is waved."

"Do we have a champion here, or what?" Pennyweight asked.

No one else from the family could speak. Ruth lowered the musket.

The sheriff turned to Ruthie: "They only want your brother to tell him in person that all the charges against him are forgiven...they wanted to be the ones to tell him...they have learned whatever they have learned from some storekeeper who has papers from England, and apparently want to talk only with Mister—Captain—Lyons."

He pulled out the other letter and held it out to Ruth, who took it and gave it to her father; then Pennyweight took the musket from his daughter.

The sheriff continued: "This all started when an aide from the Baronet Halifax (he pronounced it "Ha-Lee-Faax") arrived on the late tide. The assistant governor's lamps burned all night, regardless of that infraction of the law. Earlier today they sent me—post-haste—galloping and changing horses at each post relay-station. We'll have to go back the same way: they want you there in the morning."

"Good thing you ate," Pennyweight said, slapping Ashley on the back. "You'll have more stories to tell us when you return, Captain." He reached around and shook Ashley's hand. Twenty years previously he'd promised a frightened boy he'd tan his hide if he didn't comply; now this same man was immensely proud of his stepson. Funny how things like that happen, and the years change us.

"Knowing what you know now, is there anything you'd have changed?"

Ashley nodded slowly. "Yes…I'd not have involved a boy and I'd have told Rufus I needed a ball-proof hat."

They rode all night. Ashley got three hours of sleep, then was awakened and escorted to Plimouth's Great Hall, where the functionaries of Plimouth worked their daily chores to keep the colony prosperous and religious.

Several men were waiting for him as Ashley entered the domed room.

"Stand here, please." An aide.

"I believe we have three presentations to make. Captain Standish, will you do the first honor?"

"Indeed. I want to say, before we go much further, that you, Good sir, as assistant governor of this fair colony—my previous position which I held long and enjoyed—have not only lived-up toomy personal expectation of you in this office—and I have somewhat of an understanding of what should and shouldn't be done—but you, sir, have exceeded and surpassed my best efforts and do the council proud."

Miles turned to Ashley, a rolled paper in his hand. "I gave you this several years ago and was quite hasty in taking it back. I herewith return your commission as captain of militia of Plimouth colony with my promise that if you accept this, I shall not expect you to attend every meeting." He sighed, and Ashley knew this was probably the hardest thing old Standish had ever done: retrace his steps on an order.

"We know that with that bad hand of yours you won't be able to use a musket so quickly as the militia wants, so you'd be better used to make field decisions and in scouting—as you, Captain, are a fine scout." He motioned to an aide and a box was brought over.

"This, Captain, is to replace that musket." He opened the box and there was a French flintlock pistol inside, similar to the one Johnathan had used. "Rufus

Case told me you knew how to use one of these; the governor presented it to me but I no longer require firepower and I want it to go where it'll be used and appreciated."

Standish held it out, and Ashley—tears flooding his eyes, whispered to Miles, "I...I don't think I can take either of these...I disappointed you after Anna died..."

Standish smiled fatherly, then returned the whisper: "Take them; they're yours. You came by them honestly and they're given in appreciation. I know the commission was taken unfairly, and I know you now have other interests; but take these as a gesture of thanks from an old soldier who watched you grow up and is proud of all you've one for this colony."

Then Miles beamed widely as Ashley took his offerings. "Be clean-shaven and have your horse groomed!" The Old Miles Standish was back!

"Thank you, Captain Standish; I'll do just that."

"Ashley...I lost a wife also...that first winter, here. So I *do* understand, Lyons, how that feels: the ground is taken from under you and you can't understand why. Attend the militia-Meetings as you can. The truth is, the men would rather see you have this and have you attend even once a year than think their favorite captain was taken forever from them. We've had quite a few no longer show up because of this...misunderstanding."

Ashley thanked Miles, wiped at his eyes and shook the hand of the old warrior and politician.

The next presenter was from England—the man who pronounced "Halifax" as "Ha-lee-faax."

"This is sent on behalf of the Baronet Halifax, and to tell you the truth, George is a young man and isn't able to leave England or he'd have come here himself. What he did say to me was, 'Pop over there and straighten out this colonial thing'..."

Most of them laughed.

"So I thought...George's land here is all wilderness and even though it borders that of this settlement, it would take some influence to have anyone actually settle there to improve the land...the Marquess of Halifax was given it for political reasons and really never meant to even visit it...and I have the baronet's seal..."

"And I know exactly how important that seal is," Ashley interrupted.

"So...from your sponsor, the Baronet Halifax, I have two papers. The first is a deed to a square hectare of land bordering the Post-Road in Halifax's dune-area—which I hear is a prime spot—and the baronet wishes you to build upon it and encourage people to settle there. You'll still be under the rule and protection of Plimouth's colony…Leagues away, but…"

"I know. But the tax collector and the sheriff will still come calling!"

They all laughed; wasn't *that* the truth!

"And the other paper—because the baronet wants a civil government there—is a commission for you as captain of militia of the Halifax Grant, subject of course to the Plimouth colony governor's approval."

"Which he has," the assistant governor added.

The baronet's man handed the papers to Ashley.

"A few days ago…" Ashley's eyes teared again, his cheeks now wet. "And now two commissions and land. I don't know what to say, how to thank you all and the Baronet Halifax…and all the efforts of the assistant governor, of which I assume there were many…and Captain Standish and our Lord High Sheriff and his men."

"What have I told you about the militiaman's only friend?" Standish asked Ashley.

"The art of survival. God! It's true. That's *just* what you told us repeatedly: 'The art of survival is the militiaman's only friend; he should know it, love it, practice it more than anything else.' Maybe all those lessons got through, after all."

"Then you must have been listening."

"May I tell the baronet you'll build on the property?"

"You certainly can! That's a beautiful spot there, the dune-area. You know what I'd like to see there? An elk."

"Oh…quite good. I'll inform the baronet of your plans."

The assistant governor stood next. "Captain Lyons, I'm not going to give a speech. I've been communicating with the governors in Providence and Salem and a few wrongs will be set right. And we know the men to watch…your reports are invaluable. The baronet tells us England's Navy will be restored, and that—thanks to him and you—has already begun, under the covers, so to speak; no word to our friends the Dutch. If they *do* attempt a naval surprise, it's they who will be getting the surprise! I give you thanks from a grateful colony and your homeland, and an apology for some of the more recent things we've said and done to you, but that's now all behind us." He shook Ashley's hand vigorously: this was a true politician.

"Go in God's grace," and they all managed the "Amen."

CHAPTER 39

Ashley stopped to see Rufus and brought Bess some apples and carrots, those things with which Anna had spoiled her.

"Michael loves that horse. If you ever need to sell her again, he'll buy her."

"Why does he like her so? She's little and I know she gets winded fast."

"Michael's not a large man, as are we, and very gentle. She's a perfect mount for him and he exercises her as often as he can. He rides my horses but they're huge—like the hackneys of your stepfather: bred for pulling rather than riding. He's lost, way up there on my horses."

"Michael will manage my stepfather's store in Plimouth, I hear."

"Yes he will, under my eye. I'll watch the books and the buying; can you believe Pennyweight and I are close friends now? We were fierce competitors for years. Your stepfather said he was too ill to manage both places and wanted to know if I'd buy the Plimouth store; then I realized Michael was the perfect manager for that one. He can sell things to women like I can't. I'm backing Michael and everyone wins; I have new help in this store also. I'm already kicking myself that he's going to leave me; big step up for him…just what he needs."

"You said he aspired to bigger things."

"That I did, jokingly, however. But he always has wanted to better his lot; a stableman's job is only an entry or a part-time thing for work."

"Then if Michael will manage my stepfather's store in Plimouth, he has Bess. Gratis."

"Really? He'll go crazy when he hears that! You want nothing for her?"

"Only that he loves and cares for her…what Anna would want."

"That's all he'd like to do."

"Then she's his. Anna will understand when I tell her. Oh! What will you do for a stable-hand now?"

"Got two men to replace Michael."

"Took two to replace him?"

"Yup! The first already started to learn; he's here now, breaking in. The second is going to be a temporary man until I get him settled here, my man already in the Ohio, Gerald. He's there for furs now, waiting for you to bring the trade-goods to him, then you two come back here and one of you gets to go to London with the furs. He uncovered a great amount of furs there…we'll all be rich with them."

"Well, I like the 'rich' part, but the going to London? Not me! Never again to London!"

"So…you'll make a good stable-boy."

"By God, I'd rather do that than chase after spies!"

"You're a brave man, Ashley Lyons."

"Anyone can be brave; *staying* brave is the hard part."

"That's what I have heard. Those who can, do what they can; those who cannot, do what they must. You know you've changed England's history."

"Didn't know that at all."

"Well, you have. Lord Protector Cromwell has beaten the Scot's Army and will return—if he hasn't already—to Ireland. The Navy had been given a bigger role in England's defense: my brother-in-law has written all this to me. No one knows specifically it was you…except you and us."

"I never did anything—none of that—for a medal or land or to get back my commission…and now I have two!"

"Well, we appreciate what you did, the risks you took and the information you got."

"Rufus, you tried to make ball-proof vests; could you do a hat?"

They laughed.

"Actually, I'm working now on a vest or coat which *is* ball-proof. Something to withstand those new flintlocks that the French make and the Dutch copy. You can test it for me."

"Ahhhhh…I don't think thus. Get Michael; I've already been shot."

"I heard you had a full morning; does that mean you'll stay in this area, with the new land?"

"No…I'll see someone about building a house, then do the job you wanted me to do with those furs…in that Swede-place in the forest. I think I need that for a while."

"Plenty of Indian girls there."

"God, no more women!"

"We'll see. You want to talk with Wyman Briggs and the Ellis brothers—all are the best carpenters in the colony. Stay here today and I'll set up a meeting with Wyman; no one builds a better house than Wyman, and no one builds better doors and cabinets than the Ellis brothers."

"Funny...'the Ellis brothers' and I came across the sea as 'James Ellis.'"

"They're probably related."

"Rufus..."

"Don't say it! You're about to tell me you haven't the coin to hire builders and have them construct a house."

"Remember me? I'm the one who couldn't make rent payments. How can I afford to have a house built? I'll have to ask my stepfather. I'll have the work done but not right away; after the job for you."

"You forget who you worked for. Who do you think told the Baronet Halifax about your contribution to England's political good?"

"Your brother-in-law?"

"That's who. Federated Banks wants to help build your house for you—that's part of what the baronet asked. He said he wants a decent house built there to encourage others to purchase land and build also. Has to sell-off that land somehow, so this is the best method. Federated loans the money up front to settlers, Halifax sells off the land, pays Federated and keeps the rest; everybody wins. New houses for new people in a new land with new money from a new baronet for an old bank."

"How do you keep up with all that?"

"You don't think I have a finger in the pie? When the houses become a town, *my* store will be there, the first one!"

"You *are* a sly dog!"

"With supplies from England via Federated, everybody gets a chunk of business."

"You said I changed England? What a change Oliver Cromwell has made for England! Trade, business, new laws and taxes and restrictions on cheap goods from foreign countries...people owning their own homes on a regular basis..."

"One last thing before I forget, then no more surprises."

"I'm afraid to ask."

"There's a line in an English play...Marlowe's *Edward*."

"Another of those banned plays?"

Rufus grinned. "The line goes, 'Champion, here's to thee.'"

He tossed a purse across the table to Ashley.

"What's this?"

"Open it. Twelve troy-ounces of gold."

"Gold? A pound of gold?"

"A bag a year for ten years, compliments of my brother-in-law and the Federated Banks for your house. Won't make you rich, but you can pay for some things with it...and a bit more, although I don't suggest you go back to that cabin in Duxbury." He smiled a benevolent smile.

"Ten pounds of gold. Who does this?"

"A banker. My brother-in-law sends his apologies also...he wrote that as you were leaving London you were upset, angry with him...he wants to make amends...probably is afraid you'll go back there. Do you accept his apology?"

"I guess I do!"

"Then...our business is over for the day. You can sleep in the house tonight and not the tack-room...I still want to talk with you. Oh! I almost forgot! At the packet you wrote me about your silver buckle."

"That Anna gave me; did you get it?"

"On my table, waiting for you."

"How do I thank you for that?"

"Thank God you're still alive to wear it, after what you've been through."

"Words to live by, and I shall. But I keep thinking none of this would have happened if I hadn't had to leave my wife."

"Now, *those* are words to live by!"

CHAPTER 40

Ashley arrived at Boston in time the next day for the evening meal, and spent more than an hour talking about his most recent experience and afterwards in Plimouth. After the meal he asked Ruth if she'd go to Elspeth and ask her if he could speak with her soon. Not long afterward, Ruthie was back, grinning all over.

"She says after prayer-meeting starts for her parents, on her porch." She giggled. Little sisters are like that.

When his mother was alone in the kitchen with him he went to her. "We must speak."

"Then say it or don't." That's the way she was: mercurial.

"Before I left for London, Mister Pennyweight told me I was going to be the head of the house."

"He *didn't*!"

"Yes, he did." Long pause. "My business with Rufus is done and nothing is more important to me now than you."

"I wish to God you'd have said that to me twenty years ago."

"Mum…so do I. The business I did for Rufus has given me great reward."

"Then, take it and go; I know what you're leading up to: you're leaving again; that's what you do to me: leave me."

"Not for a bit…I have been given land in Lord Halifax's Grant, on the dunes, there; and there shall I have a house for us all built."

"When rabbits fly."

"Then today they fly, as I have already contacted a man who will do that for us: Wyman Briggs."

"Wyman? Wyman is my dear friend from Plimouth! His wife passed."

"Wyman is a dear friend to all, especially the homeowners, as he is the volunteer fire chief as well as a master carpenter. You thought to marry him, didn't you? I remember some things from twenty years ago."

"Hush! What a thing to say to your mother!"

"I'm not sure you *are* my mother."

"What an ungrateful child you are!"

"Mum…I looked at the records in the Great Hall of Records in Plimouth when I was there. Your age when you arrived here is listed as eighteen. I was twelve. Who is my mother?"

"*My age* is there in the Great Hall? For people to *see*?"

"Afraid so."

"*That's* why those hens cackled at our wedding…they thought Mister Pennyweight was marrying a young girl! The laugh's on them! I always wondered why they tittered and talked with their hands over their mouths!" She smiled, lighting up the kitchen and Ashley's heart.

"Ashley, I *am* your mother. In London, when I first applied for passage to Plimouth, I didn't think anyone would want a woman of thirty over here, so I wrote I was eighteen."

"What did Mister Pennyweight say when you showed up with a twelve-year-old son?"

She sighed. "I told him…well, I *did* tell the truth…that I was widowed. I said you were your father's child by a woman—not at all a lie—and as he and I were married, you were my child as well."

"And he believed you? A woman thirty saying she's eighteen?"

"It was hard for a man to get a woman then…I was never sure he believed me…but he never said he doubted me. He's been the nicest, kindest man I've ever known."

"I have a different image of him."

"Because you weren't here! When you left…were taken…"

"Mum…the real truth is what I have said all these years: I was kidnapped by Anakapi Indians from the north, and taken there. Brendan Splaine had also been caught by them and he and I escaped and he brought me home."

"I never met him."

"He had business to do…a thousand furs left east of Mont Real to get; he was a trapper and not used to Plimouth or the English…especially the English as he was Irish…he had also been caught by the Anakapi but we escaped and he brought me home."

"I never believed all that."

"Then I'm sorry for you that you couldn't believe your husband's son."

She pursed her mouth and he though she would cry. "All that was true? You swear today before God that all that was true?"

"I swear before God everything I told you and a whole lot more I didn't was true; I swear to God and hope my soul burns forever in the pit of Hell if this is not the truth I tell you."

"You never stowed-away on Stoddard's ship to England?"

"I swear to God I was never, ever, on Master Stoddard's ship. At any time."

"That man lost the contract he had with the colony because popular thought was that he had taken you aboard or let you stay when he found you. We've done a terrible injustice to him...oh, God...all these years...I never once believed you...no one ever believed you...Ashley, I'm so sorry..." She cried openly a few moments.

"I...have done you a great wrong...all these years. I wanted another son, to take your place...and—God's justice—I got Esther and Ruth; God's way to punish me for trying to replace my runaway son whom I never believed. I pushed you out of my life because I thought you had done the same to me."

"I never thought that...only that I had a mother I loved, even if she didn't believe me."

"You ran away so many times..."

"I never ran away. I'd go look for Gair, because he asked me to be at a certain place at a certain time of the new moon, but—truthfully—I never ran away; you just wouldn't listen to me when I said I had to go meet Gair. Gair was my friend. He left...an...item with me...and I promised I'd return it, bring it to him because as soon as he came out of the caves he'd need it right away. But for all the times I went to look for him, I never found him; never saw him again."

"You never could return his item?"

"I kept it a while, then...sent it to him another way. Hope he got it."

"So you only skipped suppers and sleep to look for your friend? Not to run away or because you didn't like my cooking?"

"Mum...I *love* your coking! Anna's was..."

"Don't speak ill of the dead! I tasted her mother's cooking and I know why you turned down that invitation to visit them: she never learned to cook and couldn't ever teach her daughter. Why do you think I invited you two here for meals? I knew you were always hungry!"

"After all those years, my biggest memory of you is you chasing me with your broom, around the house, threatening to whack me if you could catch me! We had a lot of fun times."

"I never hit you with that broom!"

"No, you didn't. But you surely did chase me and give me the impression you were going to!"

"And now you're going to be the man of the house—your own house in Halifax. My son. Jesus loves me that I would live to see that."

"Then He does, and you shall. Wyman will build the house only if you tell him how you want it built. And *only* the way you want it! It's going to be your home, for all of us, so think about how many bedrooms we need…that sort of thing. Oh!"

"Oh, what?"

"Two more things: I have to have an attic room…"

"You should have a room on the first floor, an office."

"Make an office for me and Mister Pennyweight on the first floor, but give me a roomy attic with a window—the window is very important. Please…I have to have an attic room with a window, like the one here. I want to be able to overlook things…and…Gair said if he ever could visit me, it'd be when I had an attic room; he knows about this one."

"He seems to know you a lot."

"And the other thing…the land in Halifax is part of a small hill…"

"God in Heaven! A house on a hill! The dream-house your father and I talked about in Dockside, that he would build for me some day. He was a carpenter and always said he'd build me my dream-house on a hill."

"Now your dream will come true. And he'll look down on you and smile."

She hugged her son joyfully, tears streaming from them both.

"Ashley, this is very hard for me to say, dear, as I know I've said the opposite thing to you and have pushed you and Elspeth together…"

"What?"

"I was such a fool…thinking you two should marry and give me the grandchildren I wanted to have…"

"Some day I'll do that."

"No…I have to tell you about Elspeth." She paused, her mouth moving without her speaking. "Elspeth has never been married, dear. Very few people know this, but she was stolen as a girl and used horribly for a long time—years—by a man who was stabbed to death and probably by her. She made up the story of her being married so she could explain why she's not a virgin…but she's told so many men…and used that tale to have relations with them, that she truly seems quite lost as a person. Only recently have I heard this.

"When I thought Elspeth would be my daughter-in-law I asked around of the older women in her family's neighborhood and was told in secrecy all which really happened to her, and what she did out of fear and the hope to escape. God, what that girl has been through.

"I'm...God, I'm so sorry, Ashley, to have to tell you all this, but I brought her here and I tried to keep the two of you together just for me. Please forgive me for that."

"I do, Mum...It's all over between Elspeth and me, and never was going to lead into marriage anyway."

He hugged his mum for a moment, then left.

Now the hardest part of all: going to see and talk with Elspeth.

They met at her home:

"Ashley, I've ducked out of prayer-meeting to see you."

"And I surely appreciate that, Elspeth, there's a lot I must tell you."

"Later...much later. We're alone now..."

"No, has to be now. Later would...would not be good."

"Then tell me quickly and..."

Ashley heaved an audible sigh. "I must tell you...before you hear this from another source or too late in life to forgive me."

"Whatever would there be for forgiveness? That you disappeared when we had shared so much? That you weren't here for me when my brother was buried? That you never said a goodbye?...I'll tell you...I thought a lot about all that...it burned in my mind for a long while. But in the end, I told myself if you ever returned I would give myself to you freely. Now, that's *my* confession!"

"Mine is worse."

"Did you leave me for another woman? I thought thus."

"No."

"What, then?"

"I'm going to tell you the truth...I did...a lot of things...I went a few places..."

"And? Did you think of me in those places?"

"This is very hard for me to say, but say it I must if I shall ever hope for peace with you."

A long pause—she kept her eyes on him all the time.

"Three things."

"Number one?"

"I followed and killed the man who killed your brother."

"You didn't!"

"Yes I did. From here to Providence, to London and back, this past month."

"I don't believe in killing…but…I have done it and it still bothers me. But it also gives me some small satisfaction Roland's murderer was done in. I hope he knew why you did that and that you killed him slowly so he can carry that through Eternity in Hell, that he died because my brother died."

"He knew why…And he died painfully and slowly." Only a small lie; the words she wanted to hear which would comfort her somewhat for the rest of her life. God could tell her differently.

"Then, *good*! I'm glad he's dead! I loved my brother more than anything and I'd have killed that man myself, a lot slower and meaner than I bet you did."

A pause.

"There are other things I must say."

"Say them, and then let me reward you for your work."

"First…I did meet a woman in London…"

"And went to bed with her?"

"Yes, but it was…"

"What fools men are…Well, why not? Women allow it and men just go along with it. We're not married; you have made no pledges to me of faith, nor I to you. And we have no true commitment." She seemed as if she were crying, her eyes watering again. "Why not bed her? What else about her?"

"I was frightened, tired, chased by Roland's killer…I saw her on a street and she invited me into her room…"

"A street whore?"

"No! Just a nice girl…And she bandaged my hand…"

"Why? Why did you require your hand bandaged by her?"

"The men who killed your brother caught me, broke my hand, and tried to throw me into the Thames."

"What a tall tale! You tell a good story, Ashley Lyons; your mother told me that."

"No…the truth! It all happened. Then she bandaged my hand…and it was late at night…"

"So convenient…and then of course you stayed with her, the night being so late. Well…" She shook her head. "Get on with it."

"I'm not sure…"

"Of what happened or what you intended to tell me?"

"Ummmm…both. I asked her—the next morning—to…come with me…here."

"What a night *that* must have been! Did she just laugh in your face or just take money?"

"Truth be known she didn't really want to leave London, but I did give her coin..."

"And if you gave her coin, why would she want to leave there, there was so much *more* coin to be garnered from all the men she invited inside to have their hands bandaged. I wonder why, Lyons: why would such a nice girl with a room on the street leave London with all those men and their needs, to come to a colony of religious people who wouldn't let her practice her profession? Your mother said you'd never grown up and told me I'd have a time getting you to do that!"

"That sounded mean-spirited."

"I never meant it to be..." But he saw a sneer.

"Anyway, Elspeth...after I left her, the man who was following me—the one who killed your brother—found her and killed her in the same manner as he did Roland."

"Oh, Ashley."

"After that I got...became as a Woods-Indian and stalked him...went to his rooming house where his master lived and they captured me again, had a...tussle with him there...killed him afterwards, with a poker."

"I find this intriguing but not quite truthful. You killed *two* men? Who *captured* you?"

"Actually...four."

"You are the biggest liar I've ever met or the most vicious. I just don't believe you. Must have taken you a while to conjure up that tale! I almost believed you."

"It was them or me...Mostly accidents..."

"Captain Lyons: the wayward killer of four men, after he beds a whore. What inspiration *she* must have given you! This is almost laughable, but I missed you so much and prayed you'd return...And now you insult me with lies."

"Elspeth...All true, and more I will tell you later."

"Oh, tell me now! Why wait? So you asked the whore to...what? Marry you and come to Boston with you so you could show her off to me and your mother but then—conveniently—she was slain?"

"Yes."

"Yes to you asked her to marry you or yes that she was slain?"

"Yes to both."

"Why are you telling me all this? To hurt me? You poor fool…Rather I'm the poor fool, thinking so long I could be with you, that you'd change my lie forever—well, you certainly did that! Would you have told me if she came here with you? Of course you would: you're so polite and have such manners. *Would* you have told me if you brought her here?"

"Yes, certainly. We…"

"You're so much the gentleman. Sorry, Elspeth, I'm here with my new whore-bride; want to meet her? You'd like her, she's such a good lay and she wraps bandages. Lots of practice in London with street-people who just walk in on her—and *into* her! Well…I can't forget, but I can forgive. We were separated and if I do find out what you say was he truth…"

"It *was*!"

"You'll have to tell me a lot more, like, why you were involved with those four men and how much you missed me all the while that you would go to a whore…"

"I was asked to watch five men as they seemed to be doing things which could have hurt the settlement in Plimouth and everywhere along Boston's coast."

"So you are a spy, in addition to being a captain?"

"No."

"But you 'acted' as a spy, did you not? Watching men and following them…then you say they caught you but you killed four? That was all—if true—'acting'? Acting as a spy but not a spy? Do you lie to me again? I thought you were a simple Puritan colonist, a captain in the militia. I never thought you…so much has happened; I have to think more on this."

"One other thing."

"Oh, God; what else?"

"In my job—it's true—I watched others…I was watching five men on the Great Wharf, here…and Roland was in the store…" He hesitated. All or nothing.

"Yes?"

"I wanted to find out where they were going, what they were doing on the dock…and I asked Roland…"

"ROLAND? MY BROTHER ROLAND? You involved Roland in your spying? Merciful God…you sent my brother to WATCH THEM FOR YOU…and they…killed…him?"

"I…I didn't…"

"You...you SPY! Are you one of Cromwell's spies? A man who would kill a King in public? You sent my brother to watch strange men who KILLED HIM, then you took me to bed? That is the most vile thing...I hate you! You killed my brother! If I were a man I'd..." She hesitated, getting some breath. "Until now I never realized your detachment of recklessness. You made love to me, then left me to go...wherever you went. You didn't consider my feelings, my love for you; you who were FINALLY THE man for me...but before then you caused my brother's death and HID IT from us? You just went where and when you wanted!"

"My mother told me the same thing."

"Leave your mother out of this; this is between you and me!" She shook a finger at him, seeming then to shake herself all over, she seemed so frustrated. "I have never been so angry ...you are more than contemptible; you, sir, are scum! You'll burn in Hell for what you did to my brother! I have had a proposal of marriage from a Swede in Granite City and tomorrow, I ACCEPT!"

Ashley's head was already hung down. He mumbled an ineffective apology which Elspeth probably didn't hear nor did she care to...and she continued to sputter at him.

Then he said a guarded "Goodbye," not caring to hear nor give a response as she spit at him. He turned away and left her there.

Elspeth. What a shame to have to leave her. Well...The world was half-full of women—Rufus kept telling him—and there must be some who don't yell and spit. She was so confidant in her quest to marry that mere words just meant nothing to her; no amount of apologies would return her to where her mind used to be. So much for truth. But he learned that even a proposal of marriage to another woman wouldn't dampen her zeal to marry him; this was one of the stories he wouldn't tell Rufus.

He walked quickly back to Pennyweight's store and took the back steps up into his home, and more stairs to his attic-bedroom. Here was where he had watched the ships from his window when he was young, where he had hidden Gair's chest of diamonds, where he had written the poem for Elspeth. Stood and looked out the window for a long while, thinking.

Then he looked around as though to attempt to recall it all before he left for good, seemed self-satisfied, picked up his riding-coat and went down the stairs to the kitchen, headed for the rear door.

His mother cut him off. "Aren't you going to bed, dear?"

"No, Mum...I think I'll just look in on Joe, in the stable."

"Didn't you do that earlier? Before you went to see Elspeth?"

"Yes…But I thought a lot and I think I'll go out and see Joe."

"And will you give him the coat under your arm?" She saw everything: mothers are like that.

"Perhaps it shall rain…One never knows what will happen in Boston."

"No…One never does know. Ashley?"

"Yes, Mum?"

"I don't quite know how to say this, so I'll just say, 'God bless you.' I honestly thought these partings were over, where you suddenly left."

"I never said a word about leaving…"

"I'm glad you have your coat, Ashley; you may need that wherever you go. Write. I love you."

"I love you, too, Mum." The first time he had ever told her that as an adult.

He went into the stable Pennyweight used and it seemed darker than usual, inside. Normally there was a lantern left burning at each end of the building, for the place was used at all times by the boarders, but tonight, only the far-light glowed. Enough for him; perhaps just the oil was gone.

He started down toward Joe and saw a man cross behind him, now blocking the door he'd just come in.

"You're Lyons, aren't you." Not a question; he was sure.

"You have me confused with someone else, sir."

"No…you're Lyons…I watched you before and I've been waiting for you to come in here."

"Whyever would you do a thing like that?"

"Lots of reasons." He moved closer to Ashley. The man was Ashley's size: long-armed; Ashley had long legs. This man presented muscles which couldn't be hidden by a shirt, tho; years of working the quarries in Granite City. Ashley had no prominent muscles.

"What reasons?"

"To start with, I will fight you bare-handed."

"Why would you do that? I have no fight with you."

"Yes you do. I shall tell the sheriff we fought because you caused the death of the brother of the woman I shall marry. A family thing, this fight."

"Whose family?"

"When I marry Elspeth, MINE!"

Ashley's heart sank. Elspeth had TOLD this man about Roland? How could she do that? Why? Then he began to realize…She hadn't time to go anywhere to tell him; this man must have been there at her house when Ashley was there...and there was only one reason for him to be there at that time...the same reason Ashley had been there weeks ago.

"So you caused the death of my relative, my wife-to-be's brother; and I demand satisfaction of you. You will fight me." Cold. A statement. He must have said things like that before, he was so sure of himself. The man looked like he could fight and win.

No place to run; no chance to run. Thinking Elspeth would betray him like that... Well, as he had told her, he betrayed her...so...she had been busy whilst he was away, getting another groom lined up and waiting.

"I won't fight you."

"Yes you will. When I hit you across the face a few times you'll fight—or try to." He reached forward and slapped Ashley across the face, just for ample reason. More than daring: eagerly waiting.

"Ready to fight? I like to fight. I am a champion fighter; have never lost a bare-knuckled fight."

"Don't touch me."

He hit Ashley twice more, glancing blows, tearing strikes on the arm. Lots of power there.

"Oh, you will fight, and I will win."

"Stop now, or I shall become serious."

"Become serious!" He jolted Ashley with a fist to the chest: it hurt! The man was strong, capable, could place his blows; wanted to fight and knew he'd win.

"Do not do this, sir."

"Come on, Protestant; I am Catholic!" Taunting, but not effective with the reference. He swung at Ashley but Ashley dodged this one, then received a back-handed slap on the mouth which stung. When this man became serious about fighting, he'd surely win any fight.

"I don't fight."

"You will, and very soon, for I shall make you. I have more to tell about Elspeth."

"I don't want to hear anything you might have to say about her."

"But you shall...and then you will fight. I have been tasting that honey for almost two years. Does that bother you, Lyons? That she beds regularly with me?"

"It only surprises me that you would marry her if you already have had her so regularly."

"You trying to insult me, Lyons? Is that your way? Get me angry and you think to win? No...you may anger me, but I win all my fights; I am a champion fighter."

"So you say; so you brag. You think she'll marry you? She wants to marry ME!"

"You think thus? After what you told her tonight? She's just been trying to trade up with you, she told me. She'd get you for a husband and get into that store of yours…and live fine, with me on the side to take good care of her…needs, shall we say? Make you mad, Lyons? To hear the truth about yourself? Now that you've left her, I get my chance with her…after I do this for her. The things women make men do, huh, Lyons? You killed a man for the boy; I'll kill you for her."

"We talked earlier; she wouldn't have you do all this."

Another hard hit told Ashley this was the end of all the talk. And a left-handed punch caught him on his neck, rocking him back.

"Fight me!"

He threw another punch but Ashley stepped aside, catching it on his back, above the kidney—which was still sore from Johnathan's kicks.

"You're a good opponent You know how to take punches. This will be a good fight."

"You'll get no fight from me."

"I have big plans for Elspeth." He chuckled. "Big plans. She has no dowry so she'll work for it."

"You want the woman to work?"

"The night we marry she'll entertain several friends of mine…An' they'll pay me for that entertainment…Then, whoever else wants to pay."

"You'd make her a whore? Your own wife?"

"Lyons, she's already a whore; she just doesn't take coin. I have several wives; they're all making money for me. Elspeth likes to do it anyway, why not for money?"

"That's immoral; you'll burn in Hell for that!"

"Stop the talk, Lyons, and fight." He slugged, catching Ashley on the side of the face again: a hard hit making him wince and wish he had Johnathan's pistol handy.

"I'll tell Elspeth what you have planned for her."

"She wouldn't believe you, but you're not leaving here anyway." He drove a sudden punch into Ashley's face, knocking back his head and drawing blood. "Fight now! Be a man!"

"Stop it! If I get mad I'll pull a knife!"

"Then do that and stop the fight tonight. I'll kill you with a musket, from afar! You fight bare-handed now or I'll shoot you when you least expect it…maybe tonight, when you go to piss; maybe a month from now when you've forgotten all about me. Fight now, and die like a man!"

"I'll put a knife into you!"

"Pull a knife and I'll run, and tell everyone you tried to kill me because I'm marrying Elspeth. You'll be sought by the sheriff anyway, when I tell him you had that boy killed by your friends out there on that wharf. And you'll be a laughing-stock when I tell that you can't keep a woman."

He had the voice-accent of a Swede; there was a colony of them in Granite City, there mostly to work the quarries of granite-stone and do laboring jobs whilst they plied their own religion. This man looked strong, determined, a winner in life and a confident man who refused reason. But he was—although a fighter—not a hired killer. Geoffry would already have shot or knifed his victim; this man wanted to play with him like a cat toys with a mouse before the actual kill.

For Ashley, there was nothing else to do. Johnathan had taught him very well and Geoffry reinforced that teaching. Yes, the Swede was very good as a bare-knuckled fighter, but in that single instant of Ashley's thought, he realized the Swede's size and strength didn't matter…And neither did his boxing talents.

"You remind me of a man I met who thought he knew all the answers to all the questions. All you want to do is beat me up? Humiliate me so you can brag to Elspeth?"

"No, Lyons…you're going to die this night."

"I died when Matthew shot me. Everything else has been…extra."

The Swede grinned. "After you're down I'm going to kick off your balls. Then I'll kill you and afterward your family."

"What?" Ashley drew a curtain over his soul. This had become a necessity. He couldn't—wouldn't—have a man threaten his family for all his life, killing them one by one as he had just promised. Time to lock away emotion and clothe himself in the coldness of ice. For all he did, Geoffry had passed along that condition to Ashley Lyons.

This was no way to treat a man, but this man was an arrogant, threatening killer—who, by the way, had probably made enough love to Elspeth to think he cold marry her and hire her out, and himself live happily after. Elspeth was wonderful in bed and perfect as a victim, but she was a shrewd, calculating woman who fought for what she wanted. She played men against each other and took the winner. He wondered how many other "bare-knuckled fights" had been because of her.

"Then, my friend, you've become a real problem for me. Elder Otis would tell me to solve my problems permanently."

"So, you'll fight?"

"No…I'm just going to kill you."

"With your knife? Go ahead and try; pull your knife and I'll run. Throw it at me and I'll get it; hit me with it and I'll either tell the sheriff or if you kill me you'll have murdered me as I ran away. I have a witness outside already, and I will have the last laugh. You cannot win this one. Put up your hands and fight me."

"Why do you persist so?"

"Honor."

"Then, by God, carry your honor to your grave!" The fast left hand wasn't expected by the Swede and it caught him on the right eye, sending him backwards a step but not nearly down. He recovered fast, holing his hands in readiness for the now-started fistfight, coming in toward Ashley to punch and punish him.

Ashley kicked with a long leg, striking the knee of his attacker, again causing him to buckle a moment but not fall.

"You don't fight fair!"

The other leg hit the Granite City man's left knee and this time he dropped to one knee, still holding the fighter's pose; valiantly, then, coming back onto his feet and ready to strike again.

He tossed a winning blow to Ashley's face but came nowhere near as his right knee was again kicked; and he rocked in place, teetering.

Ashley ducked and suddenly—instantly—threw himself onto the Swede, bowling him over on already-sore knees and they both fell to the floor of the sable.

The knife came from its shoulder-pocket and never was seen until it flashed in the Swede's face; then he felt it on his neck.

"You won't kill me."

"I won't? So you can kill my parents and sisters as you said? So you will make me wary and cringe in fear as I leave my home each night that you're out there with a musket?"

"You're a Puritan; you can't kill. What would you say to your God on Judgment Day?"

"Your choice. You fought and lost. Promise me you'll leave me and my family alone."

"Never. I shall ever stalk you, kill you and your relatives."

"What in the bloody hell is the matter with you? Why do you do this? Say this?"

"I will kill you and your family...one by one."

"No, by God, you won't."

Ashley's eyes saw it happen but they didn't bother to report it to his mind: the knife-blade—seemingly alive and desperate for blood—slipped almost by itself under the right ear and in one constant move drove through the neck, disregarding the flesh, slicing the great artery as it immediately parted the skin, pouring a torrent of blood and driving yet deeper into the neck, under the chin, seeming to curve around but really only just moving in a straight line, its path deep and very fatal: no human could have survived it, least of all recover from it. The Swede—for all his experience and bravado and strength—was in the end the same as all those men he had beaten and killed, and his life stuttered and choked and paused forever as all those he had beaten and killed had done.

Ashley had seen enough of Geoffry's work to be aware of how a professional did it. It was actually very easy, but he had to move quickly away as the blood spurted out so fast and blew in so many directions at once.

It was a move which both thrilled and disgusted him...the end-move; the culmination in defeating an enemy once and forever: a climax suddenly physical and sensual, a payback, a strike of the owl.

How else does one stop a person who vows lifetime revenge toward an entire family, other than this way? He again had put on the cloak of the revenger of blood, and was content he had worn it well.

This Swede from Granite City was no one and everyone: no one he knew, but all those who had threatened him these past weeks...everyone who had caused Ashley Lyons to struggle over this past eleven weeks. The Swede was Johnathan and Geoffry, Miles and the landlord, Francis Lane and the posse. And in the end, it was a final goodbye to Elspeth.

Ashley dropped to his knees. *God in Heaven, this was no murder: this was saving my family. Please turn this miserable wretch's soul away from Heaven and give him a taste of what he must have done to so many here on Earth. Through the actions he showed, he doesn't deserve Salvation. Amen.*

"God, Elspeth, I've hurt you again."

He got to his feet, wondering if he now were part of it all...If the brutality of this summer had gotten inside him and now he was the same as Geoffry. He had used Geoffry's move with the knife and probably felt the same way that English assassin had felt as he drew his blade to use it.

How do you know if you're acting for God or against Him?

He thought for a moment, then answered himself: *If what you do has helped others and not hurt them, you're doing God's work.* He nodded, satisfied; that made sense to him, the most sense he'd made since all this nightmare had started.

Ashley was tired…Lord, was he so tired.

He dragged the body of the Swede to a scupper in the floor of the stable and pushed it down with the horse-waste, a drop of about two meters to the water. The tide was in or at its neap, so it wouldn't be long before the sharks and the crabs completed the job.

"What will I say to my God on Judgment Day?" he asked aloud, as if in answer to the last question the now-dead Swede had asked…"I will tell Him the same thing the great bears used to tell Father Bear when they'd already done something they couldn't take back: 'It has been done.'"

Then he went over and lit the lamp which had been extinguished, and kept walking over to see Joe. Joe whinnied when Ashley came near.

He saddled the big horse from New Hampshire and led him outside and shut the stable door. A figure from the darkness rushed up to him and he spun around, grabbing again for the skinning-knife and putting his back against Joe.

"Oh!" A woman's voice.

"Elspeth?"

"I didn't…"

"You didn't think it would be me coming out?"

"Whyever would I not think it would be you? I came here to see you; you just surprised me."

"I bet I did." She was good: too good.

Sometimes it happens; sometimes it just doesn't, no matter what you say or what you do or how you want it to go. You throw the bones and you get the numbers. Maybe you win; maybe you lose. Just like that. Luck? Probably. Maybe God's on your side this time and maybe He's looking away; you'll never know. Maybe He's answering another prayer and too busy; maybe you didn't pray at all.

"Nice to see you again, Elspeth."

"Are you alone?"

"Yes, I am."

"I mean…"

"I know what you mean, Elspeth…he's gone."

"Who's gone?"

"You can stop playing your little game now; he's gone away."

"You've killed him? That's the only way he'd have left here."

"I think I know what's happened tonight...I got some experience in figuring out things after London. You told your friend what's happened tonight, what I told you; you probably told him I'd leave Boston after we argued...he told me he was there with you when I arrived at your house tonight."

"No..."

"He accosted me and we spoke awhile, as men are wont to do...then I gave him a rather large bag of gold and a pocket-full of silver sovereigns and he left...happy."

"He was going to kill you. He NEVER would have left without doing that! I think he's dead in there and you killed him!"

"Elspeth..."calmly, "he *was* here, wanted me to fight with him, struck me a few times as you might see in the daylight, and upset me so much I gave him a bag of gold I was going to take away with me; and he cleaned out my pockets of silver, but then he left and said I was never going to see him again, he apparently was that happy—at my expense."

"He's inside."

"Go look for him."

"You did kill him." Her voice was as cold as the North Sea in winter. "I'll tell the sheriff."

"Please do. And all your little secrets will come out: that you've had a lover for the past two years who was going to turn you into a whore after he married you, and that you only wanted to marry me to get into my family's store for yourself and you'd have your lover when I wasn't around. Is that what you want the Lord High Sheriff to hear? That a woman who murdered her kidnapper years ago now has another dead lover? Think about it. Think who the Lord High Sheriff will believe: the captain from Plimouth with a business-family here in Boston or the estranged lover who suddenly has lost a man again."

He had learned how to think and talk to his advantage. It had taken a while, but the past eleven weeks taught him a lot about what people thought and said and feared.

"I'm leaving Boston now, Elspeth, but I'll be back. Don't talk with any of my family and don't go into my father's store. If you do, I'll tell the sheriff something happened to your lover from Granite City and *then* you'll leave Boston, afoot or in chains."

"How can you be like this after..."

"We all do things... We have to do. Some we want and some we don't. You know that; you said that once.

He held a long silence and she didn't volunteer to break it. "I've been away—as I told you—taking care of business for myself and thinking of you. I realized after all this started between you and me that... I'm not ready to have another woman in my life."

"What about the London woman? You asked *her* to marry you!"

"You had to have been there...I was beaten up, dragged around, had a broken hand, almost tossed off London Bridge...had a fight with a man...a girl gave me shelter from a killer and I wanted to get her out of the single room and sad condition of her life."

"So you asked her to marry you. I didn't know you were a knight of Arthur's."

"I admit I got carried away; it won't happen again."

"Is that your apology and proposal to me? Then, I accept!"

"No...No proposal. I'm already married to Anna. No more marriages for me, even tho' I really enjoyed our time together."

"Ashley...you don't have to marry me—I told you that before. Just...be around for me."

"That's not what you want and it's not what I want. I loved you when I loved you; that's over and it won't start again. Anna is dead; Margaret is dead; you and I are dead."

She put a hand on him and he pulled away from it.

"The London girl is dead?"

"Killed by the man who killed Roland, and tried hard enough to kill me."

"You need a woman's love. I..."

"No! The women I love seem to leave me, so I'm putting a stop to that."

"I'm here for you."

"And I'm not staying!" He pushed at Joe, who swung around, and Ashley grabbed at the little saddle.

"I know you killed him. Anyone else would be in panic right now, but not you. Not Captain Lyons. I misjudged you. You're too...calm. You've already killed him, to spend this amount of time talking with me; that's why he's not here right now...he's dead somewhere, probably in there, or maybe where they put Roland.

"Lyons, I've never met so calculating a man as you. I thought I was cold and sure of myself, but you make me look like a woman without a Bible at a prayer-meeting: embarrassed, but not willing to go home to get it." She sighed. "I guess this is goodbye...so...goodbye."

She turned and left.

Ashley waited a moment beside Joe, letting her go in his mind and feeling deep-down the relief that her leaving honestly gave him while still wanting to bring her back, chase after her, tell her everything would be all right...remembering that night with her and the way she looked and the poem he had written with love for her.

She was another lost person. God. He'd been lost and thought she never was and it turned out she was worse than he, worse than she made out to be, worse about everything except the way she behaved in bed.

Well, he'd miss that!

But now he had ended it finally with Elspeth, tho' she protested, insisted she loved him all the while she was carrying-on a romance with the Swede and probably several others, getting ready to chose the lucky (or unlucky) one. They probably also had written her letters and poems to which she never responded. Hell, HE was the lucky one!

Now all he had was Anna: the perfect wife. She'd never leave him, be upset with him, ever hurt him at all no matter what he did or said or thought. The perfect wife.

Is the memory of desire still desire? Or just memory?

"Just memory," he answered himself...Only memory. Desire is real and earnest and present; memory is only recall. Still...He warmed in his thoughts of her: Elspeth—the prettiest name he'd ever heard.

Still in his mind; still in his life.

He swung onto the small saddle and urged Joe on, not paying attention to the direction Joe was heading (Joe remembered the apples and carrots he'd received when Ashley was away and wanted more). Ashley was just memorizing.

A figure which had been standing by the lamp at the corner of Pennyweight's store came out of the night.

Ashley sighed: another fight?

His stepfather reached out and gave Joe a carrot and halted the two of them instantly: Joe a happy, munching, spoiled horse.

"I heard you left and was hoping to catch you."

Ashley got off the saddle and stood beside Pennyweight.

"We still have business to complete...business we began before you went to Granite City with me. About you and New Amsterdam?

"Well, about the job you offered in New Amsterdam...I wanted to speak further with you about that...Rufus has offered me a job which would take me into the interior for a short while...speaking with the Algonkin Woods-People there with his fur-trader who knows no Algonkin."

"With winter coming soon?"

"I'd stay the winter there."

"Then, thank you; you've made it easier on me. With this heart-thing..."

"I know; I understand. Here is my gift to you: I have been given land in Lord Halifax's Grant, west of Plimouth and along the Boston Post Road, and have contracted with Wyman Briggs the master carpenter and the Ellis brothers—the cabinet-makers and wood-finishers. They will take a year or more to build a fine house there—Mum knows all about this and will tell them what they need to know. The Ellises will live in the house to completion, to do everything after it is raised...fine carpentry, moldings, panels, cabinets...when they leave, there will be nothing left for you to do but move in..."

"Ashley..."

"No way out of this...You have to do it. Mary-lou will run this store here; Rufus has sent Michael to care for the one in Plimouth; you write to your partner in Granite City and sell your half of that store. Be a land-owner and Planter again in Halifax; you always loved that in Plimouth. Oh, and the soil there is perfect for growing strawberries, and there already are wild blueberries and huckleberries growing."

Ashley hugged his stepfather. "I've already said my goodbyes to the rest of the family...I'm glad I got this opportunity to talk with you privately. I'll...I'll try to get back here in two years, maybe three. Rufus has arranged to have flowers placed regularly on Anna's grave...but she'll be with me everywhere I go; I'll never be lonely again."

"You're not taking the ship to England?" Pennyweight smiled at that old memory.

"No...and, truth is, I never stowed away on any ship to England when I was twelve. I—truthfully, I swear by God—was captured and taken by the Anakapis up north."

"I never believed you."

"I have never lied to you; I won't now. Everything I said to you and Mum was the truth. I was kidnapped and taken there, and Bren brought me back."

"Then I shall pray for forgiveness and for your safe journey and return."

"Thank you."

"I talked with your mother before I came out here...however can we thank you for all that?"

"Live long and prosper in God's great love."

CHAPTER 41

He let Joe go at his own pace…moving south in the dark, along the same road toward Merry Mount and the abandoned cabin where he'd been shot and left for dead and where the big man had fallen from this same saddle and died.

Mathew, Mark, Luke and John. He'd never see another New Testament without remembering his countrymen who tried to kill him, replace Lord Protector Cromwell with a young, Scottish King, and end the only religion he had ever known and practiced.

And he'd never meet or read about another Geoffry without a sour taste in his mouth and a saddened "might have been" flicker about Margaret in his memory.

Almost on his birthday, Anna and the baby had died. A month later, he'd had that run-in with Miles Standish and all this terror and spite and death and loss had mushroomed and careened into his life after that. It hadn't seemed like much when it happened, hadn't seemed too long a time taken nor a day misspent. But in eleven weeks there were ten people killed around him and two deciding-battles fought and won by Lord Protector Cromwell. His England had held herself in place, and he—alive—was leaving all that behind. Only then came silently the frightful realization of what had happened—and the battle for survival he had fought and won.

Then he turned, passing through Granite City with all its influx of Swedish and other foreigners who were cutting and working stone there…past the river and along lonesome trails and cow-paths, headed…where? Certainly not home. Somewhere.

This early morning there was a cool wind off the ocean, still chilly inland, making him think of the coming of winter and wondering where he'd then be. He recalled only last year what he'd heard his friend from Duxbury—Russell Meiggs—say about a winter's day: "The sun is out, the ice is hard, the wind is chilly. Typical New England morning."

Almost a week later, the Lord High Sheriff of Boston announced he had found the remains of a body whom he though could have been the missing stone-mason from Granite City. Not much was left of the man, but enough to see that the throat and neck had been cut—exactly as the boy who had been pulled from under the Great Wharf and the stableman at Gold's. So the sheriff decided and told the story to all that the same man who killed the boy had killed these other men, and this person would be hunted down, captured and hanged publicly as soon as possible.

It was a good story for the sheriff and the people of Boston who didn't know the truth.

By then, Elspeth had accepted the proposal of a man from Salem and had moved there. When told, Ashley said it was the perfect place for her.

EPILOGUE

The days of Saint Martin's summer had slipped by. The nights, already cool and damp, became cold with frosty mornings. No longer was the world either red or yellow, as the changing colors of the autumn forest burst upon the eyes of onlookers. Soon, the southeast Massa-adchu-ess-et would begin to experience its first wet and clinging snow, burdening the tall pines and causing them to bow low with the beeches and birches. Then would the fairylike, crystalline appearance of early winter transform the dark woods.

But all this to come was lost on Ashley Lyons' mind as he rode the recovered Joe toward the place he had to go: the cemetery in Duxbury.

Finally, he was back for Anna…Anna of the tiny hands and beautiful face and gleaming smile. Back. Away for too long; involved in the intrigue of a Royalist who had everything to gain and played the game as a spy who got away. No longer Ashley's business. Never was his business. He had made it thus and barely beat pistols, knives and a noose in the trying. Didn't matter: all over now and he had returned to where Anna was staying in the hope she wouldn't despise him for what he had done in Boston and London: left her, involved himself in murders and death, slept with two woman and asked one of them to marry him, come to Boston with him. Stupid behaviors…she'd know before he saw her—if he saw her—how she'd feel about it right away. They read each other's thoughts and anticipated each other's actions. She'd know. She knew now.

He dropped Joe's reins on the withered grass and walked toward where he always had met Anna…by that tree with the wooden seat around it.

At first he didn't see her…but then…she was there for him…waiting.

POST-EPILOGUE

10 years later:
August 1660

Dear Rufus,

I take pen in hand to inform you of our latest business developments and to assure you—at least for the present—that out ties in trade shall maintain regardless of what has happened here.

As you probably know, Oliver Cromwell's bid to become King failed, and two years' back he died of malaria.

Charles II has been proclaimed King of Great Britain and Ireland and swears to all to maintain the commercial ventures begun since his father's death. He has pardoned "all traitors" in a General Amnesty but has had one person hanged before that declaration: a Carlos Johnathan Acores, who had publicly stated he was the elder son of Charles I and half-brother to Charles II.

So much for family ties. In this I think that Charles shall be liberal to Business: eliminate the competition, what?

Perhaps Charles II will be a good King after all.

We send our love and the latest list for furs, and your banking statement—which should please you greatly.

Our best to young Lyons.

Your brother-in-law,

Elmer Eugene Stoddard Federated Banks of London, Ltd.